PRAISE FOR *The Height of Secrecy*

"Loved it! A mystery with strength and realism. Mitchell's background leads to a blended masterpiece of plot, setting and characters complete with insider authenticity. He's got a good series going."
> —**Betty Palmer**, Events Coordinator, Moby Dickens Bookshop, Taos, New Mexico

"What Grisham does for law and the courtroom drama, Mitchell does for national parks and the politics of land and preservation. His behind-the-scenes knowledge of the sub-culture creates a believable setting that blends seamlessly with the story."
> —**Isaac Mayo**, Developmental Editor

PRAISE FOR *Public Trust*

"In *Public Trust,* J. M. Mitchell brings a richness to the wilderness mystery that's not to be missed. Fire starts the novel and it burns fast and furious, but pales to the political firestorm that becomes a battle for nature herself."
> —**Nevada Barr,** *New York Times* best-selling author

". . . so real you think you're reading nonfiction. . . . This is a good read."
> —*Ranger Magazine*

ALSO BY J. M. MITCHELL

Public Trust

THE HEIGHT of SECRECY

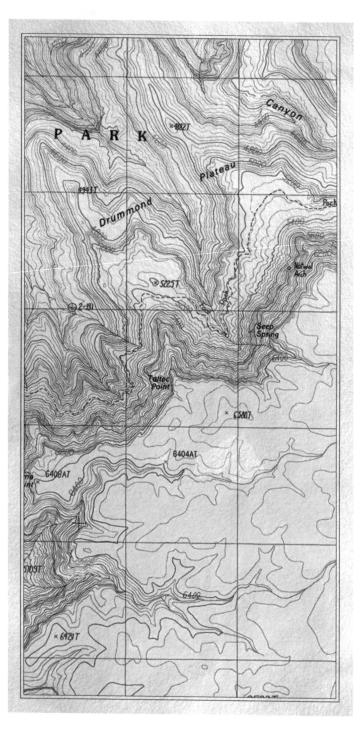

THE
HEIGHT of
SECRECY

—

J. M. MITCHELL

PRAIRIE PLUM PRESS

DENVER

PRAIRIE PLUM PRESS
P.O. Box 271585
Littleton, CO 80127
www.prairieplumpress.com
Email@prairieplumpresss.com

Printed in the United States of America

First Printing, 2014

ISBN 978-0-9852272-5-8

Library of Congress Control Number: 2014901107

Readings and author events scheduled through:
    Mary Bisbee-Beek, Publicist
    2417 SE 32nd Ave
    Portland, OR 97214
    (734) 945-7656
    mbisbee.beek@gmail.com

Topographic map produced by and courtesy of U.S. Geological Survey.

Book design by K.M. Weber, www.ilibribookdesign.com

For Cassy,
for your insight and support

PROLOGUE

It could have been a game trail. The young girl knew otherwise. This is where her clan mother had said she would find it. Warily, she scrambled through brush, past an outcropping of sandstone. She kept behind cover, cautious, checking repeatedly, making sure no one was following.

It seemed she was alone, but she could not be too careful. A Spanish soldier, maybe a suspicious priest, someone from another pueblo or tribe, even someone from another clan—it did not matter. None of them were to know. None were to be allowed to follow. Especially the Spanish—because of their intolerance of traditions— but it was little different for the others. If they knew, there could be consequences. They could inflict such damage. The reason she was here, the lessons she would learn, the blessings with which she would return, they were not to know.

She crept higher, toward a break in the canyon wall. Needing to catch her breath, she stopped in the shadow of a pine, dropped her parcel and sat. She watched for movement. She saw none, yet she continued to watch. Her heart began to slow and her breathing quieted, letting the songs of the wind fill her ears. Whispers, from Mother Earth. She looked around. The rock and ground, the pines, the jays, the seed-laden grasses—the Creator living in all of them.

She nodded.

She knew not what she would find on this journey and yet she did. Her clan mother's clues were unfolding with answers. And insight. Into responsibility. Into role.

What she would find and gather would become offerings for herself and her clan. Those offerings and prayers would help bring rain and harvest, health and wellbeing, not just to her and her clan but to the pueblo. Would she remember the stories? Would they come to life? Enough to bring insight to do what she needed to do?

She had her prayer sticks. Would she know where to place them?

What of the collections needed by the medicine society? Would she know where to find them?

And the collections of pigment for sacred paint? The pigment she would grind, that priests would offer to others and back to her, to paint faces, hands and feet for ceremony. If she could not find it, what would happen? To the traditional dance? To rain and harvest?

And most important—the mystical flowers only a few were blessed to find. Would she remember the stories? Had she understood them well enough to return with the most sacred of blessings? Pollen—to bring the butterfly to the garden and carry prayers to the Creator.

She turned her mind from worry. She imagined her mother, standing before her, holding a small ceremonial pot, watching proudly as she prepared for ceremony, then painting dark streaks across both her cheeks. She was at that place in her learning, and, yes, her mother—her teacher and protector until now—would be there, proudly bringing her to this point in her life.

The girl picked up her parcel and stood. She followed the trail to a dry creek bed, then down, to the beginnings of a ledge. She stepped onto it, then followed it beyond a bend in the rock. She stopped, overlooking the canyon. Her eyes grew wide.

It's real, not just a story!

She followed the ledge forward, knowing now where her journey would take her.

— · —

PRESENT DAY . . .

Early evening moonlight bled into the room and onto the floor where elders, both men and women, sat around the glowing coals of a fire, discussing the welfare of their people. One space sat empty. It represented a clan that tradition said would provide a leader, one who had much to do with religious practice.

"We've known this day would come," a white-haired man said.

"Yes," another answered. "But Anna was certain another would follow her. Her death is unexpected."

"But it is something we should have expected. If her clan is now extinct, we are left with a hole in our society . . . in our social fabric. Do we know why she thought another would come? Are we sure there is no one?"

A gray-haired woman sitting to the east nodded to herself, then spoke. "There are no men. None initiated into religious societies, none with teachings or authority. It is possible there is no one surviving who knows the traditions and secrets of the clan. But, there is a girl. One girl."

— · —

A FEW MILES AWAY:

The moon peered over the canyon rim, casting light over the pool. A wall across the way stood in shadow, but flickers of light intruded even there from the shimmer of moonlight off water and travertine. The sounds were of water falling, of tree frogs and birds calling, of gentle down canyon breezes in the leaves of the cottonwoods. A man and woman floated in the shallows, giving attention to none of it.

The night was warm, as was the water, but in time the water would bring chill and they would need to escape it. When that time came, Jack Chastain swam to a flat-topped boulder, gave a kick, and hefted himself up on both arms and out of the water. No trepidation, he stood, tall, his lean shadow cast over the rock. He watched Kelly Culberson swim to water's edge and emerge. She brushed her dark hair back and blew the water from her lips. Her skin glistened in the moon light, and droplets trailed down the length of her body. She noticed him watching. She smiled.

She came around to the boulder, climbed up and stood, and gave him another embrace, then lay down and sank into the warmth of the rock.

He sat beside her. She rolled onto her back and closed her eyes to the moon. He stole the moment to enjoy the sight of her.

She let minutes pass, then turned onto her side. "Tell me what happened in Montana."

Jack looked away.

"You can't keep secrets."

"Don't intend to. But I don't want to talk about it."

"Look at what's happened in the last forty-eight hours, in the past few weeks, in the past year. The fire, the warring factions, the trust you lost, then regained tenfold. You're past all that. Surely you can also get past what happened in Montana."

"Hope so." He stared into the shadows. "But I'm not sure all wounds heal."

"Why can't you let go?"

"Some things are harder than others. When there are those you count on, that you want to count on you, and things happen that tell you they're in it for themselves. When it should be obvious, but isn't. How do you get over that?"

"Who are you talking about?"

"No one you know."

"Tell me about Montana. It might help you forget."

"Forget? Sure, let's forget it."

"No, I mean, it would be good to talk about it, right?"

He kissed her forehead. "I do not want to talk about Montana."

CHAPTER
1

Jack Chastain tipped the drip torch forward and burning oil dribbled out, setting fire to a clump of sagebrush. The flames grew, engulfed the sage, and flashed toward a thicket of oak brush. He dipped the torch forward again to the same effect.

Wind, from nowhere, pushed back, blowing heat in his face. He stood up right. The holding crewman to his left stepped back, ready to stand his ground, but looked more surprised than prepared.

The wind died away.

Between the fire line and advancing front of flame, the strip of black was no longer narrow. It was growing. That could be good or bad, a buffer to stop the main body of the now-named, *Pistol Creek Fire*, or a potential problem. With so much fire on the ground, it would be hard to control if winds came early. The forecast said tomorrow, not today.

Jack raised his eyes to the horizon.

A gray zone of smoke rose up along the ridgeline. Two columns poked up above the trees, trying to come to a boil.

This had better work. The fire cannot be allowed to move this direction. Not this close to the boundary. Even doing good things to the west, there would be hell to pay. Explaining why this fire was seen as potentially good after starting under suspicious circumstances—a pickup found burning on the desert and quickly extinguished, but not before starting a spot fire on the plateau—would not be easy. Explaining the decision to manage the fire—or allow it to burn—would be difficult with evacuations occurring or houses burning. Heads would roll.

Johnny Reger's plan seemed good, until now. The small number of firefighters from which to draw hadn't seemed a major concern—it was so early in the year, before the worst of the fire season. A few firefighters from nearby parks, reinforcing the fire staff from Piedras Coloradas National Park, and a little help from Jack, and that seemed enough. Until now, with the wind.

One day. That's all that's needed. One day to secure this stretch before forecasted winds arrive. Then the fire can move north and west. Monitored and allowed to burn. Allowed to do good things.

But not if we lose it here.

Jack checked the others. As the wind died back, the firers pressed on, their line of fire heating up, flames lapping back. The holding crews leaned into their shovels and waited, ready.

Up the way, outside the line, a firefighter stood between the fire and a scratch line cut to protect a sandstone outcropping and a small population of rare plants, a wallflower, proposed for endangered status. It had to be protected. Once the burn advances past where the woody-stemmed plant grows—its roots penetrating cracks at the base and up the face of the rock—the firefighter can move down the line to help elsewhere. Procedure. Johnny was being thorough.

Jack moved northwest, along the edge of the black, lighting off more brush. The sweat on the back of his neck turned cool. Another wind shift. He stopped and raised the drip torch.

He exchanged glances with Johnny Reger, who gave him a serious look, the sparkle gone from his usually jesting eyes. Sweat matted dark strands of hair falling below the brim of his helmet. Nerves.

"Where did this come from?" Jack shouted.

He shrugged. "Phantom winds. Said nothing about 'em in the forecast."

Tops of ponderosas swayed.

"Should we stop?" Johnny asked.

"Don't know. Feels like we're committed, and only so much time till tomorrow."

A hot, dry wind bit his face.

Tree tops buffeted.

Not good—not with this much fire on the ground.

Jack checked up and down the line.

A gray-bearded firer raised his drip torch and stopped, he too, seemingly concerned. Looking up, he appeared to be watching the tree tops.

A tall, gangly firer stepped past Gray Beard and lit off a patch of sagebrush. Fire ate through, crackling, moving with the wind. The young firer backed away from the heat, a moment later stepped past it, and tipped his torch forward. Gray Beard grabbed his arm, and waved over a man from the holding crew.

The wind died away. Tree tops grew still.

Gray Beard watched for a long moment, then signaled the young firer to proceed. He lowered his own torch and lit off the brush at his feet, pushing the fire through a swell. Smoke moved aimlessly back up the hill, mingling among the trees on the edge of the opening.

Jack exhaled, and looked over at Johnny. Johnny shook his head and smiled. He pointed a firer on. Progress had to be made.

Jack watched Gray Beard approach a downed pine and dip his torch. Dry, red needles popped into flame, and raced along the length of the tree. It was fully involved in a moment. Gray Beard stood back and watched.

Jack studied the heat waves. Shut the burn down, or take our chances? Can the Pistol Creek Fire be caught at this stage of the game? No, best odds are with finishing this burn. He dipped his torch forward and moved down the line.

Near the top of a rise, wind bit his face. A wind shift.

A firer moved into the sagebrush near the rare plants. Blonde ponytail flowing out from under a red helmet, it had to be one of the park firefighters, Christy Manion. Fire ecology diploma only freshly minted, but fire boots well worn, she was a veteran firefighter. Jack watched her coax the burn through the sage, then into the needles at the base of a monarch ponderosa. She slowed and watched. Abruptly, she turned and signaled the firefighter on guard, waving him over.

The fellow ambled toward her, shovel on his shoulder.

Wind burst into the opening. Flame climbed into oak brush. Leaves flashed. The man stepped back.

"Hit it with dirt," Christy shouted. "Winds are shifting!"

The big man let the shovel head slip to the ground. He settled into his lean and watched.

"Hit it!"

Burning leaves tumbled along the ground, through black, into green. Grass burst into flame. Sagebrush ignited. Flame and heat marched at the scratch line.

"Hit it! Put it out!"

Jack bolted.

The man stood watching.

Fire rolled over the scratch line, igniting woody-stemmed plants at the base of the rock.

Manion dropped her torch and dashed past the spectating firefighter. Shielding her face, she danced on the flames, grinding her boots into burning undergrowth.

Flame lapped up the wall, stepping from plant to plant, each bursting into flame.

She grasped at dirt with her hands, flinging it up the wall, slowing the fire—but it was too late. She dropped her head.

Stunned, Jack watched.

Christy slowly pointed. "Get a line around it," she muttered.

The man stooped over and gave the ground a scrape. A token scrape.

"Line it," Christy demanded.

"It's done. Besides, there's nothing left."

"Do it anyway," Christy said, sounding near tears. She dug in her boots, kicking dirt at the remains of the plants. Smoke wafted from scorched stems. "How could you let that happen? Why didn't you stop it?"

The man settled back into his lean. "Would've been hard."

Jack's bile rose in his throat as he stepped up behind the light haired man.

"You could if you tried . . . but you didn't," she said, continuing to kick at the dirt. "They're . . ." She raised her head. "Get over here. I'm bustin' my butt."

The man cocked his head. "I'd say keep it up sweet cheeks. It's not hurting you any."

Christy slowly stood up right and glared, then noticed Jack. She shook her head.

Johnny Reger stepped out from the shadows, following the line. He stopped. His jaw dropped. "What? What happened?" His eyes darted from scratch line, to smoldering plants, to rock outcropping, to Christy, to the other firefighter. "What did you do?"

"Nothing?" Christy said. "He did nothing."

The man smirked. "Don't expect miracles."

Johnny turned to Jack, mouth slowly moving, no words coming out.

"You can't work," Christy shouted. "You're a lazy ass."

"And this is the . . . only . . ." Johnny said, barely managing the words.

"The only known population," Jack said. "Might be fire adapted, but we don't know for sure. The botanist who described the species thought it might be found elsewhere, but so far . . ." He let his words trail off.

"This plant was . . . ," Johnny said, sounding in shock. "What do we do now?"

"Not sure. This is bad," Jack muttered. "We'll need to do a review of some kind, but I'm not sure we can think about that today."

"It's this guy that ought to be in trouble," Christy said, pointing at the big man.

"Your problem, not mine," he said. His smirk grew into a smile.

Johnny cocked an eyebrow. "A little smug, aren't you?"

"Your fire, not mine."

Johnny's eyes moved between the fire and the crewman. "I don't have time for this shit. I need everyone here. If I didn't, I'd put your ass on the first train home."

The man threw back his head and laughed.

"Forget that. You're out of here," Johnny said.

The man sobered up and stared back. "I don't think so." He turned. "Hey, boss man," he said, in Jack's direction.

Jack turned toward him. "You talking to me?"

"Yes, boss man, you need to get involved with this."

Something about the man's green eyes. "Do I know you?"

"No, but I know you."

"How?"

"Stories." His smile grew. "My brother's stories. Remember the name Foss?"

"I know a Foss," Jack said, not at all pleased.

"I'm sure you do. Mover and shaker. Superintendent of a park so close to Washington, he drops in on the Director just to say hello. I'm his brother, Carl."

"What does that have to do with anything?" Christy groaned. "Doesn't explain your lazy ass."

Foss kept his eyes on Jack. "Clint Foss' brother. Makes you think, doesn't it?"

Christy's mouth gaped open, incredulous.

"I'd get these two under control," Foss said. "You don't need more trouble. You know, trouble? Like in Montana?"

"I don't know what you're talking about." Jack turned away. "It's Johnny's fire. Take it up with him."

"What should I do, boss?" Johnny asked.

"Johnny, you said he's out of here. He's caused enough trouble. You don't need his disruption."

Foss turned to Johnny. "He's hanging you out to dry. Letting you get your ass in trouble, saving his."

Jack spun around and stepped forward. "Johnny, strike that. I'm pulling rank." He turned to Foss, and pointed toward the trucks. "Get the hell out of here. Get your stuff. Go!"

Christy pointed in the direction of the vehicles.

Johnny managed a smile.

The man stood his ground. "You're not exactly overstaffed. Don't be stupid."

"Go," Jack shouted. He took a quick step toward the man.

Foss recoiled. He threw down his shovel, and kicked the ground.

"Go!"

Foss stomped off.

"When you get back to your park," Jack shouted after him, "tell your boss to expect a call. To talk about your reputation. What's left of it. Count on your name coming up in a review of what happened today."

"Jerk," Christy muttered. "We don't need him."

"Actually, we do," Johnny said. He turned to Jack "Love it when you pull rank. Way to kick some ass by the way. What's that about another Foss?"

Jack sighed.

"Someone mentions Montana, you stop talking." Johnny spun around to the smoking remains. "Makes me sick but I can't think about this now. Got wind to worry about. I need an updated weather forecast. Tell me later what I'm in for on this review."

He reached for his mike. The radio popped first. *"Johnny, one of the crew just walked off the job. He's in a truck, hauling ass out of here."*

"We released him."

"We did? The folks from his park aren't exactly heartbroken, but they wonder how they'll get home."

Johnny keyed the mike. Before he could answer, Christy shouted, "I'll drive 'em."

A deep tone bled over the radio, then, *"Reger, this is Dispatch."*

"This is Reger. I was about to call you, Molly. I need a fresh weather forecast."

"Stand by, Johnny. Prepare for instructions regarding personnel."

Jack picked up his drip torch, but paused to listen.

"Go ahead," Johnny said.

"Regarding that person you released," Molly said, then ended the transmission.

Jack turned toward the two-track. Dust hung in the air. Could Foss pull strings that fast?

"He was a problem," Johnny said. "Had to send him home."

"Understood, but . . . stand by."

Johnny dropped his hand. He kept an ear to the radio.

The radio popped and Molly came back on. *"We've got a bigger problem. Luiz needs help. He needs you to keep him."*

"The guy's worthless. Plus he's gone. What's up?"

"Rescue. We're short-handed," Molly said, a slight crack in her coolness. *"We need all the help we can get."*

"He won't be much good."

"You're not gonna like this, but we need him. And, we need some of you."

"No way."

"No negotiating. We need people. We've got a man stuck on a wall."

CHAPTER
2

Johnny shook his head as he keyed the radio. "You want the guy we released, stop him at plateau junction. You're welcome to him. His name's Foss."

"I'll get someone there. Plus, we need two more. Maybe three. Raising system experience. People to lift the load."

"Are you crazy? We can't give you bodies. We only have so much time to keep this fire from visiting town. If we give you people, we risk losing everything, maybe today."

"Sorry Johnny, we need people. Orders from the Superintendent. Chief Ranger says change plans or whatever you need to do, but we need two more people."

"Stand by." Johnny rubbed his eyes and turned to Jack. "Can you see if we have anyone with rock rescue experience?"

Jack clicked over to the crew channel and started calling squads. Within a minute he had answers. "None of those folks," he said to Johnny. "How about you?"

"A little training, but I live by a strict set of rules. Never leave terra firma, unless it's by helicopter."

Jack keyed the radio. "Dispatch, this is Chastain."

"Go ahead."

"Johnny has training but no experience, and he needs to be here."

"We'll have to take him. Tell him find a replacement. Anyone else? We desperately need someone with experience in raising systems on big wall rescue."

"One person. Dated experience. It's been a few years."

Johnny glanced over. "Thought you said no one?"

Molly came back. "I copy. Give us those two. We'll catch Foss at the road."

"The other person is me," Jack said, an eye on Johnny. "We can't give you both of us. We risk losing the fire. Take me, leave him."

"We understand your concern but this takes priority. Luiz needs muscles. It'll help if he gets people with know-how. Stand by for directions to the site."

Jack caught a strange look from Johnny. "Don't look confused. Makes you look stupid. So, what are you going to do?"

"You have big wall rescue experience?"

"Long time ago. The fire! What are you going to do?"

Johnny shook it off. "We're short-handed. Can't do much."

Jack looked around. "Taking us leaves seven. I'd check Grey Beard."

"We need to shift to suppression," Johnny said, sounding defeated. "What an idiot. I thought this was such a good idea. Good fire. Don't overreact, I said."

"I'd ask Grey Beard if he's comfortable leading initial attack. If he's not, ask Christy. She can do it. You might ask her anyway. She knows the country."

"Is it fair to them to . . . ?"

"Johnny, you can't worry now. You have to keep it together, make a change in plans, give 'em responsibility and the flexibility to make it work. Have confidence it will."

He nodded.

"Go."

Johnny backed away, and waved Christy over. "Stop firing, everyone," he said into the radio. "Change in plans. Holding crews, stay put. Firers, come to my location."

"Chastain, this is Dispatch."

Jack sighed and keyed his radio. "Go ahead, Molly."

"The rescue is off the rim of the Little River Canyon. Luiz thinks you'll get there faster hiking in from Falcon's Bluff Trailhead. It's a three mile drive from your location, then a two mile hike. Luiz will use orange flagging to show you where to leave the trail. He and the rest of the team are en route. They'll pick up Foss en route. They should get there before you do."

"I copy."

Christy stood waiting for the others to assemble. Jack slipped behind her and whispered, "Keep an eye out for Kelly. She threatened to drop by with cookies. I told her not to, but she's got a mind of her own."

"Women!"

"Tell me about it. Let her know about the rescue, but tell her not to worry. It's grunt work. They need muscles. Someone to pull rope and lift the load."

"Load?"

"Body or person rescued, plus the rescuer."

"Cheery."

"Yeah."

The crew assembled around Johnny. Jack pulled back to listen as they made their plans. They would line the burn and hit the fire with direct attack on the eastern flank. None were happy about it. "Not much choice. That's all you can do," Johnny said in conclusion. "Good luck."

In the distance, plumes of smoke rose in the hot, now still air. The afternoon hours were ahead. The fire would get active.

— · —

They parked at Falcon's Bluff Trailhead, jumped out, and took off at a fast pace.

Jack fell behind, fighting to keep up with Johnny. It felt good not to be breathing smoke.

Johnny picked up his pace.

"Anxious to see Foss?" Jack asked.

He slowed. "No, just want to get done and back to the fire. Foss . . . that'll be fun."

"No, it won't."

On the backside of the plateau, they stopped, caught their breath and studied the downhill stretch of trail. It hugged vertical faces of cross-bedded sandstone. Switchbacks chipped out of rock descended through a layer of strata and disappeared beyond a bend. The trail would level off with some distance still to go. On the horizon, the rim on the other side of el Cañon de Fuego peeked over erosional remnants, hinting at what they knew lay ahead.

"What did that poor bastard get himself into?" Johnny muttered aloud.

"What did he get us into?"

They headed down, the rock jarring their bones, the slope pulling at their pace.

— · —

Luiz's orange flagging hung on branches of Wood's rose. It couldn't be missed. They left the trail and thrashed through serviceberry and oak brush, following broken limbs left by others as they penetrated the thicket. Poor slobs—they'd been carrying full packs with heavy gear.

Johnny charged across the steepening slope, brush high above his head.

"Careful," Jack said.

The thicket opened up.

"God," Johnny gasped, and jumped back.

Jack grabbed his pack, steadying him. The wall across the canyon, beyond the void, faced them down. Never had it seemed so massive.

Perched between strata—sheer wall above them, sheer wall dropping away below—they stared out into the canyon. Faintly, from somewhere, came the distant sound of crashing waters. Jack stepped around Johnny, eyes to the ground. He weaved through boulders and talus, avoiding the distraction of the canyon. The drop was too sheer, too disorienting, the edge too close for mistakes.

They waded through another patch of serviceberry. Ahead were the others, in climbing helmets, green uniform jeans and T-shirts—except Foss, still in his yellow, nomex fire shirt. Perched on a slope twenty to thirty feet wide, one man worked near the edge, seemingly oblivious, fearlessly reaching around the trunk of a piñon pine. The others stood back, appearing full of trepidation.

The person at the edge turned—it was Luiz Archuleta. The law enforcement ranger, in T-shirt and minus his bullet proof vest and service belt, looked more lanky and muscular than usual. He sidestepped over to another piñon, stretched a piece of red webbing between it and the first, tied it in, then tested and tethering himself in with a runner clipped to his climbing harness. He turned to the others. "Listen up. No one, and I mean no one, steps past the red webbing without being tied in. Either to it, or another anchor. Got it?" He waited for head nods, then turned and gave a hard look at his new arrivals. "I need you two to put on climbing helmets."

In a canvas bag they found the helmets. Jack pulled out a yellow one, slipped it on, and plopped down near the wall to wait.

He glanced at Foss, sitting twenty feet away.

The big man scowled. "Yeah, glad to see you, too."

Jack ignored him, and watched as Luiz methodically chose what would be used for anchors. A ponderosa pine near the wall. A table-sized boulder just below it. An old piñon, off to the left. Pointing, Luiz directed others to put wraps of webbing around each.

With webbing double-wrapped and knotted around each anchor, locking carabiners clipped in, and kern-mantle climbing rope ran between them, Luiz now took over. Jack watched him lace together a complicated configuration of knots and carabiners—the self-equalizing anchor. The runs of rope would shift dynamically with the load and the line of decent, keeping weight evenly distributed on the anchors.

Luiz knew what he was doing. It was a redundant system. Nothing attached to only one anchor or only one piece of rope or webbing. All knots and carabiners were backed up with a second.

If anything failed, another part of the system would take over. In theory.

Luiz stepped back and gazed over the system. He moved forward and tugged at a rope, then another. Suddenly, he stopped and abruptly turned. "Okay, which one of you has rock rescue experience?"

Jack raised a hand. "That would be me."

"Figured as much. Trained in all facets of this kind of rescue?"

"Yes."

"When was the last time you operated a z-rig raising system?"

"Oh . . . maybe ten years ago. Maybe fifteen. Somewhere in there."

"Were you an expert at it?"

"It'll come back to me."

Luiz's eyes sank deep in their sockets. He faced the canyon and rubbed his eyes. He spun around. "Okay, you're at the end of the rope."

"But . . . ," Jack said, looking toward the edge. It fell away to nothing. "Luiz, I'd be better on the raising system."

"Ever been rescuer on a big wall rescue?"

"Not as big as this!"

"But you have?"

"Long time ago. Max of about two hundred feet, maybe three."

"Not important," Luiz muttered. "Two hundred, two thousand, it's all the same." He dug into a green canvas bag, pulled out a climbing harness, and walked it over. He held it out.

"Luiz, I'm not the right guy."

He sighed. "You are. Only two of us have any experience whatsoever. One of us has to go over that edge. The other has to stay up here and run the lowering and raising systems. The more complicated job is here. The guy who goes down on that rope has to know he can trust the other guy to get him down there and back. You can trust me." Luiz smiled. "No offense, but I'm sure as hell not trusting you."

CHAPTER
3

Luiz tugged at the rope and groaned. "This isn't right."

The words sank in and Jack turned, suppressing a shudder.

Luiz probed at the knot. It came easily undone. "Who did this?" No one answered. "Who tied this knot?"

Foss raised a hand.

"Get your head out and get over here."

Foss picked his way across the slope.

"Watch. This is how you tie a bowline."

Foss watched him methodically retie the knot and hold it out for inspection. No time for reassurances, Luiz turned his attention to the knot at the end of load rope.

"Looked good to me," Foss said, in Jack's direction. He flashed a smile, turned, and worked his way back to where he'd been.

"Inspect all you want, Luiz," Jack said, laughing nervously. "No rush."

"That's not what the guy over the edge is thinking."

Jack watched his fingers trace the rope through knots, then thumb knots, and then on to equalizing ropes and anchors. He rechecked everything. No one seemed to take it personally. Only Foss saw humor in it.

Jack let his eyes fall on the caver's rappelling rack, sitting ready to lower him down the cliff face. The rope wove in and out, around the cams on the device. His eyes widened. It's wrong. It looked right only a moment ago. He closed his eyes and looked again, following the rope as it went around one cam, disappear behind the next, then emerge before the next, feeding in and out. Okay, it's right. It'll work. Quit looking.

"Listen up," Luiz shouted. "Everyone has their role. Take your positions."

Half the team moved into the shade of the wall, out of the way. They would not be needed during the first part of the operation, the lowering. During raising, everyone would be needed. All four of the others, all their muscles.

Foss plopped down at the lowering station, reached around and clipped himself into an anchor. Johnny settled in at the belay line.

"Luiz," Jack shouted, and then waited as he made his way over. He whispered, "I'd rather have Johnny on the load rope."

"Foss is bigger. He's the bulkiest guy we got."

"Let's just say I trust Johnny's training, even though it might not be much."

"Foss said he had a little training and we've got Johnny on belay, but it's up to you. You're the man on the rope."

"Johnny on the load rope."

"If we need more rope and need to pass the knot, Foss will be on belay, holding everything, at least for a moment."

Didn't think of that. "Just keep an eye on him. Johnny on load."

Luiz spun around. "Foss, I want you on belay. Insurance, if anything happens. Johnny, you're on the main rope."

Foss shook his head. He twisted around and disconnected from the anchor. Luiz pointed him over to the belay line.

Reger moved over. He clipped into the anchor, braced his feet against a rock and took hold of the rope, pulling it around his body, practicing moves to give it more friction, to stop or slow the load.

The load. Jack cringed. Johnny knew the moves, but would he be instinctive in using them?

Quit worrying. The cams on the rappelling rack do the work. Johnny's strength is insurance. Anyone can do it. Luiz is in control.

The amount of rope coiled beside Johnny, the sheer mass of it—scary. Was it really that far down?

Jack dropped his eyes and caught sight of his shaking fingers. He ran them along the buckle of his climbing harness. Then the buckle on his helmet, then his radio harness. Everything's fine. Still.

Luiz stepped under the safety line and clipped himself in. He studied the knot at the end of the load rope, and tested the locking carabiner. He spun around. "I need the belay line." A young ranger carried the end of the other rope to Luiz. He clipped it into Jack's harness, locked it down, grabbed the knot on the load rope and tugged, jerking Jack forward. "Good. Harness is tight." He took hold of the sling draped over Jack's shoulder. "Let's see what you got," he said. "Runners, several sizes. Carabiners. Good." His eyes narrowed "What's in the bag?"

"Harness for the victim. Helmet. A few tools."

"Good." He sighed. "The guy doesn't look injured, so this should work, but he looks scared as hell." He motioned toward the orange, body-shaped litter, stashed off to the side. "If we need it, we'll use it, but we might have to haul you back up and do it again."

"If he's on a ledge, I can get him into a harness."

"Take your time." Luiz stepped over to the edge and looked over. "He's still there. He ain't movin'." Luiz turned to the others. "Final rehearsal."

Luiz quickly walked the others through their use of the assembly of ropes, webbing and pulleys. "The most difficult and confusing phase will be converting from lowering system to raising system," Luiz said, once again. "We'll secure the load rope to the anchor, take it out of the rappelling rack, and attach to the z-rig, all while the load is on the rope."

The load. Jack cringed.

"Are you sure everything won't go tumbling down the cliff when we take it off the rack?"

Jack turned to see who asked, but all the eyes on Luiz had the same look of uncertainty.

"Trust me," Luiz insisted. "But there's no room for mistakes."

"If I get an itching to go home, don't go missing me," Foss said, to Jack. He flashed a smile.

"Quiet," Luiz said. He turned back to Jack. "You just worry about getting that guy off the ledge without him taking a screamer."

The guy on the ledge. The big unknown. Would he freak out? The victim—apparently not a climber. Apparently no equipment. Not a jumper—Luiz didn't think so anyway. Probably stumbled onto a ledge, went too far while exploring, got scared. But how the hell did he get on that ledge? He's lucky visitors saw him, dark hair, spot on the wall, several hundred feet above the canyon floor. Probably sitting there now, wondering if he'll ever see another day.

Jack leaned back to look. Too bad there wasn't enough rope to lower them all the way to the canyon floor. Be easier, if it wasn't so damned far.

"Jack, you ready?" Luiz asked.

"Ready." Jack locked eyes on Johnny.

Johnny gave a thumbs up.

Luiz raised a hand and held it as if on a control knob. "Let out a little rope. Slowly."

Jack stepped back, putting his weight on the rope.

Johnny let the rope slip through his fingers.

"Want another bar in the rack?" Luiz asked. "Either of you?"

"I'm fine," Johnny answered.

Jack checked his eyes. "Uh, me, too."

"Good!" Luiz shouted. "We're lowering. Slowly."

Jack sat back as rope fed out, his butt sinking out over the edge. Sound washed over him from the left. The waterfall. He'd forgotten the waterfall. How had he blocked that out? The rope kept coming.

He glanced over. Hundreds of yards away, Sipapu Falls poured over its hanging alcove, splattering onto the rocks below.

"Stop," Luiz barked, moving edge rollers into position. "See the guy?"

Jack looked down. Through his legs he could see the man. Black hair, white-shirted shoulders, blue-jeaned knees. Back to the wall, he sat on a tiny section of ledge, a little off to the left. At least he wasn't directly below. "He's there."

"Good," Luiz said. "Lowering, Johnny."

"So much for terra firma," Johnny shouted, as he let rope slip through his fingers.

Jack shifted on the balls of his feet. "Plenty firm. Only vertical."

Rope speed increased, and Jack dipped below the rim.

Luiz leaned out over the edge, watching.

The wall extended forever. The man was a hell of a long way down.

Jack backed down the rock, descending smoothly, rope in his face, legs parallel to the ground, back parallel to the wall. He ran his eye down the fall line. When he reached the man, he'd have to kick left to fight gravity. Only a little. Shouldn't be hard.

"Everything feel right?" Luiz asked, his hand at the ready to signal a stop.

"Everything's good."

"Johnny, a little faster," Luiz said.

The pace quickened.

Twenty-five feet.

Step . . . step . . .

Fifty feet.

The amount of wall below him didn't seem any less.

Step . . . step . . . step . . .

Almost a hundred.

Step . . .

The rock in shadow was cool. Gritty at his feet—like sandpaper. Grains of sand. Thousands of them, staring back. The wall—millions of infinite millions of them.

Step . . .

The radio popped, then carried Luiz's voice. *"Looking good."*

Still a hell of a long way down.

Step . . .

Skies sure are blue against the red rock in shadow.

Half way. Maybe. Maybe not. He looked down. Lots of wall. He looked up. Lots of wall. If not halfway, close. The rope kept feeding out.

Step . . .

A fissure slid past. Feathers. Nesting materials. No sign of a bird.

Step . . .

He looked down. The ledge. Jack couldn't remember ever seeing it. He looked to the right, where it emerged from a chasm in the wall, hundreds of feet above the canyon floor. A hanging canyon. How did this guy get in there, much less onto the ledge? This guy's got bad luck.

In the other direction, the ledge ended near Sipapu Falls, below an edge of the hanging alcove, above mist-darkened rock. Never noticed the ledge before. Not from below, not even when sitting there watching the waterfall. Strange.

From below the lip of the fall, water seemed to launch out over the edge.

Step . . .

Nearly close enough to talk to him. A little more.

Step, step . . .

"Hold on, guy," Jack shouted. "Almost to you."

The head tilted up, slowly, in jerky moves. A face. Scared eyes. Dark hair. Pony tail. He looked Native American.

"I'm coming to you. You don't have to do a thing. Stay where you are."

Twenty five feet.

Jack studied the ledge. Tiny—a few feet wide at most. Either direction from where he sat—ten feet or so—the ledge was wider. Scalloped edges. A piece of the ledge must have broken off sometime in the past. The guy must have gotten halfway through the gap and froze.

A few feet. "Almost there."

The man shivered, his back to what was likely cool wall. Hands behind him, fingers in cracks, he had his knees at his chin, his feet set close.

Jack keyed his radio. "Slow." He looked up and watched as Luiz—hanging out over the edge—signaled with a hand.

The descent slowed.

"Stop," Jack said.

Complete stop.

Jack kicked left and set his feet on the ledge.

The man sat hunkered against the wall. He pushed back with his feet.

"How are you doing?" Jack asked, leaning closer. "Hurt in any way?"

"I'm not hurt," he said, an accent suggesting English wasn't his first language. He winced, and pushed again with his feet. He took in a breath. "I think my legs are falling asleep."

Jack sorted through webbing runners on the equipment sling. He found a long one. Reaching up on the load rope, he wrapped it several times, slipped the tail through the loop, and pulled it tight. That should be secure enough to hold the man's weight. Just in case.

Jack keyed the radio. "Give me another couple of feet." The rope slithered down. He stooped on the ledge.

Jack clipped a carabiner into the runner. "Do me a favor. Let me put this around you . . . up under your arms. That way I'll know you're safe while I get you in a harness." He stretched forward. "Ease up, left arm."

The man relaxed his hold on the crack at the back of the ledge. Slowly, he raised his arm and reached out his hand.

"No, you stay put. I'll do it." Jack leaned in, reached behind him, and threaded the runner and carabiner between his back and the wall. Reaching in from the other side, he grabbed the carabiner and pulled the runner through. He tied a quick knot to keep it from cinching, then clipped it around the man's chest. "Relax your arms."

Slowly he lowered his arms.

"If anything happens, you're safe. Uncomfortable as hell, but safe."

The man, dark eyes wide, moved his feet and pushed back firmly against the rock.

"Relax. You're safe."

Jack pulled the helmet from the mesh bag, placed it on the man's head, and buckled it under his chin. Now the harness. He keyed the radio. "Luiz, give me three more feet."

"*Three feet?*"

"Make it two."

Jack placed his feet on the lip and sat back over the edge, dropping as the rope fed out. He took a step down the wall and came to a stop. He kicked out with his right leg, moved left, and propped his leg against the fall line. He fished the harness out of the bag. "What's your name?"

Wide-eyed, he opened his mouth to speak. "T-t-thomas." He pushed back hard with his feet.

"Thomas, what?"

"Too complicated for white man," he said, self-consciously. "You'll never remember, I promise."

"Okay, then, Thomas it is. I'd ask how you got in this mess, but let's worry about that later. Relax. You're tied in. Okay?"

He nodded.

"Give me your legs one at a time."

He nodded.

"Okay, left leg first."

He pressed back hard with his right foot and lifted the other.

"Relax," Jack said. He pulled the leg loop up over Thomas' boot, and slipped it up his leg. "Okay, give me the other."

He set the foot down, pushed back hard with both, and slowly raised his right.

Jack reset himself on the wall, put the right leg loop over the man's foot, and worked the harness up his leg.

"Now, raise your butt a little, so I can pull the harness around your waist. And relax."

Thomas reset his foot on the ledge and pushed back with both, hard. Placing his hands behind him, he sunk his fingers into a crack, and slowly lifted himself off the rock.

Something moved.

The ledge floated closer. The wall drifted away.

Jack focused his eyes. What is . . . ?

The ledge peeled away, hinging from the wall, floating, dropping, coming toward him.

Thomas kicked his feet, trying to get back to the wall. He twisted, catching the rope with his leg, sliding it along the edge, slipping it into a crack in the rock. The knot caught.

"Thomas, let go."

Rope stretched.

"Thomas!"

The rope! The slab kept coming.

Jack grabbed Thomas' legs and kicked back, hard, jerking him out of his hold. The rope snapped free.

The slab passed beneath them.

They kept moving.

The slab grew smaller, tumbling toward earth.

Smaller.

Smaller.

The rock crashed into the ground.

— · —

Luiz rubbed his neck.

Waves of sound and shock rolled over him.

He eyed the rope, then Johnny, afraid to look down. "What the hell just . . ."

Slowly, he looked.

— · —

Their movement stopped.

Sound filled the canyon. Echo rose up and reverberated through it.

Movement started, slow at first, then gaining speed.

The wall soared toward them.

Jack cringed, knowing. "Thomas," he shouted. "Lock your arms. Brace yourself. This is gonna hurt."

CHAPTER
4

The wall came out and clobbered them, slamming them with its face. They bounced, then rolled across the rock.

Echo pulsed through the canyon. Air shook.

Cold stone ground into them, taking skin, leaving pain, throwing them back into thin air. They glanced off the rock, slowed, and swung back.

The spinning. Jack reached for his nose, trying to protect it, subjecting his elbows to blows.

The spinning slowed, then stopped. They slid plum, and settled against the wall.

Bone and skin, shoulders, knees, and hips, it all hurt.

Quiet. No shock waves. Nothing.

Jack pressed his hands to his face.

The radio squawked. *"Jack, are you okay? Jack? Answer!"*

Damned radio. Miracle it still works. Dizzy and fighting through pain, Jack keyed the radio strapped to his chest. "Stand by."

He glanced down. Thomas hung at his feet, not moving.

The radio popped. *"Jack, what happened?"*

"Thomas?"

No movement.

"Thomas?"

The helmet shuddered and tilted up. Bloodied face, Thomas opened his eyes.

"You okay?"

"Hard to breathe."

"I bet."

Thomas took a shallow breath. His lips weren't turning blue, yet. If he passed out, he could easily slip out of the sling.

"Jack, talk to me?" the radio screamed.

Jack keyed the mike. "Yes, Luis, we're hurting, okay. But we're all in one piece. Stand by."

The radio went quiet.

"Thomas, do you still have . . ." Jack stopped and stared.

Red vaporous movement, below them, rising, reaching. Dust from pulverized rock swirled below, slipping closer, slowly, but without stealth.

Jack shook his head. Got to get . . . But what can we do? We're sitting ducks. We're helpless.

Dangle. What else is there to do? We'll smother in the dust. No way in hell they can raise us in time to keep us out of that cloud. Dust that fine, that pervasive . . . It'll be impossible to breathe, especially for Thomas, bound in that damned sling. "Is the harness still around your legs?"

"I feel it. Got big thighs."

"That's a good thing—today anyway. Can you pull it up around your waist?"

"I'll try." Thomas struggled. "Can't reach it with both hands. Have to try with one."

"Come on, Thomas. You've got to get a move on."

"Don't rush me. I can hardly breathe."

He hasn't seen anything yet. "Just do it." Come on!

Jack strained to watch. Thomas' jerky movements pulsed through the webbing and rope. "What are you doing?"

"I have a strap. I'm trying to slide the harness up my leg."

"Is it moving?"

Quiet, then, "Got one leg. Got to switch arms."

Jack watched as the cloud reached higher, closer.

"Got to move the carabiner. It's keeping me from using my arm."

"Careful. Keep your arms locked down."

"I'm trying." He reached up the runner and pulled, lifting

against his weight. "Got to move this strap." He squirmed, inching the carabiner around.

"You're scaring me," Jack murmured. "If you raise your arms over your head . . . you'll . . ." He held his tongue.

Movement shook the rope. "Got it" he said, finally, fighting for breath.

"Quick, cinch the waist strap."

"I'm trying."

"Do it quickly. When that dust cloud gets here, breathing will be even harder."

Thomas' movement stopped.

Jack looked down. Thomas appeared frozen in place.

"Don't stop. Get your ass in gear."

Jack could smell the dust. He could taste it.

Thomas fumbled with the buckle, his breathing growing louder. "I don't understand this. Where do you put the strap?" Thomas relaxed his arms, throwing his head back and pulled in a long, deep breath.

The radio came on. *"Jack, tell me what's happening."*

Thomas took another breath and lowered his head. He groaned, and fussed with the buckle. "Okay, got it," he said, sounding relieved.

"Good." Jack looked up.

Luiz craned out over the edge.

Jack keyed his radio. "We're getting . . ." He coughed. "The air, hard to breathe. We're getting Thomas secured."

"Copy. We're switching to the raising system. We'll try to keep you above the cloud."

"That won't happen, but give it your best shot. Hurry."

"Not wanting slow anymore?"

"No, but I do want to kick your ass for sending me down here."

Jack pulled a runner from the equipment sling, quickly wrapped it several times around the load rope, threaded one end through the other, and pulled it tight. He took another, clipped in a carabiner, and lowered it to Thomas. "Now, we need to get your weight on the harness."

Thomas grabbed the carabiner. "What do I do with this?"

"Feel the loops sewn into the waist of the harness? There on the front." He grabbed the ones on his own harness. "These."

Thomas coughed. "Yes."

"Clip the carabiner into both loops. Do one, roll it around to where you can get the gate in the other." Jack held onto his end of the webbing and watched. Specks of red dust hung in the air, settling on Thomas' helmet and shoulders.

Thomas coughed.

He'll be coated, soon. Come on, Thomas!

"I think I got it," he said.

"Lock it down."

Thomas turned the nut on the gate. He coughed deep and hard.

"Cover your mouth and nose."

Thomas raised his hands to his face.

"Now, my turn." Jack fought back a cough. He braced his legs against the wall, and pulled. Thomas hardly budged. "Now why in hell did I think I could lift you like this?" He tried again, straining against the load. He sucked in dust, and the stench overpowered him. He spit it out. "You're more than I can lift. I don't have any leverage."

Silence.

"Thomas?"

Silence. Then low, rumbling. "Can't breathe."

"Hold on. I'll do something else." He felt along the sling and found a short runner. He clipped it into the one coming from Thomas. On its other end, he clipped into the runner hanging from above, on the load rope. "Now you're tied in. Don't be shocked by what I'm about to do."

Thomas coughed and let out a groan.

The dust grew thick. It stung. Jack batted his eyes. Tears welled, and gummed in their corners. He blinked hard. They refused to open. He reached into the mesh bag, and groped along the bottom. Where is it? He slid his finger along something stubby—the knife. Found it.

He fought to open his eyes. Darkness loomed over them, like evening turning to night.

He blew the dust from his lips. "Don't panic. I'm about to cut you loose." He grasped the knife with both hands. Can't drop it. Carefully, he pulled out the blade and locked it in place. Unable to open his eyes, he felt among the rope and webbing. Only the tight webbing. Stay clear of the rope—or we'll both die. He slid the knife along the tightest webbing. It splayed. He held the blade in the splay and sliced. Threads popped away, abruptly letting go. Dead weight dropped and bounced at the end of the webbing.

Thomas gasped, and broke into a cough.

The radio came on. *"Jack, what was that? Everything okay?"*

Jack keyed the radio. "Had to cut some webbing. We're okay. Get us out of here." He pulled his hand off the radio. "Thomas, keep your mouth covered. I'd lower a second line for insurance, but let's just sit tight, let the cloud pass." He brushed the dust from his sleeve and buried his face under his arm.

Luiz came on. *"We're about to start raising."*

"Copy," Jack muttered, his face still covered.

A muffled voice rose up from below. "Why are you here?" Thomas asked.

"What?"

"Why did you come down here? Why did you do this?"

"I was under the impression you needed a little help."

"It could have killed you." Thomas coughed, sounding like lung was ripping apart.

"Don't talk now, Thomas."

"Why did you do this?"

"I don't get to choose what I do. That question, I should be asking you."

The radio popped on. *"Jack, we're about to take your weight off the rappelling rack, in three . . . two . . . one."* They slid down the wall and stopped.

Now in the hands of Carl Foss. What a reassuring thought.

Minutes passed. Then Luis came on. *"We're raising."*

Jack keyed the radio. "Copy. The faster, the better."

"Do I need to remind you how emphatic you were about being slow and deliberate?"

"I'm in no position to engage in clever conversation. But in no mood to hang out, either." He took his finger off the transmit button. "Hang out. Good one, huh, Thomas?" He coughed.

The rope inched up the wall, tenuously, then moments of speed, then a gradual stop.

"Why are we stopping?"

"It'll be this way all the way to the top. And get ready, we're about to drop."

They waited. Then the drop—about three feet. Thomas gasped.

"Get used to it. It'll be that way all the way to the top. Up, then stop, a few feet down, and then up again. They have to lock in their gain, and stretch out the z-rig to do it again."

They began to ascend. When it seemed they were moving quickly and smoothly, they stopped. Then dropped.

After several rounds the dust cloud seemed to diminish. Jack rubbed the dust from his face and batted his eyes, finally managing to get them open. He looked down. The cloud hung below.

Orange haze hung in the sky.

Jack contorted himself to get a look at Thomas. His helmet faced the direction of Sipapu Falls. Orange also hung in the mist at the base of the falls. Strange. All of it was strange. "Thomas, why the hell were you on that ledge?"

He didn't answer, but turned, seemingly tracing the ledge from the falls, all the way back to its almost invisible origins in a hanging canyon.

"You okay?" Jack asked.

"Yes."

"So why were you there?"

"Trying to help. Trying to understand. Doing something maybe it wasn't for me to do."

"What does that mean?"

"Nothing. I've said too much."

CHAPTER
5

"It's everywhere," Jack complained. "In my hair, on my skin, my clothes, everywhere." He pulled off his T-shirt and gave it a pop. Dust hung in the air and drifted toward the abyss. He coughed.

A young ranger stepped back to avoid the drift. "You're alive, man. Count your blessings."

"Not till I get some air, and not till I kick Luiz's ass."

"Jump in the river when we get there."

"I'm not going to the canyon."

"You mean we're lugging this stuff down by ourselves?"

"You got it here." Jack coughed and fought for a breath. "Have him give you a hand." He nodded at Thomas and gave his shirt another pop.

"Sure as hell should," the young ranger said, turning to watch the man Luiz was attending.

Thomas sat upslope, behind the safety line. Luiz swabbed alcohol on the scrapes on his nose, then taped on a piece of gauze. It glistened against his skin.

"You stay here," Luiz said, as he stood and turned to other matters.

Jack watched as Thomas sat back and stared. Unengaged, he seemed to have little interest in what the others were doing. Instead, his attention was faintly on the canyon. What the hell was he thinking? What was he doing on that ledge? And why is he being so damned coy?

Hell, he's Luiz's worry now.

Jack knelt at a boulder and kneaded a knot loose. He tossed the webbing and carabiners into a green canvas duffle.

The team disassembled the raising system, belay lines, anchors, and safety lines, breaking them down and packing them away.

When done, Luiz made one last check, walking cross-contour, making sure no equipment would be left behind. He found none.

"Okay, you two get back to your fire," he said. "Jack, I owe you one."

"One?" Johnny howled. "And what about me? What about my fire? You've got a debt to repay, dude, like tonight. Night shift."

"I don't do fire."

"Yeah, right. Like I don't do rescue. See you at seven."

"By the time we get to the cache, I'll be wasted. And I'm not letting him drive home," Luiz said, nodding at Thomas. "I'm taking him. Plus, I need to stop at that pickup that caught fire on the desert. When this call came in, I was investigating. Left in a hurry. Need to stop and get some things."

"You're making excuses."

"I'm not, and there's something strange about that pickup. No bodies or anything, but I wouldn't've been surprised. Gotta check something. It'll be late when I get back."

"Then we'll see you late. Ask dispatch for directions."

"But . . ."

"And, that one you owe Jack. Hell, there aren't enough beers at Elena's Cantina to pay him back. But give it a try."

"You're right. Next time at Elena's, I buy."

"Deal."

"Do I get any say in this?" Jack asked.

"Don't blow the deal, boss."

Luiz bent down and hefted a pack frame loaded with rope coil, slipped an arm through the strap, and slung it over his shoulder. He pointed Foss at another pack, ignored the big man's grumbling, and turned to Thomas. "Let's go," he said, starting into the brush.

Somehow it felt there would have been more war stories, more rehashing of details, more trading of barbs, but Luiz wasn't that way.

Thomas extended a hand. He held Jack's eye.

"Take care of yourself," Jack said.

"You, too, my friend." Thomas turned and followed after Luiz.

Jack waited, watching until the others disappeared into the brush. "Our turn," he said, to Johnny.

Backing, Johnny took hold of a serviceberry branch, steadying himself. "You're not waiting on me. And you owe me. You're lousy at taking advantage of negotiating position. Luiz is a cheap bastard. You would have gotten off with nothing, maybe one beer max. Which means, your rope man would've been buying his own. You gotta keep your priorities straight, unless, of course, you're buying."

The old Johnny. "Quit talking. Start hiking."

—·—

Back on the plateau, the sense of urgency returned. Smoke sat over the terrain, and the smell of it mingled with the stench of dust. Breathing became harder.

They reached fire line with sun glaring down through pockets of smoke. Orange skies sat over the tops of ponderosa pine. No firefighters were to be seen, only line with green on one side, smoky, barren landscape on the other.

Johnny reached for his radio. "Manion, this is Reger."

No response.

"Simons, this is Reger."

"Go ahead."

"We're back at the fire, near where we left you. Which way do we go to get to your location?"

"Either direction. South, then west to get to me. North, then west to Manion."

"Who needs bodies? And how's it going?"

"Other than changing plans multiple times, okay. Christy, need them your way?"

Another wait, then, *"That would be good."*

Johnny, listening closely, said, "What do you mean, changing plans?"

"*No luck putting line around what we burned this morning. We were lucky to get around both flanks. Afternoon winds. All we could do was try to keep up. We herded it north and west. We're moving as fast as we can on the south side, no problem. Christy's squad is pushing it west. She's got all the heat.*"

Johnny looked at Jack. "Guess we're heading north." An ear still to the radio, he took off at a fast clip. "Christy, we're on our way."

They found the squad, pushing northwest. With two extra bodies it wasn't long before they hit slickrock. To the south, Luiz and another ranger arrived after sunset and helped Simon's squad reach the body of the fire.

Tied in, Johnny plopped down to assess the situation.

Jack watched him. Not exactly as planned. Not exactly bad. Tomorrow's winds will be make or break.

CHAPTER 6

Jack stood on open ground, burned-over grass at his feet, black all around. He stared across at the next ridge. Open flame tore through small pines and oak brush, but few of the big trees. The flame at their feet burned well, and some would possibly die—their growth producing cambium layers boiled—but most would survive.

Wind whipped under the back of his helmet and he quickly pulled back the flap of his belt weather kit, slipped out the anemometer and checked the wind speed. Gusts to thirty.

Gray Beard—Simons—appeared, walking the line, carrying a paper sack. He handed it over. "Special delivery. Lunch, sent up from the canyon."

"Thanks. Ready to get back to your park?"

"Whenever. Did Foss make it back?"

"I'm sure. We'll get you home, don't worry. Hope we didn't make your life harder."

"Hey, you dealt with his bullshit. Don't see that happen much. Last year he was a pain, this year he's arrogant. Something about his brother becoming a bigger big shot. Somewhere back east. Throws it around like he's next in line for some big job. Intimidates the hell out of the Chief."

"I can imagine."

"Know his brother?"

Jack's jaw tightened. "Unfortunately."

"Any good?"

"Guess."

"Not surprised. The cut of the cloth."

"Wind is supposed to drop off in the next hour or so. We just might make it through the burn period."

—·—

After changed plans, bracing for the worst, and enduring a day of winds, all of that was now past. Johnny's original plan again made sense. The Pistol Creek Fire could be allowed to burn, or, as said in bureaucratic-speak, 'managed.'

—·—

Johnny drove, and hardly slowed as he steered the truck onto Culberson Ranch. One of the firefighters held onto the dash board. He looked blue in the gills.

"Quit worrying, Pete," Johnny said. He nodded at the blackened trees in the headlights. "See that. Last year's fire. Liquor me up and I'll tell you war stories. Jack could tell ya more, but it'd take a hell of a lot a liquor to get him talking. I'm cheaper, plus I tell better stories."

Jack groaned.

At the bottom of the hill the truck bounced onto the meadow. Johnny slowed only when they neared the ranch house. "Element of surprise," he said.

Hardly surprised, Kip Culberson met them under the cottonwoods at the front of the house. "Come in, boys." Gray hair combed back, denim shirt crisp, the rancher pointed them toward the casita's courtyard patio. "We want to hear what happened. Everything. The fire, the rescue, everything."

One truck of firefighters had already arrived, and since Christy and two others had stayed behind to monitor the fire, the wait was on this truck. "Sorry we're late, Kip," Jack said. "Contrary to appearances, Johnny actually does have a responsible bone in his body. We had to drag him away. But it's nice of you to feed us."

"Our pleasure. We thought it'd be better than army rations or sack lunches."

Kelly's mother scurried out a side door, carrying a tray of food. The streaks of gray in Juanita's hair only made her an older version of Kelly. She was a beautiful woman of Spanish heritage. With her constant air of contentment, entertaining suited her. She saw Jack and stopped.

"Juan!" she shouted.

"Juan?" Johnny whispered. "Is she talking to me?"

"No," Jack whispered back. "Our little joke." He lit up. "Juanita." He walked toward her, trying to hide a limp.

"Are you hurt?"

"No." Jack gave her a peck on the cheek, careful not to brush against her.

"Do I have leprosy or something?"

"No, I do. I'm dirty. Dust and smoke. You don't want me touching you."

"Don't be foolish." She handed her tray to Johnny and smothered Jack with a hug.

The side door swung open, and Kelly stepped out, a bottle of wine in one hand, long-stemmed clay goblets threaded through the fingers on the other. Her eyes opened wide and she rushed through the horde.

Jack grabbed her shoulders. "Whoa, careful."

She pushed back his arms, and wrapped hers around him. "Ooh," she said, looking taken aback. "You smell of all sorts of things."

He laughed. "Mind if I jump in the shower? I'd breathe easier."

"Tell us about the rescue first. We're dying to know."

"I promise, it'll be better if I can breathe." He pulled away. "Kip, can I borrow a shirt?"

"I'll hang one on the door knob."

— · —

Stripped down and standing at the mirror, he checked for bruises. One on each shoulder, one on a hip. Both elbows. Both knees.

He climbed in the shower, washed away layers of dirt, dust, and sweat, then let the warmth soak into his muscles and down to the bone.

— · —

Jack returned, his hair wet and combed, wearing a shirt too big in the body and short in the sleeves, but it was clean.

"How are the enchiladas?" he asked, approaching the long, plank table.

They were going over well. He filled his plate and took a seat with Kelly and Johnny.

Kelly took a whiff in his direction. "You've lost all your character." She smiled and squeezed his arm. "Tell us what happened."

"Johnny didn't tell you?" Jack cut into an enchilada, savored a bite, and tried to decide where to start the story.

"You should tell it, but speaking of losing things," Johnny said. He turned to Kelly. "He coulda lost a lot more than character yesterday." He raised a brow.

"What's that mean?" Kelly asked.

"You coulda lost your man." He flashed her a look.

"Go on."

Jack shook his head. "Thought you wanted me to tell this."

"Hey, you saved a guy."

"Don't."

"Okay, it's your story. Tell it any way you want, unless you want to hear how masterful I was on rope. That's about the only part I can tell with any authority, except for hearing that crash, and how it echoed up and down the canyon."

Kelly's eyes grew wide. "You're joking right?"

"Yes, kinda. Except for that part about the crash."

Her brow furrowed. "Start talking."

Johnny attempted a smile. "I'm just pulling your leg."

"Is he?"

Jack opened his mouth to speak but saw something fearful in her eyes.

"Hey, I didn't see it, but you should be proud," Johnny said.

"Proud of what?"

"He saved a guy. A big rock came peeling off the wall. Made a hell of a noise. Echoed up and down the canyon. Sounded like the world coming to an end. Shook everything."

Kelly's mouth gaped open.

Johnny turned to Jack. "You tell her."

Jack held his tongue.

"You two were bouncing around on that rope . . ."

"Shut up Johnny."

"Hey, everything worked out, I promise. Besides, I was on top, on rope, had 'em the whole time. No way I woulda let go." He flashed a smile. "But it felt like I was fighting a hundred pound bass."

"Ha, very funny," Kelly growled. She turned to Jack. "Your message for me was, you were helping lift the load. The load, you said. Turns out, you were the load. You lied."

"I guess it turned out that way."

"Cristy told me you were there for muscle. That's all."

"I didn't know I'd be put at the end of the rope."

"Tell me the whole story. Everything. Don't leave anything out."

"It's not a long story. They lowered me down to the guy. He was on a ledge. I got him tied in. The ledge cut loose. I managed to kick off the rock and get us out of the way. It missed us. We were hurt more by swinging into the wall than we were from the rock falling into the canyon."

Kelly's mouth slowly gaped open, speechless.

"They raised us to safety. That's pretty much it."

"I'd a been cleanin' out my underwear," Johnny said.

"Shut up, Johnny," Kelly said, tears welling up. "I can't believe you'd put yourself in that kind of danger. Were you trying to get yourself killed?"

"No, I . . ."

"That's the second near miss I know about. You and ropes. A year ago at Caveras Creek, and now this! How many more are there?"

Johnny leaned toward her. "Kelly, I'm sure I made it sound worse than it was. That rock falling in the canyon. I'm sure it was no big deal."

She ignored him. "Why didn't you let someone else rescue that person?"

"I had no choice. I had the experience and training, even though it was dated."

"Dated!"

"It was either me or Luiz. There was no one else to do it."

She clenched her jaw. "So, you pulled rank!"

"No, Luiz did. He was in charge. He knew more about another job. It was more complicated."

She looked confused. "What could be more complicated?"

"The raising system. Getting us back to the top."

She wiped tears from her cheeks.

"Kelly, I'm sorry," Johnny said. "Didn't mean to scare you. I was trying to give Jack a hard time. Let you know you should be proud."

She patted his hand, avoiding his eyes. "I know, Johnny. It's just . . ."

Jack put his finger under her chin, and forced her eyes up to his. "Kelly, I would never do anything I wasn't trained to do. And I did try to resist, but that's where Luiz needed me."

"But you . . ." She noticed others watching. She held her tongue and waited as they turned back to conversations. "I'm sorry," she said. "We'll talk later, when we're alone."

"Now the silent treatment," Johnny said. He took a sip of beer and smiled. "You're not doing too well in sustaining conversation. First that Indian guy, now Kelly."

"You're not helping."

Kelly eyed them both. "Native American?"

"Some guy named Thomas," Jack said.

"His last name—what was it?"

"Didn't say. Said it was complicated."

"Where was this?"

"Near Sipapu Falls. On a ledge I never ever noticed before yesterday."

"Mother!" she cried. Frantically, she stood. "Mother! The rescue. It was Thomas. At the falls."

Juanita ran to her.

"What?" Jack asked.

"Thomas had a sister," Kelly said. "She died at Sipapu Falls."

"You've said enough," Juanita whispered, wiping away Kelly's tears.

"Why was Thomas there?" Jack asked.

"I don't know," she said, slipping a hand over her mouth.

"But you do, don't you?"

She said nothing.

The firefighters drove off, some to return to the fire, some to rest before the next shift. Jack said his good-byes and stayed behind. He would have Kelly drive him home.

She seemed to expect a round of questioning and stuck to her mother, helping clean up. When done, she found new things to do, until busy work started getting hard to find.

"I'll be in your studio. I want to see what you're working on," he said, in code she undoubtedly understood to mean he would be waiting to talk.

Muscles growing stiff and pains showing themselves, he hobbled down the hall and slipped into the room. In the moment before switching on the light, he noticed the lights of Las Piedras in the distance. Dark, wild ground occupied the space between. He left the light off and stepped over to the window.

The door swung open. "You in here?" Kelly asked.

"At the window."

She slipped in and closed the door. Darkness settled back over the room.

"I take it you're not studying my latest masterpiece."

"No, but I want to see it."

"It's not coming together. Maybe another time. What are you doing?"

"Thinking."

"About Thomas?"

"Yeah, and the stars."

"But we're not going to talk about stars, are we?"

"We can, but that's not all."

"I don't have much to tell."

"But more than you're saying."

"I haven't seen him in years. He's an old friend, but we both moved away for so long."

"Just tell me."

She sighed. "He was born and raised in the pueblo. Great guy. He can be quite funny or quite serious. He's very bright. His mother encouraged him to get an education, which he did. He's married, has a son. I heard he recently moved home."

"Why?"

"I don't know, but I suspect he wants his son to grow up in that culture."

"Tell me about his sister."

Kelly stepped back from the window, and picked up a brush. She twisted the handle. "After her death Thomas pulled away from who he was. It seemed to shake the foundations of his very being. After college he was teaching in Albuquerque."

"What was he doing yesterday?"

She seemed to expect the question. She didn't answer.

"Why was he out on that ledge?"

"Jack, I can't say, or rather, I shouldn't say."

"I assume the waterfall had something to do with it."

"I shouldn't say."

"Kelly, I saved his life. It could have cost me mine."

"It's not my secret to tell. It's Thomas'. It's something I know a little about, and so does Mother, but we shouldn't. We shouldn't know."

"That makes no sense."

"It doesn't sound like it, but it does, and I can't tell you why."

"Why would he risk his life in the place that killed his sister?"

She shook her head. "If anyone tells you, it should be Thomas. Ask him."

"He wouldn't talk. Except to say it might be something that was not his to do. What would he be doing that he shouldn't be, and why would you and your mother know about it?"

"Oh, Jack," she whined. "If I answer you'll just keep going. You'll make me tell you everything."

"I won't. Promise."

She sighed. "Before starting his own practice, my grandfather was a doctor with Indian Health Service. He worked at the pueblo and made many friends. Mother and Thomas' mother played together as kids. They became lifelong friends. She died a few years ago, complications from diabetes, but when Thomas' sister died, Mother went to comfort her. I went too. Thomas and I are about the same age. We became friends. When Lola Polly was grieving, she said more than she wanted to. Later, she asked us to respect and honor her by keeping those things to ourselves. We promised."

"Something to do with traditions?"

"I won't say."

"I need to know."

She sighed. "Ask Thomas. You did save his life. He might tell you, but I won't. I won't break that promise."

"But what if he . . ."

"No, it's not my secret to tell." She smiled and put her arms around his neck. "How do I get this off your mind?"

He laughed. "Good luck at that. Kind of hard letting go of something after bouncing around at the end of a rope, looking at a long drop into oblivion."

"You smell better than you did earlier. Let's go to your place."

"Funny. You're changing the subject."

She snuggled against him. "How about a dip in the spring?"

"I'm not forgetting about this Thomas thing."

"We'll see."

— · —

Jack ran his finger down the page and located the file code. He slammed the binder shut and placed it back on the shelf.

The bank of off-white, four-drawer file cabinets lined the wall. He scanned the codes on the drawers, found the one he wanted— third drawer on the fifth file cabinet—and pulled it open. Old files. Discolored, and in an old format. Looked right. He pulled out a file, dated fifteen years earlier, and flipped through the pages. Nothing. He slipped it back into place, and pulled out the one from sixteen years back. Flipping through pages he found it, accompanied by newspaper articles. The case incident report was heavy on details of the death and body recovery, sparse on the why. A young woman was on a hike, got lost, found herself in an unforgiving place, and fell to her death. The reporting ranger commented he had never noticed the ledge before that day.

A newspaper article gave information on the woman, but nothing about why she was there. Her name was Maria Trujillo. "*. . . survived by a husband and infant daughter. She was a resident of the Pueblo.*"

No more information than that.

— · —

Jack went up to his office and opened a listing of phone numbers for agency technical specialists. He dialed the phone.

Two rings and, "Park Service, Ethnography, Chloe Bell."

"Chloe, I need you to tell me something in your area of expertise. Oh, sorry, this is Jack Chastain."

"Hello to you too, Jack."

"Hi. I'm in a bit of a daze. This is all pretty hard to understand. We rescued a guy off a ledge. A guy named Thomas."

"And you were involved?"

"Yeah."

"A little far afield for a biologist, isn't it?"

"Long story, but anyway, this guy was scared to death, but even after we saved him—even after the rock he was sitting on peeled off the wall and nearly killed us both—he wouldn't talk. His mind was elsewhere. Happy to be alive, but he wouldn't talk.

Doesn't seem like a jumper. I later learned his sister died in the same location, sixteen years ago. Why, I don't know."

"Slow down. That's a lot to absorb. So, is this man Native American?"

"Yes."

"Where was this?"

"Near Sipapu Falls."

"Interesting."

"Really. Why?"

She laughed. "Ordinarily, with a name like Sipapu Falls you'd think it was sacred or something. Do you know what Sipapu means?"

"No."

"It means place of emergence from the dark underworld. The center of the cosmos."

"Ah . . ."

"Not so fast. There's another use of the word. A Sipapu can be the hole in the floor of a kiva, symbolizing the exit from the underworld."

"So which is it?"

She laughed. "Neither. Hate to burst your bubble, but everything I've heard or seen suggests the waterfall was named by businessmen early in the last century. Trying to create a mystique to lure tourists to the area. It stuck. The Pueblo calls it something quite un-mysterious, like 'place of falling waters.'"

"Then why did this Thomas guy go there?"

"The site still might have significance."

"Meaning?"

"I don't know. Maybe something important culturally. Maybe something else entirely."

"What do you mean, culturally?"

"Any number of things. Could have some significance to some important story, but I'm not aware that it does. Could have importance to one of their clans or religious societies."

"Clan?"

"Each clan has a role in the society of the pueblo. It takes all clans to make the society whole."

"What would any of this have to do with a hardly noticeable trail to a waterfall?"

"No idea, and possibly nothing. I'm only guessing. But if it did, it might have something to do with a ritual, pilgrimage, initiation, who knows. And his sister died, what, eighteen years back?"

"Sixteen."

"Hmmm," Bell said. "Hard to know."

"How can I find out?"

"I doubt they'll tell you."

"Why not?"

"You're not part of their culture."

"What about you? You're respected. You could ask."

She laughed. "Me? A short, blonde, Jewish anthropologist from New York? They won't share that information with me any more than they'll tell you."

"What do I do? This is frustrating."

"Let me ask you a question. Why do you need to know?"

"I was nearly killed up there."

"I understand. But why do you need to know? You've got to remember, traditions are important to these people, and in ways that you cannot understand. If you dig hard enough, you might learn something. It might end at that, or it might not. You don't have the slightest clue what the consequences might be. The social ramifications, for Thomas, his clan, his society—they could be great."

"I wouldn't do anything. I just need to know."

She laughed. "Oh, you silly Anglo."

CHAPTER 8

Jack got up and wandered down the hall.

How the hell do you forget something like Thomas and that ledge? Forget everything and move on! Easy for her to say. Cloe didn't hang at the end of a rope, slamming against the canyon wall, wondering if it'd all come to an end with a big fall.

He ducked into the Dispatch Office for a cup of coffee. "Morning Molly," he said, knowing she was aware of his presence, but tied up with morning routines.

"You have a meeting in town," the uniformed dispatcher muttered as she poured over radio logs making notes.

"Actually, two this week, but how'd you know?"

"*Gazette*. I wondered if we'd need to find someone to cover for you," she said. "Aren't you supposed to be on the fire?"

"I'm done, unless Johnny needs me. If it stays a good fire, he won't. Might creep around all summer, get snuffed out by the monsoons, but whatever happens is Johnny's to worry about."

He chuckled to himself as he picked the newspaper off the counter dividing the room. The *Gazette*—Molly was always the first to see it. Between the radio, phone and *Gazette* she had her finger on the pulse of everything. He gave the front page a scan and noticed the blurb about the meeting. "*Next round of Coalition meetings starts today.*" It gave the time and place, "*. . . Inn of the Canyons, at 10:00 a.m.,*" and a short list of probable attendees, "*Kip*

Culberson, rancher and former New Mexico State Senator, . . ." and
". . . Karen Hatcher, Director of the Trust for the Southwest." They
were quoted as inviting any member of the public wanting to
participate. The paper stated the purpose of the Coalition, *". . . to
find common ground and make recommendations on managing the
new National Monument,"* and gave brief histories of its establishment outside the National Park—by proclamation by the outgoing
President—and of the controversies that followed.

The earlier battles, to see them described, seemed rather
pedestrian, but they were anything but that six months ago. Then
came the Coalition, and the search for common ground, and with
that, a period of peace. Now, cliques were becoming common,
resulting in more and more battles.

Jack shook his head at the description. Overstated? Maybe.
Maybe not. Some issues were tough, but so far none rose to the
level of being unsolvable. But, it wasn't out of the question.

He slipped into the hall sipping coffee, and sauntered its
length, stopping at the end office. Margie, Joe Morgan's secretary,
was not yet in, so he stepped past her desk, and stopped at the
Superintendent's door, knocking three times. "Morning, Joe. Got
a minute?"

Joe looked up from his reading. "Morning." He gestured to
a chair and sat back, the image of seasoned professionalism—
uniform perfect, greying hair precisely clipped.

"Two things," Jack said, plopping down. "The guy we rescued
. . . he had a sister. Died in the same location years ago. I'll share
that with Luiz, in case he wants to follow up on it."

"Tell him to let me know if he learns more."

"Will do. Second, bad news and I'm sorry you're just hearing
this but today's my first day back in the office. A wallflower, genus
Erysimum, a candidate for endangered species status . . . it . . ."

"Tell me."

"Burned. The whole known population." Jack let out a sigh.
"Gone. A guy named Foss was assigned to protect them. He did
nothing. Let the fire burn right past him."

"The overall responsibility was ours."

"Of course, and I assure you the loss is weighing heavy on

Johnny Reger, but it wasn't his fault. He took precautions. He knows we need to conduct a review of some sort. Foss, it turns out, is brother to a ghost from my past."

Joe slowly shook his head. "We sure this plant isn't fire adapted?"

"Might be. We just don't know."

"Start the review. Keep me informed." He gave his head another shake. "I see you have a meeting in town."

"Actually, two this week. The hard stuff. Wanna join me?"

"No, I won't intrude. Might mess things up." He picked up a pen and gave it several clicks. "A year ago, half the Coalition was fighting to get rid of the national monument, the other half willing to fight to the death to keep it. Where they are today is remarkable. That they recognize the values they have in common, amazing. You need to feel good about that. I know that's hard to say now, considering you came in here with bad news, but you should. When this wraps up you'll be in demand. You can pretty much call your shot on where you want to go next."

"I'm not going anywhere."

"I'm serious, your career's back on track."

"I'm where I want to be. That other stuff doesn't concern me."

"What does concern you?"

"All I need is to be relevant. To do work that's relevant."

"You sure?"

"I'm not looking for promotions or big titles, just meaningful work."

Joe sighed. "I respect you for that, but there'll come a day when I or someone else needs you to take on something bigger, for the good of the Service. People will remember how capable you are when the Coalition report is finished."

"Too early to jump to conclusions. Too much work to do. We'll see breakdowns, maybe big ones."

"Is that the restored Jack talking? Or remnants of the one that showed up here a year and a half ago, damaged and defeated?"

He stopped himself and looked past Joe, through the window at soaring cliffs and blue skies opening up above them. What a question. "Not sure. I'm not sure I ever will be fully restored."

"Need to talk?"

"No, I'm fine."

"Jack, when I was told you were reassigned to this park, I was also told I had no choice in the matter, not to ask questions. I did ask—vehemently—because I wanted nothing to do with someone else's problem. I got no answers. Not real ones. Only cryptic mutterings from personnel in Washington, about you being the loser in some political battle in Montana. You arrived here no more willing to talk, hardly willing to come out of the office, unless to get quickly into the field, away from everyone."

"I know," Jack said, dropping his head.

"Things changed. Year and a half later, I'm glad you're here, glad I didn't let you hide in the office. I needed help. The controversy that fell in our laps, the creation of the national monument, all that. You were good. You delivered. The community thinks so, too."

"They're easy to work with."

"I doubt you felt that way six months ago. You took a beating, but you came through. It's time you opened up about your ghosts. What happened in Montana? Tell me about this Foss guy and his brother."

"I'd rather not talk about it."

"Remember, I've been through my own battles."

"I understand that, Joe. I promised I'd let go of that episode in my life. Mostly I have. I see the old me. Dedication to mission. Everything. But other times I'm not so sure. Other times I wonder if something's permanently changed. Sometimes I feel a little paranoid."

Joe nodded and set down his pen. He tapped on a page. "I'm not trying to preach, but I see no reason for paranoia."

Jack stood. "I need to get ready. I'll let you know how the meeting goes."

"Relevance, huh?" Joe said, watching him closely. "That's not necessarily the easy path."

"I don't expect it to be," Jack said, stopping at the door. "But what are you saying?"

"I'm saying, some people could care less. Hell with the humility of it. They'll paint you in ways that serve their interests. They'll see you as a pawn, your humility be damned. Your relevance be damned."

"Speaking of paranoid . . ."

"I know, but I'm not." He paused. "Takes a little courage, but be willing to stand for the truth. Be responsible. Remember who you work for."

"Those are three very different things."

"I know."

"Are you questioning something I did?"

Joe laughed. "No, and I'm not really worried that you need that advice. Some people need to hear it because they're more concerned with getting ahead than exercising any integrity. Someone like you? For you, it's a reminder that when things get hard, when you need to draw on that courage, it's okay to have a touchstone. It's okay to be wrong at times, but it's not okay to avoid blame or responsibility. You can't forget who your bosses are. We have our mission, but even those who don't understand or work against it deserve our attention. They deserve to be heard and considered. They deserve truth, even hard truth."

"Sometimes truth is hard to come by. Sometimes truth is taken to be the last word, the one that ends the argument."

"True enough. But if you want to stay relevant, you'll seek it out, and believe everyone deserves to hear it, and deserves to be heard."

Jack nodded. "I promise, I understand, but that last one may have gotten me burned in the past." He rubbed his forehead. "Not sure. Either listening to everyone, or not listening enough to the people who thought I should be listening only to them." He shook his head and gave it another rub. "That's not quite right either. Might've been because others were willing to listen only to them."

"Who did the listening?"

"May've gone all the way to the top. Maybe as high as the Director."

"You sure of that?"

"I'm not sure of anything. But I had the Director scheduled for a meeting in Montana and he never made it. There I sat, two hundred members of the public, wanting to be heard, wanting to be included, and no Director. Two days later, I'm reassigned."

"Sure it was the Director? Where was the RD in all of this?"

"The Regional Director called afterward, said he fought for us but lost. It was out of his hands. Said things were happening he didn't understand. Thought I should play it safe. Thought there were people who might come after me if I didn't. I was tired. I took his advice."

"And you're sure the Director was involved?"

"I have no evidence of anything."

"Not surprised. That high in the food chain, they don't leave fingerprints."

"That's not the end of the story. We had unexpected results in our wetlands research. Somehow word got out we'd picked up methane levels we couldn't explain. We weren't pointing fingers, but frackers felt implicated. I have no idea who finished the report, but when it hit the streets, conclusions were changed, data were altered."

"That's a serious charge, Jack."

"You want serious. Months after that, a family with a sick daughter tested their well. Full of carcinogens. Anytime a finger got pointed at the oil and gas guys, they waved that research report with my name on it, saying, 'It's not us.'"

"What did you do?"

"By then I was here. No one talked to me. But the truth? Somewhere it got lost."

"Dangerous games, politics," Joe said, sitting back in his chair. "Fact of life, but the trick is not to let it be the way you play the game. If you live by that game, you die by it." Expression left his face. "Unfortunately, the ones who play the game best don't get hurt, other people do."

"Tell me about it. And that's why staying relevant is all I hope for." Jack spun around and left.

He walked down the hall to his office and began preparations.

CHAPTER 9

"I know this is a tough topic, but we have to find a solution," said one of the ranchers, Ginger Perrette, a middle-aged woman dressed in what might have been her chore clothes. "We need water. Cattle need water. Grazing's never been allowed in the national park, but it is in the monument, per the proclamation. We've got to work through this. It's . . ." She was cut off.

"No, we gotta protect the river," said a young environmentalist named Dave Van Buren. "That's what's important. If we don't keep the cattle out of the riparian system, we condemn it to being a dead, sun-drenched, pisshole."

"There are things we can do. I want to protect the river as much as you do, but my cattle need water. Without it, I'm out of business."

"What would be the harm in not tackling this one? Maybe the perfect answer will appear on its own, later," said Lori Martinez, toying with the zipper on her polyester vest. She waited for a response, eyes hopeful. "Maybe well into the future, but that'd be okay."

"It's your meeting, your outcome, but my experience says it's risky," Jack said. He stepped toward her and stopped, centered amidst the group.

"Why's it risky? Aren't we risking gridlock, even falling apart if we can't work this out?" she continued. "We're nearly ready to write our report and yet we can't get past this."

"Let me put it this way. What's at stake?"

"What do you mean?"

"What do we risk losing? What, if lost, would make you feel you'd failed your grandchildren? For each of you those may be different things, or the same things for different reasons. If our recommendations fall apart because we failed to address this issue, what's at stake?"

"But it's hard."

"It is hard, but it's your heritage." Jack moved to his spot at the table, and leaned against it. He looked around the room at frustrated faces. People who an hour ago saw themselves as friends and collaborators, now were in irritated cliques. "Look, you've done pretty well so far. Yes, common ground was easier, and you accomplished a lot. Your recommendations on those things are good. Very strong. Give yourself some credit, but yes, you need to figure this out. I don't think you can avoid it. If you avoid the tough issues, it'll only cause problems later. But I do have suggestions." He looked around the table. "Be patient. Listen to each other. Give others reason to listen to you when it's your turn to talk."

"But when we were talking about common ground, I thought I could trust everyone," Ginger said. "Things seemed to make so much sense. Now, as we deal with this one, I'm seeing belligerence. My feeling of trust is slipping away."

"That's because . . ." Dave blurted, before seeing Jack's hand cutting him off.

"Give me a second," Jack said. "That took nerve to offer that kind of honesty." He turned to the woman. "Understood. What can we do to help?"

"I'm not pretending . . . I mean . . . Oh, just give me a chance to finish my thoughts before somebody trashes 'em."

"I promise, I'll do what I can to give you that." He turned to the young environmentalist. "Do you?"

Sheepishly, he nodded.

Jack looked around the table at the others, waiting for nods of agreement. He turned to the young man. "Do you have something to say?"

"I'll wait. Let's hear her first."

— · —

Jack drove back to the park, his mind on the meeting. The tough problems. The last issues, always the hard ones.

Beginning to wind down, the flow of adrenaline stopped, soon would come numbness, then being mentally fried.

He turned the white, green-striped pickup marked *Park Ranger* onto the scenic road into the park. After driving miles of an oft-beaten path, he turned right, onto a side-canyon road that ended behind headquarters.

He pulled to a stop, looked back, gently pushed the accelerator, and backed the pickup into a parking space.

The back door of the building burst open. Johnny Reger darted out and jogged toward the pickup, a thin stack of papers in hand. He came around to the driver's side.

Jack rolled down the window.

"Boss, we've got weird stuff going on. You're gonna freak."

"Tell me."

"That burning pickup that started the fire . . . you won't believe it."

"Just tell me, Johnny."

"No license plates, no vehicle identification number. The plates were removed, the VIN was ground off. And Luiz thinks it's an old government pickup. Looks like it had markings like ours, but melted off. The park doesn't have one that old, and probably hasn't had anything that model year for over a decade, maybe longer."

"That's odd. Who'd want to burn an old government pickup?"

"Luiz is still investigating, treating it as a crime scene. All he's found is a set of tracks out on the desert, made back to the road, and a spot where they were probably hiding when we arrived to put out the fire."

Jack sensed irritation. "What's wrong?"

"The pickup's got everyone spooked, as if folks are gonna start torching off their Caddys just for fun of it."

"Does Luiz think there's reason to believe this is the beginning of something?"

"Maybe someone playing some sort of weird game but we don't know what that game is."

"Why are you so excited?"

"Cause I'm pissed. The superintendent ordered me down here to update the plan for the fire. Torching that rare plant didn't help, but after I did the update he said he wouldn't sign till you've looked at it."

"Me?" Jack let out a sigh. "That's your job now."

"I know. I told him you'd say that, but he said you'd be back soon. He wants you to look at it."

"Let me see your plan."

Johnny handed over the papers.

Jack flipped past the cover page of signatures—all there except the superintendent's—and past pages of narrative, stopping at a map. He studied the topography.

Jack rubbed his eyes and tried to get his brain to click back into gear. "Fire behavior?"

"Projections are in the back. They look good."

Jack thumbed through the back of the proposal.

"You good with it?"

Jack gave him a confused look.

"I need you to say that it's a good plan, that you still support it."

"Oh, yeah. Let's go to my office. I'll run some numbers."

"Why?"

"See what I come up with for fire behavior and spread."

Johnny's brow furrowed. "You don't trust mine?"

"I do, but that's not the point. Joe wants you to have me look at it. If you want to give him what he wants, I should run the numbers. It's a thing called credibility."

Johnny pulled off his cap and scratched his head. "You saying I'm not credible?"

"No. With me, you're very credible. With Joe, I have no idea.

But I need you seen as credible. You need to go in there, show Joe you took him seriously, that we came up with similar results."

Johnny frowned and stepped out of the way. Jack rubbed his eyes and climbed out of the pickup. Johnny followed him up the stairs and down the hall to his office.

Pouring over maps, Jack quickly determined fuel types and calculated slopes. "Weather forecast," he said. Johnny sorted through the papers and extracted it. Jack picked it apart, finding hours that would give the most extreme fire behavior. He opened the forecasting software, input values for fuel, weather and topography, and let the model give him outputs.

Johnny peered over his shoulder at the monitor. "Your numbers are more extreme than mine." He glanced between the screen and numbers in his own projection. "I see the difference. Fine fuels. Why'd you use that number for one hour fuels?"

"I dropped fine fuel moisture a couple of points to give worst case."

"Makes sense, but your outputs, do they torpedo us?"

"Don't think so. Spread and intensity look manageable."

Johnny stood up and let out sigh. "So, supportive?"

"You're banking on the fire moving north and west. The bigger it gets, the more trouble you'll have catching it, if you need to. Could give you trouble if it whips around the line."

"It's already hit the canyon rim to the northeast."

"Do it," Jack said. He signed on a margin of the cover page.

Johnny rushed the door. "Let's go see Joe." He stopped. "You coming?"

"Nope, it's your fire."

CHAPTER
10

Late spring in Piedras Coloradas National Park. Days growing longer, warmth and seasonal rains bringing green to the meadows. Buds, then leaves to the trees and shrubs, and now, flowers making their appearance.

Jack Chastain knelt at the wildflowers at his feet—desert marigold, and a few feet away, paintbrush. The scene would only get better in days to come. Soon the canyon would fill with yellows common in spring and early summer, and as the desert days grow hotter, these would retreat and yield to a new scene of scattered whites—of asters, sacred datura, and others.

He noticed visitors ahead on the trail, looking at something on the river. He paused, not wanting to intrude on their solitude, and for a moment regretted choosing this way into headquarters. People deserve their moments, but they do not typically mind a minute with a ranger. He made no assumptions. Quietly, he approached a man and woman, binoculars to their eyes, looking elatedly at something stirring in a backwater margin of emergent marsh. Jack started to glance over, but they had neither heard nor seen him. He slipped quietly past.

At headquarters he stopped at his office, dropped off his canvas briefcase, and headed down the hall to dispatch. He pulled his cup off the shelf and poured himself some coffee.

"Morning, Molly."

"Someone must've been talking last night at Elena's. Our local conspiracy theorist heard about that plant getting torched. He's letting everyone know."

"You're kidding."

"No. And check the newspaper. There's some new player getting involved with the Coalition. Says you need to be kicked out of the process."

"That's odd." Jack took a sip of his coffee and picked up the paper. "What's their name?"

"Can't remember."

Reading, he slipped out and went to his office.

> "... Coalition will meet later in the week, but a new player says he plans to force a change, or bring an end to the effort ..."

He plopped into his chair and held the *Gazette* closer.

"Knock, knock." Marge, the superintendent's secretary stood at the door. "Joe wants to see you, in his office" She headed back up the hall.

Jack dropped the paper and followed after her.

He fell behind, but slipped around the corner, through her office, into Joe's, stopping at the door.

"Have a seat," Joe said. He spun around from the computer and stared across the desk. "I've only got a couple of minutes before my nine o'clock shows up. This Foss character we sent home. Was there more you didn't tell me?"

"It was a discipline and performance problem. On the verge of becoming a sexual harassment case."

"And this same fellow helped on the rescue?"

"Yes, he did. I didn't mention that, did I?"

"No. He's being characterized as one of the heroes of that action. And yet we fired him and sent him home?"

"Hero? I wouldn't exactly say he was. . ." Jack shook his head in disbelief. "Awkward, isn't it?"

"Yes."

"You sent him home?"

"Johnny did. No, I guess I did."

"Which is it?"

"I did. He was giving Johnny trouble. I asserted myself to protect him."

Joe sighed. "I may end up doing the same for you. I've been called to Washington to meet the Director. This and other business. Not sure why this would rise to the importance of a trip to D.C., but apparently it does."

"No!"

"Yes."

Jack felt his heart pound. "Can't believe it. Foss' brother is pulling strings with the Director." He wrung his hands.

Joe set his glasses on his forehead and rubbed his eyes. "Document what happened. Email me something by day's end. I leave this afternoon."

"I will." Jack shook his head. "Email's been jammed with rumors about the Director pulling research funding from Sand Dunes. Looks political. Now this! We're gonna get hammered."

"Calm down. You've got enough to worry about. Read this morning's paper. You've got a guy showing up at your meeting tomorrow, plans to give you some trouble."

"That's what Molly said. I'll read it. I'm sorry you're getting pulled into this."

"Comes with the job."

"Knock, knock." Marge stood in the door. "Your nine o'clock."

Jack stood to leave.

Marge slipped away from the door and another woman stepped in. Tall, slender, and blonde. Impeccably dressed, navy blue suit, a profile that looked strangely familiar. She extended a hand. "Hi Joe, I'm Erika."

Joe shook her hand. "This is Jack Chastain, one of my staff. Chief of Resource Management."

She slowly turned. "Nice title, Jack."

"Jack, this is Erika Jones, regional office."

She looked different. Hair shorter. "I know who she is."

Joe glanced between them. "You do? How do you know each other?"

"Past lives."

Erika cocked her head. "Yes, we were on a team that . . ."
He cut her off. "Montana."

"I see," Joe said. He gestured Jones toward a seat.

"What a coincidence," Jack said. "We were just talking about your boyfriend's little brother. Did you know he has a brother?"

"I don't know who you're talking about. I don't have a boyfriend. No clue what you mean by a boyfriend's brother."

"I need to get back to my office." Jack moved to the door.

"Jack, I need you to stay. There's obvious tension between you two, but I ask that you be adults. Erika, when you set up this appointment, I expected to be here all day. That's no longer the case. I'm leaving for the airport. Jack will have to be the one to answer your questions."

"I'm fine with that." She flashed a look his way. "We can work together. We have before. Many days of good work. There seems to be a little misunderstanding, but we can work that out."

Joe turned to Jack. "Can you give her some time today? Maybe the next few days."

"I have the meeting to prepare for, and things I need to do in the field, but I can give her whatever time I have left."

"Find the time," Joe said. "Jack, take a seat and I'll give you both a few minutes."

He settled back into a chair.

Jones transformed into cool confidence, her chiseled but attractive features focused on the superintendent. A dark suit like hers rarely made an appearance in Piedras Coloradas, and when it did, the skirt was typically longer. Jack glanced again at the blond hair, clipped almost short. Such a different look than the Erika Jones he remembered. What was confidence before now seemed catlike.

Morgan pointed at Jack. "Before we turn to Erika's business, I meant to ask about the fire."

"She's fine, a good fire. Johnny's plan is good, and he's got good people monitoring spread north and west."

"She?" Erika asked. She smiled.

"It—I mean it."

"Must be a dainty little thing."

"No, she's not. I mean, it's not. Has the potential to get large and complicated."

She dangled a shoe. "Complicated. What's her name, Jack?"

"Why?"

"Just wondering. Do you name your fires after women you know? Complicated ones. Hot, wild ones. Tame and controllable ones."

Joe threw his head back and laughed. "Careful."

Jack looked over, expected a familiar teasing smile. There was none. "I misspoke."

"I'll behave," she said, exchanging smiles with Joe. "Wouldn't want a fire named after me. Might be awful, or worse, a puny little thing."

Jack scowled. "I'm not ready for your sense of humor."

"So, Erika, why are you here?" Joe asked.

"I'm on a project for the Regional Director. Fact finding mostly. Visiting parks to understand their management issues. Giving him my take on how solid their planning is. Whether we should be approaching things differently."

"What kind of things?" Joe asked, suspiciously.

"Public engagement. Political pitfalls."

"Why would he be sticking his fingers into that from Denver?"

Her smile slipped away. "Oh, no, don't get me wrong. I won't be suggesting that we get involved in what you're doing at park-level, where the rubber meets the road."

"Then what?"

"We want a better handle on what's happening around the region so we can complement your efforts. Engage the right people, buy you space to operate."

"What does that mean?" Joe shook his head. "And how does it justify a trip here? For several days?"

"I'm making a sweep of several parks. Believe me, this park isn't one we're worried about. Things run well here, but you have to see the contrasts to know what help and intangibles a poorly-run park might need."

"Well, I can't give you the time I promised, but Jack's the right person. Talk to him. He'll have any information you need."

Erika re-crossed her legs. "We'll be fine." She nodded, giving Jack a glance. "I look forward to learning a thing or two. Like old times, huh Jack?"

Jack refused himself a reaction.

Margie stuck her head in the door. "Phone call. Washington."

"I have to take this. Jack, tell her what we've got going on. Send me that email later." Joe gestured them toward the door. He picked up the phone. "Good morning."

They slipped into the hall. Jack stopped at his office door and motioned her inside. She took the seat beside his desk.

She smiled and locked eyes on his. "I don't believe I've ever seen you in uniform. Only a coat and tie, maybe a suit. Looks good."

He avoided her eyes. "Identity. Tradition. All that stuff."

"Part of the team."

"I'm in no mood for small talk. What are your questions?"

"Sometimes I wish I still wore the uniform. I have one, you know. Past job, and I look pretty damned good in it. Most people trust the uniform. I like that."

"Maybe that's why you're not allowed to wear one. Might ruin it for the rest of us."

Her eyes moved to his left hand and back. "You're carrying hard feelings, Jack."

"I think about your boyfriend every day. You, I haven't given you much thought. Not sure why."

"Why do you call Clint my boyfriend?"

"You were chummy. Neither of you made my job any easier."

She crossed her legs. "I was just doing my job. Don't know about him."

"When all hell broke loose, I was the one thrown to the wolves."

"And you think you were the only one?"

"Look at Foss. Didn't hurt him any. He's now a superintendent back east, pulling strings with the Director any time he wants."

"Why do you think things were different for you and me?"

"Because they were."

"You weren't the only sacrificial lamb. When you were sent here, I was sent to Denver. I was buried so deep in the regional office that people wondered if I was dead. Put me in an office that felt like a custodian's closet. They hid me."

He stared.

"It's taken a couple of years to prove myself and get back in the game."

He sighed. "You're saying . . ."

"I'm not saying anything."

"I . . . I had no idea."

"Now you do, so cut me some slack. I don't want to talk about this anymore. It's not a time I want to remember. Tell me about this Coalition. Tell me about its work."

He looked into her eyes, and waited to see if she looked away or flinched. She did neither. Just move on. "Know about the national monument?" he asked. "Know about the Presidential proclamation that created it?" He waited for her nod, and continued. "Part of it managed by us. The rest by BLM. The two agencies work together on a management plan."

"Yes, I know about that," she said, sitting erect. "Is the Coalition doing any good, and where are they in their process?"

He flipped past pages in his mind. "They're getting to the hard work, some difficulties now, but they're good people, they'll get through it."

"Anything I can look at?"

Good question. He pulled out a file drawer, found a red file folder and handed it to her. "Detailed briefing statements." He started to close the drawer, but left it open.

She scooted closer to the corner of the desk and thumbed through the pages. She stopped, closed the file, and put it on her lap. "I'll look at this later. So . . . what's the purpose of this meeting tomorrow?"

"Continue discussion of protection measures. There'll be discussion of ranching culture, river protection, protection of cultural sites."

She twisted his way. "Sounds exciting. Can I play?"

Jack studied her eyes. The old Erika. "Obviously I didn't know your story, or what happened to you. Give me time to absorb that. Play? I don't think so."

"May I at least come?"

"Joe wants you to have the full picture, so yes."

She smiled. "All I can ask is to be on the playground." She glanced at the door. "You've got a visitor."

Jack spun around in his chair.

In the shadows of the hall stood a man—Thomas, leaning against the wall, his nose still bandaged, another now wrapping his elbow.

"Thomas, come in."

"I can wait. I don't want to interrupt," he said meekly. "Could we talk later today?"

"Yes, but I can also ask Erika to come back later."

He considered it, then shook his head. "I just want to ask a favor."

"Shoot."

He reached into a pocket, pulled out a sheet of paper, slipped a finger into the fold, and flipped it open. "Look at this," he said, drawing Jack toward him. He turned and shielded the page.

Jack looked closer. A map.

"I want to go here. Think it's possible?" He waved his finger over a spot on the page.

The cliffs above Sipapu Falls. "What's there, Thomas?"

"Please don't be concerned with that," he whispered.

"You won't tell me what it's about, but you ask me how to get there. I don't get it."

He handed Jack the paper.

Jack studied the map. The contour lines were so close, nearly a solid strip of black. Vertical cliff. Talus slope below. A few lines spreading out under the rim of the plateau. The alcove from which Sipapu Falls emerged hardly appeared on the map because of vertical cliff face above and below. "This isn't a good idea."

"Tell me."

Jack eyed a spot on the map, one that suggested an approach from the south and above, but maps can be deceiving. "I don't have a good picture of what sits to the west and south." He handed the sheet back to Thomas, and stepped past Erika Jones to a map tacked to the wall.

A hanging side canyon sat to the north of the falls—probably the one from which Thomas' ledge had emerged. There was no point thinking about that one. To the south was nothing like it, but there was the hint of an apron above. Was it accessible? How would you get there from the south? He walked his fingers down the map. A drainage, a side canyon that appeared to step gradually up to the level of the apron, below the rim of the plateau.

"Hard to be certain because of contour interval. A map can suggest one thing but you have to go there to know, and I don't want to suggest something where you could get yourself killed."

"I won't get killed," Thomas said. "I just never learned to read a map like this."

Jack shook his head.

"Do you see something?"

"Not sure I should say."

"Show me."

Jack tapped at the map. "If you can work your way up this drainage, if that's possible, and if you get on this level and cross this apron, you might be able to get to here." He tapped an open spot between contours. "That is, if there's much of anything there. If so, might be possible to rappel in from above." Jack set a finger on Sipapu Falls. "It's quite a drop if you miss."

Thomas kept his eye on the map. "It doesn't look easy."

"Wouldn't be. Know how to set up an anchor?"

"I can figure it out."

"It's not something you figure out. It's something you learn. Why would you put yourself in that kind of danger?"

Thomas kept studying.

"What's there, Thomas? I know about your sister. What was she doing?"

He didn't flinch. "She wanted to see the waterfall."

"If you go there you'll get yourself killed."

Thomas backed away.

"What could be so damned important?"

"Never mind." Thomas backed to the door. He turned to leave.

"Take him!" Erika said.

Thomas stopped.

"Just take him." She shrugged her shoulders. "Why not? And take me. Show a girl a good time."

Thomas studied her, then waited for an answer.

Jack let out a sigh. "I don't have time for this."

"In two days?" Thomas asked.

Jack collected himself. "The weekend. Will you tell me what this is about?"

"I'll tell you now. It's about three people taking a hike."

Mid-afternoon, Erika Jones left to check into a hotel.

Jack sat back and rubbed his eyes, trying to erase the tension. Headache, go away. No time for this. Not with the Director calling Joe to D.C.

The thought sent chills through him.

He made a phone call, to Foss' supervisor. Scribbling notes, he asked about Foss' pattern of conduct, at first getting confirmation, but suddenly having the supervisor become tight-lipped, as if realizing his name might be invoked in something that could come back to haunt him.

Was he being the smart one?

Jack ended the call and began to pound out documentation for Joe.

He typed, describing Foss' refusal to attack the escaping fire, his letting the protected plants burn, and his inappropriate comments to Christy and Johnny. It took more time than hoped, but this had to be thorough. It might get repeated viewings, by all sorts of audiences.

Hell of a lot of good it'll do. If big brother paints a heroic picture to save little brother's ass, and if he does as he's known to do—spare no expense at destroying someone else's reputation, especially his old buddy Jack Chastain's—then this effort is futile.

He grumbled to himself, pounding away.

Fill it with facts. Even if it's political suicide. Make the Director deal with facts. Written statements from Johnny Reger and Christy Manion would make it even harder to sweep under the rug. But why pull them into this? Why put them at risk?

Who are you kidding? The Director won't care about any of this.

The Director will listen to Foss. You're dead meat. You'll end up shipped off again, to who knows where. He shuddered at the thought of saying good-bye to Kelly, to Piedras Coloradas, to Las Piedras, to new friends and colleagues he'd learned to trust and respect.

He sighed and pushed send, emailing it all to Joe. If it left Joe's hands it would likely be seen by a cast of hundreds. Words would take on lives of their own.

He leaned back, rubbed his eyes, then the back of his head, trying to make the nerves go away.

The thoughts wouldn't leave. The image of Erika Jones strutted in to join them. Coy, bright, always a mystery. Could she really be another victim of Montana? How could he not have known? Clint Foss—he was a different story. He was no victim. But Erika?

The phone rang. He picked it up. "Yeah, this is Chastain."

"Boss, I need a favor." It was Johnny. "I let the fire monitors go for the day before I remembered I have a dentist appointment in forty-five minutes. Could you babysit the fire for a few hours?"

"Sure. Getting out of the office will help my sanity."

"I'll be back before dark."

"Take the night off. I'll stay up there tonight. It'll do me good. But I need to be back here by morning."

"Deal. I'll relieve you at sunrise. Tonight, I'll drink one for you at Elena's."

"Don't talk me out of this."

— · —

Jack reacquainted himself with the northeastern perimeter of the Pistol Creek Fire, plodding the fire line with shovel in hand. The furthest smokes to the west were settling down. Orange skies and still air sat over the fire.

When finished, he walked back to the pickup to set up camp.

The rumbling of an approaching vehicle grew out of the east. He watched, waiting for it to show. A gold sport utility vehicle hit the top of the hill and followed the road, stopping near the pickup.

Kelly lowered her window. "Can I get some help over here?"

She climbed out and popped open the back hatch, pulled out an ice chest and carried it one handed, stumbling toward him.

He jogged over. "Why are you here?"

She let him take it. "Bringing dinner. Leftovers from the other night. My painting's still arguing with me. We weren't making much progress in figuring out what it wants to say. You sounded bluesy." She grabbed a canvas bag from the back and slipped the straps over her shoulder.

"I'm okay, and I'm not sure you should be here."

"I'm not taking this stuff back."

Jack laughed. "The enchiladas can stay."

"And me?"

"Seriously, I'm okay. It's not a good idea to have you here. There's a fire I'm supposed to be watching, and you're not wearing nomex."

She glanced down at what she was wearing, hiking shorts and a white, V-neck top. "Does polyester burn?"

"It melts. How much are you wearing?"

"Pretty much everything. What if I take off everything that might melt?"

"I'm supposed to be watching the fire."

"How strict are you with the rules?"

"You're gonna get cold," he said, and flashed a smile. "Thanks for bringing dinner. I was about to eat something sealed in plastic three years ago."

"The enchiladas need to be heated."

"Follow me." He led her past the fire line, carrying the ice chest into the black, toward the smoldering limbs of a downed ponderosa. He dug out the foil-wrapped enchiladas and buried them in coals. "Shouldn't take long." He stood and new pains jolted through his back. "Hammered again by that canyon wall. Add a little stress and I feel just perfect."

"What can I do?"

"I'll live." He stretched, then relaxed, and took in the view around them. Plateaus falling away to canyons. Open flame in slow march on stands of trees, columns of smoke rising from distant layers of landscape. "I wish my days were more filled with this, and less with the things I had to deal with today. Look at that." He pointed at a nearby ridge and flames moving upslope.

"You're really into this, aren't you?"

"It can be one of the most important ecological processes with which we deal, and yet, most people are afraid to try to understand it. But this doesn't scare me. What scares me comes from people. The games they play. The politics they thrive on."

"What happened?"

"Hard to know. Maybe I'm overreacting."

"Something to do with this fire?"

"Indirectly. We sent a firefighter home, for reasons too numerous to list. He's an ass, for one thing, but he has connections. Because of those connections, Joe's on his way to D.C. to meet with the Director. My luck's not good when things get elevated to the Director."

"Did you do something wrong?"

"No."

"Then why are you worried?"

"Because I've learned that things aren't always fair. It doesn't matter if you've been right or wrong. What matters is who you know."

"Joe will take care of you. Quit worrying."

"Hope you're right."

Kelly knelt and dug into the ice chest. "Pacifico or Carta Blanca? Wait! You still working?"

"For awhile. You go ahead," he said, then, "follow me." He led her back to the fire line, then the other way, in the direction of less active flame. "Think of the good that fire does. Fuel reduction, nutrient cycling, nature's housekeeping, fresh start in succession. Those sorts of things."

She popped the cap on a Pacifico and took a sip. "Yeah. Are you rehearsing a sound-bite? If so, you're still a bit long." She smiled.

He groaned. "I don't do sound-bites."

"I've noticed."

"Now think about political games. Think there's people out there who look at political games in the same way I look at fire? Comfortable, they can see a purpose, knowing they can get burned, but with the right perspective they can put those processes to use? Are there things equivalent to fire that play out in the organizational ecosystem? That blow up on occasion, burn hot, make it necessary to start over? Can it be good, or is it always bad?"

"Are you okay?"

"I'm not sure."

"You're worrying me. You're sounding crazy, not like you."

"Believe me, I'm fine. I'll worry later, but I feel better with you being here. The gibberish was me thinking aloud, a moment of intellectual curiosity, wondering how other people tick, wondering if my biggest problem is being intimidated by something others thrive on, something others might be able to turn into good."

"Intellectual curiosity?"

"Yeah. Rather I mangle a sound bite?"

"Hurry and finish working, you need a drink. How's your back?"

"Hurts."

"Tonight I'll give you a back rub," she said. "I wonder how banged up Thomas is?"

Jack stopped on a shaly outcropping, looking out over black as far as he could see. Only small wisps of smoke. "Saw him today. Came to my office. Wants me to take him on a hike. Wants to find another way up to Sipapu Falls."

"You taking him?"

"I guess, but I don't get it. He won't tell me why he wants to go there, yet he comes to me to find a way."

"So, he still didn't tell you."

"No." He turned her way. "I talked to an ethnographer in Santa Fe. She said it might be a sacred site, or something to do with a clan or religious society, but she couldn't say much more than that, or wouldn't. Told me I had no idea what the consequences of digging into it might be." He shook his head. "What is the big deal?"

Kelly took a sip. "Their society is different than ours. Listen to her."

"Tell me about clans."

She sighed. "I don't know that much. Just that they're like orders in their culture. Each has a role, and it takes all of them to make the society whole. If something happens to one, its effects can run through the whole of their society."

"That's very much what Chloe Bell said, but it doesn't sound like a reason to keep a secret from the guy who saves your life."

"No offense, but who are you? What's special about you that should make him not worry about consequences?"

"What consequences?"

"They have reasons to be secretive. Probably good reasons. It's not just today's pot hunters. When the Spanish priests came and asserted their religion on them, they destroyed kivas, fetishes, anything they associated with the religions of the pueblos. They associated fetishes with idolatry, destroying them with great zeal. Even those who embraced the new religion remained tied to the culture and traditional ways. They began practicing traditions in secret to avoid the wrath of the priests, and they made new kivas and kept their ceremonial items in places where priests couldn't find them. They became very secretive. They had to. Even among clans there are secrets. Why? I don't know. But I'm not one of them, so I don't need to."

"You mentioned kivas. So did the ethnographer." He watched her eyes. "So does that place have anything to do with the sipapu? I mean the true meaning of the word sipapu?"

She threw up her hands. "You're not listening to me."

"I am."

"You're not." She glared back. "It's not the sipapu. Not that I know. I don't know much, but what I do, I'm not supposed to know. And, I don't understand any of it." She glared. "It's none of my business. Or yours!"

"Let's go to camp," he said, turning back the other way. "Someone risks their neck to get him off that ledge, and now he wants 'em to risk it again, and his own."

"Then don't go."

This is getting nowhere. "I have to. I told him I would. Actually, I was kind of trapped, but I promised."

"Trapped. That doesn't sound like Thomas."

"It wasn't. A woman visiting from the regional office suggested it. Thomas locked on. I couldn't get out of it. She even invited herself along."

"Why was it any of her business?"

"It wasn't. That's just the way she is. It's her . . ." He stopped mid-sentence.

"What?"

He stopped. "I'm not really sure. She's the last person I expected to see. It didn't go how I would've expected."

"How do you know her?"

"Montana."

"Was it good to see her?"

"In the end, we weren't chummy. I assumed she'd been working against the team. Turns out, she may have been another casualty. Buried in Denver when they put me here. Don't know why but I didn't know that. Too focused on myself, I guess."

"What's she like?"

"Strong professional background. Bit of a tease. She's a woman who knows the effect she has on men." He led her off the trail, toward the stash of enchiladas.

After a moment, Kelly said, "She ever have that effect on you?"

He rolled his eyes. "Hell, no, I was her boss. Didn't think I could trust her. Maybe I was wrong. Doesn't matter." He stopped at the stash.

She kicked the coals away from the enchiladas, and pushed them out of the heat. She laughed. "If you can trust her now, maybe I need to be the one who shouldn't."

"Come with us. It's on Saturday."

"I wasn't invited, and if the woman from the regional office is along, sounds like work."

"It's not. She sees it as play."

"Then go play. It might be good to talk to her about Montana. Might do you both some good. And maybe Thomas will open up a little."

"I'm too preoccupied to think about play, or any of that."

"Then, you need a back rub," she said. "I can make you forget everything."

— . —

After midnight, the Letters to the Editor section of the online edition of the *Las Piedras Gazette* received a post from a frequent but anonymous contributor who used the name, 'All Is Not Ducky':

> I've had time to think about the rumor I heard at
> Elena's. I don't believe it. You know as well as I do,
> whatever happened to those plants happened as part
> of some kind of government plan. I think they'll be
> conveniently "found" and probably on private lands
> they want to seize. Just sayin.

CHAPTER
12

Jack broke camp and was waiting at his vehicle, enjoying the sounds of morning when Johnny arrived, as promised, shortly after first light.

"Day's a wasting," he said, climbing out of his pickup. He checked the ground, and scratched his head. "That's strange. Multiple sets of tire tracks on top of my last ones from yesterday."

"Interesting," Jack said, feigning confusion, studying the tracks Kelly left in the dirt. "I must have slept right through it," he said, pulling Johnny's leg, but he didn't seem to get it. "Poachers, maybe. Somebody lost."

"They turned around here and went out the same way. Must have seen your truck and high-tailed it out." He stood upright. "Fire behave itself?"

"Yeah, nice evening. Looks to be burning hottest to the north."

"I thought so, too. Couple a days, the west flank could hit the edge of the old Elk Hollow Fire—from three years ago. That'll stop it cold. Lots of ground to the northwest though."

"Yep," Jack said. "And it needs to burn."

"Heard anything yet about a review?" Johnny asked, almost under his breath. "Am I gonna get canned?"

"You, me both. No, not yet. Left a message with a colleague at Fish and Wildlife Service. Haven't heard back, but don't worry, assume it'll be lessons learned for our program."

"But we killed off a species."

Jack gave a slow nod. "Maybe. Maybe not. We'll look for 'em. I need to take off." He climbed into the driver's seat and started the engine. "Watch out for poachers."

"Yeah, especially those sneaky female types."

— · —

After a shower and getting into uniform, Jack drove into Las Piedras. He turned into the adobe-walled Inn of the Canyons and immediately saw picketers standing at the corner. Two men and a woman, none of them young, all of them holding wooden stakes with large cardboard placards. *"Get the government out of our lives,"* one placard said. *"Give us back our freedom,"* read another.

Damn. Didn't read the newspaper article. Who is this person? What are they planning? And why?

He parked close to the door, grabbed his canvas briefcase and slid out of the vehicle.

Erika Jones waited at the porte-cochere in a dark suit, clutching her bag. Jack walked past and grabbed the handle on the massive carved door. "Morning."

"You look happy."

"Guess I am." He tilted his head in the direction of the picketers. "That's new. Not sure what they're about but I should've done some homework. I didn't." He held the door open. "Sure you're up for this? Don't you get enough meetings in Denver?"

"I love meetings. Can't say I've enjoyed all the good times you've shown me, but hey, surprise me." She breezed past. "Play me if you need me."

She strutted through the foyer.

He shook his head, inspecting her attire as she melted into the shadows of the lobby. Those legs. She always did manage to get the attention of every male in the house. Probably not any less distracting in uniform, but like this she looked like someone from out of town, and these people don't quickly trust out-of-towners. But for some, trust would be the last thing on their minds.

They turned down the hall to the Canyon Room. "Other than the high school," Jack said, "this is the only place in town big enough to hold a public meeting."

They stepped inside and stopped. Several workers busily set chairs in the back on the room. Flip charts stood ready at the front.

"Angie, Paul," Jack said, seeing his colleagues from Bureau of Land Management. "This is Erika Jones, from our regional office. Don't know if she's checking up on us or jealous of the fun we're having."

Angie Manriguez, in her bureau blazer, met her in the aisle and exchanged greetings. Paul Yazzi shook her hand, showing no sign of being compelled to speak.

Jack leaned in, and in a low voice, said, "What's with the picketers?"

Angie shrugged. "All I know is what I read in the paper. No one seems to know anything more than his name, Harper Teague."

Jack excused himself to collect his thoughts. Wait to worry about Teague till you meet him. Focus. Get ready to facilitate a meeting.

A man and woman appeared at the door. Within minutes, several others collected at the back of the room. Time fast approached. Five minutes to go.

Mack Latham, manager of the Inn of the Canyons, strolled in checking preparations. He inspected the glasses and water pitchers set on tables, then moved to the back, checking the lines on the rows of chairs. He exchanged formalities with Angie and Paul, then noticed the snappily dressed woman among them. He forgot what he was doing and fell into conversation.

Karen Hatcher, from the Trust for the Southwest, wandered in wearing shorts and a T-shirt, looking like she just finished a hike, her hair matted to her forehead. She spotted Jack against the wall. "How's the fire going?" she asked, dropping her pack at the table. She ambled toward him.

"Mostly good. Some bad. Something unfortunate happened. The only known population of a plant proposed for endangered status, torched. Pretty bad. Tell you about it later."

Her jaw dropped. "You're kidding, right?"

"Wish I was. We'll have a review, learn what we can. I'm hoping we'll find 'em someplace. Just need to look."

She shook her head as she turned back to the table.

Jack watched for new faces between glances at the draft agenda. Three were new to the process, one of them unexpected. Thomas. Even with a bandaged nose and a sling on his arm, he managed to be nearly invisible. He had slipped in, taken a chair near a corner of the table, and quietly took to waiting, looking at his hands, not attempting conversation.

Two other faces were a mystery. One seemed somewhat out of place. Slender, average height, sweater, slacks, good haircut, maybe a different kind of confidence than was common in Las Piedras. The other man—overweight, dark suit, no tie, dark serious eyes—worked the room with anxious, irritated gestures.

Jack approached the latter. The man noticed the movement and slipped deeper into the body of people. The picketers were probably his.

Jack turned to find the other man. He stood five feet away, talking to Kip. When they finished, Jack slipped in and offered a hand. "Jack Chastain."

"Mike Middleton."

"New to the area?"

"I've had property here for years, but recently decided to spend more time here. Hoping to contribute a little more to this part of the world."

Jack checked the man's shoes. Deck shoes. Expensive ones. "What business you in?"

"Technology. Was. Operations in the Midwest and Bay area. Sold most of my interests a couple of years ago. Haven't seen anything I wanted to get back into, so I'm just having some fun, getting involved in other things, using my influence where I can."

Erika Jones backed in among them. "May I join this conversation?" She leaned closer to Jack, and whispered, "Protect me."

He laughed.

The hotel manager slid away, seemingly numb from the Erika Jones experience.

"Mike Middleton, this is Erika Jones, also with the Park Service. Mr. Middleton was saying he hopes to spend more time here. Get a little more involved. Throw a little influence our way."

"Really?" she said, her interest piqued. "How do you hope to help?"

"Nothing too complicated, but I do have connections. I'm not bad at making things happen. I've acquired enough to consider myself successful, but connections are what I think I have to offer."

"I see. Honorable," Erika said. She brushed at her hair with her hand.

"I'm at a point in life where I can afford to focus on a few bigger picture things."

"Aren't you a little young to check out of the mainstream?"

He laughed. "True, but that's why I'm staying involved. I've got a few ideas, things to keep me busy. Like helping the two of you. You don't have easy jobs. You need people like me."

"Our jobs aren't bad," Jack said.

"Don't kid me. You have people demanding this, demanding that." He gave his fist a shake. "Thinking only about themselves."

Jack searched for words.

"You are so right, Michael," Erika said. She smiled. "May I call you Michael?"

"Of course, and I hate to say it, but you people could learn how to tell some of these bozos they can't have everything they want. Sometimes, you just have to say no."

"If you'd excuse me," Jack said. "I need to get ready to start."

Jones lingered as Jack pulled away.

He moved to the front corner, stared down at his agenda, and closed his mind to everything, visualizing the likely flow of discussion.

It was time to start. Karen Hatcher stood and encouraged everyone to take a seat. She sat, turned to the rancher at her right and said something under her breath, then smiled. Kip, dressed in a western sport coat and bolo tie, sat at the back line of tables. He leaned forward and said something to a county commissioner he had likely known for years, then nodded at Thomas, sitting catty-corner from him.

Jack watched as ranchers, environmentalists, business people, and politicos took their seats, attendance shaping up as expected. He stole a glimpse of the man who had likely brought the picketers, sitting to the left, a few chairs down from Hatcher. What would he do?

Karen stepped to the front. She called the meeting to order, introduced herself, and explained the purpose of the meeting. Then, asked Paul Yazzi to read his notes of outcomes from the previous meeting. His words were sparse, but like a magnet, drew the attention of everyone.

When he finished, Kip Culberson stood. "You've got agendas before you. Anything we should add?"

The man in the dark suit flagged his hand. "I do, and I'd like the opportunity to discuss this first, before everything else on the list. No offense, but this is more important than anything you've got on this paper. I make the motion we kick the government types out of the meeting. Let's get them out of our lives—since nothing they're doing has any constitutional basis whatsoever—and let's get to thinking how to restore the freedoms we need to conduct our lives without government meddling." He looked at the faces at the table. "Who's with me? Is there a second?"

No reaction—something he didn't seem to expect. Glances around the table bore only quiet.

Jack stood. "Kip, may I?"

"Certainly. I turn it over to you," he said, and sat.

Jack stepped into the center, between the square of tables. He checked the eyes before him, then turned to the man in the suit. "Would you like to introduce yourself?"

"Harper Teague, private citizen. Straight shooter. What you see is what you get. No interest in the kind of games you government people play. Behind our back, refusing to show your cards, playing with our lives. I'm here to level the playing field, keep things honest, get things above board." He looked around the table, as if expecting his words to ignite a response.

"Thank you. And you should know this is not my meeting. This is their meeting, your meeting." He took his turn looking into the eyes around the table. "I was invited to take part. So was Angie, so was Paul. A little different, I know, but fundamentally that's what we do when we work for a government agency, we work for you."

"Do you believe that?" the man said, not to Jack but to the others.

Kip waved a hand, and waited to be acknowledged. "Harper, you're welcome to join us. I suppose we could dedicate some time to your agenda item, but calm down. We're not trying to fix the world here. We're here as a community—big *c*, Community—to come to agreement on ways to protect the things we value when it comes to this new national monument."

"Community! That sounds like socialist talk for letting government run our lives. This nation was built on the back of individuals. Strong individuals, willing to fight for freedom, build their own success. Community, that's bullshit!"

Kip shook his head, chuckling to himself. "Jack, he's yours."

Jack turned back to Teague. "Have a seat, and we'll add your item to the agenda." He looked around the room. "Anything else?"

Mike Middleton raised his hand. "Yeah, something important. A land exchange. I want to propose a swap."

Others shuffled in their seats.

"Okay," Jack said. "We'll add that to the agenda. Let's start the meeting. We've got a full one. Ginger, you're first."

"This continues to be a rough topic," she started, staying seated near a corner of the table. "But those of us who are ranchers, we need water. Our cattle need water. We've got to work through this."

Jack motioned to the young environmentalist squirming in his chair. "Yes, Dave."

"Do you have options to put on the table for protecting the river?"

"I want to talk about it, yes," Ginger responded.

"Excuse me," Mike Middleton said, flagging his hand for

attention. "Is this the most important thing we have to discuss today? I mean, I'm a busy man."

"It is our first agenda item," Jack said. "And it's important."

"Well, I have something that might be a bit more important, and if you'll let me cover it, I'll duck out, leave the rest of you to discuss as many topics as you want."

Jack looked around the table at confused looks. No one offered objection. "What's on your mind, Mr. Middleton?"

"My proposal is this. I've got a piece of land. Large parcel abutting the national monument. I can put it on the market, which I'm willing to do, but think of what could happen. Anything—a mine, an amusement park, who knows what. You don't want that. This land could be in the national monument. I'm prepared to offer a land swap, twenty or thirty acres to one, maybe more. All I want in exchange is a prime spot to allow me to keep my roots in the area."

All eyes settled on Middleton.

"And?" Jack asked, giving him a chance to explain.

"That's it." He waited, but his words elicited no response. "How can you not jump at this?"

"Why the hell would you do that?" Teague grumbled. "That's the stupidest thing I ever heard. If there's anything there, mine it, frack it, graze the hell out of it, but put it to use. Do not put it in the hands of the government."

Jack looked around the room. Even those ordinarily quiet wanted to speak.

"Shut up, Teague," someone blurted.

"Get him out of here."

"Hold on, all of you. Maybe we should take a step back for the benefit of Mr. Teague and Mr. Middleton," Jack said. "Introduce ourselves, say something about our purpose, why we're here."

Teague slapped a hand on the table. "I don't need you to tell me why we're here. Listen up people. I promise, if not today, then someday in the very near future you'll be listening. You'll be saying I'm right. Do you hear me? You'll be saying I'm right."

"Harper, please," Kip said.

"Wise up. Do it now. Tell these government lackeys you don't want 'em here. Tell 'em we don't want 'em in our lives. Tell 'em we want to restore our freedoms. Tell 'em we don't need an overreaching government. First, let's kick 'em out of here."

Others, grumbling, gave him angry faces and dismissive waves.

Teague stepped back, eyes wide.

Jack raised a hand. "Order, please." He turned to Karen Hatcher. "Would you introduce yourself?"

Middleton flippantly shrugged, and shouted, "Whoa." He waited a moment, and continued. "Hell with Teague, but I agree that we don't need to waste our time talking about why we're here. Let's get down to business. Time is money. Let's expand the thinking. Talk big things. Put the time to good use."

Grumbling rose again, filling the room.

Erika Jones raised a hand from her seat at the back of the room. "Mr. Middleton, Mr. Teague, please give me a moment of your time. Jack, please excuse us." She stood and walked purposely into the hall.

Mike Middleton stood and took pensive steps after her. Harper Teague squinted, studying faces, then slipped out of his chair and followed him out.

— · —

Erika Jones turned, stepped a few feet past the door, and waited. She watched them enter the hallway and turn to find her. She held her tongue until both men were finished giving the other distrusting looks.

"Gentlemen, what you're failing to see is that Jack Chastain is your only friend in the room. He's the one willing to give you a chance to talk about whatever. Interesting, isn't it? You're geniuses, both of you."

"You're nuts," Teague mumbled, his anger seething.

"Hey, do what you want. I'm just offering a little insight."

"We're listening," Middleton said.

"I don't work here, so none of this matters to me, but I've known Jack Chastain for a long time. He knows how groups behave, better than anyone else in the room. If it were me, I'd let you both self-destruct. He won't do that. He'll give you a chance, but you've both tried to assert your agendas on a group that's already worked past an initial set of difficulties. You've come in, both of you, full of ego, demanding to be treated like the most important person in the room. Good for you, you're special. What you couldn't see—and kept shooting yourself in the foot over—was that Jack Chastain was willing to reset the group dynamics, just to give you a chance to be heard." She threw her head back and laughed. "Ironic, isn't it?"

CHAPTER
13

For a Saturday morning, the number of visitors enjoying the canyon of the Little River was anything but heavy. Their loss. Jack turned the pickup off the highway and onto a graveled road. "This place grows on you," he said, turning to Erika Jones, sprawled against the passenger side door. "Mysterious, quiet, deep canyons, dark shadows."

He stopped at a gate of welded pipe. He stepped out of the truck, walked to the front, and swung open the gate. Up canyon, he saw it—the side canyon, hanging well above the river. Dark reaches—getting up into it might not be the hard part. He checked the skies. No clouds. Good. Not the kind of place to be in a thunderstorm.

He climbed in, put the pickup in gear, and followed the road at a slow clip. He turned to Jones. "I didn't need your help yesterday."

"You wanted to watch that pair of egos tie themselves up in knots?"

"They would've figured it out."

"Maybe. Maybe not. No big deal. I just pointed out a few things."

He considered her words. "Probably helped."

"You're welcome."

He pulled alongside an old Dodge pickup and stopped. "Told Thomas to meet us here. Wonder if he got here first."

Erika Jones opened the door and stood on the running board, head above the cab. "I don't see anyone."

She carried no more weight than the last time he saw her. Her choice of hiking shorts—canvas, and indeed short—did little to hide the tone in her thighs. Everything in the tight-fitting henley looked just as fit.

She stepped down and slipped to the front. She leaned against the fender.

"Might not be him. We might be waiting."

"The sun feels good," she said, lying back on the hood, soaking it in.

Jack climbed out and turned away. The sun. Why the hell did Thomas want to wait till ten? Would've been easier starting early. Could've been a day hike. Less weight.

Under the cottonwoods, a man moved through the underbrush. He broke into an opening, and veered toward the Dodge.

"You're here," Thomas said. "Sorry, I thought I'd be back before you got here." He took off his daypack and tossed it in the cab.

"I thought you couldn't get here any earlier," Jack said.

Thomas ignored the comment. He dragged out an overnight pack and set it on the tailgate. He went around, pulled something from the daypack, and slipped back to stuff it in the other. "I'm ready. You?"

Jack pulled his pack out over the gunnels of the truck. He reached through a coil of rope, unzipped the top pocket, and pulled out a topo map. "See that side canyon?" He pointed at the slice in the wall, and studied the map. "No guarantees, but let's see if it gets us where we want to go."

Thomas glanced at the side canyon, then upstream.

Jack followed his eyes.

Erika grabbed her pack and hefted it up, onto her shoulders. "Let's do this." She started up the trail. She stopped at a junction, glanced back, then veered onto the trail toward a footbridge to the other side of the river.

Her pack was one Jack remembered seeing only once, in a high end gear shop in Santa Fe. It wasn't cheap. "Nice equipment," he muttered.

"She seems to think so," Thomas said. "A little skinny for my tastes."

"No, I mean, she's carrying quality gear—that's a nice pack."

"I know what you mean." He laughed. "And I'm sure she just likes being in the lead."

"Kelly told me you're funny."

"Funny, ha ha, or funny funny?" He started up the trail. "Either way, I'm not quite the same man she knew before. Kelly's a good friend, a good woman. I doubt that's changed."

They started across the bridge, footsteps clomping on the boards, drowning out the gurgling of the creek below. On the other side, Erika waited.

"Go left," Jack shouted.

They followed the river downstream. In a half mile, Jack stopped and pointed upslope. "Let's leave the trail here."

A short climb and they were on a bench above the river, crossing through sand dropseed and desert marigold, in an area more extensive than obvious from below. Piñon juniper woodland grew thick. A dry creek bed plunged in from above, cutting through talus. They followed it up, scrambling around boulders and over strata, giving each other hands and pushes, eventually making it to the cut in the wall. Jack jammed hands and feet into the crack, and pulled himself into the opening. In hefts of bodies and backpacks, they joined him.

The sandy floor of the side canyon slithered into darkness. Vertical, layered walls reached up, letting only a ribbon of blue peer in from above. They moved forward, eyes adjusting to the shadows. The sandy bottom came to an end and rock rubble began.

The way to the unknown. Impassable obstructions? Very possible.

Jack stepped out and took the lead, scrambling up and over rocks and debris. They followed, different strides, different paces, past stretches of rock, around boulders, across terraces, and through shallow pools—some deep enough to nearly require swimming. In wet clothing with no sun, the hike became chilly. After an hour, the blue skies seemed closer. The canyon grew shallow.

Another half hour and they could go no further. Near vertical rock face, reaching up to blue skies. So close. No way to get there.

"We can't do it, can we?" Thomas said.

Jack spun around, eyes on the rim. "Not with the equipment we have. Don't give up yet." He backtracked, keeping an eye to the north. He stepped back down the last bit of rubble, stopping every few feet to assess. On a large flat rock he pointed. "There!"

Above them stood a three-walled chimney. A vertical climb of well less than fifty feet. "That might work."

Thomas fought to catch his breath, and studied the slit above. "Where are we?"

"Unless I'm all turned around, somewhere near where we want to be. We'll start from the ledge at the bottom of the chimney."

Jones stepped around them. Hand over hand, she crawled through a boulder strewn chute, managing not to be pulled over backwards by the weight of her pack. She squirmed onto the ledge, and eyed the slit of blue above. She turned back. "I think it'll work."

"I'll bring up the rear," Jack said to Thomas.

He stepped forward, more deliberate in choosing foot placements and handholds, as he worked his way up to Erika. She stepped back as he shimmied onto the platform.

Jack took long steps and quickly joined them.

They studied the chimney.

"Let me go first," Jack said. "And let's hope that's the top." He pulled off his pack, unlashed the climbing rope, and dug out three pieces of webbing. "Know how to tie a Swiss seat?" He handed them each one, and kept one. He made a wrap around his waist, tied a half knot, and waited as they did the same. Taking the two strands down, through and around his legs, he laced them back into the loop and squatted, pulling the strands tight. He put another wrap around his waist and tied it off. He watched them loop their legs. "Squat," he said. They did, looking like frogs about to leap off the ledge. "Tie 'em off."

They stood. Jack grabbed at Thomas' webbing and pulled. Tight. He grabbed Erika's. Loose. Settling down over her pelvic bones. "Needs to be tighter. You'll slip out if you flip over."

"Would you do it? I'm not good at knots."

He glanced at her eyes. She's serious. Delicately, he worked the slack out of the loop around a leg. "Maybe you should do this part?"

"You're fine, but quit tickling me."

"I'm not tickling you . . . squat down."

Behind her, Thomas smiled, arching an eyebrow.

She squatted. Jack jerked on the strands. She reached back, bracing herself. He pulled in the last bit of slack and retied the knot.

"If you're done with the equipment checks," Thomas said, turning away, "this space is getting claustrophobic."

Jack reached for the rope, grabbed the tail of the butterfly coil and looped it over his neck, letting the coil drape over his chest. He stepped into the chimney. Pressing back against cool rock, he placed a foot against the opposite wall and pushed, then planted the other foot on the wall behind him. Feet locked in place, he raised his body, then pressed back against the rock, repositioned his feet, and did it again. "See how it's done?"

Both nodded. Thomas glanced nervously up the chimney.

Jack continued up.

On top, he jammed his hand into a crack in the rock and swung his legs up and out. Panting, he rolled over and settled on the ground. He looked around. Not quite the top. He stood and plodded upslope, breaking over the rim onto a terrace. Beyond was talus slope, rising toward the heights of the plateau.

Just where we want to be.

He sidestepped downslope, laid out the rope and lowered an end down the chimney. "Tie on my pack." He positioned his feet, planting them against rock.

"It's on," Thomas hollered.

Hand over hand, Jack pulled. The pack reached the lip, and he slid it over beside him. He dug out a carabiner and clipped it into a loop at the end of the rope. He stood over the chimney and lowered it down. "Now, your packs."

First Erika's, then Thomas', and with all three packs in a pile behind him, he lowered the rope again. "One of you, clip the carabiner into the wraps around your waist."

Thomas' eyes inched nervously up the chimney.

Erika grabbed the rope, clipped into her Swiss seat, and locked down the carabiner. She jammed herself into the chimney and started to climb.

Jack sat, and gathered in the slack, maintaining tension as she made her climb. Within minutes she appeared and held out a hand. "I'm not gonna try that move you made."

Jack grabbed her hand and pulled. She rolled out of the chimney, and sat on her knees, sucking in air. "Takes it out of you." She let herself recover a moment, then unclipped the carabiner.

Jack lowered the rope back to Thomas. Erika stepped between Jack and the edge. "He's got it," she said. She leaned over her knees. "Okay, he's clipped in and climbing."

Jack pulled in the slack.

"He's not moving too quickly." She looked back over her shoulder.

He managed to meet her eyes.

"Think that Mike Middleton guy is half the big shot he thinks he is?" She turned back to the chimney.

"Hard to tell. Does it matter?"

"You're such a boy scout. Oblivious to the games, or at least you try to be. Politics, gamesmanship, influence. You try to ignore it. Just gets you in trouble. Gets your team in trouble. You so hung us out to dry."

"It felt that way to you? Like I was hanging you out to dry?" He pulled in a little rope.

"You sure didn't have us playing defense in Montana. Countering moves, anticipating politics, schmoozing the people who coulda helped, buying time to understand what was really going on."

"Would it've made any difference?"

"Maybe. Maybe not."

"How's Thomas doing?"

"He's fine. How's your love life? I heard Ms. Courtney stayed in Montana."

"I don't talk about my personal life. You know that."

She flashed him a wink and turned back to the chimney. "I know. You're such a boy scout. She was a bitch. I thought about jumping your bones just to give you reason to ditch the bitch." She glanced back and smiled. "Would have done you a favor. Might have been fun."

He pulled in more rope.

"Sorry. Going quiet on me, huh?" She turned her eyes back to Thomas. "You've always struck me as a man who needed an impetuous woman. She wasn't impetuous. Just a bitch."

The lines of blue webbing tightly circled her legs, nicely outlining her backside. He looked away. "Thomas having trouble?"

"He looks tired."

"If he wants a rest, I can hold him."

"Need a rest?" she shouted down the chimney. "Jack can hold you."

"I'm fine," he responded, sounding not too far below.

"Don't worry, I'll watch him. You concentrate on the rope."

Yeah, right. He reset his feet. "Sorry I didn't know they buried you in Denver."

"It worked out. I don't mind it there. I didn't do any checking on you either. Let's hope something like that doesn't happen again."

"Yeah. When do you go back to Denver?"

"When the Regional Director calls me home, probably in a week or so. He has me going to Chiricahua next. I leave tomorrow or the next day."

Jack nodded. "So you felt like I hung you out to dry?"

She turned. "Yes." She glared. "You should've seen it coming when that slick-ass spin doctor arrived from Virginia. The one in the five-inch heels. Said she was from some Mountain West think tank. Bull. The heels should've been a clue. Women in Montana don't wear five-inch heels. I don't know if you were hypnotized by her rhetoric or just watching her ass, but we put up no defense. Nothing to absorb the spin. Nothing to counter."

"Counter isn't our job. Spin isn't our job."

"You're so naïve." She turned back to Thomas.

As he reached the top, Erika offered a hand. "Got me?" she shouted to Jack over her shoulder.

Jack reached, missed the webbing at her waist, and caught a loop around a thigh. "Wait, I don't have you . . ."

"You're fine." She gave Thomas a pull. He lurched up over the lip, staggered, and settled on the ground, fighting for air. She let go, reached back, and pulled Jack's hand from its grip.

Thomas caught his breath, and collected his things. "Which way?" he asked.

Jack pointed northeast. "Sipapu Falls is somewhere north of here. We'll work our way around till we find it."

He took off, assuming the lead.

Slickrock. Desert scrub crowding only pockets of sand. The day grew hot.

Cross-country travel, going where topography allowed, increasingly keeping the sun to their left.

Beyond a scattering of trees, the foreground dropped away. A void stood before them, a massive wall of stone rising beyond it—the opposite side of the canyon, facing them down. Erika saw it last—and gasped, stopping in her tracks. Thomas and Jack carefully approached the edge. The falls thundered, and came together below to form Little River, not much more than a rivulet on its way to the confluence with the main fork of the river, now below its peak spring flow.

The hanging alcove sat below and to the left, extending north along the disconformity between strata. A gush of water emerged from solid rock, flowing toward the edge, pouring into the void. Sipapu Fall—in all its glory. The alcove was at least twenty feet wide and two hundred feet long, narrow on each end, larger than Jack expected. It looked so small from below, dwarfed by the walls of the canyon. Boulders scattered across the ledge were not so little–some had to be a couple of meters in diameter.

Jack moved upslope and sized a ponderosa perched above the alcove. One—large enough to never budge—would do for an anchor. He checked what would be fall line for the rope—it'd do. A mistake would be deadly.

Thomas plopped down and reflected, looking from end to

end. Jack stopped and watched him. There was something he knew to be there.

"Thomas, why are we here?" Jack shouted.

"Show me how to do this. You don't have to go. You can stay here, enjoy the grandeur of Mother Earth."

"I'm not worried. Why are we here?"

"Thank you for doing this."

"You're welcome. This is dangerous. It wouldn't hurt to know why we're taking this risk."

"You said you weren't worried."

Jack pulled a long piece of webbing from his pack. Reaching around the big ponderosa, he flipped the end of the webbing and caught it in the other hand. Two complete loops and he knotted the ends, then clipped in a pair of locking carabiners. He uncoiled the rope, found the midpoint, tied a knot, and clipped it into the anchor. Two strands, ready for a rappel.

"Swiss seats," Jack commanded, handing them back their lengths of webbing.

"I'll go first," Thomas said, as he made the wrap around his waist.

"Not a good idea. It's a forty foot rappel onto the narrow end of a ledge."

"I'll go first."

Jack slipped the strands of rope through the rings of a figure-eight rappelling device, and clipped it into Thomas' Swiss seat. "Know how to do this?"

"Yes," Thomas said, wrapping the rope around to the small of his back, to regulate flow.

"Be careful, walk down, don't jump or bounce. Keep right, make sure you end up on that shelf."

Thomas backed up, the rope tightened, and he readied himself to descend. Not exactly confident, he didn't lack in determination. He checked the line of descent, then his footing, then let the rope slide through his fingers. He moved quickly down the rock.

He safely reached the end of the shelf, stepped back from the edge, hit resistance from the rope, pulled several feet through the figure-eight, and backed past a boulder to a wide spot.

"What do I do now?"

"Sit and unclip the carabiner. I'll take it from there."

Thomas sat, spun the locking ring loose, and disconnected from the rope.

Jack pulled it up. "You're next," he said to Erika. He grabbed the webbing on her Swiss seat, and jerked.

"I love it when you play rough."

He shook his head, and clipped the figure-eight into her Swiss seat. She set her feet, took the rope in her left hand and backed down the rock. She had done this before.

As she neared bottom, Thomas stood, inched over, and waited.

"Thomas, stay back," Jack shouted.

Erika slowed, then stopped.

Thomas crept over behind her.

She looked up, confused.

"Thomas!" Jack shouted again. A whiff of something hit his nose. Something burning. He scanned the horizon.

Thomas stepped back. Erika gave him a suspicious look, then disconnected and moved away from the edge.

Jack pulled up the rope. The smell hit again. Burning sagebrush. He spun around. Is that fire misbehaving? Hell of a place to be if it is. He saw nothing.

He reset the figure-eight, stepped back, and began his rappel. As he neared the shelf, Thomas crept over.

"Stand back," Jack said, turning to watch him.

Thomas clutched something bound in white thread. Its tip smoldered. Thomas swept it past Jack's feet, up his legs, over his body and head. Wisps of smoke settled over him.

Thomas spoke softly—prayer-like words Jack tried to understand but could not. He finished, and settled against the wall.

"What were you doing?" Jack whispered.

"Smudging. Its purpose is to cleanse, to purify."

Jack looked around. The alcove. Thomas. The water pouring over the edge.

Strong medicine filled his nostrils. He had to be imagining things. Something now felt very different.

CHAPTER
14

Maidenhair fern spread from the opening. Water issued from the wall, and followed a shaly depression before plummeting over the edge. At some point in geologic time, the flow would cut through the impermeable layer of shale, creating something somewhat less spectacular. For now, it was a celebration, a launch into thin air.

In awe, the three of them beheld the marvel. Well placed stepping stones—the only suggestion of past human presence—crossed the short run of the creek. Distances between stones left little room for mistake. If caught in the ribbon of water as it made its brief crossing, they would be swept over the edge. Launched.

Jack watched as Thomas' eyes moved methodically along the wall, over the water, along its edges. Jack saw nothing other than watercress in still water, sedges and rushes in scarce sediment. Thomas abruptly stopped, returned to his pack and dug into it.

They followed him.

"It's bigger than it looks from below," Jack said, for reaction. None came. "Now what?"

"Anything you want. I'm setting up camp."

"Here?"

"Yes, here."

"Wouldn't it be safer up there?" Jack said, pointing a finger up the climbing rope, back to the ponderosa pine wrapped with blue webbing. "Why am I asking? Yes, Thomas, it'd be safer up there. Take care of your business and we can get the hell back up where we can sleepwalk in relative safety."

"You sleep walk?"

"No, but . . ."

"We'll camp here."

Jack exchanged glances with Erika.

"I guess we're camping here," she said. She tapped a toe on solid rock. "Thomas, mind if we check out the place?"

"No. Be careful."

"Be careful," Jack mumbled to himself, slinking away behind Erika Jones.

They jumped the stepping stones, crossing the ribbon of water, and crept along the sliver of ground, an eye on the edge, feeling like they were visiting more than fallen rocks and wind-deposited sand spits. The far wall of Cañon de Fuego peered in, looming over them, but that wasn't it. Something felt there in their midst.

They came to the end and paused. Jack spun around, looking closely at the rock at his feet.

Why did Thomas go to all this trouble? There's no substantial evidence of activity, no sign of past visitors—other than stepping stones—at least none to be seen. No pictographs. No habitation sites. No rock caches. Nothing.

Not even the ledge from which his sister had fallen can be seen from here.

What does it all mean?

When sunset's flame on the canyon wall was gone, and with darkness settling in, they traversed back across.

They found Thomas waiting, lying quietly beside a rock-encircled campfire. He had managed a fire of pine limbs and needles that had fallen in from above. The fire cast a lazy shadow of him against the back wall of the alcove. He stared the other way, beyond the fire, beyond Jack and Erika, toward the vast, growing black of Cañon de Fuego.

Jack plopped down at his pack and dug out bags of tortillas and cheese. He offered a tortilla to Thomas.

"No thanks. I'm not eating."

"Aren't you hungry?" Jones asked, as she got into her own pack.

Thomas put another stick on the fire.

"Wow, I'm famished," she said. She bit into an apple. "You expecting rain?" She cocked her head, glanced up at the sky, then at the rather odd tent sitting against the back wall of the alcove. Its fiberglass poles, bound at the top and again at the bottom, were covered not with nylon but with clear plastic sheeting.

He ignored the question.

"Well, are you? I didn't bring a tent."

"It isn't a tent."

"What the hell is it?" Jack asked.

"Sweat lodge."

"You're kidding," Erika said. "Very cool."

Thomas remained quiet.

"Maybe we shouldn't intrude," Jack said.

"Oh, Thomas, you wouldn't exclude us, would you? We've all had a workout."

He chuckled, and looked up from the fire. "You can join me."

"Great. Jack, how about you?"

"We'll see."

"It's okay," Thomas said. "You should know this, however. Sweat lodge brings you into the womb of earth, to be cleansed. You should behave as you would in church. Sweat lodge is a ritual of purification, spiritual renewal, healing."

"So, something kind of sacred?" Erika asked.

"I am still relearning what it means to be traditional. I've lived away for many years. But for my people, there is no separation between the sacred and the ordinary."

"What does that mean?" she asked.

He seemed unsure how to answer.

"Is this a sacred place?"

Jack lay back and turned an ear to listen.

"I'll say this, because I do not want to enter sweat lodge with a deceptive heart. There are things I will tell you, things I will not."

"C'mon, Thomas. Is this the Sipapu?"

Jack watched Thomas closely. Erika knew the meaning of the word, and Thomas seemed to be having trouble selecting his.

"It is, isn't it?"

He smiled.

"Tell us the story, Thomas."

He shook his head.

"Thomas . . . tell us the story."

Amazed at her persistence, Jack watched. Uncomfortable as it was, he did not want to stop her.

"Please," she cooed.

"There is much meaning to the word, Sipapu."

"I've heard it's the hole in the earth, from which your people emerged."

"From which the ancestors of humans emerged, yes."

"Tell us the story."

He seemed befuddled by the pressure. "Somewhere to the north, the first humans climbed from a hole in the earth into the sunlight. The underground place from which they came is called Sipapu. It is a sacred place. Those first humans, the Great Spirit protected as they wandered the land. At long last they came upon a place they knew was meant for them. They settled there."

"That's the whole story?" Erika asked.

"That is our creation story."

"What about the mole people or spider woman?"

"Those are stories of other peoples."

"Really?"

"I have no idea who you're talking about," Jack said. "Maybe I don't need to, but I do want to know why we're here."

"You're here because you wanted to come."

"Why are you here, Thomas? Is this the sipapu?"

"No, this is not Sipapu. Your people named it that."

"Then, what is it?"

He made no effort to speak.

"Tell us a coyote story?"

"Zuni have many coyote stories, not my people. And be aware, if you are uncertain of how a story is used, then you may misunderstand and misuse it." He stared into the fire. "Our stories come from oral traditions. There is a place and a proper use for them. They are important to the welfare of the individual and the pueblo. I am not a good storyteller. Others are better."

"Are you holding out?" she asked.

"Instead of stories, let me tell you about storytellers. My grandfather was a very good storyteller. He was a leading member of his religious society. He knew much."

Society. A word Cloe Bell had used. Jack sat up.

"Grandfather told stories to help us understand our traditions and what they mean to our culture. He went to great lengths to help my sister and I understand them." He paused. "I remember his voice. He wanted us to remember the stories, to tell them to our own grandchildren. It's hard to remember them all, my mind is so cluttered by the modern world. Some stories, I remember well. Tales of mythological heroes. Grandfather emphasized their success in turning mockery on those who had mocked them. I have tried to tell them to my children correctly but I can't remember them all."

"His stories were all about heroes?" Erika asked.

"No. Grandfather would tell stories of legends, about traditions, about ceremonies and the responsibilities of our clans and society, and how to perform ceremonies correctly."

"Tell us about ceremonies," Erika said.

"No, I won't talk about that."

"Aren't they about fertility and harvest, those kinds of things?"

"They can be, but not necessarily."

Erika let out a sigh. "Thomas, you're making me work here. Quit being so coy."

He smiled.

"Okay, then, I'll make you confirm or deny," she said. "I heard a story about a ceremony, solstice I think. Sounded quite wild. Lots of dancing. After several days, unmarried girls went into a kiva and sat around a fire. Young men went inside, but only after their clothes had been torn off by others standing around the entrance and on the roof. When someone poured water on the fire, all hell broke loose. Darkness, confusion, jostling around, and if someone tried to start the fire, someone else put it out. All the while, the guys were trying to . . ." She held back, turned to Jack and raised an eyebrow.

"Don't stop now," Jack said. He let out a chuckle and turned to Thomas. "Does that kind of stuff really happen?"

"If so, it's another people," Thomas said, "but there's something you need to understand. No story, no ceremony, exists in isolation from the life of its people. There are cultural contexts for them. I said it before. If you are unaware of the way they are to be used, then you are likely to misunderstand and misuse them." He stirred the coals.

"Why are we here, Thomas?" Jack asked.

"The rocks are ready." Thomas reached back and grabbed a pair of broken pine branches stashed beside the stack of firewood. "Jack, could you help me?"

Thomas laid the limbs alongside a red-hot rock and Jack took the other ends. They pressed in on the sides and raised it out of the coals. Thomas backed toward the lodge. Heat radiated onto their arms and faces.

Thomas ducked into the opening and moved to the center. Kneeling, they set it on the ground. Dry heat began to accumulate, settling into the depths of the lodge.

"I'll be back." Thomas said, stepping into the night air. He set his sticks aside and slipped behind the boulder where he had stashed his pack.

Jack spun around to wait.

"So . . . now we do the *get naked* ritual?" Erika asked.

"Don't know. This is all new to me."

"Hey, we're all adults here." She grabbed the bottom of her top and smiled, catching his eye before going further. She slipped it off and let the glow of the fire ripple over her. "You know what this reminds me of?"

"No clue." Jack began unbuttoning his shirt.

"The long drive that night after public meetings in Bozeman. We were all coming down off the adrenaline, really tired, and decided it was unsafe to go any further. First hotel we came to, that hot springs. It was late. I talked the night clerk into letting us use a grotto. You acted like you needed sleep but I convinced you to join me."

"I did need sleep." He tossed his shirt on a rock.

"You have no idea how close you came to getting lucky that night. You'd been so impressive, or so I thought at the meeting. In a year I didn't think so, but that night you were hot. I was ready to do anything. Au naturel? Hell no. You insisted we swim in our skivvies." She laughed.

"I was your boss."

She unbuttoned her shorts and dropped them to the ground. "No skivvies tonight." She slipped them off.

"This is not a good idea."

"Chill, Jack Chastain. Get with the rules. This is innocent. Thomas said, like church."

He slipped out of his shorts and tossed them with the shirt.

She smiled. "Now that wasn't difficult, was it? Let's get inside. I'm getting cool." She stooped under the flap, slipped past the rock and around to the back.

Jack followed her in, and took the other side of the rock. He sat. The ground was gritty.

Thomas ducked inside, carrying water bottles and a deerskin pouch, still wearing his shorts.

He dropped his eyes and draped the pouch's drawstrings over his neck. He set the bottles down, pulled the flap closed, and settled onto the ground.

"A little over dressed, aren't you?" Erika said.

"No."

She scooted around and leaned toward Jack. "Whoops," she whispered, then giggled.

The heat was dry, searing.

They sat quietly, breathing it in.

Outside, the fire was burning down quickly. In its glow, Thomas and Erika were becoming little more than silhouettes.

Thomas began to speak. Jack tried to understand the words

but could not. Chants—repetitious, song-like, haunting—and when he stopped, the silence grew deep.

Thomas pulled the pouch open, sifted through its contents, and sprinkled them over the rock. Dry, herbal scents permeated the lodge. He twisted open a bottle and poured. Steam hissed, and the air became thick, almost too thick to breathe, easier to taste.

"Inhale it . . . drink it in," Thomas said, reverently. He doused the rock again.

Jack closed his eyes.

Thomas sang.

Surreal. Jack pulled at the heavy air, trying to breathe deeply, searching for the bottom of his lungs, trying to get the air to satisfy them. Every pore of his body seeped sweat. Fragrance filled his nostrils. Cedar. No, piñon. No, something else. Was it something Thomas gathered along the river before the hike?

Thomas stopped singing.

Time passed.

He poured more water. More steam. Quiet.

Starlight penetrated the lodge where droplets streaked the side.

Woozy, Jack felt almost drunk, unaccustomed to the feeling.

Thomas sang, then stopped, rose to his feet, and pulled back the flap. Condensation rained down on the floor. "I will see you in the morning." He slipped out and was gone.

Quiet settled over the lodge, except for shallow, expectant inhalations from Erika.

"Now what?" she whispered.

"Not sure. I guess we can get out."

"Church is over? Can't we stay? Just a little longer?"

"Maybe we should. Maybe we shouldn't intrude on Thomas."

"Good. Pour more water on the rock. He let out the steam."

Jack groped along the ground and found a bottle. Empty. He found the other, twisted off the cap, and poured. The rock hissed, less vigorously.

Quiet. Jack could hear her every breath.

"Feels so good, doesn't it?" she whispered.

"Yes."

"Here we are. Like that night at the hot springs. I remember you going on that night about how even the antagonists deserve to be heard. I ate it up, oblivious to the fact that you were a loser. I offered to rub your shoulders, ready to do anything you wanted. You were so clueless."

"Not that clueless."

"Yeah, right. But you've changed, Jack Chastain. You were different then. Not as tentative. Happy go lucky, confident, ready to act. And an idiot. I was an idiot too, sitting there rubbing your shoulders." She giggled. "You know what? It's your turn."

"What?"

Her silhouette moved forward, over her hands. "You owe me a back rub."

Not a good idea.

She inched toward him. "Start with my shoulders." In a quick move she planted her back against him. "Right here," she said, taking a hand and placing it on a shoulder. "Hard. Play as rough as you want."

Not funny. "Only a minute."

He kneaded into the muscles, his fingers slipping on her damp skin. He bore in with his thumbs. She moaned and her muscles turned to putty. He moved to the base of her neck.

"Oh, that's good. After that, do my back," she muttered.

With one hand he moved down her spine. After a moment, he said, "That's enough"

"Oh, don't stop. More." She moaned. Her back went limp. "I like these rituals of purification. How did Thomas describe it? Spiritual renewal, healing?" She giggled.

His hands slipped to her waist. So small. The curve of her hips, so . . .

"We weren't such a bad team, Jack Chastain." She moaned. "That feels good."

"I need to stop. I'm woozy."

"Then, I'll do you." She twisted, falling against him, slipping in his hands. He fell back as she went limp and slid over him. Giggling, she said, "Trying to get away from me?"

"Erika, sit up." He grasped at her shoulders and tried to push her away.

She squirmed, twisting out of his hands. She laughed, then became still, breathing hot breath on his face. "Did you like my solstice story?" she whispered. "Someone threw water on the fire and great confusion broke out. I always wondered what that would be like." She planted her hands on his shoulders and shifted her weight to his legs, squirming against his struggle. "Jostling, great commotion." She lowered herself into the sweat on his chest. She moved her hands down his sides. "And the boys . . . or maybe it was the girls with a little something on their minds." She slid, writhing over him, mixing their sweat.

"No," he blurted, squirming under her.

She giggled and countered his moves.

He pushed her against the wet plastic. She stiffened as droplets rained over them. He slid out from under her, ripped back the flap and fled, staggering out into cool night air.

He stopped dead in his tracks. Vast void. Cañon de Feugo stared back, daring him to step forward.

He stood motionless, trapped amid two sets of uncertainties— the mysteries of Thomas' world, and the predations of Erika Jones.

CHAPTER
15

Jack grabbed his shorts and quickly moved away. This is no place to be when Erika Jones comes out of that sweat lodge.

So much for getting along with colleagues.

How many guys would be unwilling to participate in her notion of a little friendly camaraderie? Loser? Maybe so.

Jack stepped over to the wall, shivering, sweat clinging to him. He looked back. No. No turning back. You don't need a shirt, and no taking time to get into shorts. Keep moving.

But to where? Without intruding on Thomas, tempting yet another kind of spirit.

He put his hand to the wall and slid along the rock. He came to the rope. Up there, that would be the place to hide. Better than jumping that damned creek in the dark.

He stopped and listened. No sound came from the sweat lodge.

This is stupid. What's to be afraid of? She's either embarrassed as hell or mad. She won't be on the attack. Or would she? Her fire or her fury—either seems risky.

The time in Montana had been easy compared to this. That time was tempting, but not quite as dangerous. Of course I've changed. So has she. If she was another casualty of Montana, her wounds were . . . Hell, it was hard to tell how her wounds had healed.

He glanced around, looking for cover. Only boulders, and not very big ones. He backed into shadow, felt for a boulder, and sat.

"Hello Jack."

He nearly jumped out of his skin. "Thomas?" He squinted, finding the silhouette of the man a few feet away. "What are you doing here?" He quickly put on his shorts.

"No, that question is for you, ranger. What are you doing here? Tired of church?"

"I'm, uh, looking for my pack."

"It's not here. You had it by the fire. Not in the mood for white man's version of solstice ceremony?"

He cleared his throat. "You heard, huh?"

"Yeah. That is my fault. Men and women don't share traditional sweat lodge. If we do, we don't get naked, as you white people say."

"Wise."

"Tradition. You bahanas might keep it in mind. I hear you mate like rabbits." He let out a sad little laugh. "All you need is the back seat of a Chevy, and things just start to happen. Tradition, I hear."

"Touché," Jack said.

"Bahana tradition."

"Touché, already. What is that word, bahana?"

"Hopi legend, their white brother. Now they use the word to refer to white people. Some silly whites think they're saying banana, which sounds particularly apt for Miss Erika Jones. Slender and blonde, likes to slip out of her peels."

"Something wrong?"

"Why?"

"I don't know you all that well, but you sound angry. Different than I've ever heard you."

"It's nothing. Not your concern."

"If I'm intruding I can move back down the wall. Try to avoid becoming a ritual item to the hot bahana." He chuckled self-consciously. "Lesser men have . . ."

"No, stay. You're not intruding. Not now anyway."

"Sorry if we messed up anything."

"You didn't."

"Can we talk?"

"Yes."

"Ever since we pulled you off that wall, it's driven me crazy to try to understand why you'd risk your neck like that. And now, this trip, same thing."

"Can we move this way first?" Thomas whispered.

"The further the better."

"You came all this way to find Sipapu. We might as well go sit in its presence."

"It . . . it is the sipapu?"

"Hell no, I'm pulling your chain."

They started along the wall.

"Is there a reason you're hanging out here in the shadows?"

"It's no ritual, if that's what you're wondering."

"You're coming back here alone, aren't you?"

"I was. But now, maybe not."

Jack let Thomas step past a boulder. "Why?"

"There was something I thought I could find. I didn't. The stories . . . I heard them so long ago. Maybe I'm not remembering them correctly. And I'm not sure I could make the trip back alone if I tried."

"Nonsense. You did fine."

"I didn't do fine. You had a rope on me twice."

"Once, and only as a precaution. The second was a rappel."

"You got me here."

Jack stopped and studied him. "I'm sorry you didn't find what you're looking for."

"The day wasn't a waste. You got reacquainted with Miss Manipulation." He laughed long and hard. "Really well, and even better with her equipment."

Jack laughed nervously. "I'm not seeing this as funny. Why do you call her Miss Manipulation?"

"That's what we called her in high school. Be careful with that one. You never know for sure."

"What do you mean, what you called her in high school?"

"High school. Grades nine through twelve."

Jack stopped. "You're saying that day in my office wasn't the first time you'd met Erika Jones?"

Thomas stopped and turned. "I've known her all my life. She might not remember me, but I remember her. She didn't go slipping out of her peels back then. Not with me anyway, but yes, I knew her."

"Why didn't you tell me? Why didn't she tell me?"

"You didn't ask. I assumed you knew."

Jack shook his head. "I'm more than shocked. Does Kelly know her?"

"Quite well. Long history of friendship—and rivalry. Some of it not very pretty."

"Oh, great."

"You didn't betray her."

They stepped around a boulder. Thomas bore toward the water issuing from the wall. Jack stopped and looked into the sky. No moon, only stars. The heavens grew deep, casting enough light to make the canyon take shape. He glanced back at Thomas.

He sat staring at the wall and the waters. The hole from which the waters poured stood black as pitch.

Jack moved closer, knelt, and let the mist splash his face. "What were you here to find?"

"My grandfather taught me a song. May sing it for you?"

"You're changing the subject aren't you?"

Thomas stood and searched the sky.

Jack sighed. "Sure. I'd love to hear it."

His eyes seemed to settle on one place among the stars. He sang, in a low, resonant voice.

He paused. The quiet echoed back.

He continued, his song carrying across the canyon.

Jack listened, the power of it undeniable, and unexpected. He couldn't help but imagine generations of Thomas' people, his clan, his society, whatever they were, coming to this spot. Did those previous generations do the same thing? Sing from this spot into the canyon? Jack could imagine it; he couldn't understand it.

The stars seemed to brighten and the heavens opened more, revealing more stars.

Thomas stopped.

Silence.

Jack held his breath.

The universe seemed big and endless.

"The song . . . What does it say?"

"It's a song, a prayer."

"But the words?"

"There are no words." Thomas turned away.

"I don't understand," Jack mumbled, his eyes still locked on stars, and heavens deep.

"I tried," Thomas said.

"Tried what?"

"I thought I could help. Maybe it is not for me to do."

"Why not? Why not you?"

"After my sister died, I distanced myself from everything. I had no interest in continuing to learn. I had no interest in following the teachings of my clan or seeking initiation into religious society. Those, I stopped."

"So? You're interested now."

"The initiations I would have had, the learning I would have gained . . . it's too late."

"Thomas, you're a good man. That has to be good for something," he said.

"You don't understand, and I don't expect you to. The secular and religious are two different paths. I can help my people, but in secular ways. I'm not initiated and don't have the religious teachings to help my people along religious paths."

"I don't understand any of that Thomas, but if that's the way it is, that's the way it is. Do what you can, where you can."

"It's more complicated than that. I can't tell you why." He stared into the canyon and let out a sigh. "There are things my sister would have continued that need to fall to someone. I wanted to help. I can't."

"Why?"

"I don't remember the stories. Not enough to carry on traditions, or help others understand them. Or help assure our presence in this canyon never ends." He sighed. "Too much time has passed. Some things I remember. Some things I don't." He looked at Jack. "Two times you have helped me. Thank you."

"Why are we here, Thomas?"

He turned away.

"Was something supposed to be here?"

"I suppose you could say that."

Jack crept toward the opening. Water dripped from the moss around the hole. Fern growing at the opening cast shadows over it. Starlight flickered on the emerging waters. "Is this where you looked?"

He didn't respond.

"May I?"

"Yes."

Jack reached inside, above the waterline. Wet rock. Mineral deposits. Moss. Slime. No place to hide something, whatever it was. He felt deeper. No good place. Nothing. Thomas would have been this thorough, surely.

Jack stopped and stepped back, studying the opening. Maybe he's just a little off on what he remembers. Jack ran his eye onto the wall. Other little features. A drip line, running either side of the hole. A hanging garden, chest high, with fern, possibly monkey flower.

Hand to the wall, he felt along a crevice, then inside, then swept along a nook, then probed a hole. Nothing. He felt along the edge of the hanging garden. Nothing. He moved left and felt again. Still nothing. He squatted and probed along the strip of ferns that clung lower. Wet—from droplets sprinkling down from the hanging garden. He plunged his hand into a depression in the rock, amidst the ferns. Shallow. Nothing. He stepped to the left and felt again.

The depression grew deep. He withdrew his hand. Powdery. Dry. It glistened in the starlight.

Thomas stood as Jack moved to the next depression and

plunged his hand under the next row of fern. He pulled it out. White, covering his fingertips. He touched a finger to his tongue. Salty. He dusted off his hands.

Thomas followed. Jack sidestepped left, slipped a hand through a matt of fern, into a hidden crevice. The depression grew deep. Nothing. Only dirt and dust.

He slid down the wall, reached through fern, and found another hole. Only chalky dirt, dark. He dusted off his hands. Thomas stepped closer.

Jack looked higher, and stopped. Is that. . . ? Is that *Erysimum*? He glanced right, then left. Individual plants, woody stems, spaced along the wall. He pointed, and spun around to Thomas. "That plant. Do you see flowers?"

"No flowers. Why?"

"Too dark, but there's a plant we thought we killed it off. A real butterfly magnet."

"I don't understand."

"I'm sorry, I'm distracted." He laughed, and composed himself. "Forgive me. Maybe if we look on the other side, across the water."

Thomas placed a hand on his shoulder. "Friend, stop."

"If something's here," Jack said, finding another slot, "we can . . ."

"I know."

Jack slowly dropped his arms. "What?"

"I know. You want to help and you have. Go. Leave me now."

"Just tell me a little more. Maybe I can . . ."

"No, you've helped, and I will not say how. I trust you, but sometimes even those most trusted do things—or are forced to do things—that have unintended consequences. It's best you not know. Go."

"Can you at least tell me why this place is important?"

"Why is everything. Now, let me have some time to myself."

Jack read his eyes—their sincerity, their gentleness. "I'll go. We'll talk later. Don't know what will happen back in camp, but I'll survive."

Thomas laughed. "Please, this is not something to discuss with Erika, or anyone. I ask that you not tell others what you know."

"That's not hard. I don't know a thing."

"You know more than you think. This is a sacred place. These are healing waters."

CHAPTER 16

"Erika? Where are you?"

Is she in her sleeping bag? It lay sprawled across the ground, no one inside. Her pack was open, no evidence of anything more having been taken out.

He followed the wall to the rope, glancing behind boulders.

He slipped back to the door of the sweat lodge. The plastic flap was pulled closed.

"Erika?"

No response.

"Erika, are you in here?"

"What do you want?"

"Checking on you. Making sure you're safe."

"I'm safe, go away."

"Maybe we should talk?"

"About what?"

"I'm coming in." He pulled back the flap and slipped inside.

"I don't have clothes on. Aren't you afraid I'll attack?"

"I assume you won't."

"Assume! Okay, assume you're safe, for now. What do you want? Say it and get out."

"Maybe this isn't a good idea." He stopped and studied her. The sweat lodge was just barely warm, and enough of the condensation had dried away that distorted starlight cast an interesting light upon her. Sweat had dried from her skin, matting strands of hair against her forehead. She sat, legs to one side, watching him, not catlike, not as prey, but watching. He had seen her angry, but not stripped of confidence. She seemed smaller. "I didn't want to leave it on that note, especially since . . . We're in a dangerous location. Avoiding each other might lead to one of us doing something unsafe. We need to be able to talk."

"Then talk, and get out."

"We've known each other for a while, been through some tough times. I don't want to make an enemy of you."

"How sweet," she said, sarcastically.

"It's hard not to succumb to your advances, Erika. You're a beautiful . . ."

"Don't go there. Get out." She crossed her arms and covered herself.

"I'll change the subject. You should know that if I did anything in Montana that hurt you and your career, I'm sorry."

"Sure, that fixes things. Get out."

"Not gonna make it easy on me, are you? About what happened in Montana. I really haven't had a chance to talk to anyone about it. You said I'm different. I am. Things are better now but there are still times I'm not sure I know myself. You're different too. Harder, a tougher exterior."

"What do you expect? A woman has to survive. Adapt or die. I chose to adapt. I'll not be accused of being some easy to control, cuddly woman. Yuck." She dropped her arms.

"That you're not. Why didn't you mention you grew up here?"

"Why does it matter?"

"At the meeting the other day, I would've liked to have known some of the people in the room might've known you."

"I wasn't much more than a kid when I last spent much time here. They wouldn't remember me."

"Someone who looks like you is hard to forget."

"I'm not sure that's a compliment. I look different now."

"I probably know people you know." He sighed. "Erika, Montana isn't my favorite subject, but I was convinced you were part of the effort that got me canned. In the final days, you and I weren't talking much."

"We were busy, all of us."

"I know, but it seemed you were off working alone, freelancing, maybe working against my efforts, against the efforts of the team. I had no clue what you were doing."

"In the end, everything was spinning out of control."

"I know, but why were you spending all your time with special interests? In private, rather than keeping your activities out in the open where everyone could see them, knowing what you were trying to do. You know what happens when people think we're playing politics."

"I was trying to find someone to go to bat for us. Didn't work. Those organizations were seeing our support slip away. They'd talk, but they had no interest in putting themselves out there. Not visibly. They weren't willing to risk their standing at that stage of the game, supporting a lost cause."

"But it wasn't lost. Not till it was."

"Dammit Jack, you were always the optimist. It was lost. Long before you accepted it. I don't know if you were blind, or slipping something in your coffee, but things were lost for a long time. You focused on engaging everyone, the whole body public, oblivious to the fact that we were toast. Support from the right people evaporated. I tried. I tried appealing to them with stories of your boy scout idealism, your interest in hearing everyone. I couldn't turn it around."

"But support hadn't evaporated. I mean, it was their cause, we were responding to their proposal, their needs."

"The support of the power people had vanished. You were oblivious. I was trying to fix it. It was just too little, too late."

"So those two organizations . . ."

"Listened till I was blue in the face, but were determined to stay on the sidelines. Took all my time. Sorry, you didn't know that."

He shook his head and sighed. "Water under the bridge. I'm sorry about my assumptions. I should have given you the benefit of the doubt."

"They broke up the team so quickly. We never had a chance to talk."

He leaned over, and rested on an elbow. "Will we be able to work together?"

"We won't have to worry about that. I'm leaving tomorrow, driving south."

"We'll cross paths in the future."

"Maybe, maybe not."

"So, will we be able to have civil conversation?"

"About what? Sitting around naked, telling stories while some Indian guy gets his jollies on a ledge in the middle of the night?"

He chuckled. "Sure. We can talk about that."

"Sure as hell won't want to talk about Montana."

"Not my favorite subject either," he said. "So, friends? Buddies?"

"Sure. Buddies." She nodded, and sighed. "Shake on it?" She leaned over her hands and walked them past the rock. She raised a hand, reached quickly past his outstretched arm, and gave his chest a push. He fell back. She straddled him, and laughed. "Give me your hand."

"What're you doing?" he said, holding them back.

She reached down and took hold of a hand. "Handshake, re-claiming a modicum of pride." She shook his hand and held it. "Now I can lie to myself that you came back for more." She laughed.

He didn't respond.

"Oh, chill, Jack Chastain, I'm teasing you. Laugh."

He managed a bit of a chuckle.

"Good. Now, I want both hands." She grabbed the other, linked fingers on both, and lowered his arms to the side, wing-like, setting them on the ground. She settled her chest over his, and brought her lips to his ear. "Remember this moment—buddy," she whispered. "And tell Kelly Culberson I said she can have you."

CHAPTER 17

That old saying . . . how's it go? Hell hath no fury like a woman scorned?

Fury sounds easy compared to this. Hot, cold, calculatedly quiet, coolly confident, knowingly distant, or shrewdly flirty—what emotion would she conjure next? Would it be accompanied by the buddy treatment or the one for worthless trash?

Jack shifted his feet on the rock, locked his legs, and settled into belay position. "I can lower you. It'd be easier."

"No. I'll climb down." Erika squared her feet, glared, smiled wryly, then studied the sky, suddenly almost oblivious to his presence. She squirmed off the shelf and slid her back into the chimney. "On belay?"

"On belay."

"Okay, I'm climbing."

She started down. "You can drop the packs when I get there."

Just yesterday she seemed a novice. Today, skilled, efficient, an expert.

Jack let the rope slip through his fingers and slide around his body.

She disappeared down the chimney.

"Might be good you're going last," Thomas said, under his breath. "If you went first, she might drop a rock on you."

"You noticed."

"Yes, but she and I are best buds." He flashed a toothy grin.

"Yeah."

Thomas laughed.

"Get any sleep?" Jack asked.

"Not much. Enough. Saw Erika come out of the sweat lodge, run around buck naked grabbing clothes and her pack. She disappeared behind a rock and I didn't see her till morning."

"Yeah, I was inside the lodge when she left, making peace."

"I see. Nice job."

Jack rolled his eyes, and checked the amount of rope already fed out. She was moving quickly.

"What do guys like you see in her?"

Jack gave him an incredulous look.

Thomas threw back his head and laughed. He stepped to the edge to watch. "The plant you saw last night. Why did that get your attention?"

"Long story, Thomas. I thought it might've been a very rare plant we may've killed off on our fire. I looked again this morning. Hard to tell but I don't think so. One was starting to flower. Early, but it looked yellow."

"Is that important?"

"The one I'm looking for has flowers so orange they're almost red, bright yellow veins. Quite beautiful. Lots of pollen. Real butterfly magnet. A wallflower. Called a suffrutescent plant. Herbaceous parts die back each year to a woody base." He sighed.

The rope went slack, resistance gone.

"She off the rope?"

Thomas leaned over the hole. "Erika, you off?"

"Yes," she shouted. "Drop the packs."

Jack retrieved the rope, clipped all three packs into the carabiner and lowered them down. After a moment, he asked, "She done?"

"Erika?"

Silence.

"I can't see her."

Jack pulled in the rope.

"You're next."

Thomas clipped in and made his descent.

Jack retrieved the rope, coiled it and followed, making the descent unprotected.

At the bottom, he set both feet on level ground and turned to Thomas. "Where's Erika?"

He shrugged.

Lying in a corner, neatly coiled, was nylon blue webbing. No Erika Jones.

—·—

The pickup hit the meadow, and Jack slowed, seeing the Culberson's adobe casita across the way. He crossed the stone bridge, took a look at the water trickling past, and studied the late afternoon shadows set into the sandstone cliff face. Later than he thought. He pulled up to the house and got out.

"Knock, knock," he shouted, entering the French doors overlooking the canyons.

"In the studio," she shouted back.

He found her staring at a canvas, dabbing color at an unsettled foreground, beyond which, canyon walls already stood, looming almost angrily. "Ready to go?" he asked, settling in behind her. "Interesting."

"No, it's not. It's just not coming together. Started with cottonwoods, then changed it to desert, but nothing seems to talk to me. Not sure what to do. May have to put it aside for awhile. Want a beer before we go?"

"I can wait till we get to Elena's."

"Have one while I get ready. I can drive." She disappeared into the hall and returned with a San Miguel. "Good hike?" She handed him the beer.

He plopped down in a leather chair. "Yeah, interesting. Dangerous, in lots of ways."

"How did Thomas do? Was the trip worth it for him?"

"Didn't look good at first. He was pretty disappointed, but then something changed, and in the end he seemed satisfied." He took a long hit off the beer. "For a while, I thought he might open up about why we were there, but then he went back into full secret mode. Made me leave and let him do his business. Made me swear not to tell anyone. I'm feeling a little guilty just talking about it now, but I have no idea what we found."

Kelly straddled his legs, relieved him of the bottle, and took a swig. "Good. Now you know how I feel. Maybe you'll cut me some slack."

"Maybe. I respect that his culture is different than mine, that there are people to be wary of, but why the big secret. If it's important enough to make people like me risk their necks, not once, but twice, you'd think he could share a little information."

"But, again, why do you need to know?"

"You keep asking me that. I don't know. Maybe I don't, but if whatever it is needs protecting, we're the ones to help him, and you'd think it'd be good to know a little something about it."

"You're not of that culture. Be accepting. Try to understand, even if you don't."

He laughed. "What does that mean?"

"Drink your beer." She squirmed out of his lap and stood. "Maybe I'll go as I am. I'll grab a jacket." She moved toward the hall.

"Why didn't you tell me you know Erika Jones?"

She stopped, and slowly turned. "How do you know Erika Jones?"

"Work. Why didn't you tell me you know her?"

"Was she the woman who invited herself along? The one who knows the impression she makes on men?" Color left her face. Eyes wide, seemingly disconnected from her thoughts, she mumbled, "That's Erika." She looked away then back. "You didn't tell me her name," she said, answering his question. "So she was on the hike. Yes, I know Erika Jones. She's a friend, I think."

"You think? Thomas said friend and rival. Said things sometimes got ugly."

"That's not exactly right, but close. Erika's complicated."

"Is she a friend or not?"

"She will do something so shocking, so unfaithful, you think the friendship is over. Then, someone will do something, attack me or try to ruin me, and out of the blue she comes in and destroys them."

"So, why are you bothered by hearing her name?"

"Erika's moral compass points south. I haven't seen her in years, and the last time was the end of one of those shocking episodes."

"What kind of episode?"

"I don't want to talk about it. It's complicated. She's complicated." Shoulders stooped, she took in a deep breath. "So now she works for the Park Service? Did she work for you in Montana? How well did you know her?" She seemed to study his eyes, awaiting his response.

"Well enough, I guess."

"What's that mean?" She watched a moment more, then said, "I guess we better go."

"Grab your jacket."

She looked down. "Give me a moment. I need to change and put on some makeup."

"You don't need makeup. You look great."

She attempted a smile, and disappeared down the hall. She returned in well-fitting jeans, makeup that made her eyes pop, earrings and a necklace. Almost a different woman. A very beautiful, different woman.

"Wow, you look great."

She forced a smile. "You said that already."

— · —

"Got a place by the window?" Jack asked the hostess.

"Or the fire," Kelly said.

The young girl picked up two menus and walked them down the hall, veering toward the fireplace. Through the window, Elena's vegetable plants seemed to be getting their height. At a quick glance nothing appeared to bear fruit or vegetable, but it would only be a matter of time.

The restaurant was nearly full, with a fair number of locals and an equal number of tourists—or visitors, as Jack was conditioned to say. Wrangler jeans and cargo pants in the latest high-tech fabrics marked opposite ends of the fashion range. The hostess walked them past couples in quiet conversation, some studying the Spanish colonial splendor of the great room—worn pine planks on the floor, vigas and latillas crossing the ceiling, artworks of importance to the Hispano and Native American locals, some of it religious and set in nichos in the whitewashed walls. She stopped at a table halfway between the nearest window and the kiva fireplace. "How's this?"

"Perfect," Kelly said.

They sat and waived off the menus—they knew what they wanted—and the waitress met them with glasses of water. They ordered and the waitress hurried off to the kitchen.

Kelly took a sip. "I can't believe you work with Erika Jones."

"How flattering," a voice whispered behind her. "Speak of the devil, and here I am."

Kelly whipped around to face Erika Jones, smiling, a margarita in hand, wearing tailored pants and a white silky top, partially unbuttoned.

"Saw you walk through the bar. So, Kelly Culberson, you bitch."

Kelly glanced at Jack, then back to Erika. "Good to see you, too, Erika."

Erika laughed.

"You two are friends? Are you sure?" Jack asked.

"We are," Erika said.

"We are," Kelly agreed, reluctantly.

He shook his head and turned to Erika. "You disappeared this morning. You shouldn't do that."

"Sorry if I worried you, Jack. Planned to wait at the pickup, but ended up catching a ride with a couple of guys I met at the trailhead. Nice guys. Couldn't wait around all day. Had things to do." She gave him a smirk.

"A little communication would have been nice."

"I know. Oh well." She turned to Kelly. "He doesn't learn very quickly does he? Did he tell you we've known each other for a while? A few years in fact. Small world, huh? Doesn't know me as well as you do."

"Is that a fact?"

"He knows me pretty well, though. How have you been?"

Kelly nodded, slowly. "Good. And you?"

She turned back to Jack. "You're probably amazed at how glad we are to see each other. Give her my little message?"

"What message?" Kelly asked.

"Something silly," Jack said.

"What message?" Kelly asked again.

"Tell her. Go ahead."

"She said to tell you, you can have me." He chuckled self-consciously.

"I see," Kelly said, without humor. She turned and glared at Erika. "Which is code for, she's finished playing her little games and you can have him back. If you want him."

"You know me better than anyone," Erika said. "But are you sure? My messages may have changed a little over the years."

Kelly rolled her eyes.

"Nothing happened," Jack said.

"Well, something happened," Erika said to Kelly. "Just not what you think happened." She turned back to Jack. "Kelly tells me my moral compass points south. She's not exactly right, but I've learned life's a little more interesting if you shake the needle a little. Did you tell her I wanted to jump your bones in Montana?" She turned back to Kelly. "He learned that one this weekend. I guess he was a little clueless at the time."

"Clueless? You don't exactly drop clues. What else did you two do in Montana, besides your little games?"

The smile disappeared. "Seriously, Kelly, it's good to see you. It's been awhile."

"It has been."

"I heard you'd had enough of life back east. I heard your art is in demand. Congratulations. I'm proud of you."

"Thanks. What's it been, five, six years? Where have you been all that time?"

"Lots of places. A good part of it Montana. I'm in Denver now."

"What can you tell me about Montana, that Jack won't?"

She gave him a glance. "I don't talk much either. It's not a pretty story. Ended ugly."

"How long have you two known each other," Jack asked.

They looked at each other. "Awhile," Kelly said, joylessly.

"Oh, Kelly, you don't hate me that much, do you?"

"I don't hate you. I don't know what I feel. You're my friend, let's leave it at that."

Erika sat her margarita down, pulled out a chair, and sat. She turned to Jack. "I'll take you back to the good times. When we were teenagers, we were always there for each other. Not quite inseparable. Kelly was in Santa Fe so much of the time, but some of my favorite memories are of us on their ranch. By the way, I saw your father the other day," she said to Kelly, then shot a glance at Jack. "At the meeting. He didn't recognize me."

"Maybe not," Kelly said. "He didn't say anything. Could be the short hair."

"Remember going skinny dipping down on the creek? We thought we were so naughty."

"We were."

"Not very."

A smile broke on Kelly's face. "Quit talking. I don't need Jack knowing my secrets."

"You don't have any secrets."

They laughed, and as Erika's laugh fell off to silence, she stood. "Gotta go. I'm heading south first thing in the morning. Need to get packed and in bed. Long drive tomorrow."

Kelly started to say something, stopped, then said, "Will you be back?"

"Don't know. Might not be for a very long time."

"If you do, let me know. We can get together over a bottle of wine. If it's summer, we can go down to the creek." She looked over at Jack.

"I'll let you know." Erika flashed him a smile, gave Kelly a hug, and turned on her heels, walking quickly toward the bar.

Food was delivered and finished. They paid the bill and stood to leave, and as they walked the hall toward the entrance, Kelly grabbed his arm and pulled him out through the side door, into Elena's garden, into the cool night air. She pushed him against the wall, pressed herself against him, and pulled him into a hard kiss. She let him come up for air.

"Wow," he said, and sucked in a breath. "What's that about?"

"Listen to me. This Erica business caught me by surprise."

"Don't worry about her. She's leaving.

"I know, but she sent a message with that little code of hers." She sighed. "Erika wants me to wonder if she's inside your head. But I'm okay. I know she's not. There's no room. I'm already there."

CHAPTER 18

In the company of crickets and the sounds drifting out of the bar, explanations were made complete. After describing the episodes in the sweat lodge, and the time at the hot springs in Montana, Jack shut up and waited for Kelly to speak.

She watched him closely, but seemed to have nothing to say.

"Are we okay?"

She laughed, but caught herself. "I'm sorry," she whispered. "You poor guy."

"You make it sound like I couldn't take care of myself, and doesn't it bother you?"

"It's a predicament more typical for women. Are you embarrassed?" she asked.

"It doesn't just happen to women, and the more embarrassing image is me fleeing into the night."

"You poor guy."

He laughed. "I wish you'd quit saying that."

"Would you rather I ask how you came to be there with no clothes on, Erika climbing all over you?"

"Well . . . no . . . but that does seem the more likely thing to say."

"I'm afraid I know Erika too well." She giggled. Holding his arms tightly around her, she gazed over the darkened rows of the garden. "I'm sorry I wasn't there to protect you."

—·—

On Monday morning, Jack stopped first into the superintendent's office.

"Marge, can I see Joe?"

His secretary looked up from her work. "He isn't here, and I'm not sure when, if ever, he will be."

"What's that mean?" He flashed a perplexed look. "He still in D.C.?"

"He is, and it doesn't sound good."

"Director beat him up over our sending the troublemaker home? Am I in trouble?"

"Apparently it came up. I'm not sure if you're in trouble, or Joe, or who. He didn't have time to talk. He said the Director is creating some kind of assignment in D.C. Permanent or temporary, it's not clear at this point."

"No. It's happening."

"What?"

"What happened in Montana. The Director's involved. Things are going to hell."

"Don't over react. He said if it's temporary, it's likely a couple of months. If it's permanent, he's stuck there." She laid her hands on the desk. "Look, I'll let you know if I hear anything."

"Just get Joe back home."

She laughed. "I'm not sure the Director listens to me."

—·—

Erika Jones felt a vibration, pulled out her cell phone and slipped past the ranger on her side of the conference table. She ducked into the hall. "This is Erika."

"Hello Erika. Are you available to talk with the Regional Director?"

She glanced at her watch. "I'm in a meeting we need to wrap up post haste, but sure, connect me." She wandered down the hall, found a door to the outside, pushed it open and slipped out. Phone to her ear, she waited for Nick Sanders to get on the phone, and studied the pinnacles in this place the Apache called the 'Land of Standing up Rock.' An acorn woodpecker flew by and she turned and followed its flight into the oaks.

"Erika," the Regional Director said, getting on the call, sounding more subdued than expected.

"Hey, Nick. What's up?"

"You in Chiricahua?"

"I am. In a meeting. I didn't know you were back in Denver."

"I'm changing your plans. Forget the meeting."

"Just got here."

"This is important."

"Of course. Anything to do with your trip to D.C.?"

"What a pain that was. The senior leadership meeting . . . what a disappointment. The Director's a political hack. I'm not sure we can survive his games. He'll drive this agency into the ground if we can't find a way to get rid of him."

"What happened?"

"You don't want to know. It was ugly. Pissed me off. Overruled me, several times. I'd committed funds to research at Sand Dunes. The Director said no. In a meeting of my peers he overrules me, to embarrass me. It's science for God's sake. How can he not support science in a national park?"

"Unheard of."

"Damned right it's unheard of."

"What'd you do?"

"Kept quiet, watched everyone suck up to him, him just letting 'em do it. I could hardly stand it. Someone has to step up and do what it takes to get him out of the job. He'll ruin us."

"Calm down, Nick. You called for a reason. What is it?"

"Sorry, but you asked, and my reason does have something to do with all that. When I was in D.C., I paid a visit to Congressman Hoff. He loved the Yellowstone trip by the way . . . nice work. Gives me a favor to call in at some point."

"Good to have favors." She glanced around, saw a trail and ambled toward it.

"I may need to double down, generate a few more, which means a project for you."

"Where, Washington?"

"No. This relates to why I diverted you to Piedras Coloradas."

"Yeah, tell me a bit more about that," she said, plodding slowly up the trail. "Your email was cryptic."

"Did you make it to the meeting? Did you get me a name?"

"I did. His name is Mike Middleton. Made his fortune in high-tech. Spoke with him briefly. Took it no further. Thought it best to wait for instructions."

"Good."

"So why are we interested in this guy?"

"Bear with me. Rumor in D.C. says the Congressman has aspirations. He's the most golden of the golden boys and girls going into the primaries and he knows it. Supposedly thinks this President can't get reelected—something with which I tend to agree."

"So?"

"He's making plans. If he becomes President, he'll need a Director. He dropped a few hints."

"What kinda hints? And what does it have to do with me? Or rather, with you."

"Simple. Hoff's hints were directed at me. I may have to take him seriously. No one else seems to be willing to step up, and we need leadership."

"Then you need to keep your nose clean."

"It's not that simple. Imagine the Director as lame duck, purging our best people till he's out of office. The Congressman thinks he could drive a wedge between the Director and the Interior Secretary, maybe even make him a liability to the President. I can't play it safe. The Congressman needs to be convinced to act now, to drive his wedge. We can't wait."

"Got that picture, but what's it got to do with Piedras Coloradas? Hoff's from the Midwest. What's he care about things going on there?"

"The Congressman mentioned a constituent interested in what's happening at Piedras Coloradas. Hoff was short on information and time, but asked if he could get back in touch, to follow up on some things. The story seems to be, the constituent wants to insert himself into the meetings, push some things he's interested in."

"That's Middleton. I talked to him, heard him introduce his proposal." She checked her watch. "So, what do you need from me?"

"The Congressman's out of touch for a few weeks. Foreign policy junket to show voters and the world that he's presidential. When he gets back he wants to talk about follow-through."

"Gotcha. Could be dangerous, and bold at this stage."

"There's too much at stake. Someone has to step up and do something. Anything, to stop the political games. If nobody does it, we could see fundamental change in this agency. It won't be pretty."

"You'd be good," she said, and left it at that, "If we're waiting for the Congressman to get back before you talk, what's there to do? Other than approach Middleton, and start building a working relationship?"

"Ordinarily, that'd be enough, but the situation calls for getting out front, getting things moving, finding out what Middleton wants, and taking care of it. If I demonstrate some initiative—proactive initiative—give the Congressman satisfaction that his constituent has gotten the right attention, then maybe he can be convinced to move forward, first, to get the Director removed, second, to follow his instincts on who should be the next Director of the Park Service."

Erika chuckled. "You make that sound easy. So, when am I coming back to Denver?"

"Be here tomorrow. You won't be here long. I need you in Piedras Coloradas."

She stopped and stood upright. "C'mon. I just spent half a week there, most of it with Jack Chastain. I don't want to see him again for a very long time."

"I need you there."

"Have Jack work on it. He's apolitical. You won't have to worry about his motives."

"Unfortunately, Chastain is damaged goods. You know that."

She sighed. "You're right. He's naïve, and got a chip on his shoulder."

"That's why I need you there. I don't need apolitical. I need someone willing to do what it takes. Some things are not black and white. Gray areas cannot be allowed to cause inertia or paralysis. There's too much at stake."

"Nick, I'm uncomfortable working with Jack Chastain."

"Is there something you're not telling me? More history than I'm aware of . . . an old relationship, something in that realm?"

"Hell no," she said quickly. "I don't want to talk about this. Let's just say our approaches are different."

"And that's why I need you there. Ironically, Joe Morgan's been given a special assignment. There's been a dust up concerning an employee from another park. The Director got pulled in, and for some reason he's keeping Morgan on a short leash. Given him an assignment. Probably punishment, but that's okay. I was never sure Joe was one of my more loyal superintendents. If things get tough, I need to be able to count on who's there to do what's needed. I've been grooming Linda Showalter for a bigger stage, and it might be time to reshuffle the deck chairs."

"Don't know her. Why her?"

"Admittedly, she's got a touch of the same thing that afflicts Jack Chastain, but she's dependable. Showalter might be a good one to deliver on this favor to the Congressman."

"She knows the full story?"

"Not yet, just the basics. Knowing too much might put her at risk. I need to protect her. With a little encouragement, I can see how she does. You'll be there to make things happen."

"When does she arrive?"

"Tomorrow."

"Wow, fast."

"This is important. Requires fast. Too much at stake."

"I may have to do things you can't know about."

He sighed. "Understood. It might be necessary."

"Any special requests?"

"Yeah, if we're gonna beat the Director, we have to beat him at his own game. Get me photo ops with Congressman Hoff. Make 'em good ones."

—·—

Erika stepped back into the meeting room. She grabbed her briefcase, moved to the head of the table, and flashed a smile. "Sorry gentlemen. Another time." She slipped into the hall, dug out her cell phone, and pulled up a phone number saved only a few days before.

After three rings it was answered.

"Mr. Middleton, this is Erika Jones. I assume you remember me. We met last week in Las Piedras."

She nodded as she hurriedly made her way out of the visitor center. "Yes, that was me. Very kind of you, but I didn't call for compliments. In fact, I'm calling to stomp on your ego a little." She smiled to herself. "So, a little advice. You have a proposal you want to move forward. It got nowhere. But did you happen to hear the issues that interest the others in the room?" She listened. "I didn't think so. Well, I did. Their big issue—the one that's make or break—is water, and the conflict between ranchers and those who want to protect the river. Find a solution that makes their problem go away and everyone will love you." She slowed as she approached her rental car and looked around, making sure she was alone. "I know, but you're a smart guy. Figure it out. One other thing. The park has an acting superintendent, beginning tomorrow. Her name is Linda Showalter. Make an appointment, be the first person with whom she talks." She leaned against the car. "Yes. Let's talk later. Bye." She put her phone away.

She unlocked the car and slipped inside. She took one last look at the pinnacles.

Another time.

—·—

The press release made it official. Joe Morgan was on assignment in Washington D.C., at agency headquarters. Another superintendent—Linda Showalter, from a park in Arizona—would assume responsibility in an acting capacity, effective immediately. She would arrive within days, maybe as early as tomorrow. The press release from the regional office described her as bold and talented. The quote from Nick Sanders, Regional Director, called her a mover, an up and comer.

The word first went to division chiefs, who passed the word down to supervisors, who passed it on to everyone else in Piedras Coloradas National Park.

— · —

Marge stopped at Jack's door, her bag in hand, and knocked lightly.

Jack looked up.

"I'm surprised you're still here," she said. "The offices are otherwise empty."

"Playing catch up, but my concentration isn't any good. Keep worrying about Joe. Might as well go home."

"I know. I just got off the phone with a Mr. Mike Middleton, wanting to set up an appointment with Linda Showalter. Tomorrow. I'd hate to get her in over her head on her first day. Sounded like something I'd ordinarily send to you, but this guy insists on meeting with the acting superintendent. Is that okay?"

"Sure. Tell her I can help. Even join if she'd like."

"Good. Joe called and left a message while I was on the phone. Apparently, the Director wants a briefing on everything going on here. He's asked that it be you. Later in the week. In D.C."

He rolled his eyes. "Here it comes. This can't be good."

"Calm down. Joe said, 'briefing.'"

"Yeah, right."

CHAPTER 19

Linda Showalter arrived mid-morning, ready to take the reins. She slipped in through the public entrance to headquarters, somehow avoiding contact with employees, but the word was soon out.

She brought little more than a cardboard box of things for her office, and—according to Marge—emptied and refilled it with Joe's, packing it away in a closet.

An impromptu welcome was quickly arranged, and maintenance staff brought in extra picnic tables for a quick coffee behind headquarters. Employees began assembling well before Linda Showalter emerged from the office and made her way to the gathering.

Jack watched as she shook the first hands and settled in for conversation.

Middle-aged, medium height, brown hair, she had a strong presence in uniform and a quick smile—all outward hallmarks thought necessary for a successful superintendent. But, as Jack watched, he tried remembering what he had heard about her over the years. Her reputation, her work experience, and, most importantly, whether as a leader people would actually follow her. He mostly drew blanks, their paths had been so different. Different tracks, different networks.

Jack wandered over to Marge, who had planted herself at a picnic table, drinking a cup of coffee.

"So?"

"What?" Marge asked, continuing to sip on her cup. "If you're asking my impression, she seems good. Seems capable."

"Good."

"Interesting time isn't it. When there's a change in superintendents, it brings out all sorts of strangeness."

"How so?"

"The true nature of people comes out when there's a change in the boss. Pessimists predict bad things to come. The optimists see opportunity for new beginnings. Some people struggle with uncertainty. Some people thrive on the change."

"Hell, we don't know if Joe's really gone or if this is for a few months."

"Correct, but just in case, some are hedging their bets, setting up appointments, hoping to make good impressions, hoping to paint themselves as the go-to people on everything, especially budget."

Jack laughed, and shook his head. "Budget . . . guess I better set up an appointment."

"Don't worry, you've already got one. She asked that you be available sometime after three."

"About?"

"No clue." She took a sip. "Hope she isn't like the superintendent before Joe. That one ruled by keeping everyone off balance. Kept the door closed and the staff grew paranoid of anything coming out of that office."

"And that's what you're hearing about Showalter?"

"No." She smirked. "I'm letting my pessimistic side show. What I've heard is, she's dynamic, gets people around her who make her look good."

"That's not bad."

"No. Guess I'm just missing Joe."

They watched as Showalter moved quickly—energetically—between sets of hands. She stepped up to a young male naturalist and thrust a hand forward. He offered his, carefully. She exchanged a few words and moved on.

In a hasty skate to the side, she stepped past others, and stopped in front of Jack, and without an obvious glance at his nameplate, locked eyes on his. "Jack, I'm Linda Showalter."

"Uh . . . pleased to meet you."

"I know your reputation. And, I've been wondering about you."

"Me?"

She glanced at Marge. "Did Marge tell you I want to meet today?"

"She did."

"See you at three." She moved on.

When all the introductions appeared to have been made, Showalter slipped to the middle, put her hands on her hips, and waited for quiet to settle over the employees. "This is my sixth park," she said, with a nod. "This could become my third superintendency. I've enjoyed every assignment, but I can't help but believe this might become my favorite." She smiled. "Maybe we should keep that our little secret, just in case I have to go back to my current park."

She soaked in the laughter as she lifted her eyes to the rim of Cañon de Fuego. She turned up-canyon, then appeared to bring herself back to the moment. "What a place," she said. "I want us to remember how special it is, and that we are champions of the American tradition that these places are set aside for all, not—as in some parts of the world—the exclusive pleasuring grounds for the wealthy and the privileged. These places belong to all. We assure that remains true." She paused. "And, also, it's become increasingly important to me that we send our children home with a connection, that we help them develop a sense of awe." She stopped, and made eye contact with several employees.

"Now, I need to tell you some things." She paused. "First, I am not part of the good ol' boy network. In every hard-fought step of my career, I've had to fight the good ol' boys. I didn't like it, but I had to do it. I'm willing to do it here. If you're ready to be part of the future, let's go. We'll get along fine. If you can't evolve, we'll find a place to let you rot." She looked into the eyes and let the thought settle in. "Let's get to work."

Jack watched, waiting for Showalter to walk into headquarters, then he turned to Marge. "That was interesting. Not at all like someone on temporary assignment."

— · —

At the appointed time, Jack reported to Marge's desk for his meeting with Linda Showalter. "Go on in," Marge said.

He knocked on the partially open door.

"Come in."

"You wanted to talk," Jack said.

"Yes, have a seat."

The chairs were in slightly different places. He selected one offset from the desk and sat. "Need me to join you for the appointment with Mike Middleton?"

"Nope, I got it," Showalter said. She stood and took off her service jacket. She threw it in an open chair and sat on the corner of the desk. "Do I intimidate you?"

"Are you trying to?"

She laughed. "Well, as I said outside, I'm not a good ol' boy and some people have a hard time dealing with that?"

"In my experience, even the good ol' boys complain about the good ol' boys."

"Is that a challenge?"

"No."

"Are you gonna have a hard time with me in this position?"

"You're talking like I'm the enemy."

"You're the typical ranger's ranger. You've had it easy. Everything you've done has gotten you notice, and you may not have had to work very hard to get it."

"Did someone say I'm a problem?"

"I've heard some things, but I'm also a good judge of character."

"So you think I dog it?"

"I think you've gotten where you are because you and others like you take care of each other. Politics and favors have gotten you where you want to go, takes you further and quicker. You've had it easy compared to people like me."

"Excuse me. I don't understand this conversation. You're the acting superintendent. You've gotten further than I have."

"Yeah, but I know your kind. Ambitious, and I'm in the way."

"You're wrong. That's not who I am."

"Then, who are you? Convince me."

"I don't know how to answer that. All I want at this stage of my career is to do meaningful work. To be relevant. Nothing more."

"Relevant?" She laughed. "That's a pretty low bar, and I don't believe it."

"I don't expect you to. Do you know why I'm here?"

"I've known your reputation over the years, but not much of late, until recently."

"There's a reason for that. They buried me here, and that's okay. I like it here. I can do the job they want me to do, but I don't play politics, which is probably my problem. As much as I may want to believe there's an unwritten code of integrity and all that, I know that's being naive, but I'm okay with naive. Getting along with the guy in the mirror is more important to me than impressing someone else, including you. There are others like me. All of us deserve a little benefit of the doubt before people like you start making assumptions about how we tick."

Her brow furrowed. "You're in no position to get high and mighty. First, I don't buy it. Second, I expect you to prove yourself."

"What does that mean?"

"I've paid my dues. You can pay yours."

"I'm more than willing to do the job. If your idea of proving myself requires some kind of loyalty that has nothing to do with why we're here, I'm afraid you'll be disappointed. My priorities are the park and the public. If those are yours, I'll follow you. If they're not . . ."

"Careful." She studied him a moment. "I'll give you that benefit of the doubt, for now. But you're off on some tangent, doing something other than your real job. What is your background, by the way?"

"Biology, and what do you mean, some tangent?"

"Maybe we should get you back to exclusively doing biology."

"I would love nothing more than to spend my days in the

field, assuring you of the health of the plants and critters, but the things I'm involved in are assignments from your predecessor. I suspect they're things you will want me to do as well."

"Why should I care about this so-called Coalition?"

"A year ago, half of them were trying to do away with the national monument. The other half were fighting to keep it. The fact that they're sitting down together, seeing they have much in common, willing to work to preserve things they value . . ." He paused. "There's no guarantee it'll end pretty. Right now, I'm just trying to keep them from falling apart over the hardest issues. Still, where they've come is remarkable."

"Well . . . I'll believe that when I see it. Frankly, I suspect you're in it for yourself. Sounds like some contrivance to build you a little glory. A stepping stone to your next big job."

"No. Why wouldn't you see it as important?"

"If I thought they were off on some tangent, I'd let them crash and burn in an instant. If they can achieve something, so be it. Charge on. If not, I'm pulling you out of it."

"Why has this come up so soon?"

"Well, frankly, it's a little matter of this request for a briefing for the Director. The Director's office wants an update and it came with a name request—yours."

"You do it. I'd rather not go to Washington."

"Yeah, right. I don't believe that. You'll be going but that should be the job of the superintendent. Considering how little I know at this point, and how much you probably do, I'll honor the request."

"If you want to go, go," he said, raising both hands. "I'll bring you up to speed."

"Don't pull that routine on me. You're going and you know it. But there are people on high who are skeptical." She moved closer and gave him a hard stare. "Now why do you think they feel that way?"

"Frankly, I don't know, but I'm not pulling your leg. I don't want to go to D.C."

"C'mon Jack, it should be no secret. If anyone knows what buttons you push, it should be you."

"What are you talking about? Are you seeking answers or trying to enlighten me? Because other than some past history when things didn't work out so well, I really have no clue what you're talking about."

"Let's leave it at that. Make plans to be in Washington day after tomorrow. Stick to hot topics, current issues, nothing more. If I hear of anything unprofessional, you'll never set foot outside this park again."

"Yes, ma'am."

"Is that sarcasm?" She looked away, stood and walked around the desk to her chair. She sat. "Come right back. I want a day or two in the field, this week, learning about this park. And Jack, I don't enjoy being hard on you, but I don't like to beat around the bush. This was all to make sure we have an understanding."

The meeting was over.

Jack trudged down the hall to his office. He stopped at the door and looked inside, then stepped in and plopped down.

What was that about?

It wasn't good.

What game was Showalter playing? And what was the real reason for briefing the Director?

— · —

Linda Showalter ran her eyes over the massive rustic table. "Quaint," she whispered. Not exactly the same as the walnut desk and credenza to which she was accustomed, but pine did seem appropriate in this backwoods location.

Jack Chastain. That might have been a bit heavy handed, but at least it's done. Maybe he'll think twice before becoming a problem.

She shook her head. Relevant? Yeah right.

— · —

Before pushing 'confirm,' Chastain took one last look at the travel plans. Leave tomorrow afternoon. Fly in, stay overnight, give the briefing—whatever time that might be—and head back to Reagan National for the flight home. Should work.

Preparations. How much effort should this take? Not much, especially if it's really so the Director can dish out punishment.

Prepare something. Twenty minutes. No longer. If the Director wants real business, that'll be enough. Then, open it up for questions. If this is all a charade, no amount of preparation can help.

— · —

Marge ushered in the man in chinos and blue cotton sweater. "Mr. Middleton, this is Linda Showalter."

He stepped inside, flashed a smile and offered his hand.

"Mr. Middleton," Showalter said, shaking the hand.

"Call me Mike," he said, personably. "And congratulations. You've drawn a nice assignment." He sat in the chair nearest her desk.

"Thank you, and you'll have to forgive me, today is my first day. My learning curve is quite steep. How can I help you?"

"It's really more of a question of how I can help you. I have a project I want to talk about."

"Mr. Middleton, I've read last week's meeting notes. I'm willing to listen to anything you have to say, but let me be frank, I couldn't help but wonder if this isn't just your little pet project, something to benefit you, and not necessarily something the public needs."

He smiled. "I see." His eyes narrowed. "I'll be frank as well. I've got something to make your problems go away, in exchange for a modicum of recompense. But you don't have to take my offer. I can go elsewhere, to someone more helpful. The Director, for example. I'm sure he'd be happy to hear what I have to say."

She leaned over her desk and cracked a smile. "We're like a couple of old bison, aren't we? Finished with the perfunctory bluff charging?"

He stared hard. "Is that a joke?"

"Now that the formalities are out of the way, let's talk. Help me understand what you're proposing."

CHAPTER 20

Jack stepped off the elevator and turned right.

He pulled at his tie, straightened his collar, and checked the shine on his shoes. They're fine. It won't matter.

Veering left, he rounded the corner into the National Park Service wing and slipped into the bathroom. He pulled a paper towel from the dispenser and wiped the sweat from his brow. Damned humidity. Checking the mirror, he felt almost surprised the gray pinstripe suit fit as well as it did, it felt so long since he'd worn it. But, it was only a little over two years. The last time, that last briefing of the Director, things seemed so on-track, going as planned. Just before everything went to hell.

He stepped back into the hall.

Hall of Heroes, or bunch of political hacks, depending on who was doing the talking.

Who occupied these halls now? He looked around and soaked in the familiarity of the scene. No different than last time. Cold. Pre-war. Wide halls. Waxed floors. Doors leading to ancillary meeting rooms. Doors with opaque glass, with elaborate titles. Titles in subtly different print, suggesting changes in occupants, subtle differences in influence, and shifting status and staying power. The cost of running with the big dogs.

His heals clicked on the hallway floor as he took a step toward the offices of associate and deputy Directors. He stopped.

A plaque to his left caught his eye. Those who had died in the line of duty. He checked his watch—he had a few minutes. He stepped closer. New names had been added. He scanned, looking for one name in particular. Found it. Memories stirred, of time in the field. Work, with a trusted friend and capable colleague. Real work, before the days of being drawn into new realities—politics. He remembered the day he was pulled from a meeting in a distant town, and told that John had died. How could he have fallen? How could that have ever happened? John had been so careful, more careful than anyone. That day, the risk must have been necessary. Necessary to step between a child and the edge, necessary to let his own life come to an end.

Of all the people to lose . . .

He shook himself back. There are things to do. Abuse to prepare for.

He continued up the hall, past the doors, stopping at the reception desk at the end of the wing. The receptionist looked up from the phone and flashed him a sign: one moment.

He glanced at the door to the right, the Director's office, then to the left, the Deputy Director's office, then dropped his eyes.

The receptionist hung up the phone. "May I help you?"

"I'm Jack Chastain, here from Piedras Coloradas to brief the Director."

"Of course. The briefing will be in the room behind you." She pointed to a door to his left. "The Director's meeting room."

"Thank you."

"If you need it, the room has a projector ready to go. The Director's running a little behind, but that's normal around here."

"I understand." He backed toward the door. He looked inside.

The long walnut table ran the length of the room. It and the executive chairs around it looked much the same as last time. The park photos—Grand Teton, Yosemite and Grand Canyon, reminders of responsibility—were the same. A woman stood in the back corner, looking out the window, into the courtyard below. Navy blue skirt, long legs, short blond hair. She realized someone else was in the room and turned. Erika Jones.

She smiled. "Hello Jack. I'm glad you made it."

"Why are you here?"

"You were right. Our paths will cross. Might be a bit soon, but we can rehash old times if you'd like. Sitting around a sweat lodge, butt naked, telling stories. Maybe the Director can chime in with a few of his own."

"I didn't know you'd be here."

"Me neither, till yesterday. I'm here representing the interests of the regional office."

"I thought you were in Arizona, and what are the interests of the regional office?"

"To be helpful. To you, of course. Provide a diversion if needed, protection if possible. And plans change. They didn't need me in Arizona. Go with it." She beamed, then looked away. "I'll let you get ready."

Heart pounding, Jack pulled the laptop from his briefcase and found a place near the cord to the projector. He plugged in, turned on the computer, and proceeded through set up.

Erika studied the plaques on the walls, working her way toward the door. She took a peek into the hall and settled back inside. "Remember when you and I were in this room together last?"

He nodded. "That was my last time here, before all hell broke loose."

She laughed. "You painted such a rosy picture. I'm surprised they let you back in the building."

"I wasn't painting a rosy picture. I was trying to give an objective view of the interests at the table."

"Objective!" she said, with a smirk. "There were asses at the table. You knew it. Why couldn't you just admit that to the Director, keep the agency from being blindsided?"

"I was giving everyone the benefit of the doubt."

"Yes, you were, and they took it and ran with it. Ran your ass all the way to New Mexico. What's the harm in calling a spade a spade?"

He stood and walked to the window. "You're right, I learned

a few things but objectivity is still important. I still don't know if I would've done things any differently. To this day, I don't really know why they were playing the games they were."

"Does it matter? They had ulterior motives. We should've been suspicious and seen it coming. They burned our asses. I'm tired of this conversation. Let's talk about, say, our mutual friend, Kelly Culberson."

"You two have an unusual friendship."

"I'm an unusual friend." She laughed. "I don't make it easy, do I?" She moved to the window and stood beside him. "You should try it, Jack. Shake the needle a little. You might enjoy it."

In a flood of movement, the Director appeared in the door, crossed the room, and offered a hand. Jack shook it. "Director Lucas," he muttered.

The Director turned to Erika, shook hers, and claimed a spot at the table. "Sorry I'm late. Thanks for coming." Gray hair disheveled, shirt sleeves rolled up, and tie loosened, he did a double take. "Last time I had a briefing from you two, things didn't work out so well."

"No they didn't," Jack said. "But I'm guessing you know why more than we do."

He glared, gave a muddled look, then shook it off. "Tied me up for weeks. But we're not here to talk about that. Bring me up to date on what's happening in Piedras Coloradas. Things were getting hot, then dropped off the radar. That's okay by me, but I'm starting to hear a few things. Things percolating up to my office. I don't need surprises."

Two young assistants—one male, one female—came in with pads of paper. They introduced themselves and the names failed to settle into Jack's brain. He rubbed his forehead. This is looking like an actual briefing.

They took seats to the left of the Director.

Would the Director dish out punishment with a crowd in the room?

Erika sat to the right of the Director. Of course, at the right hand of God. Jack watched her put on her game face.

He walked to the other end of the table, and stood beside his laptop. "I'll start with a recap of the Presidential proclamation that established the national monument, and provisions for NPS management of areas adjacent to the national park and BLM management elsewhere. Then, I'll give background on the conflict that followed, and where we are today."

Covering all that, he concluded on the battle climaxing with community leaders coming together to find common ground.

"At that time, they asked that I participate. I've operated not as a government employee running government meetings, but instead as a government employee invited to help in their process of discussion, working with and for them."

"I see," the Director said, furrows forming across his forehead. "I see political risk in that approach. Someone gets the upper hand, and those with the short stick come crying to me. And why are we doing this? It's a national monument, not a local monument?"

"I had the same thoughts when this started."

"Then why are we playing this game?"

"It's not a game, and yes, it could go in any number of directions. And when all's said and done, who's to say we'll have the authority to do the things they recommend."

"That's what I thought. Maybe we should back out."

"No, sir, I don't think so. There are risks, but these people are reasonable. They're trying to work together."

"It looks questionable."

"True, the Coalition could fall apart because of the difficulty of the work, or someone could try to tear them apart, and if they do, controversy returns. Then, our job gets harder. Typical difficulties. Ideologies getting in the way, us painted as the enemy, and so on."

"What if things blow up in ways we can't control?"

"How would that be different than anywhere else we have a tough issue?"

The Director sat back and crossed his arms. "Well, at least everywhere else we're not dropping our defenses, asking them to hit us upside the head with a two by four."

"As with people I've encountered in every place I've worked, in

Las Piedras there are more things that hold those people together than things that would split them apart. There are values that define them. But just like everywhere else, there are issues out there to potentially split them apart, and people willing to do that splitting. I admit, in the past, there were some who poured on the rhetoric, pushing their own self-interests, then pouring gas on their own fire, and not openly showing their cards. They riled people up to fight their fight, blinding them to everything but the rhetoric."

"Then why the hell are we going down this path?"

"Because, how is it different? Look at what happened in Montana. How is that different?"

The Director leaned forward. "Are you wanting to talk about that? I can give you an earful if that's what you want."

"No, sir, I don't," Jack said.

"Then go ahead, continue the briefing, but somehow this is all sounding a little too familiar."

"No sir, it's not," Erika said. "Jack's not the same guy, and this isn't the same briefing you heard concerning our operations in Montana."

"Prove it."

Jack kept his eyes on the Director. "I know there are risks, and I know something could go very south, and I know the agency may choose to distance itself from anything that comes out of this effort. The agency may want to distance itself from anything I'm involved in, but I don't think you should. I think we should have faith in these people. We should do what we can to help them come together as people, to tell us what's needed most from us. Their cultural and natural heritage is as important as anything in this nation. We can help."

"No argument, but you're making me nervous. What will you do if things get messy, like we both know can happen?"

"We'll do our best. That's all we can do, our best. The answer may sound simplistic, but I can't see us giving it anything other than that. We have to deserve their respect."

"Sometimes it takes a little more than that."

"Joe's been supportive. Ask him."

"Joe's busy. He's out of the picture."

Jack glanced at the aides, and settled his eyes on the Director. "If Joe Morgan is in trouble, if I'm in trouble, I would like to say something."

"I'm not talking about any of that. Not here, not now," the Director said, slowly shaking his head "That's none of your concern."

"It is, if it's precipitated by something I did. I sent that fire-fighter home, not Joe."

The Director looked around the room and back at Jack. "Not here."

"To get us back on subject," Erika said, "let me say that acting superintendent Linda Showalter is now on the job. If she has concerns when she gets up to speed, we'll change strategy. I've also been assigned to the park by the Regional Director, effective immediately. I can suggest changes as the need arises."

Jack stared at her, trying to hide his reaction. "You're assigned to . . . ?"

The Director tapped a finger across his lips.

"If I see the need for a change of course," she said, "or a need to abandon the effort entirely, I'll work with Jack and others to make those changes."

"But . . ."

The Director continued to nod. "Mike Middleton. Know him?"

Jack and Erika glanced at each other.

"He came to our last meeting," Jack said.

The receptionist appeared at the door, knocking three times. "Excuse me, I have to interrupt. The Assistant Secretary asked that you come to his office. The deal's off. It might take some effort to get things back on track."

The Director scowled and stood. "Very well. I'll be right there." He looked over at Jack. "I don't need surprises. Don't screw things up. Don't do something that makes it necessary for me to get involved."

"What about Middleton?" Erika asked.

He turned to the aides. "Fill them in, would you?" He moved to the door and was gone.

One of the aides collected her papers and stood. "Mr. Middleton called to schedule a meeting. We're trying to find a day that works with the Director's calendar."

Erika stood. "About what?"

"Something he wants to see happen." She turned and left the room.

Jack exhaled.

Erika Jones picked up her briefcase. "Count your blessings, Jack. You were saved by the Assistant Secretary." She moved to the door. "Gotta go. See you in Piedras Coloradas."

— · —

Erika Jones rounded the corner and slipped into the elevator. On the first floor, she scooted around security and exited the building. Out in the sunlight, she stopped, drew in a breath, and looked out toward the National Mall. Past other buildings, flags flapped in the breeze. She pulled out her cell phone and brought up the number for Nick Saunders.

He answered.

"Nick, it's Erika. Got a bit of a surprise. Middleton contacted the Director, wants to meet about his project."

"Damn," he said. "How do they know each other?"

"Didn't say."

After a moment of silence, he said, "Let's not panic. Is anything set up?"

"Not yet. Director's calendar doesn't permit."

"If the Director would just stay home, he might get some work done."

"Nick, you're not exactly camped out in Denver," she said, watching a string of taxis pull up to the curb, men and women in suits jumping out.

"Erika, that's different. I'm getting things done. He's playing games, but maybe that's to our advantage. Get your head out and help me figure out what we should do."

"Nick, we haven't done anything yet, so no harm done. We can drop our plan and no one will be the wiser. You can see what comes of the conversation when you talk with the Congressman. We can make a new plan then."

"Do you know what you're saying? By then it's lost opportunity. Hoff's beholding to the Director. Someone has to do something now. We have to get the Director out of the job. I'm willing take a risk to advance the cause."

"What do you want me to do?"

"Talk to Middleton. Learn what you can. Influence his approach if you can. If you can't, we'll drop it."

"Will do."

CHAPTER
21

Linda Showalter looked across the desk and steepled fingers beneath her chin. "Talk," she said to the two before her.

Jack turned to Erika.

"Go ahead," she said. "It was your show."

"I guess it went okay," he started. "Director mainly wanted a status. We talked a bit about the process, how I came to be involved, and what my role is."

"And the risks of assuming that role," Erika added. "He had a lot of questions and concerns."

"Before we go any further, tell me how you two know each other," Showalter said.

"We worked together in Montana," Erika said. "A failed and miserable effort, but don't blame that on me."

"I don't need war stories, but I do want to know why I need a special assistant from the regional office."

"Uh, the Regional Director simply wanted to help you get your feet on the ground."

"Right. And has anything ever gone on between you and Jack?"

"Why would you think that?" Erika said, looking shocked.

"The tension in the room, which often means one of two things. Relationship gone bad, or sexual harassment. Has he ever taken advantage of you?"

Jack looked over. He waited for her response.

"Do I look like a woman who can't take care of herself? You're thinking too hard."

"Good." Showalter turned back to Jack. "Back to the briefing."

He was slow to find words. "Other than concerns over how it's structured, that's about it. Except we learned Mike Middleton wants a meeting with the Director. Wants to talk about his proposal."

"You're kidding."

"I don't think we want the Director meeting with Middleton," Erika said.

"Agreed, but if he sets it up, we don't have much of a choice," Linda responded. "He seems pretty confident of his contacts and his influence. If they're good, and he's barged in the door, what can we do?" She turned to Jack. "What do you think? And what do you think of what Middleton's proposing?"

"I don't know that much about it. Just met him at the last meeting. Presents himself as wanting to do good things, but the way he introduced his proposal wasn't received well by others."

"Why?"

"Ego," Erika interjected. "But that might have been a misstep. The Regional Director wants to see him given some consideration, at least to hear him out."

"I know. He mentioned it when he gave me my marching orders. How is Nick involved in this?"

"Uh, . . . he's not. I gave him a few details when I was back in Denver. He sounded interested, that's all. Ask him."

"I will. You stay out of it." Showalter sat back. She shook her head. "What do you think, Jack?"

"Doesn't hurt to hear what Middleton has to say, but remember, in these meetings we don't own the process. We're just invited to participate."

"When is the next meeting?"

"Tomorrow. On occasion we meet at night to reach a larger audience, but tomorrow's meeting is at ten."

"I'd hoped you'd show me some things in the park tomorrow."

"If you don't mind a late start, we could still do it. To see what?"

"You decide. I'd like to see this Pistol Creek Fire, but other than that, your choice."

"That might require an overnight?"

"That's fine."

"Am I invited?" Erika asked.

"No, you're not. And if you're going to be here, I want you in uniform."

Erika looked down at her tailored gray jacket and black skirt. She smiled sheepishly. "I wondered. I brought a uniform."

"Good. Wear it. Jack, unless you tell me otherwise, I plan to attend the meeting to listen in. To help me understand. I'll sit in the back. Erika, you can join me for that. Now, both of you, out." She pointed to the door.

Once they were gone, she turned to a two day old email from the Regional Director:

> Do what you can to be helpful to Mr. Middleton. I'm anxious to learn more about what he has in mind. Be sure to use Erika in any way you can. She'll negate any weaknesses you have on staff. –Nick

— · —

Karen Hatcher welcomed everyone to the meeting, inviting them to find a seat among the tables, arranged as usual in a square.

"Permit me to introduce Linda Showalter, Acting Superintendent of the park," Jack said. He gestured toward her, sitting at the back wall.

She stood. "Don't mind me. I'm here only to observe and to learn. I look forward to meeting each of you." She sat, Erika Jones beside her in uniform.

Kip Culberson went over the agenda and asked for additions. He underscored a return to Robert's Rules, and glanced at Mike Middleton and Harper Teague. They sat facing each other, neither giving the other attention, but they promised to play nice. Thomas joined again, and sat in the same seat near the corner.

The meeting started by ticking off discussion of items that had required outside homework from subsets of the group. The status of their work was presented and accepted.

Middleton's proposal was next on the agenda. Jack gestured for him to proceed.

He stood, smiled, and straightened his collar. "Thank you and I apologize for my impatience at the last meeting," Middleton said. He smiled and made a sweep, establishing eye contact around the table. "My exuberance stemmed from my excitement for what I want to offer. To help. I can solve many of your problems." He waited, as the point settled in. "I mentioned a land swap. I mentioned my willingness to give the government twenty acres for every one I receive in exchange, maybe even more. I failed to mention my property's ideally located to address your many issues. The land's ideally suited for water storage. Water diverted from the river could be stored in ponds and reservoirs. The linear lay of the land could give ranchers access to water over an extensive area, allowing conservation interests the opportunity to move forward with river protection measures. Do you want to know more? Shall I go on?"

A smile came over Ginger Perrett's face. She looked almost relieved. "Please, yes," she said, flashing a glance at Dave Van Buren.

Dave gave her a nod.

"Thank you," Middleton said. "And if any of you think this would be difficult to make happen, suffice it to say, I have a little influence in a few of the right places."

"My god, people," Teague muttered. "That means he's playing games. Giving and taking favors. Political favors."

"Connections require certain discretions. Do not worry. I'm here to help."

"Cards on the table, Middleton. I for one want everything above board," Teague looked around the table, his bushy brow furrowed. "With me, what you see is what you get. Before you trust this guy, you need to expect the same from him. No games. Everything above board."

"Let's listen to what he has to say, Harper," Kip said.

"He's a government enabler. What he's saying keeps government's fingers in places they don't belong. And protections . . . hell, that sounds like regulation, to sap away our freedom."

"Harper, hold your horses," Kip said, impatiently. "People want to hear this."

"We do," Dave agreed. "Harper, you don't speak for all of us."

"Because you have no clue what freedom means. You want life in the nanny state, but when you lose what's important because government takes control, denies you access to something you love, you'll remember this day. If anything from this charade moves forward, you'll remember my words. You'll be saying I was right."

Middleton tapped his fingers, looking around the table.

"Go ahead Mike," Jack said.

"Thank you. As I was saying, my land is on the edge of the national monument. Beautiful stretch of desert. At first I enjoyed the thought of ranching but learned it's not my cup of tea. I've got several stock ponds, and it's ideally suited for construction of others, allowing river protection along a two-mile stretch adjacent to my six hundred acres." He looked around the room, making eye contact with everyone, jumping past Teague. "Like the idea?"

Ginger looked across the table. She nodded at Van Buren. "That's a solution."

Dave returned her nod.

"You called it a swap. What do you get?" Karen Hatcher asked.

"A little place to call my own, that lets me keep some roots in the area. That's all I want."

"Do you have a place in mind?"

"I do. And the deal may hinge on whether we can work this out but I have negotiating room. I can tweak this a little." He paused and glanced around the table. "Twenty to forty acres, that's enough for my needs."

"Where?"

"Beyond the end of the south road, right on the edge of the monument, where it adjoins the park boundary. Below Sipapu Falls."

Jack glanced back at Showalter, and caught her eye.

She flashed a look of shock, and sank back against the wall.

"You realize, depending on where you're talking," Hatcher said, cautiously, "that location could be a deal killer. If in the monument, it would be difficult. If in the park, impossible. The difficulty increases exponentially. Opposition would come out of the woodwork. Legislation might be required to make it happen."

"Legislation can be arranged," Middleton said.

"You mean, through Congress?"

"Of course. Through the right people, anything can be made to happen, but let's not worry about that now. This is really up to you, this group. If I can help you solve a major issue before it derails your effort, I'm confident you'll be more than willing to voice support for an exchange. We can make it happen. After all, it's twenty acres to one."

"No! Not there,"

Jack turned to the voice—Thomas'. He gestured to give him the floor.

"I have nothing more to say. Just not there."

Ginger flagged her hand, and leaned forward. "I say we study this before we toss it out. It solves problems. We're struggling. If we can find a solution to this one issue, we're ready to write our recommendations. If we can't, we may never get there."

"Not there."

"Why?"

Thomas held his tongue.

"Why not that location?"

"Hell, I'll speak for him," Teague shouted. "No, and hell no. He doesn't need a reason. Toss it out, bad idea."

"But it's not a bad idea." Ginger raised a hand and turned to Jack. "I make the motion we study Mr. Middleton's proposal."

"A second?" Jack said.

Hatcher raised her hand. "I second."

"Discussion?"

Thomas slowly shook his head.

"This is only a vote to study it," Kip said.

"No."

"Can you give us a reason not to study it, Thomas?"

He shook his head.

"What do we do?" Jack asked. "More discussion? A vote?"

"Pull my second. I suggest we hold off on a vote," Karen Hatcher said. "Some of us don't want to take it off the table, and some of us need to think about it."

"A vote's not binding," Middleton interjected.

"Hell no, no vote," Teague said. "Get rid of it, admit defeat. Shut this whole scam down. Let's talk about something important, like kicking the government out of our lives. We can start by kicking the lackeys out of the room. Why should I need his permission to speak?" He pointed at Jack.

The meeting stalled at that point.

———·———

As the meeting broke, Mike Middleton stood and moved quickly toward the door. Linda Showalter intercepted him. "Mike, you and I spoke for an hour, and never did you mention the trade would involve a parcel inside or along the park boundary."

He flashed a confident grin. "Oh, did I not?"

"No," she said, returning the smile. "What you've proposed would create a great many difficulties."

"Don't worry, Linda. This is going to make you look so good."

"Good? It's crazy. It'll never happen."

"No, it will, and you can look good or bad. Shall I tell the Director you're helpful, or difficult? Which will it be? Only takes a phone call, and I'll be making that call, either now or later. Which will it be?"

"You and I need to talk."

"About what?"

"Things."

"Great. I love working with you people." He turned, and scanned the room as the others started to leave. "Good meeting. A few holdouts, but all in all I feel good about it."

———·———

Kip Culberson slipped alongside Jack, and joined him in watching the cliques in conversation. "Not sure what I think about all this."

"Not sure if that was good or bad," Jack said.

"Yeah, but Thomas didn't help. If he's opposed, he needs to say why."

Kip stepped away.

Jack waited as the last of the others said their good-byes, then he followed them out. Linda Showalter and Erika Jones waited in the hall.

He glanced at his watch—a little after noon. He gave his eyes a rub. "Bring your pack? I'm ready to go."

"Me too," Showalter said, looking disengaged. "Before we leave, tell me, did either of you know what Mike Middleton had up his sleeve?" She turned to Jack.

"Not a clue. Caught me by surprise."

"Erika?"

"Part of it. I think we all need to remember his primary motivation, to help. To solve issues, as he said. I'm sure we can suggest some change to his thinking."

Showalter looked stunned. "Let's get some fresh air."

They followed her down the hall and out of the hotel. She took a deep breath and stared into the distance, out over plateaus and the mountains beyond them.

She pulled her eyes away and faced Jones. "Now. What changes?"

"What do you suggest?"

"Never mind." Showalter turned to Jack. "I'm ready. Let's go."

CHAPTER
22

The trailhead came into view.

"We jump on the trail here," Jack said, slowing the pickup.

At the end of the two-track road, boulders demarked wilderness and the beginnings of trails leading in different directions. He pulled off the road and turned off the pickup.

Their trailhead sat near the largest rock. The trail took a straight line east and upslope, through piñon pine and juniper. Without words, they exited and pulled out their packs. Jack tucked his radio into his, and they struck out, past a sign saying, "Trail Closed. Prescribed Fire."

On a shaly outcropping, Jack stopped and let Linda Showalter catch up, his eyes focused forward, on canyon breaks. "We approach along the opposite flank from where it's been worked so far. Rather than starting at cool, burned-out control line, I thought you'd prefer a little excitement."

She sucked in air, fighting to speak, but gave it up and waited a few moments more. "Out of shape. Too much time at the desk."

"I'll get us there, you set the pace."

"I'm fine, I think." She laughed. "You said excitement?"

"Fire's moving north, but also along the western flank." He checked the angle of the sun. "It's the burn period, the hot part of the day. We'll see the fire making some moves, but don't worry. It's a little early in the year to get exciting."

"Got it." She pulled in another breath. "When we get there, let's talk objectives."

"If we see one of the fire staff monitoring the fire, I'll let them cover it. Good experience, briefing the superintendent cold."

"Are you setting me up to scare some young person to death?"

He let out a chuckle. He took a step, then paused. "I'm setting you up for a briefing. How you play it is your call." He moved on.

She followed, taking measured steps. "Tell me again. What did the Director say about Mike Middleton?"

"Not much. Assistant Secretary had him pulled from the meeting. He didn't have time to get into it."

"What are you not telling me?"

"Nothing."

He noticed her falling behind. He slowed.

She caught up. "Why did you let me get blindsided by Mike Middleton?"

He glanced back. "Today?"

"Yes, today. Why didn't you tell me he had designs on a parcel inside or along the park boundary?"

"Why are you wondering about me? You've talked to him more than I have."

"You have a vested interest. If the Coalition finishes its report, you're in the running for glory. You get your shot at the big promotion."

"I don't think like that?"

"Yeah, right. Middleton's proposal can help the Coalition achieve success. If it doesn't achieve success, you're nothing." She sucked in a breath. "Before today, what did you really know about his proposal?"

"That he wanted a land swap. That's it. He didn't get much of a chance to say more than that the first time we met."

"Okay, I'll accept that as true. If it is, what was your reaction today?" She fought for air, then said, "Don't tell me what you think I want to hear. Tell me what concerned you in that meeting."

"Why would you think I wouldn't tell you that?"

"Answer the question."

"Three things concern me, all coming from new players. Mike Middleton started out sounding helpful, gave people something they wanted, a solution. Then he put us in a tough position, asking for something we can't give."

"Glad you think so. It's a non-starter. Craziest thing I've ever heard."

"Thomas can potentially eliminate the tough position for us, but puts the Coalition back into dealing with a tough issue. And he won't say why."

"Yeah, what's he protecting?"

"Don't really know. Harper Teague supports Thomas in his opposition, but for no good reason other than being a pain in the ass."

"Why wasn't Middleton's proposal seen as helpful before? And is it really that helpful?"

"His presentation was totally different today. He gave no detail before. Today, he emphasized something to help the Coalition. Actually quite elegant."

"Elegant, hell. He was manipulative."

"Yeah, but he addressed an issue dividing the Coalition, and yet, all he said was, here's a place to water livestock. He made no mention of water rights, his or anyone else's."

"Why is that important?"

"Not sure. Without water rights, he really might not be offering very much. But even without addressing that detail, he's given most of the group a reason to clamor over his offer, even people who would ordinarily oppose any threat to the park."

"Why are they so eager?"

"Because they've worked hard. They're nearly finished. If they can find a solution to this issue, they're done. They've succeeded."

"Why did any of that surprise you? And are you shooting straight with me? You had no clue he planned to blindside me like that?"

"No, and what does it have to do with you?"

"Well, numbskull, I happen to be superintendent of this park. If anything goes south under my watch, who do you think's responsible?"

"Acting superintendent, and we're a long way from taking any action. For one thing, remember Thomas has concerns."

"Rather impotent ones if he doesn't open up. With Harper Teague agreeing with him—the kiss of death in my opinion—I see that Thomas guy as no help. No help whatsoever. All the burden of saying *no* falls to us."

The trail plunged into an aspen-filled draw. A creek ambled through. They splashed through shallow waters, skirted the edge of the grove, and climbed back to higher ground.

They topped a rise. In the distance, haze sat over the tops of ponderosa pine and quaking aspen. Further north, a column of smoke marked the head of the fire.

He pointed toward the nearest edge. "When we get there, I'll get on the radio, have 'em meet us. And by the way, Thomas has a reason. He just won't talk about it."

"And you haven't shared that with me?"

"I don't know the reason. I just know he has one. He won't share it, with me, with you, with anyone. We pulled him off the wall near Sipapu Falls, saved his life. Then Erika and I took him up there, and still, he won't say why. He won't open up."

"You and Erika?"

"She was here on regional business. Just worked out that way."

"I'm watching you two. There's something there. I won't tolerate you two forming some sort of power alliance, working against me and everyone else in the park."

He shook his head, amazed at the assertion. "You won't have to worry about that. You're misreading things, and I'd rather not talk about it."

They dropped lower, into another stand of piñon pine. The smell of smoke hit as they pounded their way through. Piñon gave way to Gambel oak and ponderosa. Needle cast lay scattered along the trail.

"What happened in Montana?" she said, slowing to a stroll.

"Unfortunate stuff."

"You don't like people nosing into your business, do you? You'd rather have no questions, no accountability whatsoever. Get used to the questions, and I promise, I'll find out the story about you and Erika Jones."

He stopped. "You think I want you to stay out of my business?"

"Obviously."

"No. I'd rather not be dragged through the pain. Find out all you want, but find someone else to tell you. I'm sure there are people more than willing to give you the gossip, all the gory details. It just won't be me."

He turned her way. She said nothing.

They broke into a clearing. Downslope, another stand of piñon pine. Upslope, ponderosa. He pointed. "There's the edge of the fire."

Creeping along the ground, fire burned through brush and pine needles. Upslope, the fallen needles of ponderosa pine—long and loosely packed, and burning steadily. To the south and downslope, flames only teasing the lower branches of the piñon.

They headed up-slope, and stopped at the edge. Breeze pushed it northwest, driving bursts of flame into unburned fuel.

Showalter raised a hand to protect her face from radiating heat.

"Impressive for this time of year," Jack said. He turned his back to the fire, slipped an arm out of a pack-strap and pulled the radio from a side pocket. He keyed the mike. "Reger, this is Chastain."

"Reger, go ahead."

"Johnny, the Superintendent and I are on the west flank of the fire. Who's monitoring this side?" He stuck his arm back through the pack strap.

"Christy, both the west flank and the head."

"Copy," he said. "Manion, this is Chastain, what's your location." He noticed movement, and lowered the radio. "Christy?"

The radio popped. *"This is Manion. I'm at the head, tracking rate of spread. It may take me a few minutes to get to your location, depending on how far south."*

"Stand by."

Jack squinted, picking up movement against deep red sandstone, an outcropping rising out the plateau. What is that? "See that?" he muttered, pointing. "Two hundred yards. At the base of the rock."

Showalter turned.

Wind gusted, pushing fire through pine saplings, toward the outcropping. Heat waves rose up and over it. What's that? A person? No, two people.

Jack dashed past Showalter. She followed.

Light hair, hands protecting faces from the heat. A little girl, crying. A father, eyes showing panic, evident even at that distance.

Wind shifted, pushing fire into the grass along the trail between them.

The little girl hunkered under the arms of the father, her back to the fire. The father picked her up, and backed them against the wall. With one hand, he reached up, clawing for a handhold on the rock.

"No," Jack yelled. "Don't climb. Get into the black."

Terrified eyes turned toward him. Wind blew. Heat waves shimmered. They clambered at the wall, trying for footholds.

"Don't. Get into black."

He closed the distance, and dashed around burning grass.

The little girl screamed. Fire blew through the tree tops above them.

Jack ran in, pulled the little girl from her father's arms and tossed her into Showalter's. He grabbed the arm of the man and jerked him the other direction, weaving him past a torching pine, around gamble oak, across already burned ground. He kept moving, past the flames, until a hundred feet in, black all around them, he slowed and stopped. Puffs of smoke rose from smoldering duff, but no flame. He glanced at Showalter. She held tightly onto the little girl, smiling, dabbing at her tears.

"There, there," Linda said, consoling her. "It's okay. You're safe."

Jack turned to the man, who leaned over his knees, sobbing.

"I almost killed my little girl," the man said. Tears rolled down his cheeks.

"She's safe. You're safe," Jack said.

The man caught his breath. Sobbing, he fought to regain composure.

Jack backed away, giving him space.

A long moment passed. Eyes on his daughter, he wiped the tears from his face with the tail of his shirt.

"Where were you going?" Jack asked.

"Following Trader John trail. Hoping to find a place to camp."

Jack leaned closer, smiled, and whispered, "Talk to me privately for a moment." He backed the man away from Showalter and the little girl, stopping on a rocky ledge where it dropped away, overlooking a dry creek-bed. "No need for your daughter to know this," he said. "This is not Trader John Trail. Trader John goes west. This is Pistol Creek Trail."

"You mean . . ."

Something caught Jack's eye below. "Yep, wrong turn somewhere. This trail's closed."

"Closed?"

"Because of the fire. Did you see the signs?"

Tears welled up again. The man dropped his head. "I saw them, but the rangers said Trader John was open. I assumed . . . How could I make such a mistake? I just wanted to give Sunny a special trip, get her excited about the mysteries of Piedras Coloradas."

"You're safe. No harm done," Jack said. "The reason you're here . . . that's important." He squinted, picking up details in the distance. "Mysteries of Piedras Coloradas?" He pointed. "Will that do?"

Beyond blackened trunks of ponderosa pine and vegetation now burned away, clinging to rock on the far side of the drainage, a cliff dwelling stood perched over the shallow canyon.

— · —

Jack dropped to the ground and sat, watching, ash and black all around him.

Sunny and her father, awestruck, walked the canyon bottom, talking, gazing up, imagining Anasazi children hundreds of years before, a world of nature all around them.

Sheltered under an overhang, the dwelling—made of rock and mud—sat defensibly above the canyon bottom, probably built around a small cave, and likely hidden over the years by oak and the brush now burned away.

Stopping at the base of the wall, Sunny reached as high on the rock as she could, seeming to want to find the way up, short by tens of feet. She laughed, and it echoed off the overhang, as if other children sat above, wanting her to come up and play.

Whole families had lived here, coming and going, living life, hunting and providing.

Jack scanned the walls, looking for hand and toe holds in the sandstone. He saw something to the left, but held his tongue. If here alone, maybe. Here with someone who might get hurt, no.

He dug into his pack and pulled out a compass. Mostly south-facing. The house stood in shadow, but in winter, the sun would likely peek in with warming rays. In summer, the drainage would funnel up and downslope breezes, bringing cool to the sheltered canyon.

Could anyone know of this place? Maybe. Maybe not. Might be undocumented.

He twisted around, checking the walls, looking for woody stemmed plants, rooted in crevices. No reddish orange flowers with bright yellow veins. No swarming bees or butterflies. Too bad.

Water? In the downstream direction, a patch of lighter green grew at the base of the wall. Possibly a spring.

He looked upslope, to the other side of the draw, where Linda Showalter sat over a map, listening to Christy Manion. In muted voices, he heard Christy briefing on objectives, having covered the size of the fire, its history of growth, and the fire ecology of the area.

Christy doing well was no surprise. The experience would do her good.

Showalter looked up, noticed she was being watched, and shouted, "Hey, if you've got time on your hands, while you've got that compass out, see if our friend wants a lesson in map reading."

Sunny's father—Dave—turned and laughed. "Yes," he said. "Sunny, too?"

Never too young to learn to read a map. "Sure, when you're ready. Take your time."

—·—

Evening settled in, and the sun set. Noses so accustomed to the ash and smoke that it no longer mattered, they made this their camp for the night.

They chose a relatively clean patch of ground and threw out bivy sacks and sleeping bags. The young father and daughter set up camp nearby, pitching a popup tent, and pulling out a camp stove, starting dinner with water from the spring below.

Jack dug out a bag of veggies, and another of tortillas and cheese, and plopped down on his bivy sack to watch.

"Well, Jack Chastain, you promised excitement," Showalter said. "Don't know how you arranged that, but you did."

"I'm a man of my word," he muttered.

"We'll see, but it has been a good day." She plopped down on her bag. "You wouldn't have reason to know this, but I love working with young people. Recharges the batteries. Seeing them value the world around 'em, that's rewarding. Can't think of anything more important in what we do, than interacting with young people, helping 'em know these special places."

"Agreed."

"How did we get off on the wrong foot?"

He held his tongue.

"I'm wary," she said, explaining herself. "I'm careful. I've heard all sorts of things over the years. Justifications, rationalizations, excuses, stories, and lies."

"What are you saying?"

"I'm saying I've seen the way people justify themselves. I've seen the politics they play."

Darts of light hit his eyes as flashlights came out in the fuss over dinner. "You hardly know me," he said, holding a hand to block the light.

"True, but I've known people of every persuasion. Politics of every kind. I am the way I am because of other people rushing to judgment. People who were wrong, I might add, and people who caused me problems. Ironically, I learned to be wary because of them, and I'm rarely wrong. Fire people like you, for example. You're quite a fraternity."

"I'm not a fire person. I know fire because the places I've worked were fire ecosystems."

"Your point?"

"They needed fire. If they needed something else, I would have acquired the expertise and experience to address that. I'm not here to be in some fraternity."

"Yep, I've heard that one." She paused. "Sorry. You've earned the benefit of the doubt. Hey, I've known good people, I've known not so good. You appear pretty good. And today is the best time I've had in a very long time, thank you very much."

He turned, looking for her eyes. Dark shadows lay over her face. What game was she playing? "So, you no longer hold this morning against me?"

"Oh, yeah, this morning. I wasn't holding that against you, but I have to be careful till I know who's on the up and up, including you."

"Mike Middleton and Harper Teague are the ones you need to think about. They worry me."

"I'm *your* bigger worry. Don't work against me," she said. "No playing politics." She paused. "Sure, I'm worried about Middleton. More than I worry about the Coalition, but if you think it's important, I'll play along. If Middleton can be helpful, we encourage him to give up his stupid ideas. We appeal to his reasonable side."

"If there is one. And Teague?"

"What am I missing? He'll self-destruct."

Jack looked away. He caught a light—a star—sitting over the cliff dwelling. It alone seemed to put the structure in peaceful shadow. "Think the Anasazi would be getting ready for bed about now? Or starting a good fire, sitting around, telling stories? Or, maybe watching the stars?"

"No clue. I'd say, getting ready for bed."

"I vote they'd be watching the stars."

"Why do you think that?"

"No good reason. Romantic imagery I guess."

"I think they were much more practical than you're giving them credit."

He searched the skies over the tops of the piñon. "I don't disagree. I wouldn't say they weren't practical, but I've often wondered what role the stars had in the evolution of who we are."

"I'm sure stars and evolution are not part of the same science. Earliest man? Hell, they were just trying to keep from getting eaten."

"Maybe, but hear me out," he said. "Imagine earliest man, long before the Anasazi, sitting here, looking into the depths of the heavens, wondering who he was. Pondering deeper and deeper questions. Imagine how that might have shaped us."

"The dreamer, maybe, but not the most practical. He was probably the first one eaten."

"Could it be that looking into those stars, pondering not just the obvious, but also the possible, he expanded his capacity to consider more than just the obvious? Could a state of wonder have played a role in learning to think?"

"Not nearly as effectively as staring down a saber tooth tiger."

"What if through that state of wonder he learned to consider possibilities, and to plan, to plan better ways of not getting eaten, and by surviving and sharing that with his children, and because his children survived more than the children of the next guy, our guy's genes show up in the next generation, thus influencing the evolution of the species."

She laughed long and hard.

"And if that were true," he continued, "what might be the implication for our species, if that quit happening now." He pointed at Sunny and her father, a few feet away eating dinner, their eyes now pulled to the stars. "What if our children never saw those stars, never exercised that sense of wonder, only watched reality television. Where might the species evolve?"

"We're toast," she said, now sober.

"Yeah, but back to the Anasazi . . ." he said. "There's much we don't know, but this I do. They sure knew how to pick a great place to live."

She turned her eyes to the sky. "You are a thinker. So if I shut up and let you think, what would you be thinking now, staring up at those stars?"

"I am thinking. About Thomas. I'm wondering why he's not serving his own cause by telling us why he opposes Mike Middleton. I'm thinking about Sipapu Falls and what in the hell could be so important that he'd risk his life, not once but twice, and I'm thinking about how to convince him to open up and talk."

"Good things to think about, but you need to give serious thought to how you're gonna stay on my good side, and not cause me any trouble."

"Linda, I'm not a trouble maker, but you won't find me guilty of blind allegiance either. I don't look for trouble, but sometimes it finds me. That's just the way life is."

"You're not putting my mind at ease."

"Not trying to."

CHAPTER 23

The phone rang.

Erika Jones stumbled out of the shower, grabbed a towel, and attempted to dry off as she dashed to find it.

She waited for the next ring, her eyes scouring the temporary housing, typically home to seasonal naturalists, and one with furnishings so contrary to what she would choose for herself that they confused her. Where is the damned phone?

It rang again, behind her, from the corner where her bag was stashed. She reached down, picked up the bag and lost the wrap on the towel. It fell to the floor as she flipped open the phone. "Hello," she said, not checking the caller.

"Erika Jones?"

"Speaking."

"This is Mike Middleton. Did I catch you at a bad time?"

She let out a laugh. "Only if you're concerned about my state of dress, because I'm not. I was in the shower."

"I'm sorry. I can call back."

"No, go ahead. If I get cold, I'll let you know. By the way, know what time it is?"

"You struck me as an early starter."

"Yeah, right. If you say so." She slipped into the hall and sauntered toward the kitchen. "Since we're both up and ready for business—and I'd be fired if I conducted business looking like this, by the way—I'll go ahead and ask the tough opening question. What's up?"

"Wanted to see what you thought about yesterday, and how it went."

"You played your cards better than last time," she said, starting to fill the coffee pot. "You know what? You caught me by surprise. I had no clue what you wanted in trade."

"A bit of a surprise to me, too. Just came to me. I thought hard about your suggestion and you were right. Made so much sense. Think about what I can do to help them, you said. Solve their problem. When I realized I had the perfect way to do that, I also realized something else."

"What? And by the way, my goose bumps are getting a little impatient."

"I'm sorry. Really, I can call back."

"They'll be okay."

"I realized my cards are not only helpful, they're essential. Almost necessary to move things forward. Knowing that, I came to appreciate the respect my offer deserves."

"You're saying it wasn't your original plan?" She pulled the coffee from the refrigerator.

"No, but I like it. Makes me feel even better about my contribution to the cause."

"I'm sure it does," she said, spooning coffee into the filter. "You realize, you're proposing something we'll have to oppose."

"My, my, and apologies to your goose bumps for my belaboring the subject, but why would you oppose something so helpful to the Coalition?"

"Linda Showalter was taken aback." She turned on the coffee pot and started back down the hall.

"As I said to Linda afterward, why would she be opposed when I can make her look so good? I can brag on her, on all of you, your goose bumps included, to all the right places, to all the right sets of ears."

"I see," she said, stopping at an open window. "That does merit giving it some thought. But regarding who gets those kind words . . . may I offer my suggestions on whose ears would be most helpful."

"Certainly. I trust your advice."

"Good. For now, I think it best to let things simmer. Work with me. I'll give you names later. At this point, reaching out to others isn't important."

"It's not? You sure? No calling in favors and greasing skids?"

"Not yet," she said, feeling some relief. "It's not crucial at this point. I'll tell you when it'll have the most effect. And when that time comes, leave my goose bumps out of it. They work best behind the scenes."

—·—

Jack Chastain woke to the sun peeking through the pine boughs. He rolled onto his side and looked around. Sunlight on the cliff dwelling gave it a red glow.

No one else was up.

The knots in his back slowly loosened. He stretched, and gave himself a moment to get used to the idea of getting up. Damn pad. Might be time to get something thicker.

He unzipped the bivy sack and crawled out, slowly standing. Coffee. He dug out a pot and started to the spring to fetch water.

—·—

"Pick up," Erika muttered into the phone. She pulled her towel tighter and tucked in a corner to hold it around her.

It was answered. "Why are you calling this early? I'm not even to the office."

"Nick, I just got off the phone with Mike Middleton. I'm not sure where we stand. This could be good news or bad, but it warranted a call. Sorry."

"It's okay, go ahead. You're on my project."

"First, Middleton played his hand yesterday. I would have called but it seemed unworkable. Wasn't sure what I'd tell you."

"What happened?"

"Land swap. He's willing to give much more than he gets, but where he wants it could be a problem." She stepped over to the near-empty closet and dropped her towel.

"Why would the Congressman want to help him on that?"

"No clue." She pushed aside a brown woolen suit and pulled out a hanger holding a uniform shirt. "Middleton seems sure of legislative support if he needs it."

"Of course. Is that the good news or bad?"

"Neither. Linda Showalter might not play ball. If she doesn't, Middleton threatens to go straight to the Director. If she does play ball, he promises to make her look indispensable, and unfortunately, again to the Director." She slipped on the shirt and glanced around. Badge. Where is it?

"Not good. We may have to abandon this whole idea. The last thing we need is to make the Director look good," he said. "If it had the potential to put someone else in a positive light, then it'd be worth the risk. But, it's looking more and more unlikely. Depressing."

"Don't give up yet, Nick. Here's what may be good news. Middleton just called me."

"You two getting chummy?"

"I dance on his ego a little. He seems to like it."

"Of course, but don't insult this guy."

"Don't worry, I know his type. Anyway, I let him give me the song and dance about whose influential ears he could either brag or complain to. But then, I may have convinced him to take my advice on when and to whom to direct those words."

"Really?"

"Yes." She grasped the knob on the top drawer of the bureau and pulled. She saw the glint of gold. There you are Mr. Badge.

"Think he'll really listen?"

"Why wouldn't he? My first bit of advice was helpful."

"Of course. Should I ask?"

"Don't. It's not something you should know, plus I may have created a little bit of a monster, and Showalter probably won't go along with any of this . . . but at least we're still talking with the guy. Your favor to the congressman may still be in play."

There was quiet on the other end. Then, "This will require finesse. If things start going south, I'll have to cut bait and let

Showalter go adrift. In that case, who cares if Middleton goes to the Director. Gives me room to distance myself, even blame the Director for tinkering in our affairs."

"But what if things don't go south? What if they work out perfectly and he gets everything he wants." She pinned on the badge and turned back to the closet.

"We need to convince Middleton there are more effective places to go than to the Director. He needs to know where to give credit when credit is due, but only if things work his way."

Pants. "It looks like we may have a chance to work that, but playing both scenarios won't be easy." She pulled green slacks off a hanger.

"No, and here's where it becomes a three dimensional chess game. Middleton could be working more than just Congressman Hoff. He could be reaching out to other members of Congress. House, Senate, who knows. When Hoff announces his run for the Presidency, he'll have people getting his name on primary ballots, building an organization, and spending money. If he's courting Middleton as a contributor, he'll be less than pleased if one of his colleagues beats him to the punch. Hoff needs to know where he can get results when he wants them, visibility when he needs it. We may not have much time. Things need to start happening."

"That makes this tricky." One handed, she slipped on her pants, an eye on the mirror. "I need to give this some thought."

"Think fast. We might not have much time. Stay close to Middleton. I'll nudge Linda Showalter when I get to the office."

"She's in the backcountry till this afternoon."

"I need her in the office, not off playing around."

"She's getting to know the park. She's with Jack Chastain."

"Hope she's not wasting time. When you see her, tell her I said this needs to get moving."

"It'd be better if she heard that from you. Hey, don't you want to know what Middleton wants in return?"

"Tell me later."

—— · ——

Jack Chastain stepped over newly exposed rock, his feet kicking up ash. He trudged up the last of the hill, rejoined the trail, and waited for Linda Showalter, moving in her more moderate pace. She hefted herself up on the trail and stopped beside him.

"Would you ever guess?" he said.

She turned back. "Where is it from here?"

He pointed, but saw no hint of a creek or a cliff dwelling. He rechecked his bearings. "In there somewhere. Couldn't prove it from here."

"Which way did you send our new friends? I told Sunny her father has lots of adventures for her. I lied and told her he's a master map reader."

"And adventures he does have. Proud of him for that." He spun around. "I pointed him to the trail, told him to head west, get back to the trailhead and take the other trail. From there, the first trail junction puts him on Trader John Trail."

"Where now for us?"

"We'll cut through the fire, skirt around to Falcon Bluff Trail, then into the Canyon. We can take a look at Sipapu Falls."

He moved out, going north, paralleling the escarpment, through the area where the Pistol Creek Fire blew through the afternoon before. Only smoldering duff—too early—but afternoon would bring flame.

Staying on the trail, they passed through patches of burned and unburned vegetation. Islands untouched, followed by near consumption of everything but the larger, older pines.

Late-morning, having crossed through the skinny, midsection of the fire, they hit the edge. Cold. Nothing to worry about here. He looked north. Smoke. It would soon be on its daily march.

He dropped his pack and dug out a belt weather kit. "Let's see what the relative humidity is." He wet the wick on the sling psychrometer and started it swinging. A minute later he stopped and read the mercury lines. He pulled out the charts, walked the numbers across and down to a reading. "Twenty-seven percent."

"Is that bad?"

"No."

"Where's Christy working today?" she asked.

"Probably up where you see that smoke."

"She's a smart young lady."

"Yes, she is."

"You've given her chances I never had."

"You have them now."

Showalter laughed. "I'm well past this. This is what I wanted to do when I was younger. Now, I'm focused on getting things done. That's my place in life now."

"Getting things done. What would you call this?"

She looked him in the eye. "This *is* getting things done. But I have you and Christy to do it. If I didn't, my place would be to find someone who could. My place is to make things happen, in the big picture."

"Is that what motivates you? The big picture? Or being in charge?" He put away the red, nylon weather kit and zipped his pack closed.

"What are you suggesting?"

"Multiple questions. Some might not apply." He picked up his pack, stuck an arm through a strap, and hefted it up and on."

"Multiple questions, or one major challenge?"

"No challenge, just curious. What motivates you? Why are you here?"

She gave him a quizzical look. "Because of the park. Because of the mission." She turned to look the other direction. "How long will it take the fire to reach the other side of the plateau?"

"Weeks. If the right storm cloud parked over that ridge and started throwing down-drafts, maybe hours, but that won't likely happen."

He turned and ambled off-trail, veering along a stretch of fire line, stopping at the base of a rock escarpment. He turned his attention to the ground at his feet, running his eye past breaks in the rock and charred woody stems. No sprouts. Yet. But it could take some time, if there's a chance of their coming back. "I need to show you something. Something bad that happened. Something unfortunate."

She stepped closer, and followed his eyes.

"This was the only known population of a plant proposed for endangered status. One of the crew was positioned where you're standing. That scratch line was intended to protect it. The crewman was here just in case. The wind shifted. The unexpected happened. The crewman just stood there and watched."

Her mouth gaped open.

"He wasn't one of ours. He couldn't've cared less. Long story, but we sent him home." He let out a sigh. His shoulders dropped. "Bottom line, we may've killed off a species. Too early to tell, but it was our responsibility and this happened."

"Uh, . . . what do we do?"

"For the species? Maybe nothing we can do. If it doesn't re-sprout, we can only hope to find another population elsewhere, but there might not be another. I thought I found one, but . . . probably not. Wrong flower."

"What happens now?"

"I've got a call into a colleague in Fish and Wildlife Service. I'll let you know what she says. We need to conduct a review of what happened, learn from it, try to keep something like this from happening again."

"Why are you telling me this?"

"It may not have happened on your watch, but it'll come up. You need to know. Reger feels responsible, it's his fire, but it wasn't his fault. He took precautions. My opinion . . . his only mistake was choosing the wrong guy to put here. The guy was lazy. Also an ass."

"Were you here?"

"Yeah, in fact, I'm the one who sent the guy home. Wanted to protect Johnny." He looked away. "Unfortunately, my action may have snagged Joe Morgan. I think he's paying the price for what I did. That's why they called him back to Washington."

"I'm here because of something you did."

"I suppose."

"Who was this guy?"

"Name's Foss. Well connected. Brother's big in the agency back east."

"I know the name. I appreciate your honesty on this. Unfortunate." She slowly shook her head as she ran her eyes across charred ground. "Conduct the review. Fix things if they need it. Don't hold back on this Foss guy. May take some political will, but we'll do what we need to do. If nothing more than a bad reputation, I'll make sure he gets it."

He gestured back to the trail, away from the fire. "You lead."

She moved out, across the plateau. As the elevation dropped, ponderosa pine petered out, turning again to piñon juniper woodland.

Hours later they came to the edge. Trail, decades ago chipped from the layers of sandstone, hugged the wall, descending. Showalter turned her attention to the change in terrain. "We're going there? Looks wicked."

"Tough on the knees, but not really dangerous."

Showalter drew in a breath. "I was hard on you yesterday. I owe you an apology."

"None needed."

"I made snap judgments. Some of them undoubtedly wrong. I'm entitled to a few mistakes along the way. It's just part of the job. I deal with politicians, the bureaucracy, the regional office, Washington. Not everyone puts their cards on the table."

"I'm not hiding any cards."

"I have a better sense of that. I needed to know what makes you tick."

"Fair enough. So, what makes you tick?"

She looked north and sighed. "I owe you an answer. What do you want to hear?"

"That you want to make things happen for a reason, not because it makes you feel in control. That you're not here just to get your ticket punched."

After a long moment, she said, "Did you ever feel like you had a calling?"

Jack didn't answer.

She glanced over, caught his eye and self-consciously looked away. "To save the world." She chuckled nervously. "The world is a big place, so many needs." She sucked in a breath and let it out. "Out of college I didn't want a job, I wanted a calling. I wanted to make a difference. I interned for a congressman I adored, and later lost faith in because he was unwilling to take on the hard issues. He couldn't muster the political will to do what was right. I took a job in an agency, hoping to make a difference. I found myself among others like me. Like-minded, young, inexperienced kids who thought the best way to save the world was in Washington, D.C., writing policy. Beautiful far-reaching words that protect places like Piedras Coloradas from greedy bastards and inept government bureaucrats." She shook her head and laughed.

"What's wrong?"

"After a year I realized none of us had any real experience, that we were all really part of the problem, not the solution. One day it dawned on me everything was turned around. Places like Washington D.C. didn't need more starry-eyed, young people who didn't have the experience to apply their idealism. Washington needed people with experience, who know how to apply their idealism. Bold, and wise enough to muster the political will to get it done. My friends in Washington thought I was crazy. They thought there was no way to make a difference in a place like Devil's Tower, but I packed my Datsun, left Washington, drove to Wyoming, took a job as a ranger, and started getting experience. Thought someday I'd go back to Washington, this time with experience, prepared to change the world. Six parks later, I have that experience." After a moment, she faced him.

"Sounds like this is just a stop along the way."

"Won't happen."

"Why?"

"A decision I made. Not the wrong one—it was the right decision, but I was on the fast track, now I'm not. I can look myself in the eye, but that's about it. It'll have to be enough."

"What do you stand for?"

"What?" Her eyes sank back as she flashed a confused look. "What are you suggesting?"

"Maybe nothing. You first said *save* the world. Then, *change* the world."

She frowned. "What's the hell's the difference? Never mind. You wouldn't understand."

"The difference? Maybe nothing. Would I understand? You might be surprised."

"I don't think you would."

"Depends. On what you stand for."

"I'm not gonna try to prove myself to you."

"I'm not asking you to. And I'm not asking you to be a certain way. I just want to know who you are and what motivates you. When the battle begins, and the bodies start falling, it's good to know whether you're there with us defending the fort or sneaking out the back door."

"That's the question I should be asking."

"Yes, you should, but realize it or not, people working for you ask that same question."

She stared hard. "I believe in service, duty, and responsibility. I believe in getting the facts. I want my decisions to be wise ones. Nothing pisses me off more than political expedience. I want people to say I have the will to do what needs to be done, regardless of personal consequences."

"Heard that before," he said, holding back a smile. "But, I hope so."

CHAPTER
24

Erika Jones bit down on her pencil, and read the words she had put on paper. She reconsidered one scratched out sentence, scrawled 'okay' across the margin, then expanded on another.

She sat back and considered her thoughts. Might work.

She heard footsteps.

Behind her, someone entered the temporary office she shared with one of the naturalists. "Adam?"

No response. She glanced back. No one.

She studied the page, committed the words to memory, then put the paper through the shredder. Time to get to work. She picked up the phone and dialed.

"Mr. Middleton," she said, when he answered. "This is Erika Jones."

"Call me Mike. How are those goose bumps?"

She smiled. "Fine. I'm not sure if I should be glad you asked, or not."

"I assure you, my concern is sincere."

"I'm sure it is. I'm calling to talk about your little proposal. And by the way, notice what time it is?"

"A little after eleven."

"Correct, a proper time for conducting business."

"Any time is good for conducting business, but let me make it up to you. Lunch, at Elena's Cantina."

"I'm not letting you buy my lunch, but I'd be delighted to join you."

— · —

Jack slowed and took a shorter step, reducing the jar of the rock. He looked ahead. Showalter rounded a bend and disappeared from sight. In the distance, beyond the foreground, he noticed a rim, the first hint of one particular landform among many, one that would startle at an unexpected moment. For now it was hidden. Cañon de Fuego quietly waited, to surprise.

— · —

Erika Jones parked on a side street, cut past the earthen church and hurriedly crossed the square. She dashed inside Elena's, gave the tables in the bar a quick look and, not seeing him, approached the hostess. "I'm meeting someone, a Mr. Middleton."

"Yes, he's waiting for you," the young woman said. She turned and led her down the hall to the dining room.

Middleton stood as Erika approached. "Good afternoon, a woman in uniform. Distracting."

Game on. She put on an appropriate smile. "Good seeing you, Mike."

"I'm having sangria. Like one?"

"Love one but no, I'm working." She pulled out a chair and sat.

He retook his seat. "Okay. All business. That's fine. Shall we order first, or dive right in."

She opened her menu and scanned the page. She felt him watching. Good. She flashed a look. "We can do both," she said. "I'm here on a mission. I have an assignment."

He gave her a curious look. "I assume I know what it's about."

"Of course, your proposal. I'd love to smack you around for what you want in return, but I've been asked to help more with the execution than the actual plan."

"Excuse me?"

"There's someone very interested in seeing you succeed. They appreciate your support, but where you lack experience, I can help."

"Experience?" He pushed his chair back from the table.

She held his eye. "Sorry, I misspoke." She let recovery slowly settle in. "You are very experienced," she said, risking sounding sarcastic. "You put my experience to shame, on every front except one, the inner workings of government. While I lend my insight on that, you can teach me a thing or two about the ways of your world, from the perspective of all your valuable experience."

"Take you under my wing, sort-a-speak? Of course." He raised a finger and tapped his lips. "Even with you dishing out that cute little, irritating, caustic edge of yours?"

She smiled and looked away. "Oh, yes, I forgot who I'm dealing with." She turned back and bored in with her eyes. "You deserve so much more respect than I'm giving."

"Well, yes," he said, looking uncertain. "But, I know the game you're playing. You're putting me off balance. You want to convince me Sipapu Falls is a bad idea."

"No, I don't," she said firmly. She dipped a chip into salsa. "No doubt you'll hear that from Linda Showalter or Jack Chastain. I'll let you work that out with them. If you wanted another site in exchange, things might be easier, but that's not my concern. My assignment is larger."

"I don't understand."

"The skids have been greased. At the right time, I'll introduce you to someone."

"Who?"

"It wouldn't be hard to figure out, but for now let's leave it at that. He's the one who makes things happen and he's looking forward to meeting you. When the time's right, there will be nothing wrong with having that introduction in the most visible way possible. Until then, my assistance to you is strictly behind the scenes."

"Interesting."

"We have work to do. Undoubtedly your proposal will need legislation, and yes, I heard you say you have contacts in all the right places, but the agency can either oppose you or quietly let it happen. You want the latter. In addition to your contacts, I have mine, possibly working for the same members of Congress—which would make it easier, but it's not imperative."

"It's not?"

"No. I'll work with mine to draft the legislation and get it in the right pipeline. Your time would best be spent working on details of the trade."

"Won't those details require pulling some strings?"

"Maybe, but I'm not sure that would be helpful now. I remember you telling Linda Showalter you could go to the Director. Your influence is hard to ignore, and that line about the Director is very persuasive, but the timing isn't right. I'll listen to the internal chatter and let you know when that kind of effort would be most effective."

"You're saying I shouldn't approach the Park Service Director?"

"Not now. If the opportunity presents itself, why not, but you have more of a supporter in the person giving my marching orders."

"I see. Then near-term, my focus should be on the Coalition, Jack Chastain and Linda Showalter."

"No. Linda Showalter and the Coalition, in that order. And it might help if I gave you talking points for your next Coalition interaction."

"Talking points? I was damned smooth in that meeting."

The ego needs a stroke. "You were perfect. I'm referring to procedural matters. Ones we'll encounter in future rounds of negotiation." She flashed a smile, and picked up a menu. "What are you having?"

"I'm a little confused. We need to talk more about this."

Set the hook. "How about tomorrow night? Or even tonight, when I'm off the job. I won't feel so constrained by the uniform."

— · —

Jack made the bend and waited for Showalter's reaction. She took a few steps before it hit. Then she stepped back, her arms rising to brace her. "Oh," she said, shocked, as if she was about to faint. "Have you ever seen anything so . . ."

He walked up beside her and smiled. ". . . beautiful?"

"You knew this was coming didn't you? I have to stop."

"Take all the time you want."

She dropped her pack, dug out a camera, and clicked off several shots—the depth of the canyon, then its width, one with a century plant in the foreground, another of a canyon wren. Then, she held the camera at arm's length, capturing herself with a canyon background.

"Want me to take that?"

"I think I got it," she said, self-consciously. "Oh, sure." She handed him the camera.

He raised it and said, "Don't step back."

— · —

Erika Jones dialed the Regional Director's cell phone and waited, wondering if his meeting schedule would allow him the opportunity to answer.

"Erika, what's up?"

"Operation 'Undermine the Director' has been escalated."

"Excuse me?"

"Just kidding. How about this? Operation, 'be careful what you ask for.'"

"What are you telling me?"

"Things are under control, but don't ask me for details."

— · —

On the move and lower on the trail, Jack caught sight of a piece of orange flagging hanging from a branch of Wood's rose. He stopped to untie it. Linda gave a quizzical look.

"We forgot to remove this after rescuing Thomas."

"Let's go see where you guys were working."

"It's not a safe place. Can't see much of the wall, and it's a hell of a scary view of the canyon. If we drop a little lower, we'll have plenty of places to see everything, including more of Sipapu Falls."

"I don't mind the heights. I was a climbing ranger in Teton, and I mentioned already having worked in Devil's Tower."

"We have time?"

"If I'm back in the office by three, I'll be fine."

They bushwhacked across the slope and slowed where the brush stopped and the view jumped out and asserted itself. Jack found a spot to sit and take off his pack. Linda stashed hers, and worked her way to the edge. She took hold of a piñon limb and peered over.

"So this is the place?" she asked, taking it in. She looked down, then over to the water fall. "Hell of a view." She stepped back. Looking across the canyon, she said, "Where is this place Mike Middleton wants?"

"Not sure. He wasn't precise in his words."

"Come here a minute," she said, waving him over.

"I'm okay. Not sure I like the idea of risking my neck here twice."

"You wimp, get over here."

He stood, and worked his way down, stopping a few feet from the edge, on an open slab of rock. He shifted his weight to his inside foot, and looked over. He cringed at the sight.

"Why the hell would Middleton think he could trade for any of this? Is he thinking here in the canyon, or down by the mouth of the Little River?"

"He didn't say?"

"Where's the boundary?"

"It jogs around the base of the cliff. Follows old homestead lines. At the mouth of the canyon, it butts against the new national monument. He could be thinking out there, but it didn't sound like it."

She craned her neck to see. "If you're there, can you see the waterfall?"

"Not from that direction. Not in the canyon bottom. Have to be higher. Off to the north, you can."

He watched her move her gaze up-canyon, along the river, past confluences with dry washes from side canyons. One—with an extensive delta, and serpentine meanders emerging from darkened, vertical walls—held her attention.

"Hope he doesn't have designs on that one," she said. She cocked her head, seeming to study the side canyon a little longer.

"That one's in the park. From here, it looks major. From there on the canyon floor, you have to be looking to notice."

"There or down canyon, either place could cause us problems." She sighed. "Can you imagine a monstrosity of a mansion, or a huge hotel, or some other building, right where people come for pristine beauty?" She turned away from the canyon. "So, where was Thomas?"

"Just below you, on a ledge that makes its way over to Sipapu Falls. One of those miracles of nature. Never saw it before that day. And as a miracle, its time may be coming to an end. Part of it was already gone—killed his sister years ago. Part of it fell into the canyon while we were trying to rescue him."

Her eyes grew wide. "And you were there when it happened?"

"I was."

"Brave of you to go down there."

"Wasn't my idea. Luiz put me on the rope."

"Similar thing happened to me on Mount Owen in Tetons. I was on the rope. Someone kicked a rock loose. I watched it roll off the mountain, right at me. Thought I was dead. It went screaming past. Swore I'd never let 'em put me on the rope again, but I did."

He shook his head and let out a chuckle. "Guess you do what you have to do."

"That's right, we do what we have to do. Guess we're kindred spirits, Chastain."

"Scared shitless?"

She laughed. "So, what's your theory? Why's this place so special? Other than the sheer beauty of it?"

He turned to the sight of the hanging alcove, and Sipapu Falls pouring over the edge. "It's sacred for some reason. Tightly held secret. Drives me crazy. You'd think a rock coming off the wall, almost killing me, would be reason to let me in on the secret, but apparently not."

She slipped back from the edge and sat on a boulder among the talus. "You don't have to stand there. I was giving you a hard time."

He took a step back and sat. "With Middleton's proposal, the reasons for needing to know are now different, and more important."

"Oh, don't worry about Middleton," she said, her eye on the canyon. "That's just crazy. It'll never happen." She paused. "Convince me the Coalition's important. Convince me it matters."

"A year ago, we had fighting, and nobody talking. We were outsiders to everyone, and political opposition to the monument was growing. Today, people are talking, willing to listen to each other. They see the monument as preserving the things they value."

"What are the implications of Middleton's proposal?"

"Hard to say. Even though his proposal smacked of self-interest, it pushed the right buttons. We have to be careful. We can't look like we're minimizing the concerns of those whose problems it fixes."

"We need to protect you in your role as objective arbiter."

"What are you thinking?"

"Let me say this first. On this trip, I've beaten up on you. You've beaten up on me. That's good. We've gotten it out of the way. Now, we need to get to work. We can't work against each other."

He nodded, eyes on the canyon.

"What do we do about Thomas?"

"I'll call him . . .underscore how things have changed. The seriousness of it. We need to know why this place is important, at least enough to protect it."

"I'll take Middleton. Get him thinking about a different piece of land."

"What if he won't budge?"

"Then we say *no*, simply based on impacts to the park. But first, I'll appeal to his reasonable side. Show him how much we appreciate his help, but tell him to put his sights on another piece of land."

"If someone has to piss this guy off, maybe it should be me. I have nothing to lose."

"I appreciate the offer, Jack. But doing the right thing is what I live for. Why should you have all the fun?"

CHAPTER 25

Linda Showalter shuffled into the office at a little after three. Dusty, sweaty and achy, she stopped at Marge's desk, picked up her phone messages, slipped into the office, and dropped into her chair. She settled back and stretched her legs. Looking through the messages, she made two stacks. After calls to the most important, it might be time to go home and soak.

Two messages were from the Regional Director. "Marge?" she shouted at the door. "Why did Nick call twice? Did you tell him I was out of the office?"

"I did, but a couple hours later he called back. I told him again."

Showalter shrugged and dialed the number scrawled on the message.

"National Park Service, Regional Director's office."

"May I talk to Nick. This is Linda Showalter, returning his call."

"Yes, he's expecting you."

In a few moments, he was on the phone. "Linda, how was the backcountry?"

"Beautiful. I wanted to check . . ."

"Good," he said, cutting her off. "What I'm about to ask for requires leadership." He paused. "Mike Middleton. He's important. More important than you might expect."

She sighed. "Nick, this guy may be wanting something he can't have. Important or not, I may have to take him on. I'd prefer not to, and I might lose, but I'm hoping he'll play nice."

She waited in silence, then,

"Move slowly, please. Be persuasive, not insulting. We need him willing to work with us. There are things I can't tell you, but if he does work with us, good things can happen. If he works with the bad guys, the politics are only gonna get ugly."

— · —

Kelly gave a knock at the cabin door and waited, the evening light and her cotton dress giving hints of a perfect silhouette. "How was your hike?" she asked when Jack answered the door.

He gave her a peck on the cheek. "I need to talk to Thomas," he muttered. "Soon."

"Hello to you, too, and I don't have a number for him."

"How do I get in touch?"

"We'll drive over."

— · —

They turned off the highway. The blacktop died away. The road became dusty, rutted and red. An old pickup up ahead moved slowly. Kelly steered past, then punched the gas and sped up.

Scattered along the flats and hillside were simple houses, more modern than where they were going, but not at all indicative of a modern world. Electrical lines were intrusions on the landscape. Houses sat amidst gardens, animal pens and outbuildings.

Kelly kept her eyes on the road. "They live on the other side of the pueblo," she said. "Well, what you might think of as the pueblo. Actually, the whole community is the pueblo."

The adobe village sat up ahead, and Kelly slowed as they approached. Spokes of trails came from every which direction toward the main earthen structure. Houses, tied together with thick adobe walls, layers high, seemed as one huge abode. "This is the center of pueblo culture. We won't stop here," she said. "We go only where we're invited."

"But we weren't invited."

"I know. If Thomas is home, you can set up a time to talk, then we'll leave."

"Perfect."

Skirting past, they encountered little houses, some looking absolutely the same, probably built by Bureau of Indian Affairs as part of a government initiative. Kelly pointed to a reddish brown box of a house, sitting far off the road. A grey Dodge pickup sat out front. "That's it."

She turned down the road and slowed to a crawl. Dogs ran out as they approached. She pulled behind the pickup and stopped. A University of New Mexico Alumni sticker was pasted in the corner of the truck's rear window.

Dust settled.

A door on the house opened and Thomas stepped out, waved, and walked toward them. A young boy followed him, looking like a small version of Thomas. Someone stood at the door, in shadow.

Kelly jumped out and scurried over, first giving Thomas a hug, then scooping up his son. "My, you are big," she said. She hugged a bashful smile out of him, and turned to Thomas. "Michael, right?" She waited for his nod, then motioned toward to the house. "Jack, that's Rachel."

He turned, expecting to see Thomas' wife, but instead saw a young girl. No, a young woman.

In jeans and T-shirt, hair pulled back, she stepped timidly forward and greeted Kelly. Kelly hugged her, then grasped her shoulders and looked deep into the girl's warm, dark eyes. "How are you, sweetie?"

She nodded.

"I'm so happy to see you. This is Jack. Has your uncle told you about Jack?"

She nodded, looking his way. "Is your given name John?" she asked.

"Yeah, but I've always been called Jack."

"I will call you John. You deserve a biblical name."

He chuckled. "Okay. If I don't answer, say it louder."

She giggled, and looked away, self-consciously.

"Come in," Thomas said.

"We don't want to intrude," Jack said. "I just wanted to set up a time to talk. There are things I need to discuss with you."

"Come in. We can talk now." He pushed them toward the door.

Kelly reached for Michael's hand, stooping toward him. "Do you know the story about how the earth got rain?" she asked.

"No," he said, eyes bright. "Will you tell me?"

"We'll have your father tell you," she said. "May I listen, too?"

He nodded excitedly.

Entering, Thomas behind him, Jack noticed a small shelf, on it a small Saint Mary figurine, cobs of corn, small weavings and carvings. Incongruous. Why are they . . . ?

"Sacred items," Kelly whispered.

He looked away, realizing he was being obvious.

In the corner, in a simple kitchen, a small, compact woman in jeans and flannel shirt worked without looking up. The smell was of onions, garlic and herbs.

"This is Suzi, my wife," Thomas said.

She acknowledged them. "Have you eaten?" she asked Jack.

"We'll eat later in town."

"You are our friends. You eat with us. We have plenty." She turned back to her work.

"Thank you," Kelly said. "May I help?"

Suzi looked over her shoulder, shaking her head. "It's almost ready."

"Thomas, would you tell Michael the story of how the earth got rain?" Kelly asked.

He laughed. "Why are you trying to make a storyteller out of me?"

"Because . . . ," she said. "You brought your family back to be part of this culture, and to reconnect." Kelly smirked. "You'll be a great story teller. Which is your chair?"

He pointed.

"Sit."

He laughed, and pulled the chair back from the table.

"Michael, go sit on your father's lap."

Thomas scooped him up, and put him in his lap.

Kelly sat on the floor. "Michael, tell your father to tell you the story."

"Tell me the story."

"This is a story your grandmother told me when I was your age," Thomas said. He glanced at Rachel.

She moved closer.

"Your grandmother told this story to your mother and me," he said to her. "Did your mother ever tell it to you?"

She shook her head.

"Too young. Did your father?"

She nodded.

"Want to hear it again?"

She nodded.

"Sit here," Thomas said, patting the pine bench beside him.

"A time long ago . . . ," he said, and gave a glance at Kelly, then settled his eyes on the children.

He set into the story, telling of a time when it never rained, when it was very dry. He told of Rabbit telling Snake and Frog that he hoped water would fall from the sky, and of how, when it did, Sun did not come out. He told how they worried about Sun and why it was not out, and how they asked Owl to fly up into the sky to see what was the matter. Owl saw Cloud crying, because Sun would not come out.

"The next day, Sun came out, and that is how earth got rain," he said, beginning his conclusion. His eyes moved between theirs. "Now, when the sun does not come out, there is always rain."

The simplicity. Jack glanced around, wondering if he'd missed something.

Kelly sat smiling, looking pleased. Michael and Rachel, in rapt attention, waited. Jack noticed Thomas studying him.

"It's okay, Jack. No story exists in isolation from the life of the people who tell it. Someday, you will know us better."

"Is that a typical story?"

"In some ways. A story has a message it is meant to convey, and a way it is meant to be used and told."

"Are they lessons?"

"They can be. Oral traditions are important to the welfare of the individual and the pueblo."

"When we were at Sipapu Falls, you mentioned stories and uncertainty about remembering them correctly. Were those stories related to lessons? Or to the welfare of the individual and the pueblo?"

Thomas smiled, and laughed quietly to himself.

"And it's not the Sipapu?" Jack asked, belaboring previous questions.

"Jack," Kelly said anxiously. "Stop that."

"Would you like me to tell you our name for that location?"

"That might help."

Thomas smiled patiently. "Our name means place where water flies."

"That's it?"

"That's it. That's what it is. A place where water flies. Out of the rock, into the sky."

Suzi placed a pot on the table. She dropped her eyes and backed away.

"Smells very good," Thomas said to her. "Posole stew," he told the others.

Suzi got everyone seated at the table and Thomas said a prayer. When finished, he offered the serving spoon to Kelly. "Let our Aunt start."

She eagerly accepted the spoon and dished up the stew, passing filled bowls to the others.

Jack took his and dipped out a spoonful, raising it to his lips. Hominy, beans and pork. He sipped. The taste of onions, garlic and jalapenos, a menagerie of spices.

Suzi sat a plate of bread beside the pot. "Fry bread," she said, pulling off a piece for herself.

Jack ate, eyeing the room. A piñon pole was suspended below the ceiling, against the wall behind Thomas. Draped over it, several colorful items. One, a beaded sash, likely ceremonial. Another, a deerskin pouch, maybe the one Thomas had at Sipapu Falls.

"Must be nice having Rachel living with you?" Jack said, making conversation.

"It is, but actually this is Rachel's house." He exchanged looks with her. "In pueblos to the east, the men own the houses and gardens. In our culture, the women do. This was my sister's house. It became Rachel's, as did her grandmother's two room house in the pueblo."

"Her father . . . should I ask?"

"He died a few years after her mother. Rachel first lived with her grandmother, then with us in Albuquerque. Suzi and I went to college there and stayed to teach."

"And you moved back so Michael could grow up in your culture?"

"Yes." He looked across the table. "And Rachel."

"Interesting," Jack said, nodding as if he understood. He looked around, and then dropped his eyes to the posole. "This is very good."

Suzi smiled and returned her eyes to her meal.

"What did you want to ask me?" Thomas asked.

"It can wait. It's about the falls."

Thomas looked away, then settled his eyes back on Jack. "I'm happy you came, and happy you came with my friend, Kelly. I know you want to know more, but there's really nothing more I can tell you."

"I know it's important for you to maintain this secret. But look what happened this week. Mike Middleton has eyes on a parcel very close. We're not sure where, but we think it would help us convince him to look elsewhere if we only knew why the site was so important."

"I understand. Thank you for considering that significant. Is this the one thing that stands in the way of that man getting what he wants?"

"Well, no," Jack admitted. "We can shut him down on any number of things, tell him no based on impacts to the park, the fact that legislation would be necessary, etc."

"Then why don't you tell him that?"

"We will, but look at it our way, Thomas. If we just tell him no, we run the risk of looking like we're belittling the issues his proposal is designed to address. Those other people and their issues . . . we don't want to look like we consider them unimportant. If on the other hand, we have the information to go to Middleton, reason with him, appeal to his better side, we can ask him to look at some other piece of land."

"Better side? With information important to the future of our culture—our culture, not yours—and you hope to appeal to him as an honorable man?"

"Uh, yes . . ." Jack lost his train of thought. "Uh . . .we wouldn't have to tell him everything. We could be selective with information, tell him enough to appeal to his better judgment, leaving out the details. But if we don't know what we're trying to protect, how can we protect it?"

"You said you could be selective with the information. Wasn't that what I was doing at the meeting? I said, no, not there."

"Yes, but, . . ." He lost his thought again. "How can I work to protect the site if I can't explain its significance for you and your people? I'm a biologist. I can argue to protect the plant life at the base of the falls, or I can give you the rationale to restore a river channel, or do any number of things for the natural world, but Sipapu Falls is important to you for a reason I don't think has anything to do with things scientific or natural. Help me here, Thomas. I'm ill prepared to defend that site."

Thomas took the ladle and spooned out more stew. "Jack, we do not see those things as separate from one another. They are intertwined. We are intertwined."

"I'm sorry, I missed something."

"We are part of nature."

"That doesn't help me."

"I don't understand why. I do know this. You have reasons to oppose what that man wants to do, and you know that we oppose him, too."

"Is this opposition just you, or the pueblo? Who is this body that opposes him? Can we get a formal statement from them?"

Thomas looked across the table.

"I mean, how do you govern yourselves? How would we get a formal position from the pueblo?"

"I could talk to the council and see if I could get a letter from the pueblo, but that would bring attention to the site."

"From?"

"Other clans and societies."

"I'm sorry, what does that mean?"

"It means it is not their tradition. It is ours. You know more than you should, and even more than others in the pueblo."

"Me? Know something? I don't know anything. Are you saying we're dealing with only your clan?"

"You know more than you know, and technically, yes, one clan." Thomas locked eyes with someone across the table.

Jack glanced over. It was Rachel.

"Can you consult the clan, get something from them?"

Blank stare on his face, Thomas seemed to look through him. "Yes, but . . . I'm not sure what to do."

"You mean this secret is a secret to them?"

Thomas jarred himself back. "No."

"One clan. This is about one clan?"

"It takes all to make our society whole. Each clan has a role."

"Does this role have anything to do with what's at Sipapu Falls?"

Thomas didn't answer.

Jack looked at Michael. "Someday will your son be fighting this fight?"

"No, Michael is of his mother's clan. He is a child of my clan. He will carry forward the traditions and roles of Suzi's clan." Thomas took a deep breath.

Jack turned and set his eyes on Rachael.

She looked away.

"Jack, enough," Kelly said.

"Yes, enough," Jack replied. "Thank you, Thomas. I hope I didn't ruin dinner. Anything you can tell us other than simple opposition would be helpful."

He nodded.

They finished their meal, Kelly pronounced it late and that they should let the kids be put to bed. Good-byes were said, and Jack and Kelly stumbled out into the night.

Dark and starry, and crickets loud, the night was interrupted only by the few dim flickers from other houses, blinking shyly across the way.

"Interesting," Jack said, groping in the dark for Kelly's Toyota. He waited for a comment, but got none. "Here it is," he said, touching the hood of the truck. He opened the door. The interior light came on.

Kelly climbed in the other side. "I think you were hard on him."

"That was not my intention. I just need enough to help him. He doesn't seem to understand that."

"Be patient," she said. "Remember, you're the government. You see yourself in one way. Thomas' people have reason to see you in another. Obviously Thomas trusts you, but you can't get past all that history on your own."

"But if I can't do something to address this issue, I'll just be another bad story."

CHAPTER
26

Linda Showalter's mind churned as she walked the trail to the office.

What had Nick Saunders been trying to say? If he's never met Mike Middleton, why's he so damned sure he can be trusted? Stay close, he had said, find out how Middleton ticks, create opportunities, make a friend for life. Clichés. There's got to be something going on.

The canyon walls caught her attention. The morning sun. Reflections off the walls in reddish orange.

Such a nice morning, and cool enough to almost need a jacket. Quiet, except the sound of leaves in the cottonwood trees, rustling in the down-canyon breeze.

Such a pretty place.

So much prettier than any other recent assignment. But this might come to an end, and soon, if the Regional Director isn't happy. This had seemed like a way out, a way to get back on track. Maybe that's not to be.

The price of doing the right thing.

Middleton can't be allowed to pull off some backroom deal, as if entitled to privilege, entitled to close off the many. But Nick didn't say he expected that outcome.

If Middleton were kept happy, yet convinced to set his sights elsewhere, the Regional Director would surely celebrate it.

Even if something else is going on.

— · —

STAFF MEETING

Jack walked in, the last to arrive. He took his seat, and Linda Show-alter—at the head of the table—watched him closely.

"Set up a call?" Showalter asked him.

"More than that. Met with him last night."

"Good. What'd he say?"

"Nothing. Still unwilling to say why it's important."

Showalter shifted anxiously in her seat. "Unwilling to fight for his own cause. That's so damned strange."

"Doesn't see it that way, but yeah, I agree."

"Would he say what's there?"

"No," Jack said. "I encouraged him to get some kind of formal statement of position from the pueblo."

"Not sure what good that will do without substance, but it's better than nothing. Let's talk later." She looked around the table. "Let's get started. Adam?"

The naturalist put a hand to his beard, and stroked a few strands. "Nothing to report."

"Erika?"

She looked up from her scrawls. "Nothing."

"Have you interacted with the regional office in recent days?"

She cocked her head and gave it some thought. "Not that I remember. Why?"

"No reason," Showalter said, watching her closely.

"Oh, I did speak with Mr. Middleton yesterday."

Showalter drummed the table with her fingers. "How'd that happen?"

"Saw him at a restaurant. He invited me to join him for lunch. He said he was looking forward to having conversations about a land swap."

"What'd you say?"

"I told him to talk to you."

"Good. That's precisely what I want to do, talk. Can you set that up?"

She made a note. "I'm sure I can. What day?"

"Today, tomorrow, doesn't matter."

"Consider it done," Erika said, making notes. "One thing of concern. He says he's getting lots of positive feedback, especially from Coalition members."

Showalter glanced across the table at Jack. "That's what I was afraid of." She turned back to Erika. "Let's do it sooner."

"Done."

Linda moved on.

— · —

Erika Jones stuck her head in the office door. "How about lunch today? Elena's Cantina, main dining room."

"That'll work," Linda said.

"Need me to join you?"

"No, I can handle it. Thank you."

— · —

Linda Showalter approached the hostess. "I'm meeting a Mr. Mike Middleton for lunch."

"Right this way." The young lady led her down the hall, into the dining room, to the table where Middleton waited. He stood as they approached.

"Good afternoon. A woman in uniform. Quite distracting."

"I'm sure you can see past it, and thank you for meeting on short notice."

"Not at all. I'm having sangria. Would you like one?"

"No, thank you, not while I'm working."

"That's precisely what your Miss Jones said yesterday. You people are very predictable."

"Are we? I suppose I should be glad to hear that."

"Shall we order first, or get down to business?"

"Whichever. How are you doing, by the way?" she said, forcing a smile and picking up her menu.

"Fine. Enjoying late spring in Piedras Coloradas, and, I've been hearing lots of positive feedback on my offer."

"We sincerely appreciate your interest in working with the Coalition to find solutions. With respect to your offer, that's precisely what we need to discuss."

"Good. My favorite subject."

"Mr. Middleton, what you propose as a use for your land is admirable, but the land you've requested in return . . . that will be a problem."

"I don't see why."

"Well, I'll tell you."

"No, I'll tell you. An exchange of acreage, twenty to one, thirty to one, an exchange that addresses an issue the Coalition is stumbling over, an issue that could make them fall apart . . . well . . . a man is due a little respect."

"I understand, and I agree, but there are other issues, one of which is the fact that what you want in return is either in the park or abutting the boundary. We're not exactly sure."

"We can talk about that."

"Good. The other issue is one of cultural sensitivity, something of concern to the pueblo."

"I see. What's the issue?"

She took a sip of her water. "We're not exactly sure."

He laughed. "You put your reputation on the line for something, and you don't even know what it is?"

"That's correct."

"When I talk to your Director, I can either say good things or bad. I'd rather say good things, such as, what a pleasure it is working with you, and only you. Will you allow me to do that?"

"Love to, but it might not work out that way." She took another sip and cleared her throat. "Before we go there, I hope to appeal to your charitable side."

"I am charitable. Remember why I made this offer. And why wouldn't it work out?"

"Because I may have to say no." She took a gut check and smiled. "But let's talk about your charitable side. If the location you want is important to the pueblo, wouldn't you want to know? Wouldn't you want to take that into account, be charitable with them as well?"

He raised his eyes, staring into a corner, cogs turning. "Of course," he said, finally. "If it's a good reason, something substantial. Learn what you can, we'll talk. Otherwise, I've fallen in love with a little meadow sitting at the mouth of a side canyon with a great view of Sipapu Falls."

—·—

Showalter knocked on the door.

Jack looked up from email. "Come in." He waved her to a chair.

"Had lunch with Middleton. Tough, but I may've made some headway. He's promised to talk if we have a substantial reason. If the pueblo can say why it's a problem, he'll listen. Otherwise, he thinks he's fallen in love with a meadow with a view, maybe the one we were looking at yesterday."

He shook his head. "Lordy. Tell him we'd have to oppose him?"

"I did. Didn't pound on the table. Focused on what it'd take to get him looking elsewhere."

"How'd he take it?"

"Well, he knows. Not sure I wore him down, but he's willing to talk. If we can find out what's special about the area, he claims he's not one to, quote, 'walk all over the Indians.'"

Jack sighed. "That means I need to force the subject with Thomas."

"Want me to talk to him? I can. What's his number?"

"No phone. I can drive you there."

—·—

Nick Saunders closed the most recent communiqué from the Director's chief of staff.

Tough questions. Less than obvious motives. If the Director sticks his nose where it doesn't belong, outcomes might come unraveled. If he reverses anything, old fights will start anew. Deals will be broken. Things could become dangerous.

Got to get rid of that guy. Soon. Got to make sure something happens. No missed opportunities.

He picked up the phone and dialed. "Linda Showalter, please."

—— · ——

Marge found Linda Showalter in the hallway. "Regional Director called. He said to call him, pronto."

She went to the office, sat, picked up the phone, and dialed. "Regional Director, please."

He answered.

"Returning your call, Nick."

"I was calling to see what time line you have for getting things wrapped up with Middleton. Got a schedule?"

"Excuse me?"

"Middleton. Schedule. Timeline. Sharp people like you don't let things happen, they make things happen. Leadership. That's what it's about. If I've figured you wrong, if you're not up to it, I can bring in someone else."

"No, Nick, I don't have a schedule. This may require more finesse than hammer. It might be great to work this through quickly but what Middleton wants he can't have. I told you that. I need to convince him to be just as excited with another place."

"Can you do that and make him think it's his idea?"

"Too late for that, but I think I can make him feel good about helping someone else not feel stomped on."

"I'll give you a day or so. Then, put a bow on it. Wrap it up. I'll explain why later. It'll make perfect sense. You'll see it's necessary."

—— · ——

Nick Sanders hung up the phone. There was a knock on the door, and he turned.

"Your two o'clock is here."

"Give me a moment first. And close the door."

The door swung closed.

He turned to his email. He typed in Erika Jones' personal email address, not her government one. 'To be discreet,' she had told him. "Why the hell do I need to be discreet," he mumbled aloud to himself. "I'm the Regional Director, for God's sake." But it might be wise. Ridding ourselves of the Director might require a covert operation. He exited, opened his personal email account, and started a new message.

He began to type.

> I need to know. What makes Linda Showalter tick?
> Find out quickly.

He pushed send.

Thinking of something else, he retyped her address, then,

> And do something to nudge this along.

CHAPTER
27

Jack Chastain and Linda Showalter drove past the old pueblo and followed the dusty road to the brown box house, bringing the white pickup with arrowhead and green government markings to a stop beside Thomas'.

The door to the house opened and Thomas stepped out, meeting them at the vehicles.

Politely, he nodded, shook Showalter's hand, then put both of his hands in his pockets.

"The reason we're here," she said, "is I thought my presence might underscore how important this is. Preserving whatever it is about Sipapu Falls and the area around it—for your people and your culture—is important to us. But we need information."

He nodded. He seemed to be studying her.

"You were there of course, but I'm sure Jack explained the gravity of the proposal made by Mike Middleton. Generous offer, one with the potential of garnering public support. It's incumbent on us to move quickly, convince him there are more appropriate places for a land exchange than in that part of the canyon. We need you to tell us what's there."

He stared back.

"You do understand, don't you? You need to tell us what's there."

"Excuse me. May I speak privately with Jack?"

"Sure." She exchanged looks with Jack, turned, and walked back to the pickup.

He waited, then said, "I'm sorry. I will not talk to that woman."

"She's trying to help."

"I'm sorry. I will talk to you. I will not talk to her."

"I see. Regarding that subject, have you given it any more thought?"

"You and I talked only last night. Nothing's changed. I'll let you know if I figure anything out."

"Understood. Sorry to bother you." Jack turned and started back to the truck.

Thomas stepped inside and closed the door.

Linda, leaning against the hood of the truck, followed Jack with her eyes. "And?" she asked, as he approached.

"He only wants to talk to me."

She scowled, then softened. "I understand. Doesn't know me from a hill of beans."

"And he hasn't figured out what he's going to do. Hasn't had time, we only discussed it last night." He climbed into the driver's seat, and waited as she got in the other side. "I guess things take time."

She sighed. "Back to plan A. I've got Middleton. You've got Thomas."

— · —

Erika Jones slipped out of her uniform and into running shorts and her newest sweat-wicking pullover. Looking in the mirror, she studied the tone of her thighs, and nodded, satisfied. She sat on the bed, put on her shoes, and tied the laces.

Her personal cell phone gave the dull rattle of a newly arrived email.

She popped it open and read both messages. She glanced at her watch.

Too late to do anything about the first one. Might not be too late for the second. She leaned into the door frame for a stretch.

What would work?

Charm offensive.

She picked up her phone and dialed.

"Mike, is it too late to commandeer the next Coalition meeting? When is it?"

Silence, then, "It's tomorrow, why? What are you thinking?"

"Your place. Walk-through. Wine and cheese."

— · —

An email went from Karen Hatcher to everyone in the Coalition.

> Mr. Middleton has graciously agreed to host a 'walk-through' to discuss his proposal. Meet at the gate to his property (map attached), 10:30 am tomorrow, thirty minutes later than our usual time, giving anyone who doesn't see this the additional time needed to get there from Inn of the Canyons.

She also went to the online edition of the *Las Piedras Gazette* and posted the information as a comment on the newspaper's article about the upcoming meeting.

Later, another post was made:

> Heard people at Elena's talking about this guy Mike Middleton. Some love him, but if he's been here for years, why don't we know more about this guy. I think he's a government plant. A Trojan horse.
>
> Posted by, All Is Not Ducky

CHAPTER
28

'Change of meeting location,' said the subject line on the email.

—·—

The drive took them past the west desert, around the furthest reaches of the national monument—portions the Bureau of Land Management had long managed, but with the establishment of the monument did so now with new mission and directives. Jack forced glimpses at soaring views of sagebrush flats, canyon country and layers of distant mountains.

Linda Showalter picked away at a stack of papers.

Minding his business, he watched for evidence of creeks or water of any kind. Finally, he broke down. "What are you working on?"

"Letters Margie put on my desk. Don't worry, you'll get your share."

"Lucky me."

She ran a finger across a line on a page. "I've been invited to speak at the high school. Career day. Think I should do it?"

"Enjoy that sort of thing?"

"Absolutely. Young people. Love working with 'em. Could plant a seed. Could find the next generation of you or me."

"Then, do it."

"I will. Margie can make the arrangements." She took her eyes from the page. "If I could be known for just one thing, I can't think of anything more important than shaping the next generation of stewards. Young people who value their cultural and natural heritage."

Jack nodded.

She put the papers away. "It's hard to imagine what might live out there," she said, eyes on something distant.

"Did Molly show you an online post from our local conspiracy theorist?"

"No clue what you're talking about," Linda said.

"Person that posts under the name, All Is Not Ducky. Sees conspiracy in everything. Molly's followed him for years—her favorite entertainment. Last night he posted something about Middleton being a government plant. Someone to be suspicious of."

"I'm suspicious." She shook her head. "Too bad we aren't half as good at making plans and carrying them out as people think we are." She laughed. "People don't have a thing to worry about."

"But worry, they do."

They turned off the highway onto a graveled road. Gradually, the terrain turned hilly, and after a fork in the road, a gate of tall, standing timbers rose in the expanse of desert. They neared, and slowed. A split-pine crossbeam said, *'Virtual Empire'* in letters chiseled out and painted black.

"What does that mean?" Showalter asked.

"I think it's a nod to where he made his money. Online something or other."

"I see," she said, sounding unimpressed.

Jack steered through the open gate. Tacked to the fence was a sign. *'Come up to the house. Leave the gate open.'* On the hill sat an adobe home.

Jack pulled up, killed the engine and sat, studying the house. Vigas jutted from the walls high above a veranda that circled all but the portion of the house where tall windows looked out over what was likely a dramatic view to the north. Not exactly the best direction for solar but certainly the best one for the view.

He counted the vehicles. Seven, mostly pickups.

"Party's waiting," Linda said, climbing out.

Jack followed. As they approached the heavy wooden door, it swung open, and Middleton stepped into the opening, a glass of wine in hand. "Come in, please. Welcome."

"Beautiful home," Linda said, avoiding eye contact, sounding unwilling to be impressed. She walked past, and Middleton followed.

"Glass of wine?" he asked. "Red, white, sangria?"

"Can't. We're in uniform." Showalter turned to shake hands with Karen Hatcher.

Karen, mouth full, hand holding a long-stemmed goblet filled with berries and wine, nodded her greeting.

"You're among friends, loosen up," Middleton said, moving with Linda as she shook other hands.

"Wouldn't want to be anything but consistent." She spotted the serving table. "Oh, I'll have some cheese. Maybe some water."

"I don't have water. Only wine."

"Then I'll do without."

He shrugged and circled past a birch wood counter, ducking behind a whitewashed wall. He returned with two glasses of water. He handed one to Linda and turned to Jack. "I suppose you, too, are having water."

"Only till five."

"That's the spirit."

"Only if you're out of uniform," Showalter said. "When does the tour start?"

Middleton turned to Hatcher. "Karen?"

"We need a few more minutes to let everyone get here."

"And no talking business," Middleton added. "I expect you to enjoy yourselves."

The room started to fill. A pair of wine bottles were empty when Kip Culberson arrived, in jeans and boots, forgoing his usual western sport coat.

Another bottle was empty when Harper Teague knocked on the door. A smile cracked at the offer of wine. "White, I guess."

The bottle of white was being opened when Thomas slipped in.

"What may I get you?" Middleton asked. He flashed a smile and recited the options.

"I don't need anything, thank you."

A few more arrived and Karen Hatcher chimed her glass with a spoon. "I think we're all here. Mike, thank you for the hospitality, and what do you propose?"

"Load up."

— · —

A third of the vehicles were chosen to carry passengers. They piled in and followed Middleton's Land Rover past the house and a pair of smaller outbuildings, then along a low earthen wall and a larger building that appeared to be an indoor horse arena. A stock trailer sat parked beside it.

Jack looked all directions. No horses. No cattle.

The road climbed a hill and took a line alongside a straight stretch of barbed wire fence. They drove up and over several more hills before encountering a dry arroyo. The road veered right and followed it downstream. The terrain began to open up. A stock pond came into view. An earthen dam sat at the far end. The water body appeared little used. No sign of use by cattle or horses, water fairly clear, reeds and equisetum growing in quiet margins, sheltered from the waves that lapped at the dam, kicked up by downslope breezes.

The brake lights on Middleton's Land Rover flashed, and it came to a stop. The driver's side door opened and he stepped out, and waited for the caravan to converge. Karen Hatcher climbed out of his passenger side.

Once all had stopped and exited, he shouted. "We won't linger. This is the little pond."

They continued on, arriving at a larger one, and then made a lengthy drive along a ridge above a wide ravine. The caravan stopped at the end of the ridge, overlooking the river. Middleton waited as they climbed out and assembled in a circle. He pointed at the river. "I was thinking water could be diverted from upstream, put in a ditch along the contour." He pointed mid-slope, "If another earthen dam was built about there . . ." He ran a finger across the scene before him, along a line upslope of the mouth of the ravine. ". . . a considerable amount of water could be stored for livestock."

Kip Culberson studied the terrain. "That might work," he said. Others agreed.

Jack watched Ginger Perrette spin around. "What are you are looking at?" he asked.

"Thinking about how much range this would serve."

"It can all be yours," Middleton said.

"What about the house?" came a voice in back.

"That can be part of the deal."

"Serious?"

"Why not. Use it as a nature center."

Ginger turned back to the conversation. "What would it take to make this happen?"

"Just the land swap," Middleton said. He eyed Linda Showalter.

"No," Thomas said. "Not if it's trading something in the canyon. Not in the park."

"He's not talking about the park," said one of the women. "Or is he?"

"Don't know. Don't know where park lines are," Middleton said. "But let the Park Service worry about those details. Concentrate on whether this addresses your issues." He gave Showalter glance.

"What games are you playing, Middleton?" Teague said. "What are you not telling us? Cards on the table."

"No games," Middleton answered. "Just a desire to help. Right, Linda."

Arms crossed, she nodded. "Yeah, and I promise, he's not talking about trading for a place in the park. Because, one, he desires to help, and two, he knows that'd be crazy." She flashed a smile his way.

Eyes cold, smile big, he muttered, "Yeah, just give me a little place I can call my own."

"Stupid, that's what this is, just stupid," Teague said, growling out the words. "This is an answer in search of a question. No one needs this."

"Harper, why are you always so critical?" Laurie Martinez asked, nervously tugging the zipper on her jacket. "Can't you even try to work with the rest of us? We've got ranchers and environmentalists working together, trying to see each other as partners in protecting the things we value, and all you can do is poo-poo everything."

"Yeah," came another voice. Others shuffled, turning on Teague.

Teague's eyes darted side to side. "I, uh . . ." He cleared his throat. "Maybe I'm gotten off on the wrong foot," he said, nearly inaudibly. "I get angry. I can't seem to explain to you folks, you're on a dangerous path."

"Help us. Don't work against us," Martinez said.

"You people working together, maybe that's good," he said, sheepishly. "But get the government out of it. I've seen it before. It happened to me, my family. Lost it all. Land in the family for over a century, eighty miles from here. Now it's gone. Pa couldn't bear to face the family, ended his life rather than face the disappointment."

"What happened?" Martinez asked.

He dropped his eyes. "Thought we'd worked out a deal. Thought the regulators would work with us, let us explain what they didn't understand. But, they descended like storm troopers." He choked back tears. "They took everything."

Martinez swallowed hard.

Teague looked up. "Even if you think you can trust these two," he said, nodding at Jack and Linda, "their word won't stick. Their bosses in Washington will roll us in an instant. All it takes is their political cronies wanting something."

"Won't happen," Showalter said.

"Heard that before," Teague responded, turning away, and facing the others. "Don't let it happen to you. Deal with each other, not with these guys." He flashed a look of disdain at Middleton. "He plays games. He pulls strings. How can we trust he won't screw us? Require him to play by the rules. No games. No pulling strings. Everything above board."

Middleton shook his head. "Are you finished?"

Jack flagged a hand. "I don't know what to say, Harper. We had no idea. What can we do to earn your trust?"

"Don't think you can."

"We can try."

"May I continue?" Middleton said.

"A land exchange is not a good idea," Teague said.

Uncertain eyes met uncertain eyes.

"Well, this has been a little confusing," Ginger said, drawing attention to her. "But if this land exchange isn't an option, we're back to square one. Our cattle need unencumbered access to the river. They need water."

Dave Van Buren stepped to the front. "That can't happen."

"Dave, be reasonable," Ginger said. She gave a glance at Kip, standing a few feet away. "I'm afraid I'll have to leave the Coalition if we can't fix this. I'll have to quit. This is too important."

"But," Karen Hatcher interjected, "you'll do more good if you're involved. If you quit . . ."

"I know. I had hoped this could be constructive. But if we can't assure our stock get water, I can't stay involved."

Karen turned to Van Buren.

He shrugged. "Hey, if we cave, and decide we're not protecting the river, then I'm the one who's out of here. Choose your poison."

"You need me. You need this land exchange," Middleton said, scanning all eyes but Teague's.

"No land exchange," Thomas said.

"Thomas, I've spoken with Linda Showalter about this. If you have a reason, I'll consider other options. But you have to have a reason."

"She does not need my reason to say no. It's her job."

Middleton exchanged looks with Ginger Perette and Dave Van Buren. He smiled and said, "Let's head back."

— · —

They retraced their path across Middleton's *Virtual Empire*.

"We've got two things going on," Jack said, eyes on the road "Two or three separate battles."

"Ranchers and enviros," Linda muttered.

"That's one. Thomas and Mike Middleton."

"And Harper Teague, but he's irrelevant."

"I thought so before today," Jack said. "But I'm not sure now. Still, the key lies with Thomas and Mike Middleton. We need to get them talking, or one of them talking, the other listening."

"Got an idea," Linda said.

Jack took his eyes off the road, ready to listen.

"I don't know if this will work."

—·—

They waited as the others sorted themselves and departed in their respective vehicles. Middleton stood on the steps, saying his good-byes, waiting for the last to leave. Linda got out of the pickup and approached him.

"Do you like to hike?" she asked.

"Excuse me?"

"Hike! Can I interest you in a hike? Tomorrow."

"I suppose."

"Good. Prepare for an overnight. Pack light. I'll pick you up at eight. You'll love it."

She climbed in the truck. "He took the bait. We'll see if this works."

—·—

Jack followed Linda in the back door of headquarters, and up the hall to the offices.

Erika Jones stepped out of hers. "How'd it go?"

"For a while it went well," Jack said.

"Not well enough," Linda said. "You two, let's go to my office."

They followed her in and took chairs across from her desk. "I invited Mike on a hike, to get to know him better, and have a heart to heart about this land exchange."

"Good idea," Erika said.

"Glad you think so," she said, dismissively. "Jack, think about that place you took me, our camp, near the cliff dwelling. Maybe that's the right setting for this discussion. Let the place work its magic. Overwhelm him, get him thinking about native cultures, doing the right thing."

"Might work."

"Any concern about taking him into the fire perimeter?"

"You shouldn't be in there, but it was safe for us. I can ask if that sector's cool by now."

"Do that. It might put just the right edge on the hike. He might find it exciting, a little risky. Wanna join us?"

"Got a commitment. If you need, I could come in late, join you at camp."

"How about me?" Erika asked.

Showalter looked across the desk. "You know . . ." She thought a moment. "Okay, Erika, I'll take you."

— · —

Kelly scooted back from the table, stood, and walked to the bar for one of Elena's margaritas. She returned drink in hand, and plopped down beside Jack.

Johnny leaned over his beer. "Have you talked to Fish and Wildlife Service?"

"Not yet," Jack said. "Tomorrow."

"You worried?"

"Don't know what to think. Never been through anything like this."

"Great," Johnny said, sarcastically. "I have no credibility with Joe Morgan, and when Showalter finds out, I'll be dead meat. She'll fire my ass."

"She knows, and quit worrying about credibility. Credibility is built. You're fine."

Johnny shook his head and reached for the pitcher. He filled his glass.

"Is Linda still playing hard ball," Kelly asked. She took a sip.

"Not with me," Jack said, and took a sip of his own. "She's tough. I think I understand her now. I respect her for things she's willing to do."

"Like canning my ass?" Johnny asked.

"No, but Foss should worry. Unless . . ."

"Who's Foss?" Kelly asked. "And why the melancholy face?"

"Foss let the plants burn. Linda's willing to seek some kind of accountability—and to negotiate with Mike Middleton rather than simply tell him no. Both, because of things I said." He sighed. "Hope I'm not setting her up."

— · —

Erika Jones dropped into the government quarter's only somewhat comfortable chair, and took out her cell phone. "Good news," she said, when answered.

"I need good news," Saunders said, sounding sour.

"Showalter isn't sitting back. She invited Middleton on a hike."

"What good will that do?"

"Gives her a proper setting to discuss this land exchange, get him to go along with an option that's considerably less complicated."

"If it works in our favor, and things can move quickly, good. But keep this moving. The Director's actions are getting close to home. Got a sense yet of what makes Linda tick?"

"No, but I'm going on this hike."

"Good. Pull out the big guns."

"I'm not sure what that means."

"I'm not either, but this is important. Think of something."

CHAPTER 29

The smoke hung more lightly across the landscape, at least on the southern end. To the north, the fire was making its daily run.

The perimeter had burned nearly to the trailhead, as backing fire, flames inching downslope against the breeze. It was anything but scary.

Still, Mike Middleton appeared nervous, his eyes on flame as they approached the advancing edge, Erika in the lead. Beyond the perimeter—into the black, with smoke only from smoldering duff—he turned chatty.

"You're not in uniform, Erika?" he asked. "Why not? Linda is."

"Don't have a field uniform," she said, glancing back but charging on, a sway to her step. "Only these old things."

"And I wouldn't let her wear her badge in those shorts," Linda said, under her breath.

—·—

Linda trudged up the trail, watching for clues. An escarpment came into view. She saw disturbance—a hint of days old track across blackened ground. "We'll leave the trail here," she shouted.

Up ahead, they slowed and turned back, looking for reasons. Nothing suggested anything but trail leading forward.

Linda chuckled to herself, and peeled off to the right, into the ash. "Follow me."

She wove past scorched brush and fire-singed piñon pine, crossing an area where nothing survived but standing ponderosa. She zeroed in on a spot ahead, and approached a flat rocky outcropping that overlooked a drainage, cut scores of feet deep. "Here it is," she said.

Mike and Erika walked up beside her and stared down.

"We came all this way for this?" Middleton said. He cast an eye over the canyon bottom.

"Not that," Showalter said. "That." She pointed.

Across the way, behind vegetation now mostly burned away, cliff dwellings sat exposed, sheltered beneath the caprock.

Erika Jones, eyes wide, soaked in the sight of the earthen rooms. "Cool," she murmured.

Mike Middleton stared, saying nothing.

— · —

A sliver of a moon hung over the plateau.

Camp set up, her bivy sack and sleeping bag thrown out on the same spot she'd used days before, Linda Showalter knelt, then laid down, and watched the others mess with their own machinations.

The best place to start this discussion? Probably best to dive right in.

Middleton finished reading the instructions to his tent, and directed his flashlight toward the bundle of fiberglass poles.

"Here, I'll show you," Erika said, picking them up. She extended the three poles, slipping rods into ferrules, and guided them through nylon sleeves on the tent.

He stepped in at final tent-raising, then grabbed his sleeping bag and rolled it out inside. "Done," he shouted.

Jones snickered and settled onto her own bivy sack.

He took a seat on a rock. "I assume you want to talk."

"I do," Linda said. "Nice sky isn't it?"

"Yeah, it's great. I see it every night through my window."

"The other night, Jack was carrying on about these stars, hypothesizing their influence on the depth of our minds."

"He likes to think a little too hard, doesn't he?" Middleton said.

"I thought so, too, at first, but it got interesting, started making sense. What was scary is thinking about kids who never see these stars, only reality television and video games."

"Video games develop skills," he said. "They also keep the money rolling in."

"Yeah, but you want 'em to have opportunities like this, don't you?"

"Of course. And three squares a day, the good life, and a few years of social security. Who wouldn't?"

"Mike, let's talk about your proposal. Have you figured out why I wanted to bring you here?"

"To bond. To soften me up." He laughed. "Right?"

"The Coalition is close to self-destructing, and yet your proposal—if done right—can keep that from happening."

"True, but you could have said that yesterday."

"Things have gotten complicated. I'm hoping the cliff dwelling underscores both the magic of this place, and the fact that people have had cultural affiliations with this land for hundreds, if not thousands of years. We don't understand those affiliations. They're none-the-less important."

"The makings of a great nature walk. Bring in the tourists, fill 'em with stories, send 'em home happy."

"The point I'm making is, it's important to preserve some places. What I want to talk about, what I want to encourage you to do, is set your sights on another piece of land, something far from Cañon de Fuego."

"What'd you learn from Thomas?"

"Nothing yet, but Jack's working on it."

He pawed the ground with a foot. "Then we'll wait to talk. As I said yesterday, and previously, I'm reasonable. Get information, we'll talk."

"You could at least start looking at options. Federal lands are okay, but not in the national park. Wanting park land complicates the issue tremendously."

"Get information, we'll talk. I won't play it any other way. I've learned it best to start with the end in mind, know exactly what I want going in. Otherwise, people take advantage of me. I'm willing to adjust my thinking, but only if there's something to talk about."

Change the subject. "Your business. Where'd you get your start?"

"Boston, where I went to school, but I set up my business in Chicago, then Silicon Valley. And you? How did you get where you are?"

She laughed. "Where I am. That's funny."

"Why?"

"Oh, nothing. I'm not in a bad place."

"But not where you thought you'd be?"

"Why do you say that?"

"Your reaction to my question. Where'd you think you'd be?"

She looked at Erika. Her outlines in the dark seemed to sit a little higher, a little closer. "Let's talk land swap. That's the priority."

"How about a different question. Where do you go from here? What's next, after Piedras Coloradas?"

"That's hard to know. I might not be here very long."

"Meaning?"

"I'm on detail. I could be sent back to my old park at any time, but I love it here."

"Would you want to be here?"

"Surprised I still had a shot," she said. "Years ago, I took it for granted, opportunities would come. Then, . . ."

"What?"

"Nothing."

"You got sidetracked?"

"Let's not talk about it."

"Something you didn't plan for?"

"You might say that."

He chuckled to himself. "Well?"

"Pissed off someone, okay," Linda said. "I assumed he wasn't part of the good ol' boy network. I was wrong. My rocket sputtered. I crashed and I burned." She snorted. "No more talk about that. Land exchange . . ."

"Where have you worked?"

She looked away, then up, then back. "Lots of places. Parks mainly."

"Any place you'd want to go back to?"

"Not really . . . well . . ."

"Where?

"Rather not say. No more talk about me."

"Okay, we'll talk about me," he said, and paused. "If I had a chance to do anything over, I'd do it more on my own. Had a rich uncle. He liked saying he made everything happen. If I could do it all over, knowing I created my own breaks, with my own ingenuity, and how his money only greased the skids, I'd do it on my own."

"Can't change history," Linda said. "Erika, why aren't you talking?"

"You two talk. I'm watching the stars, wondering where my brain might be if I hadn't watched so much television."

"My uncle did help," Middleton continued. "His influence helped."

"Influence is a funny thing."

"Makes things happen. Opens doors."

"Yeah, but some of us just want a chance to make a difference. Someone else's influence game is my pain in the ass." She stood and started to pace.

"The place you'd like to go back to, why was it such a great job?"

She sighed. "I was surrounded by idealistic minds, in a place and time where we thought we could do so much good. Once I figured out how naïve I was, how much I needed to learn, I left, but always hoped to return to make a bigger difference."

"Why don't you? Return, that is."

"Won't be up to me," she said, stepping away.

"Why?"

She stopped and turned. "Going there, in the kind of position it'd take, requires more worth than I've got. Won't happen."

"There's that influence thing . . ."

"Yeah, that thing helps everyone else."

"That thing—mine—could help you, if you'll let me. And if you help me."

"Mike, it's very possible you and I will be in battle soon. If I have to tell you no, you won't like me very much."

"No, I won't, but I know where to go, and I can use my influence to get my way or destroy you, or both, but it doesn't have to be that way."

"No, it doesn't. You could play fair, work with us, achieve the right outcome, feel good knowing you're holding the Coalition together."

"True," he said, shifting on his rock, sitting a little higher. "But, influence is an interesting thing. Like muscle, it has to be used. If you don't, it wastes away to nothing." He chuckled to himself. "Use it wisely—exercise it, not too much, not too little—it grows."

"I'm picturing becoming a game to you."

"Why?"

"You know why."

"No, what you need to picture is what you want to accomplish. Start with the end in mind. Do what it takes to get there."

"Too risky."

"Why?"

"Why would I tell you? You're the one who'll try to roll me."

"I'll be the one who *will* roll you, going straight to the Director. But I can also be the guy who goes to the Director doing just the opposite, making sure you're in a place to make the most difference. And if I read you right, the Director's in just the place to do it."

She glanced at Erika.

Erika lay flat on the ground, looking up. Asleep, if lucky.

— · —

Showalter passed the spot where the rescuers had jumped off the trail two weeks before—much too dangerous to go there with these two, or at least too scary for most people. With hard rock jarring her knees, and likely the knees of the others, she made no effort to go faster and neither did they. The pace with the tug of gravity was enough.

Several more bends, all on trail chipped from sheer rock, and the view of the canyon began to open. The waterfall pounded boulders below, its sound weaving into the echo that carried across the canyon. Linda stopped, and propped a foot against the low rock wall standing between her and the plunge to the bottom.

Middleton slowed. He took hold of his pack straps and sucked in a breath. "Beautiful. Wonder if that sound gets annoying."

"You'd never get away from it," Showalter said, "For that reason alone you should think about someplace outside the canyon."

He stepped back. "Oh, I'd get used to it." He turned and studied a cavernous slice in the wall on the other side of the canyon. "But I made a promise. Learn something from Thomas, we'll talk." He turned toward her. "And work this out, and I'll talk to someone about refueling your rocket."

He started down the last of the switchbacks to the canyon floor. Erika followed. Linda Showalter waited a long moment, then brought up the rear.

— · —

Erika Jones dropped her pack on the floor, and went to draw water for a bath. Slipping out of her clothes, she checked the scratches on her legs—most were not scratches, only black streaks from brushing against ash-laden stubs of burnt branches.

She checked herself in the mirror. Maybe a little too much sun.

Several items gathered and set on the floor, she stepped into the tub and settled in. She gasped, then relaxed. Eyes closed, she took a long breathless moment to soak in the warmth.

Reaching an arm over the rim, she picked up her phone.

No answer. She waited to leave a message. "Nick, got your answer. I know what makes Linda Showalter tick. Unfortunately, so does Middleton. This is gonna be tricky."

CHAPTER

30

An article in the *Las Piedras Gazette* updated its readers on the progress of the Coalition, and the outcome of its latest meeting. Its sources were several meeting attendees.

The article was also posted online.

The *Gazette*'s online edition drew responses from readers throughout the day, including thoughts on different priorities, and the value or drawback of enviros, ranchers and others working together.

At 6:50 p.m., a response was posted from an individual wishing to remain anonymous.

> I heard the feds at the meeting were doing lots of talking among themselves. Didn't sound like they're concerned about 'river versus cattle' but they're letting it create confusion so they can carry out their plan to put everything under government control. The call to trade for Middleton's Virtual Empire Ranch is leverage to seize it when the time is right. After that, they're free to work on the rest of their plan.
>
> They're playing along with the Coalition, a ruse that makes it easy to work the back rooms. A new guy

named Teague is a straight shooter, but ineffective at
cutting through the games. He's worthless. Someone should give him the hook. He's working against
himself, but he's trying. My source wants to help, but
is afraid. I'm afraid, too, but someone has to tell the
truth.

It was signed, 'Fearfully Anonymous.'

At 6: 57 p.m., a person with a real name—Dan Romero—
posted:

I don't believe any of this. I was at the meeting. The
government employees were with us the whole time.
I never heard anything questionable. Use your real
name and have a little intestinal fortitude.

At 7: 02 p.m., 'All Is Not Ducky' posted:

I believe it, and I know why 'Fearfully Anonymous' is
afraid. Give your real name and you become a target
for the government. When they know who revealed
their plot, first thing that happens is an audit by the
IRS. After they invent all sorts of reasons to go after
your money and your home, they kick you and your
family out on the street where you don't have a voice
and can't afford to have one. Don't do it Fearfully, stay
Anonymous. Just sayin . . .

After several other posts, covering a range of opinions, 'Fearfully Anonymous' made another post at 7:24 p.m.:

Here's another thing everyone should know: There's
a special government team targeting private lands
for seizure. It's hard to know who these people are
because they're instructed to do their work without
being detected. Until I can learn more, watch for
suspicious activity.

And believe me, Ducky, I am laying low.

The string of comments were not included in the Letters to the Editor section of the next day's print edition of the *Gazette*, but word spread quickly, and by morning, many in town were aware of the discussion. They were talking.

— · —

Jack Chastain came into headquarters, dropped off his bag and went to the dispatch office for coffee. Molly drew his attention to the previous day's newspaper.

He took a sip and scanned the article. "Okay, fair enough."

"Now, come here," she said.

He came around the counter and stood behind her, as she found the article online and scrolled to the posted comments.

He read the entry and leaned closer, reading it again. "What the hell. Where did that come from?"

In the hallway were sounds of someone coming in the back door and up the hall.

"Morning, Molly," came a voice. It was Linda Showalter.

"Linda," they hollered, simultaneously.

She abruptly turned, and came in.

"You need to see this," Jack said.

She came around the counter and read over Molly's shoulder.

She finished and turned to Jack. "What should we do?"

"I think we have to say something? Or have someone say it for us."

"I'll write up something and get it to the paper," Linda said, backing toward the door.

"Wait," Molly said. "There's another." She scrolled down several posts and rolled her chair back from the monitor. They stepped forward and read.

"Secret government team? You've got to be kidding. No one's gonna believe that." Linda shook her head and laughed. She left.

Jack refilled his coffee and read it again.

Yeah, no one.

— · —

Nick Saunders stared at the Director's travel itinerary for the coming weeks. Sand Dunes. Why would he go there? Without me? What is he doing? First cancelling research, now what? Without much effort, he could undo so much. Create a political firestorm. Who's he meeting? If the park superintendent doesn't know . . . ?

A favor might be needed. A few questions from the right protector. No—Congressman Hoff is the surest way to get rid of him. Don't overreact. Keep things moving. Get out in front.

Nick checked the clock. Ten minutes after eight and Linda Showalter still hadn't returned his call. Impatiently, he punched in the numbers for her direct line.

"Linda Showa . . ."

"Linda, it's Nick. I need an update. What happened with Mike Middleton?"

"Can I call you back? Something's got my attention."

"There's nothing more important than this."

"There is. And it relates to this. Last night someone posted conspiracy theories online. I'm trying to get a sense of whether people will consider the source and ignore it, or react in some way that gives us problems."

"How does it relate to Middleton?"

"The posts accuse us of having plans to seize Middleton's property in a grand scheme to assert government control over everything."

He swallowed hard. "Has Middleton seen or heard this?"

"No idea. I plan to call him."

"Who's the source? Who posted it?"

"Someone anonymous. Posted in comments to a news story."

Saunders let out a sigh of relief. "Good. Probably a sniveler no one listens to."

"Don't know if they listen or not. Has me concerned. Rather disheartening, actually. I could tell Jack was disappointed."

"Middleton's your priority. Make sure everything's fine, that we're moving forward. Everything else can take care of itself."

"Why are you so involved in this, Nick? And why do you seem so confident about what I should do when I'm sitting here, and you're sitting in Denver?"

"I'm tuned into the bigger picture, that's all."

"What are you saying?"

He was slow to respond. "What you don't know is that there are several interrelated actions that hinge on moving the Middleton proposal forward."

"Oh, I know. And if I can't get something worked out, the Coalition could implode. Whether the Coalition's important or not, Jack Chastain seems to think so."

"Linda, I'm talking bigger things. Some that might decide the future of this agency, positively or negatively. We're trying to steer toward the positive, and we can if this moves forward. You're concerned about details—that's good. Helps things work better locally, but those details are of little consequence on the regional and national scales."

"How would our stuff even relate to what's happening on a national scale?"

"You'd be surprised. You'd also be surprised at who's watching how you handle this. People who wonder if you fit into their plans."

"What kind of plans?"

"Plans of a national kind. That's all I can say."

"And they're talking about me?"

"They are. It's up to you. If you do well in this assignment, you make a name for yourself. If you don't, it's back to your old park."

"What are you saying?"

"Your part in this is minor compared to what you're capable of tackling, but this one must be tackled. As you do, you can demonstrate readiness for the larger stage."

"We're at a particularly sensitive time. This is complicated."

"It isn't, compared to what's in store in your next position. Get a bow on the Middleton proposal. Quickly. If you wrap up the details in the next couple of days, it won't be too soon."

— · —

Linda Showalter dialed the number, her fingers tentative.

After two rings it was answered.

"Mike, this is Linda Showalter."

"Good timing," he said, angrily, his breath seething, melting into the connection. "I'm about to call the Director. It won't be a social call."

"Hold it, Mike. We didn't say those things."

"Who did?"

"No one. As we speak, I'm writing a response to the *Gazette*, rebutting everything posted."

"Convince me."

"It'll say there was no such discussion, no such plans, and we would never attempt to seize your property."

"It'll take more than that."

"You can't have it, Mike. You can't have that place in the canyon."

"I'm not sitting around waiting forever. Do something or I will."

— · —

Jack stuck his head in the door. "Need help crafting the response?"

"Sit," Linda said.

"I can put together a few points that might be helpful." He settled into a chair. "Oh—and I meant to tell you—I talked to Fish and Wildlife Service. They'll lead the review into our torching the wallflower."

"That'll have to wait." She leaned over her hands. "Get me Thomas' secret, or things could get bloody."

His eyes widened. "I need time."

"Tell him he's got till tomorrow. If he gives me nothing, I'll have to tell Middleton no based on other reasons. The result won't be pretty. If Middleton pulls strings, it'll get ugly."

"Tomorrow's Saturday."

"Then by the end of the weekend. Report to me first thing Monday."

——— · ———

Nick Saunders typed a quick message to Erika Jones. "Productive talk with Showalter. Be ready to get the ball rolling."

——— · ———

Erika Jones opened a binder of business cards, in clear plastic sleeves. She flipped through the pages, searching for one in particular, a card with the gold eagle crest of the U.S. Congress.

Found it.

She slipped it out and laid it on the desk, then dialed the number to Ethan Burke, Policy Advisor to Congressman Brett Hoff.

He answered.

"Ethan, this is Erika Jones, National Park Service."

"Who? Oh, Erika, from Yellowstone."

She smiled to herself, and put her feet on the desk. "Yes, but I don't actually work at Yellowstone. I was there to take you into the backcountry. I work for the Regional Director."

"Oh yeah, I remember. What's up?"

"I'm on a little project for my boss and yours."

"You are? What project?"

"I'm to be discreet, but it has to do with a constituent. I'm calling to get your thoughts. The Congressman wanted us to be attendant to this constituent's needs."

"Yeah, he tends to do that."

"We've learned this constituent's interests. He wants to make a donation of land, actually an exchange in support of a public purpose, willing to give twenty acres for every one he receives in return, maybe more."

"Sounds generous."

"Yes, very. He has his eyes on a specific plot of land. Only thing, it'll require legislation and it might be hard for us to show visible support for this legislation."

"Interesting."

"But behind the scenes, I can provide you the language for the legislation."

"Okay. Understood."

"Is there a way to limit the attention this gets?"

"There is a way to do it quietly. It'll only get attention after everything's said and done."

"How?"

"Simple, the Congressman's on the appropriations committee. We wait till they're in conference committee, slip it in when only appropriators and leadership are involved. Your timing's good. Things could be happening as early as next week. With the Department on continuing resolution this late in the year, everyone's tired of the fight, wanting to focus on next year. They want this budget done. Questions might come up in conference, but people there understand favors. It's more likely than not we can avoid a point of order. No one interested will notice till it's voted on and signed."

"Perfect. I'll tell the Regional Director. Hey, next time I'm in D.C., want to get together for a drink?"

"Uh . . . yes, definitely."

She said her good-bye and hung up. "I thought so."

CHAPTER
31

On Saturday morning, the *Gazette* included a letter to the editor asking why the print edition of the newspaper did not include a very important post by 'Fearfully Anonymous.' The letter suggested the online post/comment provided information everyone should know.

The editor politely replied it was the policy of the *Las Piedras Gazette* to only publish letters submitted from those willing to provide a name, phone number, and town of residence.

The letter below it—with a name—did, however, force the print edition into becoming the forum for a developing fray.

> *Thank God for Fearfully Anonymous and their willing-ness to offer reason to fight against Piedras Coloradas National Monument and the work of the Coalition, which is in cahoots with big government. Ostensibly, the local efforts are intended to find balance and work from mutual interest. However, the effort has a more insidious purpose than advertised. There is more involved than the emotions surrounding these issues that are important to the commu-nity. It is really a federal issue with the main sponsors (the president and his federal goon squad) aiming to emasculate our way of life. The local efforts are merely one step in a federally orchestrated campaign, directed by the president in this rapidly accelerating process.*

> *Why would they do this? Simply put, the federal*
> *government is preparing a war against the American*
> *people, tying up land for their enviro-nazi purposes.*
>   *The president has promised to fundamentally change*
> *the character of this nation. He doesn't want us in control*
> *of our own lives, he wants control of our lives to be in the*
> *hands of the government. The Coalition is unknowingly*
> *a pawn in the game—or maybe they know. This man*
> *named Harper Teague—though giving his best—is ill*
> *prepared to wage the war alone. It's not his fault . . . he's*
> *working against sophisticated operators. At least Fearfully*
> *Anonymous—though fearful—is brave enough to support*
> *his cause, stand up to the government tyrants, and call a*
> *spade a spade. We must show up and help in the fight."*

Hack Pearson, resident of Las Piedras

— · —

Jack stopped at the hardware store to pick up supplies. Inside, he walked past the check-out counter and followed the aisle to the back. At the paint counter, a pair of men carried on animated discussion with another in a paint-splattered apron.

"Hack's right you know," one of them said. "The only people with a lick of sense may be that Harper Teague and the person calling themself Fearfully Anonymous."

Jack picked up a bottle of lamp oil and froze at the mention of the names.

Great! Just great!

— · —

The stacked stone cairn came into view. Its rusted sign, hanging from a cedar post jutting from the side, said *Culberson Ranch* in flowing letters. Jack slowed the pickup and turned off the highway. He steered down the winding road, around the hillside, and dropped onto the meadow. Well beyond green-up, in morning light it pulled at his eyes. The makings of a beautiful late spring day.

He pulled up to the house and climbed out of the pickup.

Kelly appeared in the courtyard, in well-fitting jeans and an untucked shirt, toting her boots. Barefoot, she sat, pulled on socks, then her boots.

"Ready for breakfast?"

"I am," she said. She gave him a quick hug. "I'd love to take a ride today. Maybe a dip."

"Isn't Caveras Creek still a bit cool?"

"You baby."

"I need to talk to Thomas about something."

"After breakfast. I'll go with you."

— · —

They ordered huevos rancheros and coffee, and Jack picked up the paper he'd grabbed from the bar on the way in. He flipped through the pages and found the letters to the editor.

Finished, he sighed, folded the paper and set it aside. He tried to enjoy his breakfast.

— · —

They drove slowly past the pueblo, and turned down the road to the brown, box house. Two people were outside, working in the garden. Its level beds, in plots surrounded by built-up earth, lay along a snaking ditch that stretched past the gardens, and on to the next set of beds at the next houses.

Kneeling over their work, one appeared to be Thomas.

Jack pulled in behind his pickup and stopped.

Thomas met them at the truck.

"Good morning," Jack said. "I apologize, but can we talk?"

"I promised to help Rachel in the garden. Come, we'll talk there."

"What are you growing?" Jack asked, as he followed.

"Rachel wants to plant traditional crops—blue, red and yellow corn, squash, beans, some cotton. Chili peppers over there. A few others. Medicinal plants, some for cooking, some for other purposes."

Rachel worked in the corner of a plot.

Kelly approached and knelt beside her. "Hi sweetie."

She looked up, smiled, and continued to work, pushing a stick into loosened earth.

"Sorry to bother you again, and so soon, Thomas," Jack said. He paused, distracted by Rachel's actions. "What's she doing?"

"Planting corn. She found a planting stick in her mother's things." Thomas walked over beside her. "Squash and beans will be here, shaded by the corn when it gets taller, when the summer's hot and dry."

Jack stepped closer and watched her drop a blue kernel in the hole and cover it over with soil. He turned back to Thomas. "Linda asked me to talk to you."

"About?"

"Same stuff. What we should know about Sipapu Falls. She said tell you there's no more time. If she fights and loses, things could get ugly. She only has so many options. The Coalition could fold." Jack walked past well planned sections, into a portion more wild, but recently watered. "What's over here?"

"Bee plant, sunflower, purslane, Indian tea. Plants collected and brought here from other places." Thomas looked up, into the late spring sky. "This is a good day for this, Rachel."

She nodded and pushed the stick into the earth.

"So, could you help us? What should we know, Thomas? Linda's not telling me everything. She's obviously under pressure. It'd help to know enough to create options. Maybe even arguments to use in pushing back."

"Nothing has changed."

"Something has changed. Mike Middleton's turning up the heat."

"Jack, my friend, what you want to know is something of our

culture, not yours. You have reasons enough—reasons that come from yours.

"Isn't this important to you? Enough to help put up a defense?"

"I didn't say it wasn't important."

"Then, give us information, please. Help us!"

Thomas looked down. He toed the ground.

"This may be your last chance to easily affect an outcome without us having to play hardball, doing something that could cause the Coalition to destruct. We have to do it now."

Thomas watched his niece. She planted another kernel of blue corn.

"Thomas, we need enough info to convince Middleton to set his eyes elsewhere, but we need him to give his land to keep the Coalition together. What's there? Why is it important?"

He looked up and shook his head. "I can't."

"Thomas."

"Jack, this is difficult."

"Is it something only important to you?"

"No."

"Then to whom can I talk?"

He glanced at Rachel.

"Are you serious?" Jack raised a hand to his forehead. "Who else?"

Rachel looked up, glanced between them, then dropped her eyes.

"Who else can I talk to?"

Thomas held his tongue.

Jack took a deep breath and let it out. "What the hell am I going to do?" he muttered.

—·—

In the pickup and driving away, Kelly crossed her arms and pressed herself against the door. "Why did you do that?"

"What?"

"Push him like that? He almost said more than he wanted to."

"I need him to. He didn't tell me anything."

"It's not something you need to know," Kelly said angrily.

"I was told to speak to him. I explained why. Middleton won't talk options without some bit of information. Without his land the Coalition's on the verge of falling apart. If Linda tells Middleton no, it might. Plus he'll go to the Director. She might get rolled."

"There has to be a way to fix this."

"This was the way. Thomas isn't thinking this through."

A guttural growl grew from inside her. "Damn it, Jack," she said, her patience gone. "Don't you know what damage has been done?"

"Yes . . . but . . ."

"When my people came, priests worked to convert the pueblo to Catholicism. The converts tried to integrate the new religion with their own—their traditions were so important to them—but priests searched out kivas and anything to do with traditions and religion, and destroyed them. Destroyed them! Things were lost."

"But I'm trying to help."

"Why do you think what you're doing is different?"

"I'm here to serve the public interest."

"Don't you think the Spanish—my people, at least some of them—thought the same thing?"

"I'm not here as a conqueror."

"What's the difference?" She sighed. "There have been conquerors, but the conquerors weren't the only ones causing things to happen. Others pressured them to abandon their way of life, become *good* Indians. Indian agents, some sincere, honest, well meaning, trying to help, often causing more harm than good. Then, there were the anthropologists. Some felt so entitled to learn ceremonial secrets they barged into ceremonies, physically threatening anyone protesting their being there. When they published their findings, collectors and pot hunters went after artifacts and sacred items."

He stared ahead, not sure what to say.

She continued. "Then, there were those doling out jobs, and Indians desperate to care for their families let themselves be convinced to send their children away to school, to turn their backs on the teachings of their clans and religious leaders.

"They have a reason for being secretive" she said, her voice growing calm. "They're trying to protect who they are."

Jack felt her eyes on him.

"The effects of those earlier actions live on today," she said. "Ceremonial items and stories lost. Clans unable to initiate their young. Clans lost, and each had a role. Thomas' mother once told me the spirits are crying. I didn't understand it. I'm sure you don't either, but it had meaning to her."

Jack slowed the vehicle to a stop. "I know you're mad, but I'm trying to help. I'm trying to help Thomas, trying to help Linda Showalter, trying to protect the park. I don't know all the pressures, but I have nothing to help."

"You know enough. That place is important. The whole canyon is important. What pressure trumps doing this right?"

"Things are moving fast. Middleton's a squeaky wheel demanding grease. The Coalition's heading toward self-destruct."

"And for those things, traditions holding a people together for hundreds of years hang in the balance? No one is that important. No one is that unimportant."

— · —

The horses plodded through sagebrush flats, toward a break in the sandstone. In the lead, Kelly reined her paint pony through the slice, around a patch of prickly pear cactus, and over to the wall, into the cool of the shadows. They followed the trail deeper, stopping at a dead juniper. Kelly jumped off, pulled a rope from her bag, and tethered the horse to a limb. She waited as Jack tied his, then led him around a bend in the canyon wall, into the sunlight. She stopped on a spit of sand overlooking pools of water, surrounded by travertine, filled with the waters from Caveras Creek pouring in from above.

She sat and pulled off her boots.

Jack shook his head. "I'm . . . I'm troubled . . . and confused."

She stood. "Why?" She unbuttoned her jeans.

"I can't give Linda Showalter what she asked for, but there's got to be something else I can do. Something to help."

She slipped off her jeans. "Sometimes there's no easy answer."

"I can't blow it off. Too much is happening. The Coalition is struggling. Conspiracy theorists have people talking. Thomas and Mike Middleton are at cross purposes. An anti-government guy named Harper Teague is confusing things, but deserves more effort on my part to understand what he's about. I'm not holding this together very well."

"Again, things are not always easy. You may not know what to do now, but trust yourself. You always do the right thing." She slipped off her top and tossed it on a rock. She took hold of his shirt. "Is this good?"

"It's seen better days."

She yanked, popping buttons and tearing cotton. "There, that's better." She smiled. "It's time to think about something else."

CHAPTER
32

"Come on, Mike, relax," Erika said, watching Middleton slide down the rope. She chuckled. *If this guy gets killed, my goose is cooked.*

Middleton's eyes nervously moved left, unable to ignore the void.

"Quit looking, you dope," she shouted. "Keep your eyes on your feet. Focus on where you're going. You're safe, unless you do something stupid. If you do, I'll be scraping you off the canyon floor."

He looked up, whites of his eyes showing. He forced them down, onto his feet.

Like putty in my hands.

He dropped lower, slowly walking the near-vertical face.

Why'd he bring so much stuff? If both feet come off that rock, his pack will pull him over in a heartbeat. At least he's doing as told—walking it, slowly. "Work your way to the right. Make sure you're a good distance from the edge when you get there." She watched him adjust his line of descent. "That's good. Stay on that line."

He approached his target. The angle of the rock began to change. She watched him steady his feet, then set one on the level, then the other.

A bird flew from a crevice—screeching, wings beating against air. Middleton jumped back, reaching for his chest. "Thought something got me." He managed a laugh as he gathered himself.

"White throated swift." She flashed a smile. "You're bigger

than what it eats. Now, step back and pull a little rope through the figure-eight."

He backed up, pulling on the rope.

"Good. Now, sit down and disconnect."

She watched.

He turned the collar on the carabiner and disconnected.

"Sit tight. Stay out of trouble. I'll be right down."

She pulled up the rope, slipped the rope from the figure-eight, and reset it above her. She clipped in, locked the carabiner, and tossed the rope downslope. She started her rappel. In a moment she was standing beside him.

"How do we get back up there," he asked.

She shot her eyes up the rope. "I forgot about that," she said, panic in her voice. "Why didn't you say something before I got here?"

"You're not serious?"

She smiled. "No, I'm not. We use ascenders. They're in my pack."

He let out a sigh.

"Mike, relax. We're here." She slipped out of her straps and set the pack on the ground.

He dropped his.

"Follow me."

She led him across the hanging alcove, and carefully approached the waters gushing from the wall. She studied his expression as his eyes followed the waters from the hole, flowing through fern, past watercress, picking up speed, and soaring into air. "Pretty cool, huh?"

"Yeah, pretty cool." After a moment, he pointed past the water to the other side. "What's over there?"

"More of the same. If you want to see it, let's do it now. We won't want to cross after dark."

He eyed the stepping stones. "Maybe we should blow it off."

She set a foot on a stone, then the other. "We need firewood. There's plenty over there. Falls in from above. We used most on this side on our trip here with Thomas." She crossed, and looked back. "Just be careful, you'll be okay."

"I thought you couldn't have fires in the backcountry?"

"Didn't think of that. Interesting. Jack didn't stop Thomas, so . . ." She spun around. "We'll set it back from the edge. No one will see."

He nervously took a step, then another, then another. He stepped onto solid ground and took in a settling breath. "Starting to wonder if you brought me here to kill me."

She laughed. "You realize I could've cut the rope."

"There would've been evidence."

"You're right. Don't relax quite yet." She turned. "I might have plans. You might have to keep an eye on me."

She led him across the back side of the alcove, looking about, searching, and gathering pine branches.

"See," she said, at the end, "nothing here."

They turned and walked back, stopping at the water crossing. They tossed the collected wood across, and Erica paused, looking back over the plateau, then into the canyon. "Such a cool place."

"Who would've thought you could get up here."

She nodded.

"What's here that Thomas is so concerned about?"

"No clue. I'm guessing nothing. Wasn't with him the whole time, but you can see, there's nothing here. Probably some mystical reason."

Middleton leaned in toward the solution hole, a hand firmly grasping a slot on the wall. He looked inside, and probed with his left hand, feeling along the edge. "Mystical?"

"This is about as mystical as you can get, don't you think?"

"That's not the word I'd choose, but I suppose."

She led him across and they re-gathered the wood, carrying it over to the packs.

"You start setting up camp, I'll make a fire."

He pulled out his fiberglass poles and pop tent. "Remember how these damned things worked?" he asked, holding a pole and searching for an appropriate opening on the tent.

She shook her head.

Once the fire was started, she piled on more needles and placed another limb across the flames. She watched a moment more, enjoying the sight of him trying to figure it out.

"Start with this one," she said, picking up a pole. She strung it through a nylon sleeve, set its end in a grommet, bent the pole tight against the nylon, and stuck the other end into another grommet. Two more poles and the tent was standing. They set it against the back wall of the alcove.

Sitting around the fire, they ate a light dinner, and watched the glow of the sun on the wall across the canyon.

"So, what's your mission, Miss Jones?"

"Excuse me?"

"What mission did Linda Showalter give you?" He set his eyes on something across the way.

"Linda has no clue we're here." She scanned the canyon. Where he appeared to be looking, she saw a small meadow at the mouth of a side canyon, on the other side of river. "You think I'm here to talk you out of that piece of land."

"Crossed my mind."

She laughed. "If that's what you want, fine with me."

"Why?"

"My job is to make it work, whatever it is."

"Just like that?"

"Just like that. I'll let others worry about details."

"Why bring me here?"

"Thought you'd enjoy it." She reached into her pack. From the largest pocket she pulled a roll of plastic and a broken-down set of fiberglass poles. "And thought you might need a reminder. You take your cue from me when it's time to start throwing around influence. It's not the Director you worry about. Other names are more important."

"Whoever you say."

She assembled the poles, rolled out the plastic, and proceeded to fashion it all into a dome.

He watched, looking quite curious.

She formed a flap for a door, and flipped it open. She turned and flashed him a smile.

He looked confused.

She picked up a limb, jammed it against a rock, and pushed

it away from the fire, then lifted an edge of the tent, and set it over the rock.

"What the hell are you doing?"

She unbuttoned her shirt, took it off, and tossed it on her pack. "Sweat lodge. Wanna join me?"

He grinned, stood, and took off his shirt.

"No touching the merchandise by the way. This is like church. Thomas says sweat lodge is a place for purification." She finished stripping. Naked, she smiled. "Ready?"

"I don't think Indians do sweat lodges in the buff. And, I'm not sure men and women share the same sweat lodge."

"Really? You knew that?"

"Heard it somewhere."

She giggled. "Yeah, me, too."

— · —

Lying on rock, under the moon, they stared out over the canyon. The night grew cool and Erika reached back, grabbed her sleeping bag, and yanked it out of its stuff stack. She covered them both.

"So, what do you want to do over there?" she asked.

He ran a finger down her back. "Don't know. Maybe a big house. Maybe a hotel, or an eco-tourism something or other. Maybe a world class museum."

"You don't know? Really?"

"Really. No final plans. Nice merchandise, by the way."

"You realize, I'm under heat-related duress." She ran a hand down his arm. "Otherwise, you'd be slapped." She sighed, and relaxed. "If you don't have plans, why cause such trouble with this land exchange?"

"You know, this would make quite the attraction. Come stay at my eco-tourism something or other, or my world class museum, and while here, take a hike, learn secret Indian mysteries. That'd bring 'em in."

"Be serious. Why so much trouble?"

"I am serious. For one thing, I'm tired of my other place. I need a change. There's nothing out there but desert."

"You're not kidding."

"No. What's wrong with that?"

"Mike, what you're seeking will cause a great deal of controversy. If not immediately, at some point in time. There's no guarantee it'll work."

"Is that so?"

"I'm surprised you haven't thought of that."

"Did I say I haven't? But that's your worry, not mine." He took hold of her bare shoulders and kneaded into the muscle. "Think Linda learned anything from Thomas?"

She let her shoulders melt into his hands. "Don't know. Jack's working on that."

"Hmm."

"Where were you considering before I suggested you change your approach?"

He pointed into the darkness. "Over that way. Just outside the park."

"In the national monument?"

"I think so."

"Is that your fallback if Jack gets something substantial?"

He chuckled to himself. "Just between you and me?"

"Sure."

He ran his hand down her side, letting his fingers linger over her ribs. "It won't matter."

She found his eyes. "What are you saying?"

"It'll make no difference."

"So, you'll push for that piece of land, no matter what Thomas says?"

"You agreed it was between you and me."

She laughed. "You're such an ass. Why'd you say you'd listen to his reason?"

"Hell, I want to know. Should be interesting. One should know everything they can about their future home."

Linda Showalter's hastily written rebuttal appeared in the Sunday *Gazette*.

> *Comments made by someone calling themself Fearfully Anonymous were brought to my attention. They are complete fabrication. We've had no discussions of any kind similar to what were described. I have no clue what this person's motives are. We have no grand plans to take control of anything, and we have no plans to seize property, especially Mike Middleton's. He's too important a partner, and we would never consider doing such a thing.*
>
> *Signed,*
>
> *Linda Showalter, Acting Superintendent,*
> *Piedras Coloradas National Park*

Within hours of the *Gazette's* delivery to subscribers throughout Las Piedras, 'Fearfully Anonymous' posted more online comments:

> I didn't expect her to invite us down to her office,
> but she could at least admit they've been caught.
> She could admit to government lies. We deserve

the truth, as citizens and taxpayers. But what do you expect? She's paid to keep things secret, for as long as possible. It's time to push back. It's time to rid ourselves of the national monument.

And I also learned something else today. The fire on the west desert was started by the secret government team deciding which private lands to seize. They started the fire by accident, and had to ditch the pickup. Few people know who is part of this secret operation, but they're living among us. The Pistol Creek Fire—the one on the plateau we smell smoke from each morning—was allowed to burn to limit reaction to the burned pickup. Hundreds of firefighters would've led to nagging questions about the pickup and who caused the fire. But, while the fire burns on the plateau, keeping an eye on it became a convenient excuse to pay overtime. Our tax dollars at work.

'All Is Not Ducky' was ready to pile on:

I knew it. I knew there was something fishy going on. What have I been saying? Keep your eyes open people. The government is probably reading this now, but if enough of us are watching, maybe we can stop this abomination.

—— · ——

MONDAY MORNING

Jack pulled into headquarters, just as Linda Showalter was getting out of her car. She waited while he parked.

"Come to my office," she said.

He followed her in.

Molly met them in the hall. "You gotta see this."

"Something in the paper?" Linda asked.

"Kinda. Another online post from our friend, Fearfully Anonymous." She led them past the counter and over to the computer. The comment was on the screen.

They read.

"No one's gonna believe that?" Linda said, tapping on the passage about the secret government team. "Why would they be on public land if their purpose is scoping out private lands to seize?"

"Don't write this person off," Jack said, eyes on the screen, studying the writing for anything unusual. "There are people who believe these things. Some have explanations for anything."

"Where are we on investigating that burned pickup?"

"I can check."

"Do that. Then come to my office." She left.

Jack refilled his coffee and went down the hall to the Chief Ranger's office. Barb Sharp was leaning over her knees, brushing dust off her shoes.

"Morning Barb," Jack said, standing at her door. "Has Luiz learned anything about that burned-out pickup?"

"Morning." She sat up. "He has leads, but they're taking time to work. This one's strange. More to it than meets the eye. Seems carefully staged to confuse, maybe even suggest something."

"Go online. Read the comments after Linda's letter."

"Something related to this?"

"Conspiracy theories."

She pulled it up and read. When finished, she shook her head. "I'll show this to Luiz."

— · —

Jack stuck his head in the Superintendent's office. "Talked to Barb. Luiz has something, but not much."

"Sit," Linda said.

He settled into a chair. "She's available if you want a briefing."

"I don't have time for that! What did you learn from Thomas?"

"Isn't the burning pickup rumor a bit more important at the moment?"

"What did you learn?"

"He still won't say. Something of his culture, not ours, and we have reasons established in our culture to tell Middleton no."

"He screwed up," Linda said angrily. "He's given me nothing to use in changing this outcome."

"I know it makes it harder, and as much as I want to know, he's right. We have the tools we need. Law, policy, and the public would go bonkers if they thought we were even thinking of handing over a piece of the park. Seems to me, the bigger worry is keeping the Coalition together."

"I don't need your ramblings. I need information. I've spent the weekend stewing this over, hoping you'd come up with something to make this easy. You failed me."

"I tried."

"You failed. Now, we're gonna see how good Middleton is at playing hardball."

"Can't we slow things down?"

"Too late for that. There's a conference call at ten, here. Now, go," she snapped.

He left.

— · —

Jack came back at ten. Erika sat waiting, legs crossed, in the chair near the wall.

"Come in," Linda muttered, not looking up, eyes on the speaker-phone set in the middle of the desk.

"Who's that?" said someone on the line.

"Jack Chastain," Linda said.

"Good morning, Jack," the voice said.

"Morning," he said, then whispered, "Who's that?"

"Regional Director."

"Been a couple a years," Nick Saunders said. "Montana, I think."

"Yeah."

"Let's get started," Linda said. "Nick, we need your support."

"What kind of support?" he said, sounding clueless.

"Protection. Your backing," she said, eyes locked on the speaker-phone. "Things may be about to get ugly."

"What are you telling me?"

"I'd hoped things would be different." Linda looked across the table at Jack. "But, information I need is not forthcoming. Mike Middleton has to be told no. He can't have what he wants."

"Whoa," Saunders said. "Explain. What do you mean he can't have what he wants?"

"Middleton wants a piece of the park, smack dab in the canyon. I had him convinced to consider better options, but he gave us conditions. Insists the biggest opponent to his proposal give his reasons. Native American guy, and he ain't talking."

"Why not?"

Showalter glared at Jack. "You tell him."

"Thomas won't give his reason," Jack said. "Secret seems to have profound importance to their culture. I don't know what. I don't know why, but he won't say."

"Probably playing the sacred card," Saunders said. "Get him to understand the gravity of the situation. This is important."

"I'm sorry, Nick. We tried," Linda said, sounding resigned. "I wanted you to know before we tell Middleton. He's confident he'll roll us."

"I'm sure he can," Saunders said, under his breath, the wind coming out of his sail.

Quiet settled in as they exchanged glances.

"I have to tell him no, Nick," Linda said, breaking the silence. "He can't have what he wants. Plus, there's more." She looked around the table. "I'm still not convinced this is a big deal or not, but when we say no, the Coalition self-destructs. Their existence seems to hinge on the land exchange."

"Going to hell all over, isn't it?" Saunders responded. "Tell me what Middleton's threatening?"

"To go to the Director," Linda muttered. "I'm hoping you'll let the Director know our side of the story."

Nick sighed. "Not a good time, Linda."

"I know. It's never a good time to get rolled."

"No, it's bigger than that. I've been reluctant to share this, but there's something more going on. There are things building to a head. If Middleton goes to the Director, expect a bloodbath. Are you sure you can't fix this?"

"We tried."

A sigh bled over the speaker. "You gave it your best shot. With the three of you there, I thought we had a chance. I thought your leadership and combined abilities could turn this guy, get him focused on helping, doing the right thing."

"What are you not telling us, Nick? And, I thought the Director was involved in this."

"I didn't say that. I said he was watching. I've been keeping him in the loop, playing his game, only because I thought if Middleton was happy, the Director wouldn't be compelled to get involved. Is Erika still there?"

She leaned toward the speaker. "I'm here."

"Why are you not talking?"

"I'm listening. I have nothing to add."

"And this is your take on things?"

"I guess."

Another sigh. "I guess we have to change plans." He paused. "I'm worried about what'll happen. I'll try, but I'm afraid it'll be hard to protect the three of you."

They exchanged glances.

"Any idea what we're facing?" Showalter asked. "Wrath? Me sent back to Arizona?"

"If you're lucky. Who knows where you'll end up. This will be difficult."

Showalter gave Jack a hard glare.

"I may be the only one who can put up some kind of defense. It'll be hard," Saunders said. "I'll do what I can, but I'll need time to dig, look behind the scenes, see what the risks are, get a sense of how to control the damage, figure out who I need to protect you from."

"I promised Middleton I'd call him today," Linda said.

"Don't," Saunders said. "Give me time, a day, maybe two."

"We'll try," Linda said.

"You're sure this can't be fixed? You sure you can't put a bow on it?"

They exchanged glances. "We're sure," Linda said.

"Okay, give me some time. No talking about this, with anyone," Saunders said. After another long period of silence, he ended the call.

Linda Showalter reached over and hung up the phone. "Okay, we stall."

— · —

Numb, Jack staggered out of the building, hitting Luiz Archuleta with the door, knocking him against the wall.

"Careful, guy," Luiz said, collecting himself. "Where you going?"

"Somewhere."

"Where? I asked *where* you're going?"

"Anywhere. Doesn't matter."

"I need a ride. You can drop me out in the desert at that burned out pickup. Need to see if I missed anything. Not sure I want a government vehicle parked in the middle of nowhere, considering all the talk of secret government operations. Drop me off and pick me up in half an hour."

"Won't that look suspicious?"

"Only if someone sees us."

— · —

Jack stared down the road, jaw locked, mind on impending judgment and punishment. What goes around comes around, over and over.

Luiz seemed to know it best to stay quiet.

They neared the fire-scorched stretch of desert.

"Drop me near that culvert," Luiz said, pointing. "I'll hike in from there."

Jack glanced in the rear-view mirror, then up the road. No cars. He slowed, and stopped.

"See you in thirty." Luiz slipped out of the pickup and dropped into the drainage.

Jack accelerated, watching through the rear view mirror as Luiz slinked away from the road. Hope he knows what he's doing.

Jack reached highway speed. He eyed the desert scrub on the side of the road. Sage brush, four-wing saltbush, rabbit brush. Too bad life wasn't just about doing field work. Vegetation transects. Talking to the plants, seeing if they're healthy. Real work.

Thoughts repeated themselves. Montana, now this. The prospect of being plucked out of the park and sent to another, hidden away, put somewhere he couldn't do any damage. Again.

What could have been done differently? To get Thomas to open up. To help Linda Showalter work things out.

He checked his watch. Thirteen minutes. He watched for a road, keeping an eye out for other cars.

A dirt road came into view. He slowed, turned off the highway, flipped the vehicle around, and headed the other way. He turned his eye back to plants alongside the road. Same desert scrub, different angle to the shadows.

His cell phone rang.

Probably Showalter. He pulled the phone from his pocket and checked the number. He flipped it open. "Kip, what's up?"

"Can we talk sometime?"

"When?"

"Later. I've got men here to work some calves, but we need to talk."

"I'm out on the road. What if I drive up to your place, talk while you're working?"

"That'll do."

He flipped the phone closed.

Approaching the burn scar, he checked the mirror. No cars. He saw Luiz peeking out from the creek bed. He slowed.

Luiz climbed up to the road and jumped in.

"Find anything?"

"Confirmation, but nothing new."

"What're you looking for?"

"Anything. You better now?"

"Not much."

"At least you're talking."

"Mind if we take a detour? I need to go to Culberson Ranch."

— · —

They made the turn onto the ranch, followed the two-track around to the meadow, then downhill to the corrals. A pair of vehicles—a pickup and sedan—sat parked alongside the pole fence.

Kip stood at the head of a squeeze chute, attending a calf. Kip's hired hand, a man with coal black hair, named Benny Begay, stood on the back side of the chute, working on the calf that had Kip's attention. A man in a gray ball cap and blue western shirt pushed a pair of calves up the metal alley toward them. Another man, in a tan shirt, stood beside Kip, his back to the road.

Jack parked and exited the government pickup.

Kip looked around. "Jack," he said, in greeting.

The man nearest Kip spun around. It was Harper Teague. He raised a hand. "Give me a minute, please. I'm leaving."

"Hurry," Kip said to Teague, stepping back from the squeeze chute.

Jack rested against the pickup. Luiz leaned over the hood.

Teague's arms flew as he talked. Kip, eyes sunk deep in their sockets, nodded as he listened. After several minutes, Teague's movements ceased. Kip gave a maybe, maybe not nod of the head, and they shook hands. Teague turned and walked past the government truck, eyes to the ground. He got into the sedan and drove away.

"Had no idea he'd show up," Kip said, waving them over. "Teague's embarrassed. Something that Fearfully Anonymous person said. He doesn't realize it, but it didn't hurt him any. Not with some people. Especially those who want us to fail. Anyway, sorry Jack."

"That's okay"

"That's Sacramento," Kip said, pointing to the man in the chute. "He works at a ranch down the road. He's giving us a hand."

Jack gave him a wave. "Kip, remember Luiz Archuleta."

"I do," Kip said. They shook hands.

"I'll let you two talk," Luiz said, backing away.

"I'm gonna keep working these little guys," Kip said, as he filled a hypodermic needle. He gave the shot. "This one's done," he said to Benny. Benny released the head catch and the gate swung open. The calf bolted out. In an adjoining pen, fifty to eighty calves waited, their mothers down the hill, bellowing for their babies.

Sacramento pushed another calf up the alley.

"Things aren't good," Kip said.

"Worried about Teague?"

"He's the least of our worries." Kip picked up a plier-like tool and clicked an ear tag into place. "His story's more complex than I'd first thought. Might not be a bad guy, just jaded, bitter about past history."

"You worried about Middleton?"

"No. That Fearfully Anonymous person . . . and Thomas." Kip grabbed an ear on the calf, set the pliers and squeezed, affixing the tag. He stepped back as Benny put on a brand, and smoke and the smell of burnt hair wafted past. "Thomas saying no without a reason makes it hard to find a solution. That's a problem." He gave the calf its shot, opened the head catch, and released it. "The Coalition's strained. We're in a tough place. I'm gonna talk to Thomas, try to get him to open up and talk to Middleton. I think you should, too."

Jack nodded. "You haven't talked to Kelly about this, have you?"

"No. Why?"

"Never mind."

A gust of wind pelted them with dust. Kip turned his back.

"Viento fuerte," Sacramento shouted, in the direction of Luiz.

Jack turned, and caught sight of Luiz on one knee, head down, looking at something, shielding his eyes.

"¿Que?" Luiz said, after cupping an ear.

"Mucho viento."

He nodded.

"You okay?" Jack shouted.

Luiz stood. "Yeah."

Jack turned back to Kip.

"The main reason I wanted to talk is this Fearfully Anonymous person, whoever it is." Kip stepped back from the chute. "What he's doing is making it difficult to be associated with the Coalition. Things he says suggest he's an insider, or someone who knows an insider, but we can't prove he's not. He's making it plumb uncomfortable for some of us."

"You?"

"Hell, no."

"Just through those posts?"

"They have a life of their own. People are talking. Bev Johnson called. She's getting pressure to back out."

"What do you need from me?"

"Don't know. I'm worried. Been thinking about this a lot. You government people have to be smart. Don't do anything stupid that'll play into that Fearfully Anonymous person's hands."

"He's making things up. He doesn't need anything stupid from us."

"I know, but people jump on those things, then they come around. They'll come to see it as hogwash, unless you give 'em something that validates suspicion. That's what this is about. He's creating then preying on uncertainty and suspicion."

"Kip, what happens if we say no to the Middleton land exchange? What if we say he wants too much?"

"Could split us apart."

"What happens if it goes political, say, to the Director's office?"

"People love having the heavy weights involved, until they don't, when it feels like local influence is slipping away."

Jack kicked at the dirt.

"If the Coalition fails, we're back where we were a year ago," Kip said, "fighting over the existence of the national monument."

Jack sighed. "Understood." He backed away. "Guess I better go. See ya later."

Jack and Luiz walked to the pickup and climbed inside.

"Well, that doesn't make things any easier," Jack said.

"How's that?"

"Oh, nothing." He put the keys in the ignition and started the truck. "What was Sacramento saying?"

"He said it's windy."

"Well, that's obvious."

Luiz tapped a fist on the dash. "And unfortunate."

CHAPTER
34

Jack lay awake, eyes on the black silhouettes of canyon walls. Words played through his thoughts. Various scenarios were gamed and options tried, all to different effect. Each resulted in haunting admonition from Kelly, and ended in the worst possible way—Jack having to tell her good-bye.

—·—

In another part of the canyon, Linda Showalter stared at the same walls. The scenarios played out, and none of them seemed fair.

—·—

Jack came in the building, bleary eyed. He walked passed dispatch, and Molly hollered for him to come look at the latest midnight posts. "Show me later," he said, continuing down the hall.

He peeked in an office and saw Erika at her desk. He knocked. She wheeled around, and gave him a quizzical look.

"Can we talk? About ways to fix things."

"Not a good time, Jack. I've got to go. Got a commitment." She gave him a second look. "It's too late to fix things. And once again, you're taking me down with you."

"I'm not trying to take you down."

"But you are, aren't you? Who knows where I'll end up this time. I need to start hanging out with a better class of people." She gave a flippant shrug. "All because you couldn't find out what Thomas is hiding. Not a big job, but you couldn't do it, and frankly, I don't think there's anything there. I was there, remember. We're toast, over virtually nothing."

"Neither you nor I knew what we were looking for."

"I wasn't looking. I was there for a good time, remember? If I count swapping a little sweat, maybe I got one. I'm not convinced I did." She stood and walked him to the door. "Out. I gotta go."

"When can we talk?"

"Too late. We're toast. But I tell you what. I bought a nice merlot. Thought I'd see if Kelly wanted to join me down at the creek. You should come take a dip. We can talk then."

"I'm serious."

"Me too." She raised a hand. "You'd have a good time. I promise you would." She laughed, stepped back to the desk, and grabbed a pad of paper. "Give this to Kelly." She scrawled a note and passed it to him. "Gotta go."

— · —

Erika Jones sat in the cell phone waiting area at Albuquerque International Airport. Killing time, her mind wandered across the stock set of accoutrements. The vehicle—with government plates but no ranger markings—was stark, but the only one not in use when she left the park.

Her cell phone rang. She answered.

"I'm here."

"Pick you up at the curb." She ended the call, started the car and pulled out of the lot. She approached the terminal.

A dark-haired, dark-eyed man appeared, walking out, pulling his carry-on. Nick Saunders stopped at the curb and faced the incoming traffic. Not a hair was out of place. His black blazer and collared shirt looked crisp.

Erika stopped beside him and put the car in park. She jumped out and opened the trunk. He threw in his suitcase and got into the passenger seat.

"Nick, why are you here?" she asked, putting the car in gear.

"You know why."

"You're not changing plans, are you?"

"No. We need to get things moving."

She flashed a look in the side mirror and pulled into traffic. "On the call yesterday, you said you needed time to control damage. Why aren't you doing that?"

"This is where I can control the damage."

"Because Middleton's here?"

"That's right. That's why I need your help."

"Have you told Linda yet about the Congressman and his connections to Middleton?"

"Not yet."

"You mean she doesn't know what you're working on?"

"Not entirely. We're at a particularly sensitive time. I'm hearing rumors people are about to get hurt. Director's on a war path. The less she knows the better. Might protect her."

"I see. Actually I don't."

"You'll have to trust me," Nick said. "Until I understand her, it's best to limit what she knows. The Director's only actions of late are political. I think they make him vulnerable, but they also make him dangerous."

"Yesterday you asked for time. To do what?"

"To put a bow on things. We can't have Middleton going to the Director before Congressman Hoff gets back in the country. If Linda tells Middleton no, and he turns to the Director for favors, we're sunk. The agency's sunk." He pulled out his Blackberry. "Now, what can we make happen today?"

"We could see if Mike's available for a late lunch. We could let him know where his support comes from. It'd take some skill. We'd need to do it in a way that makes him beholden to you, even though he's more than willing to go to the Director to pull strings."

"You're confident you can make that distinction stick?"

"Yes. From the way he talks, I believe Mike's more enamored by his ability to exert his influence than loyal to any depth of connection to the Director. He knows he can get things done through the Director, but today we'll show him where his loyalties need to lie."

"Good." He turned his eyes to the highway heading north. "Legislation. Where are we?"

"I'm working a contact on Congressman Hoff's staff."

"Perfect."

"Underscores how well you work with his people."

"Good thinking." He nodded. "Anything to be concerned about?"

"A simple point of order by anyone in the Congress gets the whole thing pulled, but that won't happen. They'll never see it till it's signed."

"You're gonna make a great chief of staff."

"Chief of staff?" She laughed. "There's one other thing. A meeting tonight in town. Coalition's monthly meeting to reach as many people as they can."

"Why didn't this come up in the conference call yesterday?"

"Not sure. Jack runs the meetings. If things miraculously fall into place, and if somehow we could convince Linda to make an announcement, you'd be in a good place with the Congressman. Convincing her will be the difficulty. We'll never get there."

"I've got a plan," he said. "Plus I'm her boss. And I'm serious when I say, we need to start thinking about some kind of event. A photo op for me and the Congressman."

"Nick, it's a little early to be calling his scheduler."

"Yeah, but the call to Hoff might be closer than you think."

— · —

Erika Jones approached the hostess, Nick Saunders step for step behind her. "We're meeting Mike Middleton for lunch."

"He's waiting. Right this way." She led them to the table.

Middleton, in chinos and red sweater, stood as they approached. "You're not in uniform."

"Not today, no." She raised an arm to present the man beside her. "Mike, this is Nick Saunders, Regional Director." She watched their eyes.

He reached across the table and shook Saunders' hand. "Pleased to meet you, Nick. Where do you work?"

"Denver. The regional office. As Erika noted, Mike, I'm Regional Director," he said, exuding confidence. "You and I have mutual friends. I'm here to keep things on track, and to thank you for contributions to the cause." He leaned over the table. "I thought it important you know your efforts have the attention of the highest levels of the agency."

"You're saying you're a big wheel in the machinery."

"I guess you could say I'm a big enough wheel."

Erika studied the expressions. Good enough. Time to do it. "Mike," she said, pulling their attention back to her. "Remember I said someone was helping you, and at the right time I'd make sure you were introduced?"

"I remember."

"This is that introduction. Nick is the force, moving things forward."

"Well, thank you Nick, but things aren't exactly settled. We don't have an agreement."

"I'm here to fix that. What can I do to keep the trains running on time?"

"There's the matter of what land I get in return. There's the piece I want, the suggestion by the Superintendent that I can't have it, and the conditions I put on negotiations."

"I know all that," Nick said. He flashed a look at Erika. "Mike, the discussion today does not need to be all that complicated."

"What are you saying?"

"If you had my assurance you can have the piece of land you want, regardless of what's said and done by others in the agency, would you be satisfied?"

Middleton smiled. "You mean, whatever Linda Showalter suggests, just play along?"

"I suppose. Erika can work through the details, but I also think an announcement of some kind, maybe even tonight, might be in everyone's best interest."

"Agreed."

Erika pulled out her cell phone and punched in a number. She smiled as she waited for the call to be answered. "Margie, this is Erika. I need to schedule a meeting. With Linda. In one hour."

— · —

Jack plodded into headquarters, having had a late lunch.

Margie met him in the hall. "Linda sent me to find you. You're needed in the conference room."

"Now?"

He followed, stepping into a room full of faces. Linda Showalter, Mike Middleton, Erika Jones and Nick Saunders.

"What's up?"

Saunders rose and extended a hand. Jack shook it.

"Sit," Linda said, from the head of the table, pointing Jack to a chair.

He sat.

"Jack, the Regional Director has surprised us with his presence, but he managed to convince Mike to change his tune. He's dropping his insistence that Thomas tell his secret. He's willing to negotiate what land he gets in return at a later date."

"Really?" Jack muttered. "That's good . . . I guess. I mean, it is, it's good."

"Seems he's ready to announce tonight at the meeting." She leaned toward Jack. "This has to be done right, very right."

"What has to be done right?" Jack asked.

"Our announcement, committing to a land exchange. Jack, my suggestion is, first, before anything else, let them know we've come to an agreement. Don't go into detail. Let Mike do the talking. Then, when he's finished, you emphasize the benefits."

"Good plan," Saunders interjected. "Do that."

Jack looked around the table. "Remember, this isn't our meeting, it's the Coalition's. They may wish to discuss things first. I don't control what's said and done."

"Of course you control it. You're facilitating," Linda said.

He gave a shrug.

Showalter looked around the table, then set her eyes on Middleton. "Know what to say?"

"Yes, Erika coached me. If I'm asked which lands I receive in the swap, I say we'll negotiate it later."

"Very good."

"What if that's not enough?" Jack asked, without much thought.

"We control the message, they don't," Middleton said. "We don't have details to offer. That'll be my talking point. Control the message . . . I'm surprised you don't know that."

What's going on? "I don't do, control the message. I don't ignore people. I don't steer them only to the answer someone wants them to hear, whether it's correct or not."

"Well . . . that's how it's done."

"Not if it's misleading, lying, or both." Jack stared in disbelief. "So, Mike, what will you want? What will you press for, once you have the leverage?"

Middleton smiled. "We'll negotiate that later. We don't have other details to offer."

"Why are you making this difficult?" Linda said to Jack, angrily. "Fix the Coalition's issue. Give 'em what they want."

"I'm not trying to be difficult, but this won't be easy. For one, it'll require legislation, and two, a public purpose. Something like this takes time."

"Erika's working on all that," Saunders said.

Erika looked at Linda, then Jack. "My contacts believe we can take advantage of committee votes already on the calendar. Legislation could be said and done as early as this week."

Jack's eyes grew wide.

"Good," Linda said. She turned back to Jack. "Resolving a Coalition issue constitutes a public purpose, agreed?"

Jack rubbed his eyes. "I'm confused by this sudden change. Why has this happened?"

"Out of the goodness of my heart," Middleton said.

"Jack, you're the one who wants to keep the Coalition from falling apart," Linda said, incredulously. "Be a good soldier. Turn the meeting over to Mike. He'll make his own announcement. Never mind speaking to the positives. I'll do that. Then, you start into other business." She stared hard. "If you don't do it that way, I'll fire your ass."

He stared back. "But . . ."

"Got that?" She gave a hard nod and turned to Saunders. "Sorry you had to hear that, Nick."

"Not a problem. These moments happen, even with the best of employees," he said, looking Jack in the eye. He turned to Showalter. "May we talk a bit about an event of some kind, an opportunity to give this the positive attention it deserves, when the time's right?"

"Sure."

"Knock, knock."

They turned to the voice in the hall. Margie stood in the door. "Sorry. Just got off a call. Thought you'd wanna hear this."

"Go ahead," Linda muttered.

"The Director's office called. He's flying into New Mexico, as we speak. He's got meetings tonight in Santa Fe, another in Sand Dunes late tomorrow night. He asked his staff to touch base, see if he could drop in for a short visit tomorrow afternoon."

Middleton's eyes lit up. Jack watched confusion take hold of Linda, then Erika. Saunders' expression went cold.

"Uh, . . . of course he can," Linda said, looking bewildered. "I wonder what's on his mind."

"Maybe me," Middleton said. "Might be a social call. May I join you?"

"I don't think so," Linda said, eyes on no one thing. "Sounds like business."

"I could let him know how pleased I am with how well things are working."

Jack watched closely as Linda shook her head, seemingly confused. "All we need to know is the time. Thank you, Margie." She turned back to Saunders.

His eyes were on his Blackberry.

"Nick," Linda said. "You were saying?"

"Never mind. Not important. It's nothing we can decide today."

"Okay, we're done," Linda said. "See everyone tonight in town. Meeting's at seven."

Jack stood and waited as they moved into the hall.

Linda turned back. "Wanting me?"

"Yes."

"Can it wait?"

"There's something strange about this turn of events. Anything you're not sharing?"

"No." She put her hands on her hips. "I'm trying to keep the right things on track, and the bad things from happening." She glanced at the hall. "Mike is not getting what he wants most," she whispered.

"Why this sudden change of heart? And now the Director coming."

"Jack, you're paranoid. The Coalition's more your concern than mine. Save 'em. If you don't, you're shooting yourself in the foot. Your paranoia will do yourself more damage than it'll ever help anyone else. This helps. It's that simple."

"But what about Thomas?"

"Thomas is lucky. He dodged a bullet. This outcome protects his secret."

"You believe that?"

"Jack, you can't survive just trying to be relevant. You've got to go out and change the world, or you become irrelevant."

"Linda, look at the leverage this gives Middleton. Imagine what could happen. It could force a backroom deal that sounds like something cooked up by Fearfully Anonymous. What would that do to our reputations?"

"Jack, this saves our reputations. We, too, dodged a bullet. We were cooked, our reputations good as trashed. Me, for what I had to do. You, for not being able to get a simple answer." She let the thought settle in. "You can't ignore someone with Middleton's influence. You can't help someone like Thomas if he won't help himself. Thomas is more the enemy than Mike. Thomas would've let the Coalition crash and burn. Mike isn't."

"Thomas is not the enemy. This is complicated. If Middleton is that influential, he can take care of himself. But Thomas and the pueblo . . . we can't turn our back just because we don't yet know what they need us to protect." He studied her eyes. "I respect your willingness to take a stand, but . . . Wait, this is about you, isn't it?"

"No, it's not. This is a disaster averted."

He leaned against the wall. "After you get your ticket punched and you move on to that next big job—maybe Washington—what will you do when the black and white turns grey?"

"This isn't about that, but I've trained for that day. I'm ready. I can handle it."

"When people here in the field do things hard to defend— things that could become precedent and harm other parks—what will you do?"

"I'll tell them to stop."

"But if things blow up here, do you really think they'll listen, knowing your fingerprints are all over it?"

"Get out."

"Maybe this is a little world, but people here don't think it's little. Saving this world is important, too."

"Go to your office, close the door, and scream that I'm a bitch. Get it out of your system, because you know this has to be done. If it isn't, everything you've worked for falls apart, and you'll be to blame."

—·—

Jack closed his door and leaned against it. Maybe she's right.

— · —

Linda Showalter sat and pulled in a long breath. That was rough.

Margie knocked at the door. "Regional Director to see you." She backed away as Saunders moved past and sat.

"Need a place to make some phone calls, Nick?"

"No, I saw a couple of empty desks. I wanted to talk about tomorrow."

"You mean the Director's visit?"

"Yeah. Until this exchange is a little further along, it might be best not to bring the Director into this discussion."

"I know, but we can't keep it from him."

"It'd be best to wrap it up, give him the complete package. If you can't give him that, he'll think he needs to get involved. Then, you look bad, and you'll find yourself back in your old job."

They finished and she watched him wander back into the hall in search of a phone.

She crossed her arms and sat back in her chair.

That was strange.

— · —

Linda Showalter put on her Stetson, picked up her briefcase and walked out, closing the door behind her. She slowly walked the hall, feeling the effects of a long day. It wasn't over yet.

The dispatch office door stood open. She stuck her head inside. "Night, Molly."

"Night, Linda."

"I didn't think to ask earlier . . . Our friend, Fearfully Anonymous. Any peep today?"

"Yeah, this afternoon. Not much. Rather cryptic. All the post said was, 'for those going to the Coalition meeting tonight, expect a surprise.'"

How the hell did he know that?

Jack arrived thirty minutes early and found a quiet corner.

He made a quick count of people lingering about, expecting a slightly larger crowd than a typical meeting. A fair number already. But that's what these evening sessions are for, to give others a chance to catch up on progress to date, even if evenings were inconvenient for some of the regular contributors to the Coalition.

He breathed deeply, and worked to clear his mind. The day crept back.

What game was Middleton playing? Was he playing straight?

What will Kip say? Good—for keeping the Coalition from falling apart. Or, that it has the smell of a government back room deal?

But maybe this was good for Thomas. Maybe Linda was right.

He looked again at the gathering crowd. Unusually large for this early. Hotel staff were already adding rows of chairs at the back of the room.

Linda Showalter came through the door. He watched for Saunders, Jones and Middleton, but there was no sign of them as she moved quickly toward his corner. She stopped inches away and stooped over him. "Who have you been talking to?" she whispered angrily.

"What are you talking about?"

"Have you leaked what's happening tonight?"

"No. Why?"

"Fearfully Anonymous. His latest post said expect a surprise."

He glanced around. Who is this guy? "I didn't see it."

"You haven't talked to anyone?"

"I haven't."

She stood and eyed the crowd, rubbing her forehead.

The others sauntered in, Nick Saunders in the lead.

Linda waited for them to circle. "See the latest post from our online friend?"

They exchanged blank stares.

"It said expect a surprise tonight," Showalter said.

Middleton shrugged. "Good."

"That doesn't bother you?"

"Someone might've heard me talking. No big deal. Let's give 'em something to celebrate."

"You're not worried about this?"

"Should we be?" Saunders asked.

She sighed and raised her eyes to the ceiling. "Maybe not. Maybe I'm thinking too hard." She turned to Jack. "Just let Mike have the floor as soon as possible. Get this over with."

More regular attendees straggled in, taking places around the table. Jack moved forward and took a seat. He nodded to Ginger Perrette, then Dave Van Buren, a greeting Dave returned as he feebly messed with a note pad. Bev Johnson avoided eye contact. Jack checked the others. Enviros in force. Everyone else as well.

Kip Culberson and Karen Hatcher came in, talking. They stopped at the back of the room, gave it a look, shared a few more words, separated, and took seats across the table from each other.

The last of the regulars arrived, some shooting sheepish looks.

Middleton finished working the room and moved to the table. He pulled folded papers from his blazer pocket, and laid them out.

Linda Showalter and Erika Jones took seats on the first row at the back of the room, and settled in to wait. The other chairs on the row filled around them. Nick Saunders finished shaking hands, then made do with a seat on the back row.

Harper Teague entered at two till seven. He walked quickly to the table and claimed a remaining seat.

At seven, Jack stood. "Let's get started." He turned to Mike Middleton. He opened his mouth to speak but stopped. No, not gonna do that. He turned to Culberson. "Kip, I'll let you go over the agenda," he said, then realized he forgot the formalities. "Oh, and I'll let you give the welcome. I forgot."

Kip laughed.

Thomas came quickly in, made his way to the table, and quietly slid into a seat.

"Welcome everyone," Kip said, boisterously. "Thank you for coming. This is an important effort. It's got us working together, finding common ground, working through tough issues, and working hand in hand with federal agencies to preserve some things we all value." He turned to Jack. "How's that?"

Jack smiled. "Very good, thanks." He scanned the eyes in the audience. "This is your meeting. You decide what you want to talk about. Kip, go ahead with your agenda." He glanced at Showalter.

She had her palms open, flashing a bug-eyed, questioning look. She pointed at Middleton.

Jack looked away.

Kip put on reading glasses, picked a page off the table, and held it at reading distance. He cleared his throat. "First item on our agenda, the report on old business. We've got . . ."

Showalter stood. "Excuse me, Mr. Culberson. Jack apparently forgot to mention this, but I'd asked him to let Mr. Middleton make an announcement before anything gets started. Do you mind?"

Kip turned to Jack, looking over the tops of his glasses. He raised a brow.

Thomas lifted a hand. "Is this is about a land exchange? If it is, . . ."

Harper Teague jumped in. "Hell no. People are tired of that bullshit. If you've read the paper, you know people are talking, and it's not about what Middleton has to say. We're better off spending our time talking about how to put an end to this charade."

"Watch your mouth, Harper," Kip said. "I'll have you escorted out of here."

"Excuse me, Mr. Teague," Showalter said. "I have the floor."

"I don't know why that Fearfully Anonymous gave me a hard time," Teague continued. "I'm doing what they're afraid to do, and I'm not afraid to do it." He paused momentarily. "You've seen the papers. You've seen the expressions of distrust. Let's quit the charades and call the Coalition a failure. There are people here tonight, not to play this little game, but to help put it out of our misery." He turned to the back. "Am I right?"

Loud words—yeses, yeahs, and damned straight—came grumbling out of the front rows.

Jack looked for Showalter. She appeared startled by those around her. Saunders—where's he? Back row, shoulders hunched, head down.

"I don't care what's been said in the papers," Kip said. "This is an honest effort. All that misinformation in the paper, that's just what it is, misinformation. Now, sit down." He turned to Showalter. "You, too. If you want something on the agenda, we'll put it there, but everything in its turn."

Wide-eyed, she slowly sat.

Teague remained standing.

"Take your seat or leave. We don't need the disruption."

Teague stood his ground.

"Harper, take your seat. We want to get started. I'm ready to turn the meeting over to Jack and you're holding us up."

Teague put his hands on his hips. "You see, that's the problem. You turn it over to him, he'll turn it over to that woman in the back, and it's obvious they have a plan they've cooked up that we're not gonna like."

Culberson stared him down.

"Kip, here's an offer. Kick the government lackeys out of the room, and I'll sit down and play nice."

"Hell no," Kip shouted. "Not all of us have had the experiences you have. Be patient."

Jack stood. "Kip, let me have this." He turned to Teague. "I've asked before if this group wanted me to excuse myself, to bow out. I can do that again. I'm more than willing to leave and let you conduct the meeting yourselves. No big deal."

He looked around the room. All eyes stared back. He caught movement in the front row.

Showalter glared, slowly shaking her head. She mouthed, "No."

He turned to the table, ignoring her.

"Do I recuse myself?" Jack asked.

"Hell, yes," Teague said, still standing. "Bev?"

Bev Johnson looked up. "Might be good. No offense, but I need to prove to some people that we're thinking for ourselves."

"Understood," Jack said.

"He's not manipulating us," Kip said. "He's conducting the meeting, working with us."

"It's okay," Jack said.

"But some people are saying he could be a puppet to the government," Bev said. "What do we know about what the government really intends to do? Jack's a nice enough guy, but how do we know he's not just doing what Linda Showalter wants, helping her carry out some big government plan?" She glanced at Showalter. "No offense."

Showalter, looking shaken, said, "Uh . . . uh . . . none taken."

"Good," Bev said. "Still, if Harper's right, it might be safer to have the discussion without the perceived specter of big government manipulating our work."

"Damned right," Teague growled. "Who else? Dan?"

Daniel Romero crossed his arms. "Let's play it safe. Let's work things out on our own. Mr. Teague pointed out some things that concern me, worry me actually. Let's come up with recommendations without risking the appearance of interference, or real interference that we don't see or understand. Things we might accept but not intend."

Karen Hatcher waved for the floor. Jack acknowledged her.

"I'm not afraid of what may come of this with or without you here," she said to Jack, and then faced the others. "But, I have to stand up for Jack. He's done nothing to erode our trust. I don't see why we're doing this."

"It's alright, I understand, but thanks, Karen," Jack said. "Who's next?"

"Me," Teague said. "I have a motion. I move that we vote."

"Is there a second?" Jack asked.

"I say we proceed with the agenda," Mike Middleton interjected. "We have more important things to cover."

"Yeah, you'd think that," Teague said. "That's because you've got 'em in your pocket. Is there a second?" He scanned the table. "Just think what opportunities we'll have with the freedom of no government interference."

Bev raised her hand. "I guess I second it."

"So, discussion, or do we have a vote on a vote?" Jack asked.

"Vote," Teague said.

"All in favor."

Hands raised, some coming up slowly.

"The motion passes. We'll take a vote on whether I leave or stay."

Teague smirked, nodding smug approval.

"Okay, how should we do this?" Jack asked.

"Go around the table," Teague said. "Let's make it painful."

Jack shrugged, and caught site of the whites of Showalter's eyes. She sat on the edge of her seat. "Let's go around the table. Bev? Leave or stay?"

"No offense. Leave."

"Karen?"

"Stay."

Two 'leaves' followed by Mike Middleton's 'stay.' Ginger Perrette's 'leave' followed by Dave Van Buren's 'stay.' Two 'leaves' and Kip's 'stay.'

Jack gestured to the corner, to Thomas. "Leave or stay?"

Slowly, he looked up. "Stay."

"Hold it," Teague shouted. "Why? You should be lined up with me. I'm your best shot at stopping anything Middleton wants to do."

"I know that."

"Are you blind? He'll promise them something. They'll suck up to him, make backroom deals, give him anything he wants."

"I can fight my own battles. I'll take my chances."

"I'm your ally. I don't care what your reasons are."

Thomas glanced at Jack.

"It's okay," Jack said, "Do what you have to do."

Thomas slowly shook his head. "I vote stay."

Teague raised his hands in frustration. "I'm trying to help you man. Open your eyes. Take back your government."

"There is much you say, Mr. Teague, that I do not understand. You have many words. You tell many stories. Stories, I've been taught, do not exist in isolation from the lives of the people who tell them. There are cultural contexts for stories. Your stories confuse me. I've been taught that if I'm unaware of how a story is used, then I'm likely to misunderstand it."

"What're you talking about?"

"I'm saying there's danger in listening to you. You don't tell us your true intention."

He shook his head "These guys can't be trusted."

"Stop," Thomas shouted. "I don't want to hear your words. I have more reason not to trust them than you. You offer no reason, only ideology. You offer no truth. Only images of enemies, created to manipulate us."

"My bad experiences speak for themselves. What the hell are you talking about?"

"I'm not concerned with your experiences. I am concerned about your motives. Your stories hide what those motives are, and I can't help but wonder if you don't have more influence than the rest of us combined. I might be able to prove that, if I only knew what you were up to."

Teague looked over at Jack. "Move on. Next person."

Thomas shook his head. "No, I have more to say."

Jack smiled. "You can't have it both ways, Mr. Teague. Go ahead, Thomas."

"Fear is your tool. You attempt to control us by making us afraid. You make us fear things we should trust, and you use that fear to make us do things not in our own best interest.

"You hide behind ideology. Your stories make ideology seem more important than truth. You have an agenda, but your stories never tell us what that agenda is. You talk of evil plans, but you don't talk of the plans that are yours."

"Are you finished," Teague growled.

"No," he said. "I fear government, but because of people like you. You place yourself above the rest of us. For you, the end justifies the means. You prey on the fact that most of us don't think that way. You convince us of peril in not believing. But I'm not afraid, except of you. I want Jack Chastain here, to assure each of us is heard."

"Whatever. What's the vote count?" Teague asked, exasperated.

"Your motion is up by one vote," Jack said.

Romero raised a hand. "I'd like to change my vote."

Another hand shot up. "Me too."

"Hold it," Teague shouted. "Don't have misplaced sympathies just because he's Indian. I'm trying to help you people." He looked around the table. "That was a lot of jibber-jabber about stories, but all you get from me is straight talk—cold, hard realities—not stories. Other than telling how my family lost everything to the feds, not far from here, no stories, not from me."

"I don't believe you're from anywhere near here," Thomas said. "It feels like everything you do is part of a complicated plan. I just don't know what that plan is. Here's what I do know. The stories were yours. Stories of burned pickups and secret government plans. The words were lies and they were yours. You burned the pickup. I don't know why, but you did. You are not fearful, and you are not anonymous. Not anymore. It was you."

Teague's eyes flashed about the room.

Jack crossed his arms. He checked the others, getting a nod from Romero. "I guess the motion fails." He glanced at Showalter, who glared back.

Teague stormed out.

Through a window, he could be seen climbing into a sedan, throwing it in gear, and racing out of the parking lot. He turned onto the highway and poured it on. He might have hit eighty before reaching the edge of town.

Jack turned back to the meeting, the quiet of the room, the searching eyes. In the back, several observers slipped out the door. "Where were we, Kip?"

"First agenda item, old business, formal discussion of Mike Middleton's proposal."

Showalter raised her hand. "I think our announcement will help make that a short discussion. May we go first?"

Thomas raised his hand. "What does he get in return?"

"Patience. We'll get to that."

"No, what does he get in return?"

Ginger Perrette raised her hand. "Everything that has happened here tonight aside, the fact remains, we still need a solution to this problem. If we don't, I'll have to stop participating."

"I might have to as well," Dan Romero echoed from his corner.

Linda Showalter jumped to her feet. "People, I refuse to let this Coalition fall apart. I will do whatever it takes to resolve this issue and keep that from happening."

Startled eyes glanced among themselves. Karen Hatcher began to slowly clap her hands. "Do that and you're my hero," she said, still clapping.

Applause broke out at the table. When it stopped, Linda smiled and said, "Let's make our announcement, Mike."

He sat back in his chair. "It's late, and I'm a little tired after what happened with our friend Harper Teague. This can wait. In fact, I make the motion we conclude for tonight."

"You do?" Linda said. She glanced back at Saunders, who flashed a frustrated look.

The motion was seconded and approved.

— · —

Linda Showalter rubbed her temples. What just happened here?

She waited for Mike Middleton to scoot back from the table, then grabbed Erika Jones by the wrist. "You get Saunders. I'll get Middleton."

Middleton stood and Showalter pulled him to the back wall, grabbed him by the shoulders and faced him, trying not to be distracted by the angry look from Nick Saunders, approaching behind them. "What just happened here?" she demanded.

Middleton shrugged. "Hey, I think we should do this on our

terms, and our terms just got better. Easier, in fact. Plus, I know of a better time and place to make the announcement."

"What the hell are you talking about?" Linda said, angrily, before remembering with whom she was talking. She took a deep breath. "I'm sorry. When? Where?"

"Tomorrow, in the canyon, when the Director's here."

"Are you crazy?" she said, again losing control.

"That's what I want," Middleton said. "Great fanfare. Reporters present. Director on stage joining in on the big announcement. Your heroic move to hold the Coalition together."

"You can't have what you want, Mike. I won't let you have it."

"I know, but that's where I want to announce the deal. If you don't like it, take it up with the Director. And think about it. If you did give me what I want, the Director sees not only how much the Coalition loves you, plus he hears great things from me. Just think what that might make possible. Think rocket ships and favorite destinations, the chance to create a legacy."

"And if I don't give you what you want?"

"You still get to show off for the Director. You're welcome."

Linda took a deep breath and let the modicum of calm she could muster settle over her. "If I say yes, will you work with us, listen to us, do what we say to keep this from becoming a disaster?"

"I'd be delighted to."

She sighed. "Erika, I've got an assignment for you. Call the Director's staff first thing in the morning. Explain the event but don't confuse them with details. Tell them we want the Director taking part. Taking part, that's all." She noticed Saunders backing away. "Nick, are you leaving?"

He stumbled back. "Uh . . . no."

"And Erika, do we want big splash or little splash?"

She shrugged.

"Big splash," Middleton said.

"Erika, find out what reporters we typically notify when we have major announcements."

"I can help on that," Middleton said. "I've got a PR firm I contract with on occasion. They can send out press invitations in the morning, and work up a press package to give out at the event."

"Erika, can you work with him on that?" Linda said.

Erika nodded.

"Okay, everyone, let's talk first thing in the morning."

"This'll be fun," Middleton said. He turned and left.

— · —

Others walked past and gave accolades to Linda Showalter. She continued talking, slipping closer to the door, and waited as the last of the attendees finished talking to Jack. He moved to leave. She grabbed his arm and walked him back into the room.

"Why did you ignore my orders?"

"I take my cues from the Coalition. There wasn't a convenient time to give Middleton the floor."

"You control the meeting, you idiot. And you took a stupid chance. Why did you let that vote occur?"

"It's not my meeting."

"Hell, you were a gnat's ass away from getting us all tossed out of here."

"Would that've been bad? Would've bought us some time."

"It would've been bad for you. If you want to get tossed out of something, here's your grand bargain. We're announcing the agreement tomorrow, in the canyon, with the Director. Stay away. Do not come out of your office. Erika will handle it."

— · —

Thomas stood waiting at the pickup when Jack made it into the darkness of the parking lot. Exhausted, Jack rubbed his eyes and leaned against the fender. "Why are you still here, Thomas?"

"Not sure."

"I respect what you did tonight. If there's any risk at all, Teague was your best shot at stopping it. I'm not sure why you did it. I'm not sure why you've done lots of things."

"I don't know if I've done the right thing, but the right thing is what I've tried to do. If I'm wrong, I am a fool."

Jack looked hard at him. "Thomas, you're no fool, but I wish you'd trusted me more. I might've helped you more."

"I do trust you. I've always trusted you."

He put a hand on Thomas' shoulder. "Good night, Thomas." He opened the door and tossed in his bag. He looked back. "What you said about Teague and Fearfully Anonymous. Are you sure?"

"Yes." Thomas turned and left.

—·—

"We'll have to be prepared to cut Showalter loose and distance ourselves from the whole damned mess," Saunders said. "It's her own damned fault. If she hadn't taken so damned long to work this out, we wouldn't be in this predicament." He stared ahead, watching the stripes at the furthest reach of the headlights. "If this becomes a photo op for the Director, everything changes. The Congressman's beholden to the Director, and we have to endure another four more years of his political games. Hell, he might give Middleton the whole damned park." He slammed a hand against the dashboard. "I'll torpedo the damned land exchange. I'll leak the details to the press."

"Calm down, Nick."

"I don't understand. We talked to Middleton. We told him he could count on getting that piece of the canyon. Why does he keep trying to get Linda Showalter on board?"

"Simple. He wants her to kiss his ring."

"She doesn't get it."

"Or maybe she does." Erika looked away from the road. "Nick, we can get this back on track. Leave it to me. I can fix this."

"How? You know this isn't gonna come off the way Linda thinks."

"Trust me."

"When are the Congressman's aides expecting something from you on that legislation?"

"They have it now. I sent it this morning."

"Pull it back."

"Nick, we only have a small window to make this work."

"If you make it work and everything goes south, the Director gets the credit. We're screwed. You're screwed."

"Don't worry. I know how to fix this. And, I can ask my contact on the Congressman's staff to give me one last call before they pull the trigger. Think about it, Nick . . .if we ask them to pull it back, then this whole plan stops now. Nothing happens. The Congressman's of no help in dealing with the Director. He forgets who you are."

"Might be better than letting the Director get the credit."

"No risk, no reward. Is that what you want?"

"I don't know."

"If I pull the legislation and we decide we need it, tough luck, the package will be in the hands of the President."

"Be ready to jettison the whole damned thing. Got that?" He turned to watch her face as she answered.

She glanced over. "Got it. But leave everything to me, Nick. This can still work. I know how to fix this. Start planning where you want your photo op."

"That's looking about as shaky as something else you did."

"What? What did I do?"

"Never mind." He stomped on the floorboard. "I'm gonna kill Chastain. He ignored Linda's orders, screwed up the whole plan for the night, and lets the meeting get out of hand. Turned it into a nightmare."

"In his defense, it could have gotten a lot worse."

"I don't want to hear it." He slammed an elbow into the door. "Take me to the airport."

"You're not staying?"

"Hell no, I'm not gonna stick around while the Director gets my photo op."

In the distance, waters pounded the canyon floor, but the view from the spot Erika chose for the event was dominated by no one thing. Sheer walls, slickrock domes, the river flowing in and out of view, cottonwoods all along its path, and spring flowers giving way to summer ones. This was a beautiful spot.

The podium and dais were positioned to overwhelm the audience with that perfect vista. The sun lit across the polished arrowhead emblem, leaving no doubt as to which organization deserved credit for the impending profound announcement.

Linda Showalter circled the clearing, checking everything. Again. The rows of chairs—straight. The press table—positioned precisely opposite the dais. The press packages—now delivered. She picked one up, and gave it an inspection. Nice folder, good picture of the canyon. She flipped it open. The press release—polished. Fact sheet—thorough. Park brochure—perfect to complete the package. She nodded. They look good. Impressive, on such short turnaround.

She stretched and pulled in a breath. Relax, this will work. Quit worrying. Middleton will behave himself, the Director will be impressed, and you will be back in the game.

But what if Middleton doesn't behave?

Is this an opportunity or a trap? Coalition needing a hero, or

Middleton trying to get something he can't have. But opportunities are created in moments like these. A month ago, none of this seemed possible. A month ago, it felt as if the future would always look like the present, stuck in a park that first seemed a stepping stone, then became a boulder, blocking the way to anywhere. Opportunities. Amazing how they come from nowhere. Suddenly, you're back in the game. Everything's possible.

No, now is not the time to think about all that. Middleton must behave himself. He's up to something. But, a man with that kind of influence is good to have on your side.

Now feels like the time to create opportunity. To create a splash. To create the beginnings of a legacy. Hero to the Coalition? If that impresses the Director, it's a good start.

— · —

Jack got up from his desk and unconsciously stumbled into the hall. He approached the door to the outside and remembered Linda Showalter's order to stay in the office—surely, only figurative, surely it'd be okay to get out and do something in the field, and hell with it if it wasn't—but he turned and headed back down the hall.

He peeked in each of the rooms as he passed. Empty. Empty. Empty. Everyone's at the event, awaiting the Director. Quiet echoed loudly through the halls.

Luiz stepped from the protection ranger offices wearing dress uniform, his weapon covered by the length of the coat but his service belt obvious. "Wanna ride with me?" Luiz asked, putting on his Stetson. "I'm heading up canyon. It'll give us a chance to talk. Got a question, and something to tell you."

"I'm grounded. Not allowed to leave the office."

"You're kidding." Luiz twisted his face in confused disbelief. "Loca," he said, in a blurt of Spanish. "Well, I've got a minute now. We can talk more later."

"Sure."

"This Teague guy. Where can I find him?"

"I really don't know. Hear about last night?"

"I did. I think Thomas is right."

"Why do you think that? And how did Thomas know?"

"Investigation points that direction. Don't know how he figured it out, but I'll tell you the clues I'm following." He tilted his hat slightly right and checked his badge. "Everything look okay? I don't wear this very often."

"Looks perfect."

"Good," he said. "Shoes. Teague's shoes, or rather the tracks made by his shoes."

Jack flashed a quizzical look.

"Remember the day at Culberson Ranch? His tracks in the dirt . . . I was looking right at 'em. Almost didn't notice. Same as the one's I pulled from the creek bed out by the truck. By the time I made the connection, too late."

"Why?"

"Wind. If I'd been quick I could've gotten pictures."

"You sure the track was the same?"

"Wasn't sure then, but I got a good look. When I got back here I checked the plaster casts made out by the pickup. They're the same. If I can find him, I can try to get something conclusive. Otherwise, might be a hard case to make."

"Good luck."

"Yeah, but there's something I haven't told you. Possible connection the Chief Ranger noted when I briefed her. Sorry."

"I'm not in the loop on those things. Don't need to be."

"You'll understand when I finish. That vehicle. Hard as hell tracking down anything. Finally did. Turns out, it was sold in a government auction, bought by a company that hasn't reported it stolen, even for insurance purposes. I had someone check on their fleet. Nothing they own is older than three years. That truck was way older. Why would they need an old, beat up government rig?"

"Maybe they needed a junker for a project."

"That might fly considering the type of company we're talking about, but their headquarters, their operations, they're miles from here."

"Where? What kind of company?"

"Mining and energy, based in Montana."

Jack's eyes grew wide. His lips moved but he couldn't think of a thing to say.

— · —

Erika Jones stood waiting as Linda finished buttoning her dress uniform jacket. She held a thin stack of papers. "Reporters are showing up early. You'll want to study these."

"My remarks for today?" Linda asked.

"Yes. Top pages are your statement. Bottom pages are Mike's."

"And you got my last set of edits?"

"I did."

Linda flipped through the pages. Double spaced text. Good. "Thank you, Erika, looks perfect."

"You're welcome."

"Is Middleton gonna behave himself?"

"Yes, he will."

"Hope you're right. Where will you be, and what do we know about the Director's arrival?"

"I'll be over there, with Margie," Erika said, pointing at the press table. She looked at her watch. "His staff projected him arriving about twenty minutes from now. Three o'clock, more or less. I prepared a short statement for him, unless he prefers speaking off the cuff. I'll pull him aside when he gets here."

"Good." Linda laughed. "If he's a few minutes late, I doubt it'll matter. Not with this crowd. Can we expect everyone from the Coalition?"

"Most of 'em. They don't know everything that'll happen. They think they're here to meet the Director. They'll be pleasantly surprised with the announcement. You'll be their hero."

"Really believe that?"

"I do."

"Will Kip Culberson be here? He's a rancher, he'll want to hear this."

"I thought about Kip, but with Jack's connection to his daughter, I decided it best not to risk it."

"Connection?"

"Tell you later. Nothing to worry about . . . if Jack's professional about this." She tore off toward the press table.

Professional? He wasn't last night. He can start planning his next career. It won't be here.

You never know about some people. He was better than I'd been led to believe, and not as good as I'd started to think. He's the kind of person who'll never understand what it takes to change the world.

— · —

Jack plopped into his chair and leaned over his knees, head in hands. What was Teague doing? All that talk about playing fair, everything on the table. What was he up to? Montana—can't be.

Don't be paranoid.

It seems so long ago. So painful.

But . . . less than the pain of fresh wounds.

— · —

"You ready, Mike?" Linda asked, walking up behind him at the back of the dais.

He looked up from his reading. "Yep, this'll work. Unless of course, you're ready to announce my getting a nice little piece of land with a view of the falls. I can pencil in changes to your copy, you can read it, I can act surprised. Then, I can tell the Director how well things have gone."

She laughed. "Not gonna happen, Mike. You promised, you'll only say what Erika coached you to say."

"Little bird tells me there's a nice job waiting in D.C. Could have your name on it."

"Mike!"

"Okay, only what Erika told me to say."

"Comfortable handling questions coming your way?"

"I'm a master at controlling the message."

"Good. The Director will be here any minute."

"Can't wait to see him."

— · —

Jack wandered back down the hall and into the dispatch office. "I guess you and I are the only ones in the office," he said to Molly as he entered.

She looked up from her logs. "Always the case for me. I never get to go anywhere. Hey, while you're here . . ." She clicked open the browser, and onto the online *Gazette*. "Nothing new from our friend Fearfully Anonymous, but Ducky's weighing in on what happened last night."

"Not sure I want to hear it," Jack said.

"Sure you do." She chuckled to herself. "Listen to this. He thinks Harper Teague was set up to take a fall. Entrapment. Orders from Washington, because the government wanted him out of the way. He was becoming a danger." She laughed. "Here, come read it."

"No, thanks."

— · —

Luiz walked the event perimeter, going through the motions. Nothing to worry about here. Not with this kind of event, especially on such short notice. Nothing criminal was likely to happen. At most, security might involve asking an unruly member of the public to behave, and this was not shaping up to look like that kind of crowd. No one looked to be a demonstrator, picketer or disrupter. If someone like that made a showing, they could be given a place to conduct their business.

He checked his watch. The Director would be here any minute.

He did a quick count. Half a dozen reporters, maybe more, but there were at least that many others carrying press packages distributed by Erika Jones. Two television cameras sat on tripods behind the last row of seats, their satellite trucks parked a hundred yards away. Dignitaries—a few, mostly county officials. He scanned the crowd for park staff, those in uniform. Maybe a third of those here. Out in mass not only for the announcement, but also to meet the Director.

Behind the press table he stopped and stole a moment to enjoy the view. Sipapu Falls—the sight and sounds brought quick memories. He located the spot where he'd hung out over the canyon weeks before, his eye that day on Jack Chastain at the end of the rope, and Thomas sitting on the ledge. He traced the distance down the wall—hell of a drop—and spotted the break in the ledge, and the fresh scar, and remembered first looking through the spotting scope, confirming what a visitor first reported at the Visitor Center—that someone was stuck on the wall. He locked his eyes on the spot.

You have got to be kidding! . . . Can't be . . .

He jogged to the patrol utility vehicle, unlocked the back window, and dug out the spotting scope. Setting the tripod on the hood, he targeted the scope, focusing on the wall.

On the ledge, near the fresh scar in the rock . . .

Not again!

— · —

"Poor Ducky," Molly said. "Believes everything he writes, but won't admit to himself that Fearfully Anonymous—or rather, Harper Teague—played him like a fiddle."

Jack sighed.

The radio popped on. *"Dispatch, this is Three-twenty."*

Molly spun around to the microphone. "Dispatch, go ahead Luiz."

"We have a problem. Someone stuck on the wall or trying to kill themselves."

The phone rang.

She looked around. "Jack, answer that, would you?" She turned back to the mike. "I copy, Luiz. Where?"

"Sipapu Falls. Stand by."

Jack came around the counter and picked up the phone. "National Park Service, may I help you?"

Crackling bled over the line. "Hello? Can you hear me?" a man said, through intermittent pops on a bad cell phone connection.

"I can hear you. How can I help you?"

"There's an event in the park this afternoon, and my instructions for getting there are incomplete."

Jack pulled back the phone and stared at the earpiece. He put it back to his ear. "Is this Director Lucas?"

"It is. To whom am I speaking?"

"Molly, it's someone on same the ledge, same location, looks like same person."

Thomas! "Uh . . . this is Jack Chastain."

"Jack, why are you answering phones?"

Molly keyed the mike. "What do you need, Luiz?"

"I don't, ordinarily," Jack said. "Too many things going on—we may have a breaking rescue—so I picked it up."

"I see. Need me to call back?"

Luiz came back on the radio. *"It's Johnny Reger's day off. See if he's home. See if he can pull gear from the rescue cache."*

Molly wrote as she listened. "Copy."

"Sorry," Jack said. "I was distracted by the radio. Can I help you?"

"Should I call back?"

"No, it's okay."

"I'm supposed to be at Sipapu Falls viewpoint. I need directions."

"Drive down-canyon. It's off the main road, but well-marked."

Luiz came back on: *"I've got a list of needs. Prepare to copy."*

"Just curious. What kind of rescue?" the Director asked.

"High angle," Jack said. "Near where you're going. Can you hold a second, I want to hear this?"

"Go ahead."

"I'm ready, Luiz," Molly said, her pen over paper.

"*We need the rescue ropes, anchor packs . . . raising/lowering system pack, climbing harnesses, helmets, edge rollers.*"

"I copy," Molly said.

Jack turned his attention back to the phone. "I'm back."

"Sounds like you've got your hands full."

"We do, yes."

"I don't have time for a delay. Tell Linda Showalter I didn't want to be a disruption. Tell her I'm back in the office tomorrow late afternoon, and in Washington all next week if that's better. Tell her let's talk, and if she has a reason to come to D.C., we can talk there."

"I'd rather you had this conversation with her."

"No arguing. My schedule's tight. I have to be in Sand Dunes tonight—dinner with a county commissioner—and I fly back in the morning. Trying to do too much, but I'd hoped to talk to her. Tell her." He ended the call.

"Molly," Jack said, "That was . . ."

"Hold it," she said, still frantically writing.

The radio popped on. "*Dispatch, one more thing. Get Jack Chastain. Tell him I need him. Tell him I don't have any choice. I need him at the end of the rope. Tell him to hurry.*"

Molly spun around and pointed at the door. "Go. I'll have Johnny meet you at the cache."

CHAPTER 37

Jack floored the pickup.

He slid to a stop at the rescue cache, spraying gravel on the cut stone walls. Running in from the other direction, Johnny slapped the hood, dug out his keys, and unlocked the door, throwing it open.

Jack ran inside, jumping out of the way as Johnny headed back out with two packs in hand.

Jack grabbed the rope pack and followed him out.

— · —

Linda Showalter steadied herself against the eyepiece. The ledge came into focus. Movement. Dark hair appeared on the ledge, and dropped again below the line of sight. She pulled back from the spotting scope. "Has to be some sort of protest," she said. "He's shooting himself in the foot."

"Hard to know," Luiz said, his eyes still on the ledge. "Seems out of character. I don't know why he'd go back up there, he was so frightened before."

"Whatever. Keep this quiet, just between you and me. If we don't draw attention to it, I doubt anyone will notice."

"I can't worry about that. If he's stuck or afraid, we need to help him. To stage the kind of response we had before, I'll need several people from here to operate the z-rig."

"You'll do no such thing."

"You're kidding."

"I'm not kidding. It'll draw attention to his little game. If he's in trouble, he can sit there till we're finished, thinking about how stupid he's being. You can go after him later."

"I can go by myself."

"You will not. You are assigned to this event. At most, keep an eye on that wall. If he tries getting attention by unfurling a banner or anything like that, be sure I'm the first to know. Do it discreetly."

"I have a bad feeling about this."

"Doesn't matter what you feel. Look sharp."

—·—

"Why would he go back up there?" Jack said aloud to himself. He shook his head, hands locked on the wheel, driving the canyon road at a fast clip.

Johnny held on, eyes on the road.

"I don't have a good feeling about this."

"He's helping you keep up your skills," Johnny said.

He glanced at Johnny. "I'm not joking. It almost killed him last time. What's he got, a death wish?"

"The place has a hell of a view."

"I'm serious. Would he try to kill himself? Why else go back there?"

"Jack, I don't know. You're thinking too hard."

"When I saw him last, he was acting strangely. Just after he did something high integrity, but not exactly in his own best interest. He was in a strange mood afterward."

"I don't know what to tell you, Jack. Let's just go get him."

—·—

Luiz pulled his radio and raised it to his mouth. "Dispatch, this is Three-twenty."

"Go ahead Luiz."

"I've been ordered to call off the rescue."

"Repeat that, Luiz. I don't think I understood you."

He squinted to see what was happening on the ledge, for a moment catching a flash of black. "No, you heard me. Call everyone back. The acting superintendent says no. She thinks he's staging a demonstration or something."

"What'll you do?"

"Watch the wall. Never cared much for speeches."

— · —

Jack stared at the radio, not believing his ears. He put his eyes back to the road and sped up.

"What are we gonna do?"

He turned to Johnny. "I'll jump out and let you take the pickup back to the cache."

"Naw, I'll wait. Nothin' better to do."

They turned off the pavement and onto the dirt road to Sipapu Falls.

— · —

In the distance, dust rose up from the road. A vehicle approached, growing louder by the moment.

Showalter checked her watch. Right on time. She chuckled to herself. He doesn't have to be in that much of a hurry. She saw Erika moving toward the parking area. Good. Let Erika bring the Director to the dais. Don't look eager. Look in control. Look presidential. She walked to the dais, stopping near the steps. Mike Middleton joined her there.

— · —

They slid to a stop. Jack jumped out, moving quickly toward the trailhead.

"Wait. What gear do you need?"

He paused and looked back. "Nothing, I guess. Not sure what good it'd do. It's just me."

"No," Johnny said. He reached into the truck bed, grabbed a pack and dumped its contents. He threw in a climbing harness and a pair of helmets, dug out a short coil of rope and several webbing runners, and stuffed them inside, along with a handful of carabiners. He tossed it to Jack. "Go."

Jack flung the pack over a shoulder and took off on a run.

Johnny took a seat on the tailgate, and drummed his fingers against metal. "Hell of a way to spend a day off." He turned his head and gave the equipment a look. The long rope, a few things for an anchor, a climbing harness, more carabiners. What else? He dumped another pack into the bed, quickly filled it with equipment, and put on a helmet, clicking the strap tight under his chin. He checked that his radio was in its place, then hefted the big rope pack onto his shoulders, grabbed a strap on the other, and started off in a jog.

— · —

Dust hung in the air. Erika stopped on the edge of the parking area and checked her uniform. Perfect. Even the paper she held was without a crease, even after walking against up-canyon breezes. She scanned the length and width of the parking area. No one.

She stepped to the middle of the lot and spun around, peering into spaces between sedans, sport utility vehicles, and pickups—some with government plates and markings—and satellite trucks parked along the edge. No one.

Must've been a hiker.

— · —

"Jack, this is Johnny. Go to crew channel." Johnny took his thumb off the transmit button and turned the channel knob on his radio.

After a moment, *"Go ahead Johnny."*

"I'm right behind you. Got a big load, but I'm not sure I've got enough gear to do much good."

"What are thinking you'll do?"

"Don't have a clue. You?"

"I'm hoping to find where that ledge starts."

"Thought so. I'll go where we set up before."

— · —

"What are you listening to?" Linda Showalter asked, walking up behind Luiz.

He took his eyes off the wall and changed the channel on his radio. "Nothing."

"Luiz, would you please wait at the parking area. As soon as the Director arrives, get him to the dais as quickly as possible."

He nodded and took off on a jog. He glanced around for onlookers, then went to his patrol vehicle, opened the back hatch, and pulled out his spotting scope. He set the tripod on the hood and took a look through the eyepiece.

He reached down and switched the radio back to the tactical channel.

— · —

Please be there! Don't do something stupid, Thomas!

Jack stopped and studied the terrain, uncertain. Talus and strata stood above, the ledge to the left, but the angle making it increasingly difficult to see. Sipapu Falls, even further left. Confusing perspective.

He stepped off-trail and treaded upslope, eyes on the hanging canyon. It appeared to have no way in or out except for the ledge itself, but that couldn't be. The ledge emerged several feet above the canyon bottom, following the line between different colors of strata.

Has to be this way. No time to get lost.

Thomas, please still be there!

—·—

Johnny plowed forward, his pace set, his lean forward to counter the weight in the pack. The slope of the trail began to increase and he dug deeper, shortened his stride, and regulated his breathing, pounding through the first tough spot. Up ahead, in the distance, he could see the beginnings of switchbacks, zigzagging their way through hundreds of feet of vertical sandstone. There, it's gonna get hard.

—·—

"Do I have time to get something from my car?" Karen Hatcher said to Linda Showalter.

Linda glanced at her watch, shaking her head. "No . . . well, maybe so. I don't know."

"I'll hurry." She turned and walked past the press table. She reached her car, pulled out a sweater, and slipped it on. Walking back across the lot she noticed Luiz, elbows on the hood, looking through a spotting scope.

What's he doing?

She veered his direction and stopped behind him, lining up along his line of sight. She squinted and searched up and down the canyon wall.

She saw the ledge, then a black spot. Is that a person?

—·—

Jack hefted himself up, stepping past a flat rock that looked ready to slide downhill. The soils gave, his foot slipped, and he fell to one knee, his balance about to go. He grabbed a piñon limb, regained his footing, and pulled himself past. He looked up. No view of anything but slope, rocks, and piñon. He keyed his radio. "Johnny, where are you?"

"*Switchbacks.*" Heavy breathing bled over the radio.

"I may have to give this up," Jack said, fighting to catch his own breath between words. "May have to go down and go where you are."

"Copy. I'll have everything set up. With something. Not sure what."

"I'm not giving up yet. I'll let you know."

He continued up, grabbing limbs, stepping around rock, using hands and feet to scale where there was little to hold. He came to a game trail and stood upright, catching his breath. It climbed slightly upslope. Still low on the hill. But this will be easier. At least for a bit. He sucked in a breath and took off.

See where it goes.

No wider than a foot, more pebble and leaf litter than bare soil, it made a diagonal sweep up the slope, crossed over a ridge, and turned back. At the base of an outcropping, it stopped. He studied the rock and caught another breath. Reaching up, then jamming a foot into a crevice, he climbed through the slice in the strata. On top, he pulled himself up and sat.

Another trail. Are those foot prints? Why didn't I see those before?

He jumped up and followed, walking faster, following the tracks up and across the slope, then back the other way. The trail came to an abrupt end at an outcropping. He looked up and scanned the top of the strata. Still below the hanging canyon and nothing but vertical wall between here and the ledge. How do you get into that damned hanging canyon?

He went right, fighting loose soil, trying not to slide downslope, following the base of the rock. Nothing. He went left as far as he could. Still nothing. He saw a crevice and moved toward it. Its slice up the rock started waist high and widened higher on the wall. He felt along the edge, then inside. A depression. Like a handhold. He reached with the other hand and found another. Pulling himself into the crack, he picked his way, working up the crevice to the top of the strata. He sat and studied the ledge emerging from the hanging canyon, hundreds of feet to the left and slightly higher. Without climbing equipment, there was no way to get there.

He sucked in another breath, and searched the ground. Game

trail—where is it? He spotted it, climbing diagonally the other way, to the right. Wrong direction, but it's going somewhere. The only way onto the ledge must be from above.

He took off.

—·—

Johnny came to the spot on the trail he remembered from weeks before. Breathing hard and stooped under the weight of the burden, he plowed into the serviceberry, pushing limbs out of the way, forcing a path through. Branches grabbed at the pack, trying to hold him back.

He broke through, the void pulling at his attention. Turning his eyes to the ground, he worked his way across the slope. "Here," he said aloud to himself, remembering where he'd sat before. He dropped the packs and spun around, trying to recall where the anchors had been set up.

—·—

"Please just wait, Thomas," Jack said, pounding his way upslope. "I'm sorry I was hard on you. Just don't do anything, please."

The trail disappeared.

Where is it?

Find it. He moved left, past a ridgeline. He saw the beginnings of a creek bed. He headed down, one leg outstretched, feet across-slope. Through brush and rocks, pushing dirt as he slid, he worked his way down. The walls came together. They grew taller.

A rock kicked loose, rolled downhill, careened off the wall, continued to roll, and launched into air.

Don't kill yourself. But don't stop.

He slid into the creek bottom and followed it toward the opening. A ledge began to form to the right, on the wall, following the slice of time between erosion on one layer and deposition on the next. He moved over and climbed onto it. In careful steps, he followed it to the mouth of the hanging canyon. He looked down, at the last few feet of dry creek bed, then out, into the depths of the canyon. He stopped, took a deep breath, and pushed the sight of it out of his mind. "Okay, here we go."

He stepped around the corner.

—·—

The echo of crashing rock faded quickly. Quiet settled over the canyon. Linda Showalter listened, waiting for another rock to drop. "What was that?" she whispered, eyes darting.

"Rock fall," Erika said. "Happens all the time."

"Right. Where's Karen Hatcher? We need her here when the Director arrives. She's been gone a long time. And speaking of a long time, where is the Director." She turned to Mike Middleton. "Have you heard from him?"

"I'll see." He pulled out this cell phone and checked for missed calls. "Nothing yet."

"Where the hell is he?"

—·—

Shoulders close to the wall, Jack followed the ledge, eyes on his feet, uncertain about anything but them. He stopped, leaned into his hand on the wall, and slowly raised his eyes.

A hundred yards ahead, a silhouette in brown jacket sat perched facing the break in the ledge, and—beyond it—Sipapu Falls. Back hunched over, Thomas sat hunkered against the wall.

"Thank God," Jack muttered to himself. Better not surprise him. Get close. Don't yell. Talk him back. Don't let him do anything stupid.

Wind whistled past.

Jack took his hand off the wall and pulled off the pack. Stooping on one knee, he pulled out a helmet, slipped it on and cinched it down. He slipped a leg into the climbing harness, and stopped.

What good is a climbing harness? None, unless Johnny can get a rope down here. He slipped the other leg in, and fastened the buckle. He stuffed loose gear back in the pack.

He put a hand on the radio and turned down the volume, then keyed the mike. "Johnny, I'm on the ledge," he whispered. "Got him in sight."

"I've got an anchor set up, and the rope is tied in. Want me to lower it down."

"Sure it can reach?"

"Same rope we used last time. I can tie into the anchor and toss the whole length over the edge, or I can lower the end down, and tie it in when you tell me to stop."

"Do the latter, but go slow. I need time to get to him, and we don't want to scare him. I'm not sure what state of mind he's in. And put a knot and carabiner in the end of the rope. Make it easy on me."

"Copy. One more thing," Johnny said.

"Go head."

"I have no way to bring you up."

Jack shrugged. "We'll worry about that if we have to. The rope's just a margin of safety." He raised his head and watched the rope appear at the edge, and snake down the wall, a knot and carabiner in the end.

He moved forward, foot at a time.

The rope slid down.

He picked up his pace, hand on the wall, hundreds of feet of void and a rocky canyon bottom below him.

Rope kept coming, slithering down vertical rock, carabiner clinking against stone. Jack saw Thomas react—likely startled—and look up.

Jack moved quickly.

Thomas scooted back on the ledge.

"Careful Thomas," Jack shouted. "I'm here. Everything's okay."

Thomas' back went stiff. His head started to turn but stopped.

"Stop, Johnny," Jack said into the radio.

The rope stopped its descent as the carabiner clanged onto the ledge. Jack picked it up and keyed his radio. "Got it. Anchor it in."

Thomas put a hand against the wall, and tried to stand.

"Wait." Jack fumbled with the loops on his harness, threading the carabiner through one, fighting to get it through the second.

He stepped closer, and felt the shift of his weight on the rock. He heard a crack.

Thomas' head turned. It was not Thomas.

The rock gave way.

"Rachel," he shouted, digging in his toes as he dove toward her.

CHAPTER
38

She tried to stand. The rock dropped away. Her arms flew up as she fell.

Reaching, Jack soared, slamming against her, locking arms, knowing what was about to happen.

She hit the wall, clawing with fingers, peddling her feet, trying to find holds on nubbins and cracks. She slid down the wall, then into free fall.

"No!" she screamed.

The rope caught, stretched—nearly jerking her out of his arms—and shot them up the wall, scraping against rock.

Jack tightened his grip. Don't let go! Don't let go!

The radio popped. *"Jack, what's happening?"*

The rock hit ground in a thunderous crash.

They bounced against the wall, and slid to a stop. Sound washed over them.

Echoes rattled, then faded into silence.

Jack sucked in a breath and listened. Nothing but heartbeats and shallow, excited breaths. Hers. His. Rachel hung motionless.

"Are you okay?"

"Hard to breath. You're squeezing too hard."

"I'm afraid to loosen my hold."

The radio came on. *"Jack, are you there?"*

No way to answer. "Not sure how long I can hold you like this."

"Am I heavy?"

He let out a desperate little chuckle. "Anything gets heavy."

"You will hold me. I know you will. I have faith."

How long will that help? "Good," he said, uncertain what else to say. Can't drop her. Can't let it get her, not like it got her mother.

"Jack, answer me. You okay?"

"They will soar on wings like eagles," she said.

She slipped. He reset his hold. "What?"

"They will run and not grow weary; they will walk and not be faint. Isaiah."

"I'm sorry, Rachel. I will grow weary. I'm not sure what I can do."

She looked back. "Have faith," she said, her voice calm. "I have faith." Reaching up, she took hold of the rope, squirmed between the rock and his body, and twisted around to face him. Blood dripped from her nose and along scratches on her face. Pinned between him and the wall, she reached again and pulled with both hands, hefting herself a few inches.

"What are you doing?"

"Got me?"

He squeezed harder.

"Are you there, Jack?"

"Johnny, this is Luiz, I can see him. They're on the wall and I see movement."

Rachel pulled herself a few inches higher, waited for him to reset his hold, then released her grip on the rope. She wrapped an arm around his head, forced an elbow between him and the rope, then a shoulder. Pushing back, she slipped a knee through. "Got me?" she asked.

"Yes."

She reached down, guided a foot past the rope, and settled against him, wrapping her legs around his torso and resting her chin on his shoulder. "Easier?"

"Yeah, but if I let go of the rope, we'll flip over and . . ."

"What can I do?'

"Hold on a second." He forced a hand to the radio strapped to his chest. Rachel eased back as he keyed the mike. "Johnny, we're kind of okay. Stand by."

"*Copy.*"

"Rachel, reach in my pack and find some webbing."

She pulled back the top pocket and probed into the bottom of the pack. She pulled out a piece of blue webbing, a looped runner.

"Good. See if you can reach a carabiner." He looked down. Dust circled, rising toward them.

She forced a hand to the bottom of the pack, and pulled out a locking carabiner.

"Good. Clip the carabiner through the runner and clip that into the rope."

She did.

"Now, take it around me. Pass it between the pack and my back, and clip the other end into the carabiner."

She threaded it through and clipped it in. It hung loose, draping between them and the rope.

"Okay, take one end out of the carabiner and tie a knot about two feet from the end. We need to be tight against the rope."

"Got me?" She unclipped and knotted the rope, clipping it in short of the knot."

Jack tested the webbing. Tight enough. "Do we have another runner?"

She reached in and pulled out a red one.

"Take it around you, under your arms, slip one end through the other and clip it into the carabiner."

She did.

"That's just in case. We'll try not to test it." He looked down. The dust cloud grew closer. He keyed the radio. "Johnny, we're safe for now, but we've got a dust cloud coming our way. Looks like about twenty, twenty-five feet of stretch in the rope. We're below the ledge."

"*Copy, but I'm not sure what I can do.*"

"I don't want to be hanging out here when that dust arrives. If one of us passes out . . . then it's never mind. Stand by." He looked up. To the right, scaly breaks on the wall, where the ledge broke away. Possibly good enough for hand and foot holds, but getting there, impossible. Above, nothing. To the left, a bit of a crack, ending at the ledge, but the wrong side of the break. "Johnny, this is gonna be hard. Can you top-rope me?"

"I think so. What're you gonna do?"

"Probably wishful thinking, but I'm gonna try to get us up to the ledge before the dust gets here. We'll have to pendulum across the break in the ledge, and hope you can hold us."

"I can. I'm ready."

"One other thing. Rachel's tied in, tenuously. She's hanging on and I just don't know if I've got the strength to do this."

"Who's Rachel?"

"I'm Rachel," she said into the mike. "Hi Johnny."

"Well . . . Rachel . . . hi. Get going, you two."

Jack kicked left, propped against the fall line with his right leg. He kicked left again and reached for the crack, pulling them the rest of the way. The crevice ran vertically, a few inches wide, a foot or so deep. He stuck a toe in the crack and felt above with his hands, jamming one in up to his wrist, then the other, then set the second foot above the first. He lifted, raising himself to the height of the top foot. The rope tightened too slowly, and they slipped back down the wall. "Push the button on the radio, Rachel."

She keyed the mike.

"Johnny, I don't know if I can do this." He glanced down. The cloud grew closer.

— · —

Linda Showalter checked her watch and glared at the television cameraman focusing on the far canyon wall. A reporter stepped before the camera, microphone to her side, reading notes on a clipboard.

"Caroline, what about this?" the cameraman said. "What if we start the shot focused on them? You describe what's happening, I pull back, get the distance and height they're at on the wall, and get the waterfall without panning. End with the focus on you and your wrap up."

"That's fine," she said. "I'm ready." She raised the microphone and put on a serious face.

Showalter backed away and turned to Erika Jones. "Did you call?"

"I did."

"And?"

"No answer. Called his staff in D.C. and everyone's gone home for the night."

"Damn it. This will make me a laughing stock." She glanced across the parking lot. "Where's Luiz?"

"He's uh . . ."

"Don't tell me. I know where he is."

— · —

Rachel keyed the mike. "Johnny, can you help lift us any?" Jack asked. "Rachel's between me and the wall, and I don't have the strength to keep doing this without assist."

"I'll try, but I'm using a piñon for leverage and it's starting to look scrawny."

"Rachel will key the mike when I'm about to make a move. Let's try it."

"Copy."

"Now Rachel." She pressed the button. "First move, about a foot, starting now," he said. Wrists and toes jammed in the crack, he lifted with his arms, and pushed down with one foot. They rose, and the rope tightened. Jack felt the assist, and he pushed another few inches and rested. "Now Rachel." She pressed. "That worked, Johnny. Still over twenty feet to go and I don't know if I'll last that far, but it worked."

"Copy. Ready when you are."

He reset his hands and toes. "Okay," he said to Rachel. "Next step, now." He lifted, the rope tightened, and they moved another foot and stopped. He sucked in a breath and nodded to Rachel. "Johnny, again."

—·—

The gas clicked off. The nozzle was pulled from the tank and placed back on the pump. The man walked into the store and placed two twenties on the counter.

Pop, the owner, stood. Eyes locked on his television, he backed to the counter and picked up the bills. "You been watching this, Thomas?"

He squinted and stared at the tiny screen.

"They've been showing this part over and over."

He leaned in to see. His eyes grew wide as the camera zoomed in on rock peeling away from the wall. Human forms flew at the end of a rope, bouncing, as the sound of a crash filled the speakers.

He spun on his heels and dashed to the pickup. He popped the clutch and sped off.

—·—

"Again, Rachel," Jack said, then, "Now." He strained, pulling with hands and lifting with legs, as rope tightened, taking up the slack. How's Johnny doing that without edge rollers?

He sucked in several quick breaths and reached higher on the crack. Fingers shaking, one hand cramping, he reset his feet. He nodded. "Now, Johnny," Rachel shouted. Jack pulled. A grip gave way and they fell out of the crack. Rachel clung on as they slid plumb.

Jack pulled in a breath and glanced down at the dust. Closer. Nearly here. "Now, Rachel." She keyed the mike. "Johnny, lost my grip. Sorry all our weight's on you. Give me a second to rest," he said, knowing Johnny couldn't respond.

He sucked in a breath and kicked left, grabbed the rim of the crevice, and pulled them toward it. His hand went into spasm. He reached with the other.

Rachel's arm shot back, catching the rim.

Jack gave the cramping hand a shake as she held them steady on the wall. "Careful, you're not tied in all that well."

"I'm okay."

He reset his hands and feet. "Go ahead."

She keyed the mike. "Now, Johnny," she said.

Jack pulled them up another foot. He sucked in a breath and looked up to check their progress.

Quit looking. Keep moving.

—·—

Linda Showalter scowled at the mass of people watching the spectacle on the rock.

Erika stopped beside her. "Keeps 'em entertained," she said, glancing between the crowd and the wall.

"That's not funny. That's not why we're here!"

"No, but we're not having to explain that the Director's late."

"Yeah, but how do we reassemble when he gets here?" Linda stomped off toward the empty dais, refusing to look back at the wall.

—·—

Jack hefted Rachel onto the ledge, then pulled himself up. He coughed, and wiped away the dust beginning to gum the corners of his eyes. "Cover your mouth and nose." He watched her sink her face into the elbow of her jacket. The red dusty haze grew worse. His arm and leg muscles cramped. Exhausted, he wanted to rest, but took only a moment, quickly tying a Swiss seat for Rachel, and clipping her in above him. "Okay Johnny, let out a little slack. We've got to move fast. Getting hard to see the other side of the break so we've got to do it now . . . pendulum across, and hope we land on the ledge." He coughed. "If we miss, we'll slide plumb, have to kick right and climb to get there, so our first choice is to make it the first time. Got us?"

"Got you. Just gave you three feet of rope. I'm ready."

They stood. Leg muscles shaking, Jack backed up, taking in the slack. Rachel's feet came off the ground as he pulled the rope tight. He stepped off the ledge, and kicked out. They swung into the haze, across the break. Jack relaxed, letting his legs give on contact with the lip. They slipped over, bumped the wall, and settled onto the ledge. He coughed and keyed the radio. "Perfect Johnny. Give me two feet of rope." They backed, hands to the wall, stopped and unclipped. He keyed the radio. "Johnny, we're off the rope."

"Copy. Be careful."

"You know that credibility thing?"

"Yeah."

"You're the most credible guy I know."

"Bet you say that to all your rope men. Get out of there, before something else happens."

He followed Rachel back down the ledge. She stopped once they were out of the dust. She looked back.

"Rachel, bad stuff has happened here. Why did you do this?"

She sighed. "My clan mother told me this was the way. She's gone, but she told me so many stories, I had to come."

"But your uncle told you not to, I know. Your mother . . ."

"Yes, but I needed to come this far. For her."

"Not a good idea."

"I had to come."

"Part of me feels I understand, but really I don't. You could have been killed." He sighed, watching her closely. "What's up there that could justify that?"

She dropped her head, then looked up, into his eyes.

"What's there, Rachel?"

"Many things and some you would not understand."

"What?"

"Things, if lost, that would leave holes in our society. Stories will come to an end if others do not understand their meaning. There are rituals. Rituals that depend on understanding the stories. Understanding that comes when you reach the destination."

"What have you just told me? Is that what your uncle is hiding Rachel?"

"Yes, but I have told you nothing."

"Why is this so important to you?"

She glanced away, then back. "I am the last."

"Last what?"

She was slow to answer. "To have heard the stories. To hope to understand them. Others who learn—if others do—will learn from me, or because I came to understand." She sighed. "If the stories die . . . much dies with them."

Jack settled against the wall. He stared into the depths and shook his head.

"I had to come."

"There's another way to get there. I showed your uncle. Promise me you'll not come this way again."

"I promise, John."

"John?" He coughed and let out a chuckle. "Oh, yeah, biblical name. Must be complicated juggling two religions."

"Many traditions. White man makes it complicated, not the Creator."

"We tend to do that."

She smiled. "We flew on wings of eagles."

"Let's get off this ledge."

They headed down, following the still faint trail until encountering white man's trail of dirt between cut stone. Jack looked back. Clear as day—like a deer trail—but he had never seen it before, and would not likely find it easily again. He let his ankles grow accustomed to near-level surface, then started walking, Rachel beside him stride for stride.

Near the trailhead, he saw the satellite trucks and remembered driving past them. "Let's go around. Just in case." He led upstream, along the ribbon of cottonwood, then upslope, through piñon and juniper to the parking area. "We'll wait for Johnny in the pickup." He watched until all heads were looking another way, then led her to the passenger side. He opened the door and helped her in. "Head down," he whispered, closing the door. Going to the other side he spotted Linda Showalter, walking quickly toward him.

"Where's Thomas?" she demanded.

"He's not here."

"Tell me where he is?"

He shrugged. "Not here, and he hasn't been."

"Who are you kidding? I saw you on that wall."

"Linda, why are you still here?"

"Waiting for the Director, smart ass."

His eyes grew wide. "The Director!" He raised a hand to his forehead. "Oh, Molly!"

"What about Molly?"

"She was busy. I was waiting to tell her the Director isn't coming. His schedule was tight and he didn't want to be a disruption."

Her eyes sunk back in their sockets. "Why would the Director be a disruption? What did you tell him?"

"I told him we had a rescue."

"Why were you talking to the Director?" she asked, livid, brow furrowed. "What did he say?"

"Molly was busy. I answered the phone. He said he couldn't afford to be held up. He said he wanted to talk, but said you could call him tomorrow. He'll be back in the office late afternoon. He said if you need to be in D.C. sometime, talk to him then."

"You think you won this battle don't you?"

"I didn't do anything."

She waved Mike Middleton and Erika Jones over. "The Director isn't coming. Jack made him think he'd be a disruption. He's on his way to his next stop."

Middleton laughed, then glared. "You loser. You're going nowhere."

"There's nowhere I want to go," Jack said. He crossed his arms. "So, Mike, what do you want, really? If we knew why this place was important, would it matter?"

Middleton smiled. "What do you think smart guy? I want to know, and I'm not the only one. Admit it, you do, too."

Showalter glanced between them, looking uncomfortable as reporters came flooding toward them. She stepped closer to Jack. "Do not say a word," she whispered, gritting her teeth. "You screw things up and the Coalition falls apart, it's your fault." She turned and put up a hand. "Stop. Give me a moment. Then, I'll make a statement."

The herd slowed and stopped.

"There has to be a better solution than risk the outcome he wants," Jack said, his voice low. "We'll find it."

"You've done nothing so far to find a solution. You've done nothing but fail."

Middleton crossed his arms. "Linda, enough. I'm tired of the bush leagues. No more. I'm going to the Director."

She turned, hands moving, desperation growing. "Whoa, Mike, hold it . . . I . . ." The look of panic subsided. She smiled. "You know what? That might be a good idea."

Middleton gave her a satisfied nod. "You know what that means?"

"So be it." She glared at Jack. "And it's your fault. If you say a word, it'll drive the Coalition apart and you know it. It'll be your fault." She turned and studied the crowd. "Erika," she muttered under her breath. "Get me Margie."

Erika pulled away and headed to the press table.

"Okay, reporters," Showalter shouted. "I'm ready to make a statement."

Two cameramen quickly set up tripods and locked on their cameras. Reporters gathered around her, microphones extended, pens and pencils ready.

Karen Hatcher, Ginger Perette, and others settled in at the back to listen.

"Who did they rescue? And who was the ranger?" a reporter asked, and extended her microphone toward Showalter.

"I would like to apologize to everyone who came here today," Showalter said, ignoring the question. "We had important things to say. Obviously we won't be getting to that. We will simply reschedule. Friday afternoon. My staff will get you the time and location.

"I also apologize that my staff failed to inform me the Director decided against coming into the canyon because of the rescue. I assure you, his intensions were honorable. He didn't want to get in the way. Someone gave him the impression he would be, even with the importance of what we had planned here today. I'll see you Friday." She turned to leave.

"You've got to be happy with how the rescue ended," a reporter blurted. "Quite hair-raising. Who did they rescue? Why were they there?"

Looking annoyed, Showalter turned back to the reporters. "Yes, very happy. It worked out. There's confusion over who was rescued, and I'm not sure I want to give them the satisfaction of being identified. Why were they there? Mischief. It didn't work out too well for them."

"What do you mean mischief?"

"I'm sorry, the investigation is ongoing."

"Who was the ranger that pulled off the rescue?"

"That's irrelevant to what was scheduled here today. That's all I'm prepared to say. Now excuse me." She turned away.

"Wait," a female reporter shouted.

Showalter stopped, turned back, and glared.

"I received an email from an individual named Foss. He claims first-hand knowledge of a cover-up. Claims endangered plants were burned, all because of your own careless, reckless action. Can you confirm or deny?"

Showalter's eyes grew wide. She pointed at the reporter, and shouted, "You will not pin that on me. I was not here. I refuse to dignify the question. If you insist on pursuing it, take it up with him." She pointed at Jack. She spun on her heels, and left, waving Mike Middleton to follow.

Jack glanced between sets of probing eyes. "I, uh . . ." He stepped forward. "There's truth to all that, except the part about a cover-up. A population of endangered plants was lost. Burned by accident in one of our operations. If you insist on affixing blame, attribute it to me, but I promise, we plan a thorough review—led by another agency. Everything we learn will be made available." He waited for follow-up. There was none, despite unsettled faces. He backed away and followed after Showalter.

Catching up, he said, "Linda, there's got to be . . ."

"Not now." She approached Margie. "The Director's back in the office tomorrow afternoon," she said, locking eyes on her secretary. "Call his office first thing—no, make it six our time. Tell them I'm coming in for a short briefing of the Director."

"I can do that," Marge said, making notes.

"Don't be late. Mr. Middleton and I will be in D.C. waiting when the Director arrives at the office, late afternoon. Email me the time when you nail it down. Make travel plans for me to get to D.C., arriving before one p.m. at the latest."

"You want that done tonight?"

"Yes, and if I have to fly tonight, so be it." She turned to Middleton. "Marge will give you my flight arrangements. You can make yours accordingly."

"Of course."

She turned back to Margie. "And make plans for Erika. She's coming with me."

"I am?" Erika said, from several steps behind.

"You are." Linda turned and looked through the crowd, now starting to break up. "Karen," she shouted.

Karen Hatcher broke away from conversation and wandered over.

"We're rescheduling the announcement for Friday at three. The announcement that'll keep the Coalition together. We want as many members of the Coalition there as possible. Can you be there?"

"I suppose," she said, appearing to be getting her bearings.

"Good." Showalter turned back to Marge. "And, I want a late flight home tomorrow night. Friday we'll make the announcement at Inn of the Canyons, three o'clock. Got that?"

"You can't," Marge said. "You have a commitment Friday. Career day at the high school."

"Reschedule or cancel."

"They can't reschedule. You're the final speaker. You said those kids were a priority. I told 'em that. Told 'em you had something special to say."

"I don't have time for that now," she said. "Hold it." She rubbed her chin. "Tell 'em Jack Chastain will cover. That'll keep him busy."

A pickup skid to a stop. Thomas jumped out, eyes wide, tears on his face.

Showalter put her hands on her hips. "I knew it was you."

Jack watched his confusion grow. "It's okay, Thomas. What you're after is in the pickup." He pointed to the government rig.

Thomas looked past them, and the confusion fell away. He put his hands to his face.

"Why were you there on that wall?" Showalter demanded.

"It wasn't me," Thomas said. "It was Rachel."

"Who the hell is Rachel? How dare she pull that stunt during my announcement?"

Jack exchanged glances with Thomas. "No stunt," Jack said. "Just a girl doing something to preserve who she is. You can respect that, surely."

"Not today, I don't. I don't have time for that crap." She turned to Thomas. "What's there, Thomas? Tell me, now."

"I will." He turned and faced Jack. "I'll tell you everything."

Middleton beamed.

Jack shook his head. "No, Thomas."

"You deserve to know. You said you wished I had trusted you. I do trust you."

"I know."

Fresh tears trickled down his face. "Too much bad has happened. I'll . . ."

"No, Thomas, I do not need to know. I do not want to know. It's best that I not know."

"What are you doing?" Showalter demanded. "That information is key."

"I know. I hope this isn't a mistake."

"It is a mistake."

"Maybe so, but just how isn't obvious." He turned back to Thomas. "You once told me even the most trusted do things—or are forced to do things—that can have unintended consequences. I understand that now. I do not want to know."

Linda opened her mouth, then noticed others listening. She glared, lips moving, as she fought to muster any words at all. "R-r-relevant?" she stammered, "You'll . . . you'll never be."

"Maybe not, but I'm letting sleeping secrets lie."

CHAPTER
40

Johnny Reger came around the last switchback, plodding under the weight of the packs. He approached the footbridge and saw Jack sitting alongside a quiet backwater, waiting.

Jack met him at the end of the bridge.

"Give me a hand with this stuff," Johnny said, dropping one of the packs on the wooden planks.

Jack gave him a crippling hug.

"Hey, man," Johnny said, "a beer would do."

"Deal," Jack said, releasing his grip.

"But not tonight. I'm tired."

—·—

Jack drove toward Culberson Ranch.

Rounding a bend, he saw Kelly's vehicle beside the road at the trail to Caveras Creek. He parked, grabbed his pack, and trudged up the trail.

At the creek, he saw her, wading toward travertine at the other edge of the pool. "Hi there, beautiful creature," he said, mustering a smile.

Surprised, she turned.

He stripped down and drove in, surfacing beside her.

She put a hand to his face. "Your nose, it's scratched."

"Long story—a rescue. Tell you later. I need to clear my mind."

"But what about the meeting? Linda and Erika, did they . . . ?"

"Not now. And I forgot, Erika gave me a note to give you."

"I'll call her tomorrow," Kelly said. "I'm not sure I'm up for her silly games."

"Her games aren't silly, and it won't be tomorrow. She'll be in D.C."

"You going, too?"

"No. I'm being replaced."

"I'm confused."

"Me, too. If there's anyone who'd think holding the Coalition together is important, you'd think it'd be me. But I'm more concerned about what Thomas wants to protect . . .and it's about to get sacrificed."

"No! Why did I make it so difficult? Why didn't I just tell you? It's . . ."

"No," he said, stopping her. "Don't tell me."

"Why?"

"You know why."

"Why the change of heart?"

"Kelly, it was Rachel we pulled off the wall."

She gasped.

"Rachel's okay. Let's leave it at that. I need to clear my mind."

—·—

Erika Jones waited for maintenance staff to finish packing the podium, tables and chairs, then slipped into her car, the last to leave the ill-fated event. Press packages and boxes of supplies filled her vehicle. As she turned onto the main road, she flipped open her phone and dialed Nick Saunders.

He answered after one ring.

"Nick, the Director didn't come. Something Jack did. He drove on past, but that's not good news."

"Why?"

"We're going to Washington."

"Why?"

"To brief the Director. Mike Middleton insists on going to Washington. Linda insists on being there with him."

"Cut her loose. Set her adrift. We'll let her get shot out of the water. You come home."

"She wants me in D.C. In fact, I'm conducting the briefing."

"Great," he said, angrily. "Pull the legislation. That's an order."

"Too late, Nick. It's already part of the package. There's nothing we can do. Committee staff put it in the conference committee package this afternoon. It authorizes a larger land exchange than what we discussed. Forty acres to be exact. In the canyon. Mike insisted on it."

"You're shitting me."

"No."

"After all this effort, the Director gets the credit, the Congressman owes me no favors, and if anything, he hears from his buddy Mike Middleton that favors earned should be showered on the Director and Linda Showalter. My only gift is getting to deal with the blowback when the public hears and the shit hits the fan. I'll be the clueless oaf who has to be shocked and treat the Congressman like the enemy. It was supposed to be the Director pissing him off, not me."

"Sorry, Nick, I'll fix this."

"Don't bother. You're working for the enemy."

"I can fix it."

"Yeah, right. That sounds about as shaky as something else you promised."

"What? What did I promise?"

"Two years ago, I was looking for a nice, quiet, velvet-lined rat hole, a place to bury Jack Chastain. A place so hidden away he'd never find his ass, much less do any damage. You had this great idea. Put him in Piedras Coloradas, you said. Nothing ever happens there, you said."

"I had no idea any of this would happen."

"It did though, didn't it? If he hadn't been there, everything would've fallen into place. Instead, he gets in the way. He screws things up."

"I can fix this."

"God," he screamed into the phone. "Why do I listen to you? What else is gonna come back to bite me? And don't remind me about that damned kid in Montana that died of cancer. Just because I gave the order to change the report doesn't mean it would've made any difference. She already had the damned cancer. What I did was inconsequential."

"I didn't say anything."

"Clint Foss changed it. I wouldn't've known it was even an option if he hadn't brought it to my attention."

"I remember."

"The photo op was to be mine. The favors were to be mine," he shouted. "I'm not going down without a fight."

"What will you do?"

"I don't know yet, and I'm not sure I'll tell you when I figure it out."

Decked out in suits, they walked the hall side by side, their heels clicking on pre-war floors. They stopped at the reception desk.

"Linda Showalter and Erika Jones, here to brief the Director."

The receptionist looked at her calendar and nodded. "Good. His flight's landed. He'll be here shortly. He has a couple of things to deal with first, and he has a half hour window for this."

"Should be plenty."

"Your secretary said a Mr. Mike Middleton would be joining. Will he need help with security?"

"Maybe, but I think he knows how it works."

"Very good. I'll call down and let them know to expect him." She pointed to a door behind them. "You'll be in the Director's conference room."

"Thanks. We'll set up."

She glanced at Erika, and nodded toward the door.

They opened the conference room and stepped inside. Linda Showalter scanned the room. Large walnut table, leather executive chairs, national park photos. It all looked familiar, even after all these years.

"Need my help?" she said to Erika.

"No, I've got it."

She turned away and smiled. She moved to the door and glanced into the hall. Feels good to be back.

Doors with glass panes. Doors with lengthy titles affixed. Could one eventually be mine? Which job? Does it matter? If it's here, that's what's important. It'll be a job where one can make an impact. It'll be a job where one can make a difference. Screw this up and it's back to Arizona, lucky if you ever see these halls again.

But that won't happen, judging from the confidence of Mike Middleton.

She turned and watched Erika run through the slides. "Did Jack give you those?"

"No. They're mine."

"Good." Damned fool. You have to be more than relevant. Chastain will never understand doing what's necessary. Making the tough decisions. Seeing the big picture.

He'll spend the rest of his career stuck in Piedras Coloradas. I'll likely be here.

She picked a spot at the table, to the right of where she assumed the Director would sit.

The Director burst in the door, in sport coat and slacks, a briefcase in hand. "Linda, good to see you," he said, as he shook her hand.

"You, too, Director Lucas." She let an easy smile cross her face. "Thought you had other things to do first?"

"They can wait," he said. "Hey, you must like Washington. That, or there must've been some mix-up in my message yesterday. I didn't say drop everything and come here."

Her heart rate quickened. "Mike . . . uh, Mike Middleton insisted we bring you into the loop. He thought it was time to include you."

"Mike Middleton, huh?"

"Yeah. He insisted. Said you'd want to be involved."

He nodded and slowly smiled. "He did, huh? Good ol' Mike, how is he?"

"Uh . . . good. Very helpful. He'll be joining us any minute."

"Great. How's his business these days?"

"Uh . . . good. Well, he sold his business."

"Oh, that's right."

"Until he jumps back in, he's found other ways to be engaged."

"That's right. Taking good care of him?"

"We're trying. Doing our best," she said, glancing at Erika. Erika smiled. "Definitely."

"Good. Whatever this takes, maybe we should double it. I'm sure it'll pay dividends. Support, political favors, influence, you name it."

"You mean . . ."

"Double it. Influential men like ol' Mike, you can't find enough of 'em. Keep him on our side."

Linda glanced at Erika. "I think we're . . . uh."

"That's alright," he said. "We can wait till he gets here. We'll talk about it then." He took a seat. "How do you like Washington?"

Linda glanced at Erika. "Great. I love it. I used to work here."

"Ever think you'd want to come back?"

"Uh . . . sure. I do."

"Great. We need good people here. People willing to do what it takes to move things forward. People who see opportunities in people like 'ol Mike. People who can thrive on what this town throws at you."

"I always thought I'd come back. I just needed more experience. I believe I have it now. I think I'm the kind of person Washington needs."

"I'm sure you are. I'm looking to fill a couple of positions now," he said, nodding, a forefinger to his lips. "Hey, how did that rescue turn out?"

Linda took in a breath and relaxed. "Good. Nothing serious."

A staffer came in, closed the door, and sat at the table, setting a pad of paper in front of her.

The Director took the seat at the head of the table. "Let's get started."

"I wonder where Mike is?" Linda asked. She glanced at the glass paned door.

"He can join us when he gets here."

"Go ahead, Erika" Linda said.

Erika moved to the other end of the table and keyed the remote to the projector. A map flashed onto the screen.

She started with general background. The Director listened intently, tapping pen to pad.

Linda watched, eyes on Erika, mind on the Director.

"Linda's working on an action that will hold the Coalition together. Prior to Linda's arrival, the issue seemed unsolvable. With her arrival to steer the ship, and with what she's directed us to do, there's reason for optimism."

The Director nodded. "Very good," he said, turning toward her.

Erika clicked the remote. The slide dissolved to a graphic, *Working with Mike Middleton.*

"Okay, the good part," he said, eyes gleaming. "Whatever it is, let's double it."

Linda watched him, holding back a smile.

There was knock on the door.

Mike? She turned.

The door slowly opened. The receptionist slipped in and locked eyes on the Director.

"Excuse me a moment." He stood and moved to the door, closing it behind him.

Linda watched his silhouette through the opaque pane of glass. "Nice job, Erika," she said, ignoring the aide. She smiled nervously.

"Thanks."

The door swung open. The Director stepped in, pulling the door closed. "Sorry," he said, retaking his seat. "The Assistant Secretary knows I'm back in town. Where were we?"

Showalter flashed a smile. "Finishing our presentation."

"When Jack Chastain and I briefed you before," Erika continued, "the Coalition faced crucial issues, one in particular. Those same issues challenge the Coalition now, and threaten to drive them apart. This slide discusses the issues they face."

The Director's eyes drifted away, his thoughts seemingly elsewhere. "Well, Linda . . . ," he murmured. "We're starting to repeat things I've heard before, and I've got other issues starting to stack up. People know I'm here. Do you mind if we get to the bottom line?"

Linda shot up in her chair. "Uh . . . yes . . . no. This will take only a few minutes. I assure you, we're working closely with Mike. I'm confident he's pleased with the outcome." She smiled and watched his eyes for reaction. "And, I'm confident I've established myself as a problem solver, filling a void that existed prior to my arrival."

He stared back.

"We'd hoped to make an announcement yesterday with you in the park. I'm sorry you were led to believe you'd be in the way. The rescue turned out to be nothing."

The Director drummed his fingers on the table. "How involved is the public in this?"

Showalter turned to Jones. "I . . . uh."

Erika smiled confidently. "Very, and we're hearing positive support for Linda's efforts to hold the Coalition together. It's being very well received."

Perfect, Linda thought, remembering Middleton's admonition to stay on message. "When we have our public meeting tomorrow, we'll cement the . . ."

"Meeting? Tomorrow?"

She leaned forward. "We have a meeting scheduled for tomorrow afternoon. Mike will join us."

"Linda, I have to get serious. I don't have time to keep toying with you." He stood and backed to the door. "Everyone thinks they do things better than the last guy. Unfortunately for you, things were working pretty well. You can only mess things up. Don't. You're in an acting assignment. You don't own the keys to the car. Go back to the park. Have your public meeting if you need it, but keep things on track. Keep the Coalition together. Do not screw things up."

"But, Mike Middleton . . . his proposal!"

"Oh, yeah, good ol' Mike." The Director opened the door, stepped into the hall, and looked back. "I'm not sure I want to hear it. I'm not sure I need to."

Showalter bolted to her feet. "Excuse me?"

"Don't know him. Don't want to. Sounds like someone who wants something. I get enough of that already."

CHAPTER
42

"Meet you at the gate," Erika said, stepping right, and ducking into a bathroom at Reagan National Airport. She stopped at the door, and watched Linda Showalter march angrily on without acknowledging her words.

She pulled out a cell phone and dialed Nick Saunders. It rang three times.

"Yes," he answered, angrily.

"I hope you haven't done something stupid."

"I don't do stupid."

"Hope you're right, Nick, because I've got news for you."

"Don't want to hear it."

"Middleton didn't show at the meeting with the Director."

"Why?"

"No clue. Claims some sort of difficulty with travel, but that's not the best part."

"This better be good. Otherwise, I'm busy."

"Wait for it," she said, then paused. "The Director doesn't know Mike Middleton. Doesn't want to."

"You're kidding." He laughed long and hard. "How'd that go over?"

"Not well. Director toyed with her before squashing her like a bug. Lucky for you, he was pulled from the meeting before hearing anything about the deal. He patted her on the behind, sent her back to Piedras Coloradas, told her not to screw things up."

"You're not lying to me are you?"

"Linda's pissed. Wants Mike's hide. She's moving forward with the announcement like she has something to prove."

"What does she hope to accomplish?"

"Keep the Coalition together. Make 'em turn her into a hero. Prevent any blowback from the Coalition falling apart. She said, no negotiating, Middleton's gonna take whatever piece of land she says he'll take."

"Why doesn't she cancel?"

"She's got something to prove, a reputation to repair, or maintain, or whatever. She's gonna play hardball. Force Middleton's hand. She also told me to pull the legislation."

"What did you say?"

"Didn't say anything. It's too late."

"Does Mike know that?"

"Yes."

"Good. One of us needs to call him, give him assurances, tell him things are still on track, that he should just let Linda blow off some steam."

"Want me to make the call?"

"No, might be good if he hears it from me," Nick said, his confidence returned. "He needs to know who's taking care of him. Also sounds like tomorrow might be the day to call the Congressman. Talk to him about his world tour. Show him how well we took care of his constituent. He might be ready to talk calendars for a visit to Piedras Coloradas."

Erika slipped over to a mirror and smiled. She pumped up her chest. "Nick, I told you I could fix this."

He laughed. "Never doubted you a minute. You're gonna make a great chief of staff."

CHAPTER
43

A hotel employee straightened the last of the chairs on the back row of the meeting room at Inn of the Canyons. He took one last sweeping look at the room and slipped out the back.

Middleton's highly paid consultants wandered about, making their own final preparations. Media handlers were ready with words, slick-sheet printed materials, and press packets. Some, dressed nicely, had name tags and were ready to attract attention. Others, dressed less formally, would later blend into the crowd to help steer crowd reaction.

Uniformed Park Service employees went about their own tasks at the back of the room.

Everything was ready. The public would arrive any minute.

Linda Showalter gritted her teeth as she watched Middleton and his ants scurry about. Their finishing touches confused her. She held her eye on their moves, tuning out their words.

This has to work. It had better hit some radars. Fix some reputations—namely, mine.

She seethed, remembering the Scotch blessing she'd given Middleton, first, from the airport, then, this morning. It seemed to roll off his back, both times. The threat of something less than a parcel in the canyon seemed expected, but did not seem to worry him. She watched him work the room. Jerk. Playing with my reputation. She looked away.

She studied the podium, the dais, the chairs set in rows, the press table at the back of the room. The only option is perfection. This meeting has to come off without a hitch.

Hold this together. If the announcement's made with enough punch, enough class, the right tone, maximum impact . . . then the Coalition will be indebted. They'll consider me a hero. Their reaction might still catch someone's attention. Maybe not the Director's, but someone's.

She shook her head, still in disbelief. How had she fallen for all that bluster?

The Regional Director could still take care of her. Good or bad, Nick Saunders holds the key, whatever that future is.

A bearded television cameraman sauntered in, lugging a camera and tripod. The reporter—a woman—followed closely. They paused and scanned the room. The cameraman moved to a corner and stood his tripod. A young man in uniform gravitated toward them and handed the reporter a press packet. They were joined by one of Middleton's media specialists.

This had better work.

She caught sight of Erika Jones, in a black suit, her skirt somewhat short, her legs long. "Why aren't you in uniform?" Linda demanded as Erika approached.

"Trying to be invisible."

"Wrong answer. I need you as an agency representative."

"You don't," she said calmly. "You have park staff and Middleton's contractors. The public needs to get used to seeing them carry the message. After today, I go back to the regional office."

"Since when?"

"Since this morning. The Regional Director called, said he wants me in Denver, said he'd call you."

"I talked to him this morning. He said nothing about that."

"Must have slipped his mind."

Showalter watched Jones move toward the corner where Mike Middleton held court with a group of his contractors. Jones cut him from the herd, and moved him toward the media table.

That's odd, after what happened in D.C.

Showalter took one last look over at the mass of chairs. They were fine. The room was fine. Everything was fine. Perfect even. *This has to show them. Hold it together—no, nail this. It's got to work. With the right spin, the locals will love it. This will be a success.*

She checked her watch. Ten minutes till game time. She scanned the room. *How many people are here?*

A young man in uniform approached. "A television crew wants to get a few comments before we start. You available?"

She smiled. "Has to be quick. We start in a few minutes."

— · —

Jack Chastain slowed as he drove by the city limits sign. A gray sedan passed and pulled back into the lane. A sticker on its bumper said, '*I love my country, but fear my government.*'

The words didn't sting like they usually did.

He turned into the high school, parked, and easily found the door he was told to use. He slipped in and found a place against the back wall, looking at the backs of teenagers, in a room full of them. The current speaker—Mr. Ferguson, owner of the hardware store—was in the midst of his presentation.

Most of the students appeared to be listening intently.

They were young, some likely serious about charting courses for their lives, some not yet ready to settle on any one path, some likely considering every option. Optimistic, eager, some likely thought they would someday change the world. Or save it.

Jack forced the thoughts away, and listened in on Mr. Ferguson. Ferguson described his life as rewarding. Small business. Satisfaction but risk, challenges but independence, rewards with pride in knowing what he built.

Maybe that would have been the better path.

How can I now look these kids in the eye and tell them the path I chose offered something equally meaningful?

But that's exactly what I'm expected to do.

He shuddered, knowing the lecture he was about to give himself.

You know the words. You've said them before, many times, to many other listeners. But maybe this time the words should be different. Maybe other words are more appropriate. Maybe just telling it like it is, is the right thing to do.

But wasn't that what you did before?

—·—

Showalter stepped onto the dais and took her seat at the table oriented lengthwise across the front of the room. She checked her watch. The room seemed quieter than expected. No, there are plenty of television crews and reporters.

Mike Middleton and Erika Jones walked forward to take their places on the dais.

"You know," Jones said. "It's not important that we start right on time. A few more minutes isn't going to hurt." She spun around. "Hold it. Where's BLM? Where's Karen Hatcher?"

Linda Showalter jumped up. "We did let them know, didn't we?"

"Yes. I called BLM myself, and I reminded Hatcher."

Showalter looked at her watch, but she knew what it said.

A woman showed at the door and looked inside.

"Come in," Linda shouted.

The woman stepped in. Her business suit looked somewhat out of place but no more so than Erika's. She scanned the room and approached a reporter and cameraman.

They huddled together.

The woman turned. The cameraman released his camera from its tripod, swung it onto his shoulder and collapsed the tripod, all in one move. He headed for the door, three steps behind the reporter.

"What are you doing?" Linda shouted. "Where are they going?"

The woman turned to another reporter, said something, then walked the aisle toward the front.

"Why does she look familiar?" Showalter whispered to Jones.

"She does, doesn't she?"

The woman stopped at the table. "Hello, Linda," she said. "I have a note for you." She handed over an envelope, and turned to Mike Middleton. "Are you here for the public meeting?"

"Yes, I am," he said, confidently. "More of an announcement really, but yes." He stuck out his hand. "Mike Middleton."

She shook his hand. "Pleased to meet you, Mike. I'm Jackie Miller, Chief of Staff to the Director."

"Why are you here?"

"Not important. If you're here for the meeting, I hear it's being held at another location. Check the sign on the door."

"What do you mean?"

She let her words sink in.

He turned and flashed an angry stare. "What are you people doing?"

Linda held her tongue. She knew.

The Chief of Staff spun on her heels and picked her way through the throng of staff and consultants. "Good luck with your announcement," she shouted, without looking back.

Nick Saunders stared at the email. A little bird had told him he would be hearing from the Director with an offer he could not refuse. The little bird was right. He had a choice. Hasty retirement or an assignment to a job no one would want, hidden away in a closet in some backwater location. A velvet-lined rat hole.

He checked his watch. Any moment now, Linda Showalter would be making the announcement with Mike Middleton. He snickered, then glared angrily at the email.

At least he had his insurance—that ticking time bomb no one knew about. Legislation, hidden way in the Departmental appropriations bill, waiting for a vote by both Houses of Congress. And because of that, favors. From a powerful person no one could ignore.

The hour was late in D.C., but the Congressman was likely still in his office. Now was the time to make the call.

He dialed the number and with each ring grew more nervous.

It was answered. "Office of Congressman Brett Hoff. How may I help you?"

Nick took his hand off his heart. "Good evening," he said, his voice composed. "Is Congressman Hoff available? This is Nick Saunders."

He sat in quiet, waiting.

Suddenly: "Hi Nick. Only got a few minutes. Need to get to the House floor for a vote."

"This will only take a minute. How'd your trip go, by the way?"

"Went well. I think we made some people stand up and take notice."

"That's wonderful. I've got news regarding that constituent you wanted me to follow up on. Something good to report, and I need a favor."

"What kind of favor?"

"The Director's playing politics. I might need air cover, a little protection. The right person interjecting himself, asking questions, asserting themselves enough to protect me till the end of the Administration."

"And who might that person be?"

Nick swallowed hard. "I was hoping that might be you."

Hoff laughed. "Of course."

"And once you've heard what I've done for your constituent, I think you'll have a good idea who should be the next Director of the Park Service."

"That is, should I decide to make a run?"

Nick made another hard swallow. "That's correct. Should you decide to run."

Hoff laughed again. "Tell me this good news."

"As we speak, the Superintendent of Piedras Colorados National Park, working in partnership with your constituent, is making an announcement. In fact, we'd like to get you out there in the next few weeks to highlight your contribution to the effort."

"My contribution?"

"While you were out of the country, we took the liberty of working with your staff to craft language to authorize a land exchange. Your staff slipped it in the appropriations bill. If we can get you to the park sometime in the next few weeks, we can make a big splash with both you and your constituent."

"Great. When can this happen? Sooner would be better."

"We can do it any time that works for you. I'll clear my calendar. I'm sure Mr. Middleton can do the same."

"Mr. Middleton?"

"Uh, . . . your constituent."

"If you say so."

"Mike Middleton," Saunders reiterated.

"Okay," the Congressman said, sounding confused. "Does this guy work for Teague?"

"Teague?"

"Harper Teague, the constituent I was talking about."

Nick Saunders fell back in his chair. He pulled the handset from his ear and glared. Slowly, he dropped his arm and cradled the phone, hanging it up. He turned and stared out the window.

He would sit staring long after having heard others down the hall closing their doors and leaving at the end of the day. Then, after one last look around his walnut-trimmed office, he would pick up a pen, and begin to write.

"Dear friends and colleagues, the time has come . . ."

CHAPTER
45

The school principal walked across the stage, clapping. "Thank you, Mr. Ferguson."

Jack stepped away from the wall, ready to move to the front.

The applause fell off to quiet.

"That was great. Now, for our last speaker, a change of plans. We'll need a few minutes."

What's going on? Jack settled against the wall.

The side door opened, and a bearded man came through, carrying a video camera and tripod. A woman followed. They slipped to the back.

The door on the opposite wall popped open. People—adults—flooded in.

What the hell is this?

Familiar adults made their way past open seats, choosing ones near young people.

Jack felt a tap on his shoulder. He turned.

Joe Morgan, in dress uniform, said, "Come with me."

He followed Joe to a corner door. Joe held it open and let him pass.

Jack searched for words. "Why are you here, Joe? Are you . . . back?"

"I'm still on assignment. Might be a few more months. You surviving?"

"So, so," he said, avoiding Joe's gaze. "What's happening out there?"

"Change of plans." He held back a smile. "Fire behaving itself? Any of that rare plant survive?"

"It's creeping around, and no survivors so far. I've looked." Jack sighed. "Joe, I didn't ask for your help." He dropped his eyes, exhausted. "I can't cry to you every time I get in trouble."

Joe moved to the door and looked out into the room. "They're the ones who asked. I'm here for them." He nodded toward the room full of people. "Had a phone call yesterday." He let out a sad little laugh. "A little after Linda Showalter briefed the Director."

"What happened?"

"Can't tell you everything, but you're a smart guy. You'll figure it out."

"Too many games, even for the Director?"

"You're wrong about him. He plays in a different world than you do, but he's a good man. He didn't do the things you think he did."

"Are you sure you can believe that, Joe? Look what's happening at Sand Dunes."

"That story's more complex than you know. Nick Saunders was putting off a decision on a difficult issue, throwing money at research, suggesting it was germane. It wasn't. He's pandering to someone on a policy matter, not a scientific one. It's confusing the issue. It's politics."

"But look what the Director did in Montana. To me!"

"I put him on the spot about that. Angered him," Joe said. "Jack, he was never asked to come to Montana."

"But I scheduled it, through the Regional Director's office. I had confirmation."

"You followed protocol, and that was your problem." Joe stepped closer. "There was no way Nick Saunders was gonna let the Director anywhere near that project. He owed someone, and you were in the way. Now's not the time to explain, but Saunders ordered the change to the research results. He ordered everything. He abused his power, multiple examples, not just Montana. He suffers from a bad case of feeling entitled to do anything he wants."

Jack looked out into the room and slowly shook his head. "Not the Director?"

"I know you're confused," Joe said. "Probably confused about lots of things."

"I don't know if I'm confused or just not smart to figure it out. It's all gray, Joe." He rubbed his eyes and turned back. "And I'm confused about what's happening here?"

"Public meeting."

"The meeting's at the Inn of the Canyons."

"You're being commandeered," Joe said.

"Why?"

"Credibility. Showalter lost hers. And rather quickly."

"How? She was becoming their hero."

"Blew that responding to a reporter about that endangered plant. Two responses—hers and yours. One avoiding responsibility, one accepting it. Caught everyone by surprise. They knew the story." He flashed a twisted smile. "The grapevine's one of the strengths of this community. They knew neither one of you were to blame. The difference was how each of you handled it."

Jack looked out into the room. "They can't be here because of that."

"No, but it got 'em thinking. Made 'em worry the Middleton deal was more about her than it was about keeping the Coalition from falling apart. Made 'em worry she was in it for herself. Reputations can be fragile."

"Tell me about it. She said I'm irrelevant."

"That's funny."

"It's not. She said I set a low bar. She said I'm a failure."

"Hard lessons are being doled out today, but not that one. What do you see in that room?"

"Something you orchestrated. A change in venue."

"Not me. They did. I'm just here to protect you. They're here because you are. Showalter's the one who became irrelevant. She forgot the park is why she's here, and she forgot who she works for."

Jack rubbed his eyes and leaned into the door frame.

"Middleton's price was too high. Elegant, but maybe not the only solution. They need you to help find a better one."

"Won't be easy."

"Issues are never easy. You rarely find a perfect solution. You can only do the best you can, and keep working on it. You hope people figure it out, and trust you."

"I thought I was doing that."

"I know," Joe said, putting a hand on his shoulder. "Get over it. Go do your job. Do what you do well. Take on the issues."

"I'm not prepared for a meeting. I don't even have someone to write down what's said."

"You've got me. I can work a flip chart. If I get tired, our friends from BLM are here."

"But . . ."

"Go."

— · —

Karen Hatcher entered from stage left and walked to the microphone. She scanned the audience, making eye contact. "Kids, my apologies. Jack Chastain was slated to talk to you about work in the public sector . . . but I, your parents and others want to hijack him. Instead of hearing about his work, you'll see him at work, and get a little lesson in political science to boot. I guarantee you'll get a lot from it. After all, you'll be citizens for life."

She looked at Jack.

He took a step forward, but Hatcher waved him back.

She turned to the students. "Let me say something first.

"Ours is a nation built on laws. Some of those laws give mandates and responsibilities to those who work for us. Other laws require those people to involve us, the public, in carrying out those responsibilities. They give us opportunity to exercise our rights as citizens, to influence the public policies that affect us. Very often, decisions are difficult. There are gray areas. Sometimes balances must be made. Sometimes there are winners and losers, sometimes there's not. Sometimes those who work for us must tell us no, or tell us something we don't want to hear. That makes their job difficult.

"There's nothing that requires the rest of us to be good citizens. We vote, or maybe we don't. If we do more than vote, we do so because there's something of interest we want to see happen. It might be the greater good, it might be personal agenda.

"Watch what happens today. It's impressive to see someone who conducts themselves in a way that makes the rest of us strive to be better citizens. It's even more impressive because he makes us all feel relevant."

She gestured to the side. "Jack!"

He stood a moment, taken aback, then walked onto the floor, picked up the microphone, and stepped to the center aisle. Behind him, Joe Morgan pulled a flip chart onto the stage.

"Good afternoon," Jack said. "Do you mind if we back up a bit and talk about common ground?"

CHAPTER
46

"Okay, now you can look," Kelly said. She stepped back and picked up her goblet. She took a sip of the wine, her eyes on the canvas.

Jack set down the stick he'd used to stir the coals and picked himself out of the sand. He slipped around the easel to the front of the painting.

What were angry canyon walls now were mysterious. A faint trail in the foreground led deep into unknown, the seemingly magical.

"Completely different feeling. Hopeful," Jack said, as he put an arm around her. "The trail, that's what was needed."

"I like it. It says what it wants to say." She took another sip. "I think I'll call it, *'Having Heard the Stories . . .'*"

Jack stood enjoying it long after Kelly took his place at the campfire. When dusk turned to dark, he joined her.

The coals grew dim. Stars grew bright. His eyes settled on her, propped on one arm, a goblet dangling between her fingers. Such a beautiful creature.

"Quite a day," Kelly said, breaking the silence, sounding relaxed, effects of the wine taking hold.

"Yes, it has been."

"What'll happen to Erika?"

"No clue."

"You really think there were connections back to Montana?"

"Yes, but they don't explain everything."

"Tell me the rest of the story."

"Not sure I can."

"You can't keep secrets."

"I'm not. The secrets weren't mine. There were things that happened in Montana that I didn't know. Probably still don't."

"Tell me what you do know."

"Politics overtook us. The person playing the politics appeared to be exchanging favors. There were a number of things going on. I must have been the last man standing. That made me a sacrificial lamb. It was easier to sacrifice the work and reputations of the team, than push back. Our work had to change. They knew I wouldn't let that happen."

"That time in your life . . . ," Kelly said sheepishly. "I know it was hard. Sometimes I wonder if it took part of your soul." She sighed. "But it brought you here. I'm glad it did. Someday that part will come back to life. I'll be here when it does."

He let out a breath that seemed to come from somewhere deep—trapped for a very long time. He smiled, but said nothing, fearing the words would come trembling out.

He reached back, dragged over his pack, and dug out a roll of nylon.

"What's that?"

"Unfinished business."

He stood and stepped back from the fire, assembled fiberglass poles, and slipped them through sleeves in the nylon. In quick moves, it became a dome.

"Thought you preferred sleeping under the stars?"

"I do. I never use this old tent, so I cut a hole in the floor. Now it's a sweat lodge." He picked up a pair of branches and managed to move a rock—glowing faintly red—away from the coals. He picked up the dome and set it over the rock. Grabbing a pail, he slipped into the shadows toward the gurgling creek and returned lugging water. He set the pail inside.

He pulled off his T-shirt and tossed it over a boulder. He offered his hand, pulled Kelly to her feet, and started on the top button on her denim blouse. He finished the buttons, slipped the shirt off her shoulders and down her arms, letting it drop to the ground.

"I've never been in a sweat lodge."

"It's a sacred place," he whispered, enjoying the sight of her in the glow of the coals. "According to Thomas, sweat lodge is about modesty."

"Why do I have the feeling I'm about to be naked?"

"Sweat lodge is about purification—body, mind and spirit. It's also about letting go."

"Am I letting go of something? The only thing I need to forget is that image of Erika climbing all over you."

"I know."

"The sweat lodge will purge that?"

He smiled. "One way or another."

—·—

Kelly slowed her truck as they neared the old pueblo. She parked away from the earthen structure and killed the engine. They sat and watched as men, women and children moved past on their way to something inside. Many wore ceremonial garb—deerskin, bells, feathers, and painted faces. It all seemed remarkable.

"We're a little early," Kelly said.

"For what?"

"I'm not sure."

"Ceremonial dance?"

"Possibly."

"We're invited?"

"No, but I was asked to bring you. For Rachel."

They climbed out and walked toward a corner of the pueblo. Jack glanced toward the brown box house in the distance. No vehicles parked outside, it looked lonely and inanimate, but the gardens had green tinges, even from this far away.

Kelly led him toward a door. "Rachel's grandmother's house," she whispered. "It's Rachel's now."

The door was open. They looked inside. The outer room, simply furnished, held only chairs, a table, and rugs.

Thomas waved them inside. He embraced them both. "Thank you for coming," he said. "You honor Rachel."

"The honor is ours," Jack said.

He nodded appreciatively.

In the other room, Rachel stood in deerskins, Thomas' wife strapping bells to her ankles.

She met their eyes and smiled.

Thomas motioned them to chairs. They sat.

After a moment quietly watching, Jack leaned toward Thomas. "I've got to ask," he said, keeping his voice low. "Harper Teague? How did you know he was behind that burned pickup?"

"Teague first talked to an elder, then me. The elder did not trust him. When he talked to me, I was standing at my truck, listening, struggling with whether to ally myself with the man. I noticed something in the dirt. His tracks. The same as out at the pickup."

"How'd you know that?"

"The day you saved me, Luiz drove me home. He wanted to make sure someone kept an eye on me." He laughed self-consciously. "He had been investigating the fire when he got the call about me on the ledge. He left in a hurry, and wanted to stop and pick up things on the way to the pueblo. His plaster casts sat beside me, all the way here."

"With that you concluded Teague was Fearfully Anonymous?"

"It wasn't hard."

Jack laughed, fighting to not be loud. "So, how did Rachel do on the trip to the falls?"

Thomas smiled proudly. "Better than I did. I helped her set up the final anchor, then I left. It was her journey."

Jack turned toward the back room, and watched as Rachel put a feather in her hair. Then more bells. Something of a mask waited, a creature of some kind, but Jack felt no curiosity as to what. He didn't need to know.

He watched the impressive young woman, upon whose shoulders rested some kind of uncertain future. For herself, a clan, possibly a people. Whatever it was, she would handle it with faith and certainty. She would fly on wings of eagles.

When the preparations were nearly done, Rachel came from the back room, stooped, and pulled her uncle to his feet. She hugged him, then spun around and hugged Suzi.

She turned to the table and picked up a small leather pouch, then offered it to Jack with both hands.

Hesitant, he accepted, and timidly loosened the drawstrings. He poured the contents into a hand. A flower—so orange it was almost red, with flaming yellow veins—and a vial—filled with golden granules. He looked up, into smiling eyes.

She pointed at the vial. "To carry your prayers," she whispered.

"My prayers are answered, with this," he said, looking at the flower.

Rachel turned back to the table, and picked up a small, painted pot. "Please, John, will you?" She brushed three fingers across each cheek, and held out the pot.

Tentative, he looked inside. Dark powder—almost black, tinged with red, orange, and brown. He dabbed at the powder, and rubbed it between his fingers. Carefully, he daubed it on her cheek. Black and other colors streaked one side of her face. He dipped his fingers again and painted the other side.

She smiled.

"Is that it?"

She nodded. Her eyes glistened, and tears formed until she brushed them away. She threw her arms around him, then Kelly. She turned to her uncle. He picked up her mask. He helped her slip it on as she turned away, paused a long moment, and slipped quietly out the door. Thomas and his family followed as she led them down the path others had taken toward the plaza inside the pueblo walls.

Kelly stepped out and watched until she lost sight of them, then turned, lips quivering.

"What just happened?" Jack asked.

"It's a secret," she said, looking at him proudly. "And it was special."

Epilogue

A maid unlocked the door to a hotel room off I–25. She stepped inside. It looked barely touched. A coffee-stained page lay on a corner table. She slipped over and picked it up. She shook her head and set it down, then picked it up again and read. Four boxes, penciled vertically down the page. Four names, written beside them. Only the top box was checked. The name beside it—Nick Saunders—was written in the same flourish used on words at the bottom of the page.

"One down, three to go."

ACKNOWLEDGEMENTS & AUTHOR'S NOTES

This is a work of fiction, shaped by experiences over a long career with the National Park Service. I'm proud to say the majority of my colleagues, including those in the highest ranks, are hard-working and dedicated, their integrity never in question. However, after *Public Trust* (and the issues it explored), and before moving to the next things I hope to say, I found it was necessary to flip the mirror around on the NPS, for no reason other than intellectual honesty. Yes, there are those in it for themselves, who forget who they work for, and whose grasp on responsibility is only firm when it looks good on them. Enough said about that.

Other influences on this book:

The scene under the stars, overlooking the canyon, where Thomas sang a song he'd learned from his grandfather: that has happened many, many times, over countless generations. I witnessed it with a Hopi elder, on the Colorado River in Grand Canyon, below Nankoweap. He was a warm and sharing man, very traditional. We were there to understand their connection to the Canyon. One night on the river, he asked if he could sing us a song taught him by his grandfather. I was only marginally interested, but thought about how long it had likely been since he learned the song; this was an old man. I was unprepared for how it would affect me. As he sang, his voice echoed through the canyon. The heavens seemed to open, the stars grew bright. I was humbled, and gained a greater sense of responsibility for preserving what matters to cultures dependent on the blessings of Mother Earth.

Though I often tell people that Jack Chastain is not me, there's a scene—in the halls of the Main Interior Building in D.C., reading the plaque for those who died in the line of duty—where he was. On the list is John Ethridge, a Tennessee gentleman and tremendous ranger who died in the line of duty at Zion, after stepping between a child and an edge. Always the most safety-conscious, his death was ironic. He obviously did what he had to do. A credit to the agency, he is missed, still. He was my friend. I always stop at the plaque.

The character Cloe Bell is based on my colleague and friend, Jan Balsom. When I first transferred to Grand Canyon, I was somewhat intimidated by Jan. She's extremely knowledgeable, has high standards, and runs a good program. What can be more intimidating? In the years we worked together—me on the natural side of resource management, her on the cultural—we developed a strong working relationship that I depend on to this day. Thank you Jan for reviewing the draft, offering insights into Thomas and Rachel, and helping me write on the cultures of the southwest with the respect they deserve. If I've failed, she gave it her best shot.

And finally, my thanks to Mary Bisbee-Beek, publicist and guru—your insights, advice and support are always given efficiently, helpfully, and with a healthy dose of warmth. And to Ann Weinstock and Kristen Weber, for taking the care to make this a beautiful book. Ann, you really nailed it on the cover—it introduces the story perfectly. Kris, you made my words look great and, ahem, consistent. And to my wife, Cassy, for letting me pick your brain and tap into your years of experience, and for, when needed, helping bring the story back to earth.